THE WESTHAMPTON LEISURE HOUR
AND SUPPER CLUB

THE WESTHAMPTON LEISURE HOUR AND SUPPER CLUB

Samantha Bruce-Benjamin

Also by Samantha Bruce-Benjamin

The Art of Devotion

For a fair and delicate boy

ACKNOWLEDGMENTS

I owe a massive debt of thanks to my brilliant agent, Christy Fletcher, for her unflinching faith in this novel. From the first thirty-two pages of the novel I submitted to her, to this final version, she has offered extraordinary support and editorial insight. All of the superlatives apply to Christy, but she is, above all other things, the best champion for which any author could ever hope.

I would also like to thank the many people who have helped me throughout the process of writing this novel. To my friends; Toga Tuite, Annaig Herzig, Emma, Jennifer, Kirstie, and Colin: to Valerie Kandel at The Westhampton Historical Society for allowing me privileged access to research materials on the 1938 hurricane: to Terry Lucas of The Southampton Library for her support and guidance: to marketing supremo, Valerie Lindsay: to Samantha Spence: to Sheena Macrae: to Paul Okroj: to Mary O'Donnell: to Hillary Black and Sylvie Greenberg at Fletcher and Co., NY: and, last but by no means least, to Alexandra Bruce-Dickie, for being so special.

Finally, I reserve my greatest thanks to my husband and family, who remain my most tireless supporters, proofreaders and sounding boards. Forever on call and prepared to drop whatever they are doing to help me, everything I have accomplished is solely because of them.

And round that early-laurelled head
Will flock to gaze the strengthless dead,
And find unwithered on its curls
The garland briefer than a girl's.

           –To An Athlete Dying Young, A.E. Houseman

Like the tender fire of stars moments of their life together, that no one knew
of or would ever know of, broke upon and illumined his memory.

           – James Joyce, *Dubliners*

PROLOGUE

The Party, the Party...!

SEPTEMBER 21st, 1938

On this early evening in September, The Summer Visitors are all packed. Yet, throughout the idyllic villages of the East End, the talk continues of the plans to be made for the morning. Tomorrow, the visitors will bid farewell to the glittering alley they call The Hamptons, off to pursue another fashionable Manhattan Fall. Their mansions, nestled like diamonds into the sands of the coastline, will be shuttered, the country clubs will roll back their awnings, and the society pages that have brightly chronicled their tea parties and fetes will illumine nothing more than the coming winters' fires. But first there is to be the party: the annual event to close the season at the Lyons' fabled estate, La Doucette.

It is tacitly acknowledged in the East End that the summer cannot be permitted to die, until Serena Lyons allows the curtain to fall over that dream. Her party is as established a tradition for the Social Register as the white silk dresses of the debutantes who vacation here. As is the gathering of the uninvited – the staff and local people – who come to watch as the triumphal procession of cars, bearing the laurel-wreathed and the chosen, speed past en route to their summer swansong.

This evening is no exception. Hordes from East to West Hampton, line the Old Montauk Highway, to cheer and wave The Summer Visitors on. While those blessed by luck seem, as ever, to trail in their wake the discarded remnants of the preceding months: all of the things they feverishly coveted, forgotten now, along with so many exquisite ladies' hats left outside to be ruined in the rain.

Yet, amongst the crowd, who can only long for a glimpse beyond the magnificent walls of La Doucette, there is an evident hint of anxiety: an anxiety that reflects the habitual nervousness of people born to serve: "Hopefully, it will stay dry for them," some comment, casting wary eyes to the high fog that has lingered all day. "We'll never hear the end of it, if it doesn't. Anyone would think we were to blame for this awful summer!" still more rejoin, from behind appropriately enthusiastic smiles, trying to ignore the oppressive mugginess in the air.

For the guests who attend each year, the mood is nostalgic, if predictably irritable. The benevolent Old Guard arriving from Southampton, fresh from their day at The Bathing Corp and The Bath and Tennis Club, lament again the floods that forced the cancellation of their beloved annual fundraiser for The Southampton Hospital last week. While those from farther afield in East Hampton, fortified by cocktails started at noon at The Maidstone, bristle anew over the interminable car ride to the West. Yet, as always, in the backseats of Packards and Bentleys everywhere, women scrutinize their make-up and re-adjust their wraps, united in a timeworn theme: how to outdo their hostess. Some still imagine they can.

Over the past thirty years, the Lyons' imposing Georgian mansion has played host to the only party of any consequence in The Hamptons, The Westhampton Leisure Hour and Supper Club. Yet, its location in Remsenburg – or the "first Hampton" as it is known – has always struck their friends as an odd choice for a family seat, so far removed from its more illustrious neighbors. Founded by Bridgehampton farmers in the 1700s and generously referred to as part of the "greater Westhampton area," Remsenburg is a tiny hamlet of gambrel-roofed houses and picket-fenced fields, beyond which horses graze: a site of simple elegance that appears to offer nothing more enviable than the leafy consolation of an unchanged world. Only La Doucette has ever deviated from this bucolic code. Yet, arguably no other home here encapsulates its essence more meaningfully. And while the more critical have wrinkled their noses at Serena Lyons' seemingly simple tastes, she has also been forgiven. For at the core of La Doucette, she has existed in a class all of her own, presiding over a domain of seasonal refinement no amount of wealth could ever acquire, her remit solely the social scene of the summer colony.

Unusually for a society hostess, Mrs. Lyons does not winter in Manhattan and so has never been seen at the 21 Club, The Stork or El Morocco. Nor is she a member of The Colony Club, despite frequent invitations from the founding ladies for her to join. Indeed, very few profess to know what happens when the red front door of La Doucette closes on Mrs. Lyons each September, as equally as guests arriving at her parties each Friday of summer have no idea quite what to expect: whether their coveted pink and gold invitation will invite them to attend an intimate supper, served by liveried footmen only previously seen in Newport; or a 4th July clambake attended by the President; or a gala peopled by Hollywood film stars, and literati alike.

Although the element of surprise has long been established as her particular forte, she has never once misshapen the boundaries of propriety. Her meticulously orchestrated guest lists may occasionally deviate from the accepted norms of society gatherings, but hers is not a world of gaudy trickery. Serena Lyons has never imported trees from the West Coast to establish a Hollywood theme, or held aloft her newborn baby on a silver-dining platter to impress, unlike that fame-hungry wife of a noted East Hampton surgeon. Instead she has glided seamlessly amongst her treasured guests, inherently understanding how to bring together people of interest, breeding – and on occasion outrage – to memorable, yet impeccable, effect.

Nothing fundamental changes each week as guests arrive to be greeted by this delicate nymph of revels. Not the lamplight or The Emperor, or the trays of vintage champagne. Not the boxwood mazes, or the verandahs overlooking the dunes and bay, perennially starlit. Not the house, filled with possessions so beautiful, even the wealthiest of visitor has often paused to stare in awe. Nor the question they always pose whenever they envisage Serena placing a delicate trinket on a Regency table, like settling a child down for the sweetest of dreams, in a place of perpetual admiration. For it is at such moments, when they think of her, when they imagine her walking through those rooms, they find that they start to remember the boy... The Summer Visitor they have never forgotten.

So, of course, everyone has to attend, if only to see if he will finally return. And tonight, their attendance is considered more crucial than ever. All are bound to honor the simple promise they have made to their hostess, the only request Serena Lyons has ever made of them: to come to the party: *Always, to come.*

As their cars pass the Moriches Bay on which La Doucette sits, the sea grass bowing graciously in welcome to its crystalline waters, the question of the boy assumes a greater significance amongst the older Summer Visitors who can remember him. These guests, who have witnessed their divine world shift and crumble and resurge in ways in which they have both delighted over and despaired. Perhaps it is because of the subtle shift they detect, the unrecognizable stitch of color in the landscape that surrounds them. Yet, a collective awareness takes root that what is about to happen this evening will differ from everything that has gone before. As the illumined splendor of La Doucette emerges ahead of them, none can escape the fact that something is distinctly changing. An altering that is evident from the fog, unfurling elegantly now over their idling cars, over their expectant souls.

As they raise their eyes to the red front door, standing open like a promise kept, the memories of everything that preceded them here suddenly washes over their aged hearts like a balm. Even guests jaded by eternities of ambivalence and entitlement, find themselves involuntarily counting the priceless joys they owe to this very party; the people they met, the husbands they married, the constancy of the grace they have always cherished. So it is with uncharacteristic spontaneity that many of them decide to disembark from their gridlocked cars and walk the rest of the way: more eager than ever before to reach the consoling familiarity of the house and their darling friend, Serena, waiting to greet them.

Without warning, a hot wind whips up violently, before falling into quiet in sporadic, deceitful bursts, causing only excitement amongst the younger Summer Visitors, who impatiently clamber from their cars to follow the others. Lovely girls in organza and diamonds rush arm in arm with their friends, chattering excitedly about the grand passion they hope the party will produce. While young athletes, their crowns hanging as heavy as their curls, stride confidently forward to bask in their day of victory at

The Devon and The Meadow under the light the girls' adoring chorus will provide. All are intent on enjoying every minute of this, their last chance to make up for the fun that was spoiled this summer by the rains. A low thrum of expectation begins to emanate, projecting forward gaiety and high spirits: *"The party, the party….!"* they cry, as they run faster now toward the red front door, and beyond it, the possibility that what they most wish to find here tonight, they will.

Others, however, sense something else and somewhere deep within them hear a call home, a discomfiting awareness of all they failed to do before they departed. The goodbyes unsaid, the night-night kisses not bestowed on their children's precious heads, the horses they prided themselves on, not petted gratefully enough, one last time, before they were stabled this afternoon: It is an awareness that, as with almost everything, they left such tasks to outsiders. And so it is, with an unnerving sense of urgency, that they insist their chauffeurs turn back. "Take us home," they urge. "We should not have come. Take us home."

If they, the invited, were to listen, all might hear it. They might know what is coming from the haunting refrain that suddenly fills the air.

The birds are caroling, louder and louder: a chorus of farewell.

There will be a storm.

And so the party begins.

I
ARRIVALS

THE HOSTESS

I am the Hostess and this is our last party. Soon, we will say goodbye. Yet, I shall be the first to slip away before the rest. I am leaving in the night.

There is only one thing left to do, before I descend the staircase to meet my guests: the reason why I am hiding here, just behind the silk curtain in my bedroom. It is part of a ritual that has been my only solace for thirty years. Every Friday evening of summer, I wait at this window for the last guest. For me it is the yearning hour; five minutes before the dusk settles and the stars emerge, to watch this road before me that leads to the sea. Five minutes to know again the ancient thrill of expectation before the party begins, that the clock might mark another minute and with it bring someone I have never dared to hope for.

From this spot, I have the perfect view of the people arriving in the courtyard below; all of them dressed in their tuxedos and gowns, intent on making it into the house to sip from the crystal depths of oblivion. I can study every face expectantly, filled with delight at what I might find there. And, when none of the guests are ever who I hope they will be, no one will see me cry. For if there is one thing I have learned, it is always to hide the truth: the heartbreaking distinction between the life I long for and the one I lead.

My father used to say that it is knowing that kills us, but I cannot turn away from this sight. I watch as the heavy, gray light of early evening ebbs from my dressing room. While outside, the brilliant white of the phlox and the hydrangeas are illumined in a pale glow that seems to augur only beginnings and not departures. Despite my age, I feel young again. The silk of my dress is fresh against my skin; the luxury of French perfume dense in the air around me. My favorite song starts to play in the ballroom below, the view before me comes alive with promise...

There are only a handful of minutes in our lives that are of any importance; those ordinary moments around which choices are done and undone and paths changed. Yet, each one contains an event and a choice and sometimes a soul that determines our destinies. I have allowed nothing in my life, not children, marriages, deaths, or even holidays, to prevent me from reliving my few moments here each week. It is how I survived. For thirty years I have waited, with the unblemished faith of the hopeful, for everything I have missed.

Through this window, I have perceived the facts, sometimes even the secrets, of my life and of those I loved. It has offered an ever-shifting portrait of how things change and vanish and reappear and disappoint and even destroy. Here, I made decisions large and small and hid from the cruel and the judgmental. Here, I wished for a different life entirely and tried to forgive myself for everything I cannot change.

This ritual is the only thing I own that means anything to me now. Yet, this is the last party that will ever be held in this house and the end of the vigil that has sustained me. I can wait for him no longer. All that remains are these five minutes to pray that I will be rewarded for my faith. To pray that I will see him again on this road before me, shy stars of heaven at his back.

But this weather, it worries me so. It would be too cruel to think that he and I were separated by a circumstance at the first party and that another could keep us apart at this last.

A storm, you see, would make prisoners of us all.

THE HOST

I am an unpaid editor of better men. This is the only talent Captain Edward Lyons allows himself to claim, as he has no other. He considers himself a chronicler of the lives he was once given to protect; the last port of call for those seeking to understand the essence of the souls they loved. And so, in his life, he has been a messenger of agonies and joys, of disappointments and surprises, the recipient of tenderness and gratitude, of violence and of rage. All of it necessary, because everything we are is what we learn from those who are left behind to speak for us, he has so often upheld. How easy it is to lie, to misdirect, if only to save people the pain of uncovering the truth. I have never allowed myself this mercy. Better to know than to not. After all, the earth belongs to the living.

To his credit, Captain Lyons has fulfilled this role as diligently and methodically as if his own life depended upon it. There was only one occasion when he failed, an occasion with his wife, Serena. It was a moment they shared, one of the very few, when he could have said, *"Turn the page..."* And by so doing, she would have found the answer she sought. Yet, whether it was the answer to a prayer or a nightmare, Captain Lyons could never decide, which is why he said nothing at all. To keep her, of course, and so that he could continue to follow at the only remove she permitted, to pretend he meant anything to her.

He owns a pragmatic courage, an awareness that brings him no shame. This courage is something he made good use of during the many storms at sea he once navigated. While others under his command blustered, shouted and raged at the elements, Captain Lyons simply accepted his fate, allowing them to do with him as they chose. On countless occasions he braced himself for death, but death did not come. "I am, it seems," he once confided, "destined to survive."

Really, she should be down by now, he thinks, irritated, casting a glance towards his wife's bedroom as he pushes through the crowd gathering in the ballroom, distracted by something he has seen through the French doors to the verandah. Yet, servants' gossip has informed him that Serena will be late, which means he will be left to tend to the guests alone: a task to which he is singularly unequal and cannot stand to perform without her. For what on earth will we talk about without Serena, he despairs: Serena, who has always been able to mine the most mundane spirits for hidden glimmers of cloistered passions: People who seem to live only to eat and breathe and to wish for nothing more; who most would overlook as tedious and in whom Serena could find a spark that she would tend until it became a fire. People like me.

How he would do anything to keep her, now it is too late, despite a mutual awareness that their marriage has been nothing less than an atrocity. And whereas he has frequently found words for other men, to express the deepest recesses of their guarded souls – words he is often privileged to learn have consoled so many broken wives – his own wife remains entirely ignorant, from the first day of their marriage until this last, of his devotion. Serena cannot guess at how much he has admired, and privately wept, for her courage; the fierce pride he harbors over her capacity to hope, to give of herself to others, for nothing in return. No, Serena has not known him at all, save for one moment twenty years ago, when he might have changed this sad fact. When he might have said: *"Turn the page, my love. Turn the page."*

But he has long accepted that his lips will never speak of love to her, and so he has hidden himself away in a corner of her life: little more than an observer who watches her captivate and entertain her summer guests, thrilling to the sight of her perfect grace while mourning unutterably the terrible secrets the silk folds of her dresses conceal within her. Yet, whenever she has cast her eyes to him, he has not smiled in gratitude to own the brightest star in the room. Rather he has scowled in disapproval, allowing her to turn away from him, without remorse. Better that she hates me, has insisted: For her own sake.

As evidenced by the hordes of people surrounding him, he acknowledges that Serena is to receive her due; the party will be another magnificent success. There has never been any doubt, however, that Serena Lyons has served her neighbors well – although nobody ever asked her to. The why of it all; Serena's overriding desire to position herself at the center of this society and to, arguably, control it, has never been resolved satisfactorily. Yet, no one wishes to be excluded. And Serena, regardless of her frailties, has only ever sought to include, to hold her guests close, like anchors, almost as if she is afraid that, without them, she would cease to exist. So she is regarded as something of a mystery, despite the fact that there is not one person, in this rarefied world in which they live, who does not profess to know her by heart. But, as Captain Lyons knows only too well, it is precisely Serena's heart no one can ever know.

As he arrives outside on the verandah, a mere glimpse confirms what he sighted from inside. And he is suddenly devastatingly aware that this gathering storm, emerging at the back of the rapidly receding fog, and causing only excitement as the guests rush past him at the top of the steps overlooking the dunes, is not the only one he will be called upon to overcome tonight. In a few hours, his beloved Serena will be lost to him. And there are so many things he has to tell her before she leaves, things she must learn: an obligation that he fears, given what he understands of himself, he may yet fail in.

Serena would be astonished to find tears in his eyes, his eyes that fasten now on the sky overhead, as if searching for a sign that all will be well. But this wind howling ever more furiously with an intent few can comprehend, these lowering clouds streaming toward him with arms outstretched from the horizon, confirms the impossibility of such a wish. Captain Lyons exercises no caution as he walks out to the marquee, passing the guests who have gathered to watch the rising waves crash against the shore. He is not afraid as he sounds the alarm and commands them to re-enter the ballroom, where they will be safe. He feels almost free as he watches them go, rushing en masse away from him. He knows: He is not one of them anymore.

THE HOSTESS

I have no plans left to manage. I have nothing left to do but watch the light as it moves and dances and plays over the possessions I have treasured. The possessions that remind me of the life I might have led.

I stand in a place of simple truth: I chose this bedroom for its location in the exact spot where the original house once stood. Everything here speaks of who I truly am: the train tickets from last Thursday for a journey I did not take; a beloved first edition of poems by Joyce on my bedside table; the sacred key that will not open any door in this house, tied with a torn piece of lace…I leave these priceless tokens to be cleared away by those who will shutter the estate: Will they glimpse my private despair? Will everything I concealed become evident?

I will no longer wait for guests in the marble hallway; no longer please or amuse people for reasons fathomable only to myself. I wonder if I have mattered to them at all. Or have I been little more than a hostess who served them dinner on the Theodore Haviland porcelain my husband's mother kept for her best guests? I have no control over anything anymore: not over these possessions, or of how people will speak of me. The decision has been made.

Most of us are nothing more than shells over shells over shells; the casings we present to the world and ask others to accept. In my case, wife, mother, hostess, betrayer, failure, a diminuendo of ever darkening notes that must be suppressed, played over with lighter tunes. I have lived in this house nearly all of my life. The house looks nothing like the picture my father sent to us when I was a child: the tiny Greek Revival cottage that I tumbled into love with, imagining myself already in its rooms. Yet, nor am I still the same daughter he bore. We have been added to, papered over, to obscure the tragedies that lurk within the walls of our frames.

I did not choose to live here all these years; it was my father who gave the house to Edward and me as a wedding gift. At the time, I kindled a romantic notion that he wanted to return what he had stolen, but I expected too much of him and I've never heard from him since. What my father did in leaving me this house was to imprison me forever in a lie: In this act, and others, he has had no better accomplice than my husband. Edward willingly picked up where my father left off. The proof of this is the dress I wear this evening: a dress that Edward chose for me. You probably consider it ridiculous. I am a woman of forty-eight and this pink chiffon, floor length dress is unmistakably meant for a teenage girl. But I was a girl when I first wore it, to the first party, the evening of my debut.

At first, I acknowledged Edward's choice with a curious mixture of sentiment and surprise. I almost doubted how I've treated him over the course of our marriage. Yet, when I realized what he had not approved, I forgave myself: the art deco, diamond combs that sit over there on my dressing table. So this evening my hair, Marcel-waved according to the fashion, is held with simple, black enamel clasps that no one will notice. And the diamond combs remain there, on the table; a touchstone to the past, to that memory he will not afford me. But I cannot reach for them now. Once I might have, but I no longer have the strength to defy him.

I was not quite beautiful enough for this dress at seventeen. People were kind enough then to pretend otherwise, but I still fall far short of the mark. I have never been a beauty although there was a time – a long time ago – when I was considered to personify grace. My graciousness was all anyone commented on at that first party, but it can be a difficult thing to hold onto, considering the disappointments life often brings.

Parties invite possibility for those of us lucky enough to star: From the outset, a party promises only reward, never disappointment. The disappointment that only comes after our imaginations have run away with us and we realize that people don't show up, cake can be tasteless, the music too loud, the company a bore. Or after we have woken the following morning, shamed and hung-over, attempting to make sense of the fragmented recollections of the previous evening. Yet, a first party will always share some kinship with the last for being something special, something remarkable. I hold dear the memory of the first night I ever stood here, and I will never forget this last evening, for all that I will learn.

I would never have permitted flowers to be brought into the house, nor allowed Edward to receive my guests. Tonight, nothing is how I would have arranged it. Every detail is down to him. And if you were to peer closer, you might see the simple truth at the heart of his arrangements: Everything mimics the first party ever held in this house, as if he imagines that I am still seventeen, as if he imagines that nothing has yet been done that cannot be undone.

THE HOST

In a frenzy, her guests stream past him, back to the safety of the house, their fear subsumed by their fascination: It's something new, this spectacle, something to do; already the evening is memorable. They do not care that their dresses are torn in the rush; they think nothing of a diamond bracelet ripped from a wrist and trampled underfoot in the stampede; it is immaterial that the men's tuxedos will certainly need to be cleaned because of the foaming spray blowing in off the waves. All of it is just so out of the ordinary, almost as if this – what Captain Lyons sees – is the most marvelous entertainment.

Some of the men, holding fast against the wind to the iron rail of the verandah that protects them from the dunes below, shout over the noise and make a pretense of asking if they should stay with him – their women are watching, after all, from behind the glass doors. Those who did not fight in the Great War imagine the romance of standing shoulder to shoulder against the elements; while those who did cannot conceal the relief of being granted a reprieve, insisting that it's "just another nor'easter, a September Gale. Nothing to be alarmed about..." grateful to get back to the bar. Go, go into the house, he thinks, resignedly, make your introductions, meet people for the first time that you've already met five thousand times before, but that you forget party on party because you don't need to remember. You are not needed here.

As he is The Host and he is The Captain, it seems only appropriate that he be the last one left to confront what will come. Yet, this fact is entirely irrelevant, destined only for inscription on a tombstone. All that matters now is that he is to be the keeper of time.

He holds aloft his pocket watch and compass that has accompanied him on every voyage for over fifty years to see who has invited this storm. He deduces that it is coming from the northeast, but there is still blue around the edges of the black clouds. He knows the guests inside will take comfort from that, especially those of a more nervous disposition who pretend to be brave whilst secretly fearing the worst: In their minds, the blue will over-come the black and the clouds will move further and further away and all they will be left with is a memory of some trouble that did not come and the late sun on their faces. This is what those who are paying attention will wish for. Yet, Captain Lyons also knows there is no mistaking the furnace rag-ing behind the edges of each cloud; the copper glow around the perimeter; the too-familiar figure emerging, little by little; the petticoat ruffles of her dress, the daintily shod foot, the winking gimlet-eyes of that exquisite devil dancing.

They need no introduction: They've met before. Captain Lyons stands, as if on the helm of a ship, in defiance of her rampaging brutality, but it is only for show, so that Serena's guests can revel in comfortable ignorance for a while longer. In the moments to follow, some will benignly accept his lead, but others will panic and question his judgment, thinking themselves better leaders, and then there will be those curiosity seekers, who will peek out from behind the lavish curtains of comfort he has provided for them, at an unfamiliar world that might be better than the one they live in, perhaps even more exciting. He knows this is inevitable: He will not be able to save them from themselves.

He prays for them, as he has prayed for Serena in her ignorance. He thinks of the inscription from Psalms on the wall of the St. Andrews Church on Dune Road and winces at its irony: "Thou rulest the raging of the sea; Thou stillest the waves thereof when they arise." God will not still these ris-ing waves, this he knows:

The waves will surely want us.

But it is the wind in this storm who will go first, who will claim its prize before the rest. He fastens his grip tighter over the iron railing before him.

It has come for the trees.

THE HOSTESS

This road I love, the road that leads to the sea, starts just over there in The Lilac Walk, where my mother planted the trees when I was a child. Of the many things I cannot forgive my father, the gardens are not one of them. Before my mother died, he gave her a fortune to transform our land into a paradise reminiscent of England. I remember how lovingly she crafted the Walk, the mazes and the night gardens. They have always brought me such pleasure, never more so than in the twilight, because there is no other place on earth where the day dies as poignantly as here. The darkness falls and illuminates the gardens in a veil of monochrome where only what is beautiful can be seen. And it was on just such a night when I found the most beautiful thing I've ever seen: Kit's face. He was sitting underneath the lilac trees.

There you are, the heart cries, when we find the one face we are destined never to forget. My heart was no different. He had grown up somewhere far away and, at first, I did not recognize him as the little boy who was once my friend. Now he was a young man, poised on the edge of his seat, watching me in a ballet. Did I know then, as our eyes met, that everything in my life would return to the memory of his smile? For nobody ever smiled as kindly at me again. And *there you are,* my heart has cried, whenever I have turned to his memory, in all the years since he left me.

Does Kit think of me, wherever he lives now? Does he remember the lilacs? *Please,* I have often begged, here at this window. *Appear underneath the arbor or wait for me at the West Pavilion or be the last guest walking up this road to meet me. Smile at me once more and I will forgive you and you will forgive me.*

After he went away, the trees never flowered again. Not until this summer. I was almost pleased. I needed no reminder of what we had shared there. It would have been unbearable to acknowledge their life, their beauty. No, apart from these five minutes, I try never to look at the lilacs; I have turned away to lesser things.

THE UNINVITED GUEST

It is like this, where he has been; it is like a screen door opening into the sun, through which he cannot pass.

In the place where Christopher 'Kit' Peel has lived until today, all that exists is memory. In thirty years, he has been afforded no other concession. All he has owned is an incomplete vision of time past, of the experiences that were denied to him, but which, sometimes, he has glimpsed through that screen door, falling open and shut, guided by hands other than his.

When Captain Lyons first left him there, Kit was forced to accept that he would never see Serena again. Only Captain Lyons could have told Serena where to find him, but he did not. The decision was taken out of Kit's control; felled, as he was, by a circumstance. One that enabled Captain Lyons to take his place in Serena's heart, to lock Kit out from where he was once safe.

Around him there, the sunlight would seep through the windows, falling in pools onto the floor, but never quite reaching where he sat. And through the door would filter the voices, almost like prayers, of lives continuing, and it was in them, that he sometimes heard Serena's name. Aspects of her life passed him by, borne on the breath of others, details emerging of her parties that raged on without him, of her friends, her marriage, the dresses she wore, the diamonds he had not given her glinting in her hair, her game of Five Things. Yet, whether she spoke of Kit, he never learned nor did he ask. Only Serena could ever tell him what he had once meant to her.

They were the forgotten: men consigned there most often by misfortune, but sometimes by the careless and the pitiless, the weak and the ambivalent. *Not you*, he would silently protest, on looking up, to find a fondly recalled acquaintance in the distance, arriving. He hoped always to avoid the sorrow of such reconciliations. Yet, it proved impossible: Over the years, scores of people from his past, laid low by circumstances, Wars, the Depression, were brought to the same place; locked in together, in the same impoverished condition, to try and make sense of what had befallen them. Kit would hide his head in his hands; *Don't remember me*, his unspoken plea. He could not have them see him, not after Nairobi, but still they would arrive at his side: a constant stream of visitors, spilling forth with platitudes, as if to pay their respects: "Poor boy, no...You're too young to be here...it's too terrible... Perhaps, though; it's better this way..."

After recovering and adapting to their reality, most eventually moved on, somewhere else, outside, where they could watch, leaving him behind, to see who would come next. But it was with a pain he had not experienced in years, that he turned, one day, to find the figure of his old friend, Anthony Duverglas, being carried in. Almost immediately, he mourned his eyes: He already knew what he would find within them.

Something happened to them there. It was as if they were bled of color, because of the hope that was lost: They were shipwrecked eyes. "Not good enough for her now," Anthony said, as he reached to shake his friend's hand. For months, it was the only phrase he could utter. Yet, each morning, Kit would watch Anthony wake, and rise from his bed, renewed; resolved to tackle the day. He would dress in the same impeccably tailored suit, a perfect gentleman even in that place where his manners and refinement didn't matter to anyone else. He would move about his quarters, as if nothing had changed, make to leave, and then, something would compel him to remember, and he would slump down onto his bed, defeated. Then one day, he stopped. The only occasions he ever found to stir was when he would approach Kit, to ask a question that never changed:

"When you think of it," Anthony would say, "what do you think of?"

And Kit would reply, "I think of splendor."

Always, as if it was the answer for which he was waiting, Anthony would acknowledge the word, lowering himself into a chair beside him, his face upturned to where Kit gazed. And they would sit, in raptures to the past, as it spread out before them, the slide-like images they conjured from their imaginations, clicking into place: an homage to everything they had known, to everything they had loved.

Yes, it is like this where he has been. It is like a screen door opening into the sun, through which he cannot pass. It is married to the memory of being twenty-one, of being left behind, as that exquisite girl walked so gracefully away out into the garden where he could not follow. *Follow,* cried his every instinct, but his head said, *No. There will be other days.* Yet, now, in his heart, he only ever follows Serena out of the door: To tell her of tomorrows. "Tomorrow, we will," he has called to her. But she cannot hear him.

THE HOSTESS

Stay and watch with me a little longer. I know how you must long to join the others downstairs, but let me introduce you to them first. There will be time for you to drink, to gossip, to waltz on the lawn to Mozart, if that's what you would like. But, please, don't leave me yet.

Can we ever know who hides to spy on our souls? Who secretly wonders what we are thinking or doing behind the walls of our houses? Which of my guests spares me a forbidden thought before kissing his wife goodnight; who amongst us anticipates the morning with happiness and who with dread; or gives thanks before sleep that they are ignorant to the deepest yearnings of their partners, who lie awake beside them on tear-stained pillows?

For thirty years, I have watched them all come and go, all of these guests. I know them better than I know myself. I know the desires they bring with them, the secrets they keep; I can detect the cruelty that creeps into the corners of the seemingly kindest smiles. I can predict who will be rewarded and who will be denied. There is nothing that I miss. And everything I've seen and learned has led me here to you this evening.

Often I have found a mirror in them, to my own life, a re-enactment of every dream I have ever kindled, here at this window; what I force myself to relive each week. You see, at the start of every party, there is a story that beats in our hearts: what we anticipate, what we believe the party will bring to us. And sometimes those stories remain secret, and sometimes they lurk in plain sight. Just like the story waiting to be told for that little girl on the steps below us, where I once waited with the same guileless expectancy, when I was only seventeen.

All week she has talked of nothing but this party. It's not her first, but it is the first that means anything to her because of the promise it holds. The reason why she is waiting down there, so full of hope, her gaze flying to each of the guests' faces, oblivious to those who are watching her in disapproval, because it's not her place to conduct herself like this. Her name is Elizabeth, but she goes by Bee, because her mother loved the sound of them in summer. She's only a child, barely more than sixteen. But the name she goes by here, to remind her of just how unimportant she is, is The Little Maid.

When I first saw her, I remember how small she was and all of the usual things little maids are – cautiously excited and dressed in her best; clothes that would appear cheap to anyone else. I remember her fawn like eyes that saw only the best in me, instead of hardening into contempt. It's almost impossible to explain, but I felt a near maternal love for her. I wanted to reach out and forego the inhibiting social rules that separate us. I wanted her to think of me as someone compassionate, someone who sensed that she must be missing her mother already and didn't want her to be afraid. I wanted her to doubt everything she would be told about me, the minute she left the room.

Elizabeth has no idea that I have been watching her ever since the day she arrived in April. You see, from the beginning, even though we seem so very different, I sensed we are so much alike. I have watched her pore over the trays of diamonds in my dressing room, the Schiaparelli gowns in my wardrobes, the silk shoes nestled in boxes of tissue paper, piled as high as she can ever imagine. I have watched her feast on every story in the gossip columns about this party, about me. I have watched the dream take hold of her, the dream so many bring to this party. The dream I would give anything to spare her.

She is the mirror we must look through for you to understand the story I am about to tell. The truth I have never revealed until this evening: of what happened at my debut thirty-one years ago tonight and everything that followed after.

So come then, let me show what you came here to understand. Forget everything you've heard. There has never been a party. This is where the ritual begins, here where we stand.

It begins with a summer redbird at my window.

THE PARTY, THE PARTY!

"Do you suppose he'll come?" a venerable socialite asks her friend, brushing past The Little Maid on the doorstep to La Doucette without apologizing. "If who'll come?" asks someone new to the party. "*Him*. Kit Peel. The one Serena was so in love with. Why, don't you know the story?" The Socialite responds keenly, stopping to speak to her. "At her debut? Such a scandal! None of us could believe our eyes when it happened." "Just like last week," chimes in The Socialite's friend. "History repeating itself, right here on the same doorstep. Well, I *always* thought her husband had something to do with it," says The Socialite knowingly. "You see, they were so in love, Kit and Serena. It didn't make any sense that—" "And to think we always blamed Lucinda. So cruel, when you think about it," interrupts her friend, biting her lip in shame-faced contrition. "But then, she drinks you know," counters The Socialite, grimacing pityingly at the newcomer. "And no doubt Captain Lyons drove her to it," she surmises, nodding triumphantly and shedding herself of blame, as swiftly as the stole she turns back to deposit in The Little Maid's arms. "What time is she coming down?" The Socialite calls over her shoulder, as she marches into the house. "I heard seven," replies the friend. "Goodness," gasps The Socialite. "Just like at her debut! Now, what do you make of *that*...?"

The surrounding chatter does not surprise The Little Maid. Over the course of the summer, she has heard every story about Kit Peel and Mrs. Lyons. At any party, it has proven almost invariable that all newcomers will be apprised of "all things Mrs. Lyons" before their first sip of champagne and the first party ruthlessly picked over as if to finally understand what went so wrong at long last. Not that anyone has spoken to her, of course. Except that wonderful film star, Rupert Turner-Hume, The Little Maid remembers, smiling to herself as if she still can't believe her luck, and that horrible debutante... she also recalls, less happily. The one who asked to borrow her maid's outfit for Mrs. Chauncey's Poverty Ball: "I'm to come depicting 'hard times,' to raise money for the Depression," she had said, taking a glass of champagne from the tray The Little Maid held up to her. "So I thought you'd be the perfect person to ask..." she concluded, much to the amusement of her friends. Except for him, though, The Little Maid reminds herself, looking to the floor and flushing with happiness.

She has waited for hours on this doorstep, despite the terrible weather that everyone in town was talking about this morning, after the reports filtered through from Montauk. What the fishermen observed at dawn from the Promised Land Dock: the turbulent wind and strange, green, soup-like smog covering the area that made them think twice about setting out. Like the wind tonight, The Little Maid thinks. The wind that is causing guests to hold their coats and shawls over their heads for protection, making it so difficult for her to pick out the one face in the crowd she seeks: the face of the young man she is waiting for that suddenly appears ahead of her in the crowd.

The Little Maid is no longer a little maid as she watches him ascend the steps on the arm of his mother. In her imagination, she is just like all of the people she serves, except her dress is pale blue chiffon, picked out by white daisies embroidered in silk onto the sleeves. Even the expression she wears, so full of welcome and delight, isn't her own: It is one she has copied from Mrs. Lyons, having studied how she greets her summer guests, albeit for far longer than the years than The Little Maid has lived.

This must have been how Mrs. Lyons felt, she thinks, as her imagination leaps ahead to what will follow when the young man arrives at her side. All of the stories he has told her of the sailing parties and clubs, where pretty girls watch polo, or play croquet in the sun. And in her imagination, she will attend those parties with this guest she met here, who is good enough to pass the time of day when she runs errands in town: this gentleman who has taken a keen interest and treats her with a respect she receives from so few. And, even though he has only hinted at a romance, she has dared to dream, imagining what will happen when she sees him tonight, at this, the last party of the season. *'The party, the party...!'* she thrills, as the young man draws closer, reciting the famous line from the column by The Eavesdropper in *The Southampton Press* that runs every Saturday about Mrs. Lyons' parties, as she finally understands its meaning.

The Little Maid, still so innocent, has not yet guessed what is obvious but yet so heartbreaking to Mrs. Lyons, standing watching her from above. That this very proper young man has already seen her but is pretending not to notice her, as he busies himself with chaperoning his mother into the party, with all of the studious chivalry such mothers demand of their sons. She is not old enough to understand what Mrs. Lyons already knows: that he is only nice to her when no one else is looking, when his social circle will not judge him unfavorably. Not because he is kind, but because he is weak. Because it would be uncomfortable for him to ignore her when nobody else is around. Almost as unpleasant as it would be to suffer what will be said to him and about him, if he were to treat her as anything other than the help tonight.

It is only as he passes her without acknowledgment, despite her searching smile, that the creeping, hollow awareness begins to take root in The Little Maid: that she is not a debutante in a blue chiffon dress with silk daisies on the sleeves. She is just a maid who will always be just a maid. And the hope she brought with her to this party is just that: nothing more than a bright spot in the mind to retreat into when life seems too dismal. When she is reminded as she is now of what everyone told her when she first arrived here: Her place is only to watch.

And whipped by the elements, like a million smarting slaps across her face, she does watch, but not with expectation anymore. She watches with a mixture of envy and longing as the boy and his mother glide, tall and perfectly poised, over the black and white marble checkerboard floor, to the ballroom where their friends await them, like the King and Queen in a game of chess. "Don't tell me you're your father's son, after all…That girl can only be sixteen, you ludicrous boy," hisses the young man's mother, turning back to glare at The Little Maid. No, this isn't how Mrs. Lyons felt, The Little Maid realizes, tears stinging her eyes. Not from everything she has heard, and lived through, of Mrs. Lyons' debut. And as she contemplates the society she will never belong to inside, it strikes The Little Maid that maybe all of the warnings she ignored from the staff about Mrs. Lyons are true. Because

23

why would she ever choose these people over that boy she loved, she asks. Why would she ever choose to stay?

Suddenly, what once seemed enviable changes before her eyes as a ferocious gust of wind screams into the house at her back: a manic blast that stirs into wild life the glittering particles of comedy and tragedy, flippancy and fantasy, prospects and promises contained within, as if the revelers have been trapped inside of a child's water globe. Yet, as the wind abates and the lamplight ebbs to half-life, the garish gaiety and noise assumes a more sinister aspect as The Little Maid watches the shadows take hold of the party. Cowering in terror on the doorstep, unsure whether to enter or run, she finds herself thinking again of Kit Peel and asks if he too detected something similarly unnerving on the night of Mrs. Lyons' debut: if that was the reason why he thought better of coming inside.

THE HOST

The waves lashing higher against the dunes below him, Captain Lyons' thoughts focus, as they must, on the boy. The boy his wife has loved, and for whom her guests have searched at each party, ever since he left at the age of twenty-one. Of all the great romances conducted upon a summer stage, the consensus of Serena's society holds that the one she enjoyed in her seventeenth year was, by far, the most remarkable. And in this, as in their affection for the young man she loved, Captain Lyons knows they are not mistaken. Christopher Peel, or Kit as they called him for short, has remained in the memory as the finest of a line of the finest, because no one can forget his compassion, or his love, so obvious to all, for Serena. They've worshipped him, he concedes, like an eternal flame of youth, who has burned gently on; a testament to the tender mercies of his innocence that once so deeply touched them.

He can recall the day Kit arrived as vividly as any as he has lived: that sunny June day, the waves, white and turbulent beyond the golf course at Shinnecock Hills, and Kit, as he had been – as Captain Lyons had known him – so full of hope, hurrying over an ancient lawn to arrive at where they stood. It was the afternoon that would alter the path of Captain Lyons' life irrevocably. "Her hat..." he says quietly, closing his eyes to the memory.

The summer colony had gathered on the balcony to celebrate some young ladies chosen to pour tea for the champions. Serena was not one of them, which Captain Lyons thought entirely unjust, but she was considered something of an oddity to the presiding Social Guard. While she was as wealthy as any of the daughters of the more aged families and infinitely prettier, she did not depart for the city in the Fall and so was tellingly ignorant of their society of winter and spring. In recognition of her mother's aristocratic lineage as the daughter of a Baronet, some matrons had occasionally offered a maternal hand, but only when it did not interfere too dramatically with their own lives. So this is why it had fallen to him to fulfill the makeshift role of guardian, Serena's father being absent more often than not: It was a role Captain Lyons found himself unwittingly undertaking, and later, unwillingly, when he realized how deeply he had grown to love her. But, by then, it was too late. I've never been able to rid myself of the impulse to protect Serena, he acknowledges, despite the happiness it has ultimately cost me.

It was a protectiveness that had begun when she was a child; memories now, which never fail to sadden him. From an early age, Serena owned, what he perceived as a desperate need to be needed: She would chase noise, clamor, excitement, anything to escape the shuttered majesty of her family home: her fear of being left inside, alone, impelling her to go tirelessly out of her way to please others. As if in response to the curiosity she inspired, Serena mastered the art of making herself indispensable. She would hover at a remove from her classmates' games at the local school, listening earnestly to their conversations and catching their eye in sympathy or interest depending on their stories. She learned to profess fascination in the most mundane subjects, spending hours seemingly enraptured by humdrum tales of misplaced ribbons, or willful pets, or the minutiae of her neighbors' days, many of whom were as lonely in old age as she was in childhood. People who simply wanted to talk to somebody of an afternoon, and who came to depend on her, finding her conveniently dawdling by their fences, as she walked home from school. Not once did she ever press them for more details than they cared to share, earning a reputation as somebody discrete who could always be trusted. It was in this way that, by degree and a certain amount of contrivance, Captain Lyons watched Serena become very popular, amidst people from every type of background, although never in a fashion that could invite suspicion.

She made herself ordinary; someone who posed no threat, and everyone believed her, he remembers. Yet, few, he knew, could guess at her true motivation, the fear that would evolve into a need to control everything as she grew older: Serena was an expert at masking the sadness that inspired her every move. So this was why, on that day in June, Serena betrayed nothing of her disappointment at not having been chosen to join the other girls, only delight in their good fortune.

Captain Lyons has often questioned why he allowed Kit to visit, given the regard he held toward Serena that summer, when he came to consider her as an adult and not a child. Although neither Kit nor Serena had met for over a decade, both would talk of one another to him, the only ear that proved receptive. Was it not inevitable that they would love one another as adults, when so many thought them soul mates as children? Possibly, he allows on this last evening, but I was blind to pitfalls then, as those who are consumed by another's perfection so often are. My only thought is that it would make her happy and she had enjoyed so little of it. I hoped, too, that it might resolve something from the past: the tragedy that had nearly destroyed her. And I so needed Serena to live.

Yet, there suddenly Kit was, on that perfect afternoon, just after Memorial Day in 1907. There he appeared from a distance in the pale linen summer suit Captain Lyons had taken him into Manhattan to buy, having arrived off the boat from England in something heavy and woolen and entirely unsuited to East End weather. And as Captain Lyons watched him make his way over the lawn, he knew that Serena's love for Kit and Kit's for her was unavoidable; As soon as their eyes will meet, he accepted that afternoon, it will begin. He was almost amused by what he had done, denying himself the right to love her so that someone else could: the extraordinary mixture of pain and jealousy that he had willingly inflicted upon himself proved suffocating, as he watched Kit move closer, and Serena's heart evolve further away from his grasp.

From the first, however, Captain Lyons understood that Kit would emerge the victor over every summer heart. The young man possessed a kindly reticence, a lack of presumption, despite his evident beauty that immediately captured the interest of the women, and caused their hat brims to tilt up in unison – and to remain up – until he arrived at where they sat. Captain Lyons knew they would not be able to resist. It was as if the summer had been reborn, lit now by Kit's gratitude, his curiosity.

"I think he was one of us originally," hazarded a matron. "That's right. Or, he was," she added, rushing to correct her error before someone else did. "He used to stay with his grandmother or was it his Aunt? Yes, his Aunt, she died. There was – oh gosh – perhaps, we should not talk of it," she suddenly realized, placing a hand over her mouth. "It really wouldn't be fair to Serena…" Captain Lyons had prepared himself for the gossip, and was poised to intercede should it go too far, but the danger passed when a young girl of Serena's age asked, "He's a friend of Serena's? Why, the lucky thing." "My goodness, it's Kit," gasped May Cook, one of the most powerful mistresses of the social seas, emerging from the pavilion. "It's Ellen Peel's nephew. Why in the world did you keep it a secret, Lyons? Serena will be over the moon. Where is she?" she asked, looking excitedly around the balcony.

The beginnings of rain trickling down his face, so different a day now to then, Captain Lyons can still see where she sat: in a corner, in a white Empire dress, her parasol resting at her side; delicate in her loveliness, tiny in her form. She was surrounded by admirers, one of whom, Teddy Worthington, was rumored to be preparing to propose. He hadn't feared Teddy as a rival, however: He thought the romance would not survive the summer, given Serena's fragility and her need for stability, something Teddy was ill equipped to provide, despite how he amused her. Yet, it was her hat that day which had captured everyone's interest: an extraordinarily dramatic wide brimmed confection of lace and tulle, offset by pale blue ribbons and pink roses that perfectly complimented Serena's gold and russet hair. A hat Captain Lyons had bought for her in Paris and pretended was a gift from her father: A deceit he had permitted himself, if only to witness her joy.

There it was, on the balcony, that moment before, the one Captain Lyons returns to again, if only to fully appreciate its sorrow. For all he saw as he contemplated Serena, before she had any notion of Kit arriving, was a recollection of that morning: of the large hat box – pink and white striped, black beribboned – which he had placed on the table in the marble hall, and Serena holding the hat up to the light through the windows, unable to believe her good fortune. And "are you happy today, Serena," he had asked, inclining his head to try and catch every whisper of emotion that flitted across her face so that he might remember it later: "Oh, Captain Lyons," she had softly replied, her eyes so full of warmth, "I am so, so happy today." And as she had tilted her perfect face up to his own, it was as if the hard angles wrought by sickness, fear and worry were smoothed once more by the softness of her newfound calm, so at odds to how she had appeared not months earlier. It was the youngest she was ever to appear to him; unburdened, carefree, her only thought a gift.

It was her hat, which started the love affair: the hat that was suddenly ripped off her head by a vicious gust of wind determined to claim it. A gasp of "Oh" resonated from the others at its loss, but not a soul moved to reclaim it, not even Teddy or Captain Lyons, awed at the injustice of how someone who owned so little could possibly be deprived of anything more: "Don't worry, I'll buy you another," Teddy consoled Serena, placing an arm around her shoulder, as Captain Lyons turned to witness Serena's expression harden once more into resignation; understanding completely why she did not move, why she had to watch it go. Society had dictated her lead. It was only a hat. One none of the other girls could own and therefore were quite happy, despite their commiserations, for her to lose.

He thought to do something then, too late, a token gesture, when suddenly someone asked: "Whatever is he doing?" and all assembled turned to watch Kit racing toward the sea. "Where does he think he's going...?" they muttered, intrigued and slightly awed by his pursuit —and then they realized what Captain Lyons had already guessed: Kit was going to try to catch Serena's hat, spiraling toward the waves. "Aah," May Cook smiled, standing up to lean over the balcony, like she was watching a race. "How very curious: How unlike us, to reach.... Oh, wouldn't it be marvelous, if he were to actually catch it..." "Wouldn't it?" agreed the others, some as genuinely ecstatic as May, others wrapping their fingers tighter around teacup handles in envy, privately willing him to fail.

But Serena was not to wait for the outcome. She was hurried away by those lesser girlfriends and Teddy, too, in advance of the evening's masque, in which she was going to dance. "Will one of you bring the hat tonight," they called. "That is, if he does catch it, whoever he is?" "I'll make sure of it," insisted Teddy, the girls jostling around Serena to block her view of Kit. "Off you go," he said jovially, before turning back to survey the young man seriously, doing what he was incapable of.

Yet, isn't that so often the way of love, as it begins? Captains Lyons considers. Something lost, a problem to be solved, that somebody new fixes, when nobody else can be bothered, or else is too weak to try? He smiles ruefully at how hard the debutantes and boys in competition for Serena's position or affections tried to keep them apart. And it is almost with a sense of triumph that he acknowledges how, within a matter of hours, Serena and Kit had found one another again.

"*I knew you before*," Captain Lyons remembers. It might as well have been the closing line of the latest play, for it was widely repeated, as if it were the most romantic declaration anyone had ever heard. And who could fail to remember that evening following the afternoon at Shinnecock. An evening when, appearing in a tableau of Shakespeare's plays, Serena performed a ballet in The Lilac Walk of La Doucette, Kit watching from the front row as if she was the only thought that might ever occur to him. "He was originally one of us, you know. But isn't he charming and so exotic," everyone present agreed, thrilling to the prospect of watching their court-ship unfold. So, of course, Kit was welcomed. Of course, the audience was transfixed when Serena suddenly stumbled during her dance and Kit rushed over to pick her up from the carpet of lilac flowers, upon which she had fallen.

There it was, Captain Lyons thinks, that moment when love fastens over disparate hearts and holds, drawing them closer in. That moment when those who love has touched become aware, for the first time, how terrible it would be to live in a world without it. It was the moment when Serena looked up at Kit, as he gathered her up in his arms, and announced, with such affecting sadness, "I knew you before" and he smiled back so grate-fully, as if she was a reward for his many losses. Captain Lyons watched with everyone else, mesmerized by that boy and girl who were never forgotten by anyone present. Despite the fact that, come Fall, whatever had bound them was severed.

Captain Lyons is not oblivious to the chatter at these parties. Over the years, he has been privy to every scathing remark. But this is precisely the reason why he does attend: He comes to listen, to watch, to see what most miss. Just as he did that afternoon at Shinnecock, just as he did that evening of the ballet. It is the only way I have been able to protect Serena from herself, he believes, given what could happen if I lost sight for an instant.

There are those who thrill to romantic visions, lost in their vicarious beauty, and there are those who watch with clear sight, aware of its meretricious pitfalls: Captain Lyons is one such person. He knows that it wasn't fate that caused Serena's hat to come loose or for her to stumble at the sight of Kit, but carelessness – a hat unpinned, the ribbons of a ballet slipper untied. And what resulted did not inspire awe in him, but foreboding: For what he saw was a girl robbed of propriety, bareheaded on a balcony, yet too intent on pleasing others to ask for help. What he saw was the tiniest foot, robbed of its shoe, and stained with the blood of lilacs – in its way, a foreshadowing of an infinitely more damaging mark that would soil her flawless skin. Yet, Captain Lyons did not intervene, as he might have: I was no Kit Peel, he reminds himself again. Despite my age and experience, and anything I may have been able to teach her. In that type of competition, I would have won, only by default. So he resigned himself to their inevitable union. Even so, he could never quite shake his unease at either sight. Or forget that it was on a bed of flowers that Kit first left Serena as a child, and the tragedy that happened there as a consequence of their devotion.

Then as now he was powerless to change anything. He had no real choice but to bring Kit back here that summer and his hands were equally tied today: He had to let him go. As barbaric as it might seem, Captain Lyons has always been grateful that no one ever saw what happened to Kit, despite how insistently the boy has preyed upon him to be set free. His only fear is for his wife, what it will do to her to learn the truth. And this is why it tantalizes him, the open door that he could yet shut and spare Serena this knowledge. But, he prays, if nothing else can be resolved between us in these, our dying moments, please let there be time for her to understand why I acted as I did before she leaves. If only so that I might know some peace, after she is gone.

THE HOSTESS

It is the evening of my debut and I am seventeen again. At midnight, I will turn eighteen. The air outside is still, stifling, and downstairs the guests are all arriving in their carriages. "To be this *hot*, this *late* in the season. *Intolerable,*" I hear the emphatic Helen Fitzgerald greet May Cook, "but how *clever* of Serena to ask for her debut to be held here. Can you *imagine* how unbearable the city would be? When I first learned of her choice, I said to John, 'Good Lord, what is her father *thinking*? Does she imagine us all as *locals*? There is a time for a season to *end* and that is on Labor Day, *not* the 21st of September.' I was sure - but, don't tell her I said this – that absolutely *nobody* would come, but look," Helen exclaims, more emphatically than ever. I can't see but I imagine that she gestures grandly to the surrounding carriages crammed into the courtyard, "*That's* how popular this girl is. But she does get everything right, doesn't she, and she was so *dear* at our tennis party at The Quogue Bathing Club; she sat with my mother *for hours* and not even *I* am that much of a good Christian..." They laugh and May says something inaudible and the subject changes, "No, not particularly good. Her health is… well…." And their voices trail off as they enter the party below this room.

There have been parties before, but not like this one. This party is to be a new tradition, one I have created, and I should be so happy that everyone has chosen to come: all of the most famous families; the Astors and the Cooks, the Wiborgs and the Halseys. I am as popular as I've ever dreamt of becoming. The dress I wear is a gift from Captain Lyons, one he bought for me in Paris, and on my right-hand, my mother's ring hangs heavily. It was her favorite, a 12-carat aquamarine my father brought home to her from nowhere exotic, from New England. And I am seventeen again and there is a summer redbird at my window.

They are so rare in this part of Long Island that I haven't seen one since I was a little girl. *"They only stay for a summer and then they fly away:"* I remember my mother told me this when I was a child and I realize that I've chosen the last day of summer for my debut. It wasn't deliberate but somehow I feel closer to her: "Have you come to say goodbye?" I ask the redbird. "Goodbye," I say, resting my forehead on the windowpane, as the bird's wings beat in front of me, but the bird won't leave me.

Yet, standing here, I am not happy: I am terrified. My breathing comes in shallow gasps, my body trembles every time I think of what might go wrong, who might not come. A step too far has brought me to this window; a fear that, despite what I thought I knew, I shouldn't have dared. I have not enjoyed a second of this day because of the worry I own and I have no idea what will happen, or how I will survive it, if.... We must give to receive. And I've given: Perhaps, too much.

The band starting up downstairs startles me and, as I hear the overture of Mozart's clarinet concerto, my hands begin to shake so badly that I can't fasten the clasp of my dress behind my neck. There is no one to help me: I have no family anymore, except for my father who despises me. My mother killed herself a year after the death of my sister: my beautiful sister, Catherine, who died as I slept beneath the sweet peas when I was a child. "Where did Catherine go?" I asked my mother on a day that I didn't realize was to be her last. "She flew away," she told me. "She was like the summer redbird. They only stay for a summer and then they fly away." "And where do the redbirds go?" "They go to where it is beautiful." "And here, where we live. Is this not beautiful?" I asked my mother. "Yes," she replied with knowing sadness. "But it is not paradise."

This legacy is all that my mother left me with, the idea of some enchanted faraway place where beautiful people like my sister and her lived. So when they found her dead of a lithium overdose the next morning I didn't cry, even though I was only eight. I simply believed that my mother and Catherine were like the summer redbirds; they had gone to find another summer and would return when the summer began again for us. But they never did, despite how I waited for them each year: despite how I would peer up to the skies to catch a glimpse of their exquisite feathers, beating a song of hello.

But all my sadness suddenly falls away as I witness a promise kept. There is to be no more worry, no more fear because it happens to me now, as it should for all the girls who love the boys so fair and delicate: I see Kit arrive, that beloved companion of my youth. He has come to the party, just as he said he would. And I feel only delight as I witness the excitement in his steps as he makes his way to the West Pavilion by the lilac trees, where he hesitates on whether to sit on the bench there or stand. I feel only relief and gratitude at his nervousness because I understand it to be the hallmark of great antici-pation that I share with him: It is a fear of getting things wrong because you matter so much to someone. And I know now that I matter to him in the way I have yearned to, and never have to anyone else before.

I should run to him, I know. I must not wait here, as if thinking bet-ter of it. I must not let my fear at everything Kit signifies to me take over, regardless of how much I love him. But I do. I hesitate, I allow the voice in my head – my dear friend Teddy's voice, to whom I was almost engaged before Kit returned for the summer – to ring louder. Teddy who, after I confided my plans yesterday, soberly placed his drink down on the table at lunch, and announced, "I shouldn't be the one to…it's not that you gave me up for him, it's *not*, Serena. It's that you must be careful. He's just a Summer Visitor when it comes to it. How well do you really know him…? There have been rumors, Serena. About him and Lucinda…"

"Lucinda," I say. And at the sound of her name the summer redbird sud-denly flies away.

Yet, all I have to do is look at Kit outside to drown Teddy's warnings out. All I have to do is let myself think of what would happen if I don't go to him. No, Teddy, you are so wrong, I reassure myself, pushing the doubts he has inspired away. Look, Kit's as nervous as I am, and I do know him. I knew him before you, before everyone. Besides, I think defiantly, he has kept his promise. And the relief is so empowering that I find the courage to turn from the window. Everything makes sense to me again as I remember Kit's words to me that morning:

"We will go then, you and I, in the night."

"Yes," I say, as I turn to run to the door and the life beyond it, in that beau-tiful world where Kit waits for me: a world that seems so much like paradise.

LUCINDA

It strikes her this impulse, as her foot touches the platform and she feels the force of the wind in her face. How kind would it be just to let the wind take it, she thinks, this handbag she clutches to her chest. The blue silk beaded handbag she has always brought to Serena's parties, ever since Serena's debut on Lucinda's eighteenth birthday: the party Lucinda was never to have, the one her grandfather too readily cancelled, so as not to spoil Serena's presentation.

If she does it, if she has the nerve, she can watch it spiral away, up, up into the air, like a blue silk kite. It would almost be an honorable parting, she tells herself, like something one hears of between warriors. She could relinquish it with such affection, such gratitude, for the dreams and hopes it contained, and the consolation it has brought her, over the years, after she failed to fulfill any aspiration of her youth. Not yet, though, because that blonde man is watching and she sees him wince in recognition. Please God, she thinks, don't let there be another scene; the type of scene that always comes from men recognizing her when she's with her husband. Of course, she knows him, but she's not in the right state of mind to guess exactly where they met. Considering some of the places she's been, she knows it's probably best not to try. She grips her husband's arm tighter and turns her attention to the floor. Please God, she silently pleads, glancing up quickly again to see if this man is still watching her, don't let there be... And now, she does recognize him and, almost as if he has her arm tethered to a string, she raises her arm up and holds aloft the blue beaded handbag to the wind.

What a thing to have loved, a handbag, she thinks, as the guests swarm past her from the train to their waiting cars. How they'll laugh at me, more than they do already. But it doesn't matter anymore.... It is the only possession she has ever taken care of, and that would include herself: Lucinda has not tended herself well, which is glaringly apparent to anyone who meets her. "A complete embarrassment to her husband," as so many have commented. But then, as Lucinda's neighbors are also frequently heard to whisper from behind the rims of their glasses, "She drinks, you know." And it is true, Lucinda acknowledges, I do, you know, drink. I drink copiously, without conviction, simply to drink. That's about the size of it. I could tell them that myself, I'd be quite happy to, but then they do prefer to whisper. As it's one of the few things Lucinda considers them to be good at, she doesn't interfere.

She is seemingly one of those well-heeled, bored women who drink in the afternoon, except that she starts in the morning: Yet, Lucinda holds it rather well: She only begins to slip in the late afternoon and that is when people notice and that is when it becomes audible, the low murmur of cruel exchanges, "oh, she drinks you know." That's what they say, she considers benignly. They never ask me why, but as everyone thinks my husband is a saint, naturally it would have to be my fault.

She has behaved herself today, though. She didn't start until later in the morning, despite how sick this made her: for Serena, obviously. Although, what I owe her, she laughs, in pained disbelief, is still not entirely apparent. Yet, it is a recollection of childhood that has always impelled Lucinda not to judge Serena as harshly as she has herself. It was that day, when she was four, and no-one would play with her, when Serena let go of Kit's hand to invite Lucinda into the circle of 'a ring a ring o' roses.' That day, she remembers, when Kit started to cry, because he was only nine, and he loved her with the fearsome devotion we pray waits for us somewhere. It was the way she looked at him. She sees it now as if Serena was her age, forty-eight, with a wealth of experience under her belt: It was a glance that contained worlds of understanding, that said 'your hand will forever be held in mine, regardless of whether you are here or not,' and it was his expression, she smiles fondly, closing her eyes, oblivious to how she sways on the spot where she stands. He understood; he accepted this silent communion that existed only between the two of them. He was always so kind that way.

This is all she has ever been able to say about him. "He was kindness itself," the gentle Kit who left one day and never came back, whose love for Serena was as much an accepted part of everyone's lives as breathing. Nothing very articulate but Lucinda is of no particular interest, beyond the judgmental tut-tutting of those who observe her shortcomings and repeat them to anyone who will listen. There is something else, too, and it means so much to Lucinda and nothing to anyone else; it's that he understood her, he belonged to her. Not like somebody tethered to a lead. It's that they rolled along together with such dignity and touching consideration of every miniscule aspect of the other's feelings, that it was like watching the prettiest of landscapes or the freshest of mornings, she thinks, plunging deeper into the sadder memory, despite what she knows it will cost her. It was so nice to watch him watch her, the attention he gave everything she said. He never intruded, never criticized. Never, Lucinda shakes her head furiously. And that way of hers; that glorious smile of relief Serena would wear as soon as she finished one of her little speeches, and turned to him as if he were the only person in the world. Everything she ever did started, and ended, in him. How often do you come across love like that? And it wasn't true, she insists. It wasn't true what they said he did. It was a nasty trick; so nasty to do that to him. But then they are nasty, aren't they, people, she concludes, dropping her head sorrowfully. And then they get away with it.

Sometimes, on bad nights, she tries to talk about him and what happened to any new guest she can find – the old ones rebuff her, give a stern stare and say "Let's not bring that sordidness up now," or "someone – please – someone find her goddamn husband." Always in the same tone, too, as if the fact that she's slouched and slurring is not evident to all, but still they speak in remonstrating hisses, furious at being lumbered with her. They're never interested in her excuses. They believe of Kit what they want, or what they've been told. It's always easier to believe the worst, but I never did, she thinks, proudly. Kit is one of her favorite memories – his tears that day for Serena moved something in her that she hoped to find for herself, something to which she came so close.

Serena's hand is perfectly formed, and like many aristocratic women, she had them fashioned in marble in Paris during her honeymoon with Captain

Lyons. Sometimes, at these parties, Lucinda likes to go into the drawing room, where the sculpture sits on top of the grand piano, to place her hand in hers. She feels little else, but then Lucinda is usually close to blacking out by the time this impulse strikes. Yet, the coldness of the marble is like a balm. It takes her there, to that place she drinks to find. She does it to remember Serena's kindness, before she stopped being kind. She does it to recall the day when she belonged. They don't see that, though, those who come to usher her away, telling her not to be foolish and pathetic. They don't see that if her husband, – that long-suffering, widely sympathetic character, saddled with such a disgrace of a wife – is the one to lead her away that he will smack her to within an inch of her life, once home. So Lucinda has learned to stop feeling, except in memory, where she feels the touch of Serena's hand in her own, and that of Kit's, as they closed the circle and danced before all falling down.

Who would have held Lucinda's hand, except for Serena? Lucinda's grandfather, who raised her, never made any secret of his contempt for what she represented to him. Her mother, a celebrated beauty, who passed on none of it to Lucinda, had come undone at the hands of an unscrupulous cousin one Christmas, and it was the usual story of disgust, scandal, horror that accompanies the deaths of fifteen-year-old girls in childbirth. Lucinda's grandfather shot him and then adopted her, but the thirty-five-year-old cousin did not die. He loitered on the periphery of their family as a cripple, looming like a devil over everything she ever did: except for that time when she joined the circle, when Serena made him invisible with her compassion.

It was just one minute of her life but it's the only place she goes to in her mind. She returns to the golden lawn, parched by the heat of a boiling summer, to remember how her heart leapt – Up, up like a kite – when she joined the circle between Kit and Serena and they started to dance, faster and faster, singing like birds, *"Ring a ring o' roses, a pocket full of posies...."* To remember how Serena turned to her and laughed, as she pulled her down to the ground – *"a-ti-shoo, a-ti-shoo, we all fall down"* – and how, even then, she didn't let go of her hand, nor did Lucinda let go of Kit's. There was no one else in the world except us three, she recalls, happily. I felt as if it was the only place I should ever be, not to come in between them, but so I could watch every expression up close of those two glorious souls.

But it was only a minute, she reminds herself. That's the problem with time. You can't keep it. You've got to let it slip if you're to get by. It is easier, Lucinda knows, to let the minutes go if you drink, especially when you also know, as she does, that no other minute could ever compare to the one that she shared with them. Yet, as a child, it was some time before Lucinda would find that solace, so the weeks and months were so sad when Kit went away shortly after to boarding school, and Serena suffered her own tragedy and became terribly ill, so that by the time she did return to school, a full two years had passed. And it didn't seem right, after that, for Lucinda to remind her of that time when she was so happy.

Serena held Lucinda's hand just once more over the decades that followed. Lucinda fell in the hallway on arriving one evening, splayed and underwear showing, so drunk as to be unable to even gather herself, and her husband, forgetting himself, leaned down and gripped her arm so viciously she almost sobered up; "Get up," he insisted, that familiar note of warning in his voice, low enough but clear as a bell. And Serena, who had not spoken to Lucinda in years, since her debut party when Lucinda arrived clutching that blue silk beaded handbag with a pride she has felt for nothing since, gently but forcefully, moved him aside and looked at him in the eye with the complete contempt of somebody who knew and understood exactly what and who he was. And she held out her hand to Lucinda, which Lucinda took with the hand that did not clutch the blue silk beaded handbag that, in spite of her carelessness, she has looked after as one would a newborn – there is not a mark or a blemish on it.

It was then, there, that Lucinda saw it, that faint smile Serena had given Kit that day of the ring a ring o' roses, and she wept, locked on her gaze, for the love she hadn't received, for the love Kit hadn't received. "See, see," she said, holding it up, "I did look after it. I did." She wanted to say more, but the words were trapped in that place where she is so articulate, so profound; where she offers comfort and glistening gems of advice so lucidly and pointedly that vast crowds drop everything to listen; that place where drunks go. So Serena did not hear them: And that is why Lucinda started to cry harder because she wanted to tell her the truth; the truth she can only tell if she is drunk; that makes no sense because no-one can understand her. But then, as it has frequently been observed: Lucinda is not articulate. She drinks, you know.

Lucinda wants to conduct herself impeccably this evening. She wants to be what she could have been were it not for her weakness. Yet, already she knows this won't happen. She'll drink too much, as ever, only to forget everything about the evening, during and after, to wake up tomorrow blissfully oblivious to the minutes of the previous day, ready to forget again. I should have brought a gift, though, she suddenly realizes, opening her eyes, a farewell gift. Serena should, at least, have that. But what? What can I give her that she doesn't already have? And now Lucinda remembers.

She lets the blue silk beaded handbag go, as if a gust of wind has taken it. This gift she received by chance on her eighteenth birthday. Yet, it was the surprise of it that made it so precious; that someone could have thought of her, someone so kind as him. That's all she thought it was, a birthday present sent because her party had to be cancelled for Serena's. What they said, how everyone twisted it, it wasn't true, but nobody would believe her... Anyway... so old, so little to mourn, she consoles herself, watching it go. Her husband, his head bent against the vicious wind, glances up slightly at the cry she makes involuntarily, but he does not remark on the loss or instinctively reach to catch the handbag before it flies away. Instead he laughs, laughs while wrapping his coat tighter around him, as those people do who are amused only when the loss does not happen to them.

He's still watching, the blond gentleman. Lucinda almost thinks she sees him wince at her choice, as if he is aware of what she is giving up, but he's not coming to her, as she feared. He's leaving now, but, as he does, he nods and she can see that he pities her. Under any other circumstance, she might perceive his wince as disapproval and allow it to torment her, but she is no longer inclined to berate herself for her shortcomings. The time for regret is over. This gift is for Serena. Lucinda let the handbag go because it never really belonged to her. All it contained was a dream she safeguarded ferociously for years; a dream she unwittingly stole from someone else.

So, Lucinda, too, must let go now. She lets go of her husband's arm and allows the wind, a welcome instrument of Fate, as it happens, to propel her backwards onto the tracks. The train starts to move forward en route to

Westhampton, and there is no time for her to stop falling, to try and right herself and get up and live again. Nor is there any need because Lucinda does know him: In the seconds before she made this choice, their eyes met again on this platform in Speonk, the eyes of the boy whose memory she has tried to keep alive amidst the ambivalent. She'll never learn where he has been all this time, but that doesn't matter. He has had sorrows, I'm sure, of his own, she knows. *Forgive me*, she wants to say as she falls, as she falls, and her eyes turn heavenward.

Lucinda watches as the blue silk beaded handbag soars higher and higher above her, like a kite toward heaven, the sadness of all that they lost and didn't become, an acute pressure on her slowing heart. And she cries out, but not in pain, for suddenly Lucinda realizes that she does know where Kit has come from, that somehow she has always known. And, she smiles, it is as if a circle has opened and a hand holds mine. It is almost as if he did choose me, after all.

THE UNINVITED GUEST

There is only one question she ever asks of him, only one for which he waits each Friday evening of summer. He turns his face to the screen door and there he hears her again: "Promise me that you'll come to the party, Kit. Promise," she says, her voice chiming like the bells of distant times past, and, in that haunting sound, a reminder of the love they once shared. "Yes, Serena," he replies. "Yes, I will always come for you." And for those few deceitful seconds, he does. He rises from his chair to walk the path of lilacs to her door, where she holds out her hand to welcome him, as if there is no other guest for whom she waits. "How I have missed you. I have been thinking of you, these hours," she smiles, taking his arm to lead him inside. And somehow, in that dim place where he has been confined, the dull haze of nothing hanging leaden in the air surrounding him, Kit finds the strength to keep standing, to hold aloft that victory, that memory, and say; *"This you cannot take from me."* And he returns to that doorstep of his mind where, for just one moment more, although he is so altered to the point where she would surely never know him now, it is almost as if they are young again, and everything between them, in the late light of unanswered prayers, speaks only of joy.

He is not invited. No gilt-edged invitation found its way to him, delivered on a silver salver at breakfast. No old friend tapped on his window, interrupting his studies, and called, "Dear Kit. I almost forgot. You must come to the party tonight. Serena said you must come." He knows, he was forgotten long ago. It is a sad fact, but he has forged a peace with his lot, although there was a time, as a younger man, when he could make no sense of his exile. "Yet, how much more we understand when all we can do is watch from a distance," Anthony Duverglas has often tried to console him: Kit will miss him now. It is unlikely that they will ever see one another again.

It has been thirty-one years since Kit last arrived at this station, the promise of a party ahead of him. It had been a present of sorts: the one thing he had asked of Captain Lyons, after he graduated from Cambridge. "Well, you must have something. You've done so well," Captain Lyons had remarked, over lunch at King's, lighter than Kit had ever seen him, the burden of his care alleviated, now that he had completed his education. Noise sounded all around them, gay and babbling, – the clatter of plates being cleared, the shouts of goodbye from fellow scholars leaving, a mother and father on each arm – everyone excited on this last day of term. "I should like to go back," he said, catching Captain Lyon's eye, as he had rehearsed, determined to show how much he hoped he would let him. "You wish to see her," Captain Lyons said, inhaling heavily in response. "Please," Kit replied. Captain Lyons did not say anything else, but his habitual mood returned – serious, silent, enclosed – and he pursed his lips tighter, as if to stop himself from protesting facts that would still sting, even after so many years.

It was all Kit had ever wished for, but it seemed that Captain Lyons would still refuse him that lunchtime. Captain Lyons had assumed guardianship over Kit, after the death of Kit's Aunt left him an orphan, his parents having been killed in a drowning accident when he was a baby. Kit had never grown to know him well, as he was sent to Eton almost immediately after Serena's sister Catherine's funeral: Yet, Kit had always been inclined to like him because Captain Lyons would often talk of Serena to him. He was indebted to him for this because, save for one letter he received shortly after leaving Remsenburg for school, they had been forbidden by Serena's father to write to one another. This was why Kit had never spent the summers there: Captain Lyons had always considered it unwise.

"It's a long way away, Kit," Captain Lyons said finally, and there was worry in his eyes, but whether he pitied him or his choice, Kit could not tell. "Home is only far, Captain Lyons, when someone stops you from going there," he replied. Captain Lyons contemplated him momentarily, but Kit could not read him. "How nice it must be to be young," he said, sadly. "That you can still believe these things." He stood to leave but, holding out his hand, surprised Kit by confirming his hope "You shall have your summer. I shall give you that." Time slowed, as Kit grasped onto Captain Lyon's handshake with both hands, the intensity of his relief evident by the force of the gesture, everything about to start anew as he smiled up in gratitude. And suddenly there was no more sound of England. Nothing but the vision of Serena running toward the bay ahead of him, the flickering sun through the arms of the elm trees illuminating the brilliant white of her dress, and the pale blue ribbons, falling loose from her russet curls, touched here and there with gold.

How different a scene to the one he encounters this evening: so many people, in tuxedos and ball gowns, disembarking from their trains, screaming with laughter and fear at the howling wind, as they careen toward their waiting cars to take them to the party. Cries of hairstyles being ruined by the ladies, a handbag torn away by a particularly savage gust that its owner seemingly allows herself to lose, as her eyes lock onto his: These lucky people, he thinks, who have twirled and reveled, amidst the softness, free of Wars and Depressions and Death, and the many misfortunes that break us.

Over the years, kinder souls have counseled that it is better never to return to a place that once was loved. Better by far, they have advised, to let it reside perfectly in the past, to avoid the sorrow of how nothing ever stays the same when revisited. Yet, Kit does not regret returning here, or of seeing Lucinda. Of everyone, it seems fitting that they should have met one another again. There are certain people impossible to forget, he knows. I would always have recognized her, despite what she has become. He might have said something, were it not for what Lucinda carried; the blue silk handbag that had belonged to his mother: in itself, an unexpected touchstone to the past and the mistakes he made there. The reason why he pauses now: Does he dare to learn if Serena will keep her promise? Can he bear to know if she has forgiven him? There is nothing he can do to ensure it, no words; no explanation he might offer. Only Serena's heart can make the choice.

All he has to go on are those fragments of summers he once lived; memories in which he has placed every faith, despite how often they have twisted darkly and dangerously into uncertainty the longer he has been away from her. It is these memories he returns to, if only to find the strength to continue on his journey: memories of vistas of pollen glinting in the light and the daisies she tried constantly to weave as a crown for his head; of a star-filled season, the evening he finally came home from England, to discover her a ballerina upon a stage; of the first time he was ever to kiss her, the tealights surrounding them flickering their last; of the love he felt toward her, the type of love that permeates the soul with the foreknowledge that all we cherish alters and shifts with time, but the essence remains true. The essence he discovered once more at the very end of that summer, beneath the lilac trees – that, for some inexplicable reason, had continued to bloom – where his most precious memory resides: of the softness of her cheek against his as he held her until the dawn when she ran away from him, over the endless lawn to the house, looking back in the gray light to smile as she left. The smile he allows to guide him now, back to La Doucette, to where he prays she waits for him.

This road he shall walk has been the only road of his life; one that leads him into the heart of a sacred memory and takes him home to her. As he considers the view before him, he is consoled that the beauty of everything he has treasured has not diminished. Yet, it is with a suspension of breath that speaks only of dying, almost as if Paradise lurks beyond the corners of this picture, in front of his blue and faded eyes, that this sight of joy and vision of hope crystallizes before him for the last time. For he will never walk this road again.

He takes his first step. In only a few minutes, he will say the words he has longed to. He will say, as he once did as a young man:

"We will go then, you and I, in the night, Serena."

THE HOST

At the sound of screaming from the ballroom, Captain Lyons turns in alarm: He sees a French door blown out by the wind, its glass shattering, guests scattering in fear. Instinctively, he looks to the mezzanine overlooking the marble hallway, searching for Serena. But she is not there. And then he remembers: "Cruel," he says, conceding the truth he would give anything to forget, the memory that has led them both to tonight.

It was the evening of her debut in 1907. There was a maid who dropped a tray of champagne, glass and liquid splashing the sides of his trousers, causing the throng of people around him to shriek in horror and step aside. He remembers how he did not move, oblivious to the frantic apologies of the girl. The accident was already forgotten as his eyes flitted to Serena, emerging from the door of her bedroom on the mezzanine.

He recalls her standing there now, almost like a mirage: a figurehead for the blessed, representative of a brilliance that did not come. And once more, he allows himself to savor the exquisite poignancy of her youth in his memory; to taste again the sadness he felt at knowing that time would not spare her, her bloom would fade, just as the unsullied purity of her questing and captivating spirit would surely die. *Turn back*, he urges her, although he knows such a wish is impossible. *Turn back*. He blinks away tears as he remembers her there, poised and guileless, an innocent before the fall. So beautiful a girl, only seventeen, about to descend a staircase thinking she would find only reward at its foot.

Captain Lyons grieves again for what he knew awaited Serena as she flew down the staircase. As equally as he grieves for what she will meet there tonight: "Cruel," he repeats to himself, mired in the memory, and turning once more to the sea.

THE HOSTESS

I emerge from my bedroom, chosen. Yet, I falter in the doorframe, as my eyes adjust to the dazzling light of the hall. Suddenly, someone screams and the first thing I see is the huge imported clock from Florence, inset into the wall facing the entrance of La Doucette and, beneath it, a commotion in the middle of the marble hall. Only now as I pick out Captain Lyons watching me soberly in the crowd, do I realize that I've dressed in the twilight, so preoccupied I'd forgotten to light the candles. Where is the maid, I suddenly wonder, why didn't she come? A first shadow falls over my happiness as I realize how I must look – half-dressed, no father on my arm to escort me: And this will never do, where my impetuosity has led me. For here is the World below me, and the World has eyes: hoards of people, far more than I could ever have anticipated. Yet, all I can hear is Kit's voice, assuring me, "They will come. They will always come for you."

This will never happen to me again, I tell myself. I'll never enjoy this thrill, or be the guest of honor, or be in the company of so many who've come to celebrate my coming-out. I will only ever be Kit's wife. Kit and I are running away tonight: I'm going to marry him tomorrow morning and board the ship to Italy, where no one can ever find us. I won't come back to La Doucette or see these faces again; I won't say goodbye or even stay until the end of my party. I must go. I've always known that I must go. We have to leave the mansions and marble porticos and summer pavilions hidden around garden walls, offset by weeping Japanese blossom trees. We have to escape from vistas of sea and garden parties, where those we know move in seamless coordination with tradition and expectation and allow for nothing else. Kit and I cannot survive in this world because I know too much about its secrets: about the lives it took and those it ruined.

I start to move and it is as if I am racing through a labyrinth of shadows, everything is illuminated in a golden glow of privilege. Yet, the only fixed point is where I will find Kit. Two steps at a time, I rush down the stairs, following a path to everything I believe to be mine. The smiling faces of the guests fade in and out of focus as the red front door opens ahead of me, and I arrive at the foot of the staircase, so grateful to leave behind my past.

I am perfect to Kit. He knows nothing about what happened to me, after he left as a boy; nothing about the illness against which I've battled and frequently lost, the remorseless melancholia that has led me to ever darker places in my pursuit of peace. Every step I take toward him is filled with elation over everything I keep hidden. I haven't wished to die today. I haven't wished to die all summer. Everything is different now because he loves me. No longer does each minute constitute a small victory over an instinct to flee. I live for him. I live because of him.

Before Kit, I used to believe that life could hold only promise if it was almost lost. That moment of survival, of coming to and finding hope again, that is why I tried to die. There was no hope in just living: Any place I turned, I found ambivalence, heartlessness: a lack of compassion. My father couldn't stand to be near me after the tragedies because I was to blame. The ghosts of my mother and sister seemed to lurk everywhere and I grew so ill that I tried to leave, but not to fly away to Paradise. I tried to die so that my father would forgive me. That day when I was eleven and I stuffed my pockets with horseshoes and sunk to the bottom of the swimming pool; that evening one year later when I went to the stables and I tried... too many to recall. I wanted to be held once more by arms that cherished me, arms that clung, just like when my father picked me up from underneath the sweet peas when I was a little girl. I wanted him to rescue me, but he never did.

It occurs to me that there is a rhythm to loss, to the saying of goodbyes. *One step, two step. One step, two step,* like a pas-de-bas, I maneuver my way through the guests thronging around the entrance, thinking I will never see them again. My heart follows a simple beat, like those of a summer redbird's wings; *Good-bye, good-bye...* Soon, I think, as I move closer to the door, I won't have to witness the pain I've caused anymore. I've tried so hard to make amends: all of the parties, the friendships, endlessly trying to please, but I am only a makeshift hostess. Parties will always end, but Kit's love for me never will.

Yet, Kit's face is not the first I see. Kit's arms are not the ones that suddenly grip mine. They belong to my father into whom I accidentally rush, and in whose disgusted expression, I see the truth of what I know myself to be – how repulsive and weak, how bitter a disappointment: "Serena, you are a disgrace," he whispers into my ear. And now a darker shadow falls, submerging all my joy beneath it: a shadow filled with dreadful awareness of how quickly love can die, of how I killed my father's love that was once all consuming. He pushes me away toward the door with such force that a guest at his side gasps in shock, and I stagger forward to where he has directed me: to confront again my role in the tragedies that destroyed us both.

He's there, my beautiful Kit, waiting for me on the other side of the courtyard. He stands, his head slightly tilted to the side, wearing the familiar, consoling smile he gave me at the start of the summer, when I first danced for him beneath the lilacs. He is the only person I have ever met who has made me feel forgiven by his acceptance of me. When I am with him, I feel like there is nothing wrong with me, after all.

The loose tendrils of my hair swish back and forth against the mid-section of my back, like a pendulum, buoyed into tick-tock movements by the breeze. *Tick-tock. Tick-tock.* Very little matters as the seconds fasten around me that will dictate what is to follow. Not the weather, or the late arrivals pushing past me to get inside, who don't even realize I'm their hostess. I don't care about the guests jostling at my back, watching me and judging me, this half-dressed girl that I am. All that matters is the choice I'm going to make. I know that I will always return to Kit, hour on hour, day on day, year upon year. I know that I will never fully understand why someone so beautiful would ever wait for me. I know that everything in my life is going to be decided by this one moment, by this person across a courtyard. And all I have to do to change my future is walk toward him. Because if I don't, every other experience of my life will bring me back here with regret and sorrow – marriages, children, the color of a teacup, the whisper of a half-recalled truth flitting over me on a dull Sunday afternoon, like a breeze from an unknown origin. *Move*, I say to myself, *just move...*

Standing on this doorstep of my life, somewhere between my past and future, I finally realize that my father has been right all along: It is knowing that kills us. It kills us when we must give up our own dreams and live with the uncompromising facts of the life we lead, instead of the life for which we long. What if I can't keep up the pretense of being well? I ask myself. What if my melancholia, my lack of control, my moods, repulses Kit too? I will have nothing if I have to watch Kit's love for me die. And there will be no hope in arms that seek to rescue because they will never be his again. These past few months have been an illusion: Kit hasn't really loved me at all. I am only an actress on a stage, expertly performing my role so that he'll never guess at the truth... But just as I think to leave him, I hear something that makes me stay:

There you are, my heart cries. *There you are....*

And the music is so beautiful that I don't even realize someone has made the decision for me.

THE HOST

His memory of Serena's debut is almost photographic in its clarity, but then so are most of his memories of Serena. After all, so much of his life has been given over to studying her. He remembers how she brimmed with possibility that evening: a possibility that had been evident ever since she was a child, when he first met her.

It was the day that Captain Lyons arrived in Remsenburg, where they had moved with their two young children at his first wife's insistence. He had been resolutely opposed to leaving England, even more so considering the reason behind it. Yet, by that point, he had failed his wife so miserably as a husband that he felt powerless to refuse. His wife, Laura, had been Serena's mother, Cecilia's, best friend in England, where they had grown up together. From an early age, his wife had held herself responsible for her friend's well-being, given the relative fecklessness of Cecilia's family, who were intolerably embarrassed by their daughter's more manic impulses. Captain Lyons, however, had always considered Cecilia's antics to be little more than theatrical eccentricities and, in this aspect of her personality, thought her entirely equally matched by her husband, William, for whom he had little time either. Serena's father was the ultimate showman; a man who could turn any step, any raised platform, into a stage, unscrupulously spouting the ideas and insights he had stolen from others. An avid interloper into their world of so-called aristocratic privilege, William had been accepted by Cecilia's family only to salvage her reputation, hindered as it was by her many flights of fancy that had led her to ever more scandalous places with members of her household staff.

Over the years Captain Lyons had found himself endlessly picking up the pieces of William's follies; the perpetual failures of businesses, debts Captain

Lyons was constantly asked to repay. By the time he moved to Remsenburg, he already lacked the spirit for it. William had near bankrupted his family again, having built La Doucette as a showpiece to impress those he needed to invest in his latest scheme, dangerously impacting Cecilia's fragile mental heath in the process. And so Captain Lyons found himself once more having to manipulate the story of Serena's family to fit the flawless picture they needed to present to avoid ruin: It was something entirely at odds with everything he believed in, and that he held responsible for the tragedies that later befell Serena.

Yet, not even Captain Lyons could ever have foreseen that first day how terribly they would all be punished for their association with one another. Because the vision that met his eyes, on travelling to Hallock's Beach to meet with his wife's friends, was one of such beauty and innocence, that he almost forgot his misgivings.

He had arrived with his family at the Quogue Bathing Station to find a performance, of sorts, playing out in front of the patrons. A performance given by quite the most beautiful child anyone had ever seen: by Serena, who was barely two-years-old, playing at the edge of the shore. "Mama, beautiful," Serena suddenly exclaimed, gesturing to the waves, her unexpected outburst and intelligence stunning everyone into cries of delight. Born to hold court, thought Captain Lyons, witnessing the confidence with which she made her observation, the glint in her eyes. Like most cosseted children, he perceived that Serena was fully aware of her effect on her captive audience, although the degree of manipulation involved was not lost on him. Yet, while he would never have tolerated such showmanship in his own children, there was something about Serena, even then, that compelled him to allow her such simple pleasures. For he could see quite clearly, that even at so tender an age, Serena possessed an instinctive awareness of how best to behave in order to please her parents, somehow understanding the role she must fulfill for them: those two vapid creatures who watched their daughter in raptures, feasting off the adoration Serena received from others, believing it only to be a reflection of themselves.

Almost immediately, however, Captain Lyons began to discern the pitfalls of Serena's parents' adoration. Serena was afforded luxuries never allotted to her older sister, Catherine, who was equally as beautiful and sweet, and by far the more sensitive of the two. But the type of sister, who, alas, came first and so was destined only to provide an audience for her younger sibling, whose infancy was to be savored because of its inherent sadness – in that everything it encompassed would prove last. Like Serena, to please her parents, Catherine fulfilled the role they expected of her, proving a constant guardian to her younger sister as they grew older and, in return, Serena showered her with such love that Catherine never appeared jealous. Yet, sometimes, Captain Lyons would wince involuntarily to find Catherine mimicking something Serena had said for the entertainment of others. It never had the same effect as she was not plump and blue-eyed, rather nine and leaner, the fleeting blush of babyhood a shadow on her cheek. Always, to his ears, it sounded a striking note of the secret injustice she felt at not having been born with the same gift of amusement. And, as much as he thought that she would no doubt grow to be the kinder of the two for being overlooked, she was never to enjoy similar trappings. Doors at birthday parties were opened and hostesses were disappointed to find her first in line, scouring the surroundings for Serena. "Catherine's time will come later," William would insist, whenever Captain Lyons raised a criticism of Serena taking too much attention away from Catherine. "It's impossible to deny childhood, especially when it distracts so bonnily: Let Serena have this. She will be old soon enough."

Captain Lyons was standing at the fire at Christmas, four years after the day on Hallock's Beach, when Serena's father repeated this dire pronouncement. Why would you wish such a fate on her, Captain Lyons thought. She may not live to be old. He, who had lifted his wife, Laura, from her bed, not three months earlier, so that she could watch over the gardens where her children played: He, who had rocked her as she gently wept, knowing that, despite how she ached to stay, she would surely leave.

It was the first of the many prices Captain Lyons would pay for not having trusted his better instinct in the beginning: to leave Serena's family to their own devices, to their own ruin. His wife had died of infectious pneumonia, contracted after nursing Cecilia through her own bout, which Cecilia had survived. Yet, the greater price had been his wife's heartbreaking legacy:

Their children weren't allowed to visit and Laura had wanted to write something to them, something so beautiful they would be eternally consoled. But she couldn't find the words: It was a failing that broke her heart. And despite how Captain Lyons tried to reassure her that the fact she loved them was surely consolation enough, she could not agree. "Most disappointments can only be learned, Edward, and I have learned mine over my years with you. We're only ever a memory," she said, "left for someone to keep alive. We are only ever as good as we are remembered. And I know that you will not speak of me, after I'm gone. I know you."

Captain Lyons has never been able to escape the irony that his first wife's dying regret was that she had nothing to say, while he forgot her, just as she predicted, by marrying a woman who knew exactly what to say and when. And yet, it is Laura's words – and not Serena's – that have haunted him, figuring as the most searing he has ever heard, because they were true. Laura did know him. She understood that he owed her a debt for choosing him, rescuing him from the disappointment of reaching for girls who would invariably reject him for being awkward and ordinary. He has always recognized that she was a far better woman than he had a right to own: a protective and loving mother, possessed of a wholly decent heart. Yet, while he has savored the tenderness of their relationship, the debt he owes that someone once understood him so well, he has felt no passion for it. My first wife was a circumstance who led me to my greatest love, he accepts again, staring out to the waves. What I regret is that she guessed this.

Laura's last look to him was so full of confusion and regret, her body wracked by the disease that had drained every inch of her vitality, that Captain Lyons closed his eyes. Not because it was excruciating to witness her grief, but because he was afraid of hearing an even harsher truth from a woman who saw him as he truly was, instead of how he imagined himself to be: By the time he opened them, she had gone. He remains certain that, were it not for his cowardice, he might have observed something he could have shared with their children, but he could not watch her die: not for her sake, but for his. An action he has never forgiven himself, and one that forged an unlikely path for him to follow. What led him to make a decision on Serena's behalf, the evening of her debut, as a consequence of the lesson he was taught at his dying first wife's side.

Most disappointments can only be learned, he reminded himself, watching Serena run to the door of La Doucette, unwilling to save her from what she would surely learn, as he saw Kit emerge from the darkness of The Lilac Walk in the courtyard. Yet, when Serena rushed unexpectedly into her father's arms, Captain Lyons was awed suddenly by the callousness of the statement, as another memory returned to him, inspired by the sight before him.

Standing there, Captain Lyons recalled the last kiss, of the million showered upon Serena by her father, the day that her sister, Catherine died at twelve-years-old: a death that was caused by a borrowed gesture from Serena. Catherine had climbed up a tree to serve as a look out for Serena who had gone missing, calling her name and waving her arm in a grand wave reminiscent of the day Serena played on the shore at Hallock's Beach. As she waved, she lost her balance, so as Serena's father swooped to rescue one daughter from beneath a trestle of sweet peas, where she had fallen asleep after running away with Kit into the deepest recesses of the garden, another fell to where no arms awaited her. He remembered the way William drew back, almost reverentially, from Serena on hearing Catherine's scream, understanding that something catastrophic had happened and that he clutched the unwitting catalyst to his heart. He remembered the silence, amidst the sweet peas, when William placed Serena on the ground to run to the West Pavilion: He remembered looking back at Serena as he ran with her father to Catherine and thinking her already forgotten, an afterthought at the bottom of the garden. It was an insight that proved correct. From that day on, neither of Serena's parents could bear to think of her, nor forgive her for distracting them from Catherine: as if Serena was something diabolical, who had lured them with her charm into a life of suffering. He remembered how Serena's life had been ruined by that tragedy. Ruined until Kit returned that summer and she finally found the forgiveness in him she had craved.

Captain Lyons realized, as he watched Serena's father viciously push her toward the door, where Kit waited in the courtyard, that it was a scream – Catherine's scream – which augured the end of her childhood. Just as he realized that the scream that presaged her appearance not a moment earlier on the mezzanine would now augur the end of her youth, given what he had done: the disappointment he thought it imperative that she learn. And he thought of how terrible it is to subject those who are old to the expectations and tragedies of the young. "Cruel," he muttered involuntarily, as he confronted a different kind of death. But this time as he watched – as penance – he did not turn away.

THE UNINVITED GUEST

The red front door was closing. Kit knew that it was closing. Yet, on the evening of her debut, he did not walk up to meet Serena. For one moment more, he wanted to watch her.

There it was as it always was: there was everything, encapsulated in her gracious and benevolent gaze, which had not found him yet in the darkness. Every Christmas, every birthday, every Sunday meal: each of the rituals and joys to come, the life ahead of him embodied by Serena. He saw the simple contentment of her companionship when they would be first married; the delight of awakening and knowing that he had not dreamt her; those early years when he would go to any length to impress, to convince her of how right she had been to choose him. The many days he would have to study her, freely now, not a quick glance as she engaged another in conversation, but to examine the facets that comprised her. He would take her to Venice; clutch her hand as they raced down the narrow alleyways, the ghosts of that dying city nipping at their heels, and throw his arms around her once back on the streets, an implicit assurance that he would never fail to protect her. Then Africa, Kenya, which she would adore, anticipating that he would find her each morning on the porch watching the pink dawn, where she would turn to him in surprise, the particular light of that continent the perfect illumination for her face, and exclaim, "You were so right to bring me here!" How then, and only then, would his day begin, secure in the knowledge that Serena was where he could find her.

Yet, they would start, after several years, to think of home and this is where their deepest happiness would reside; of England again, of his late father's estate that would be passed to him when he turned thirty, which had housed every heir for four centuries. But only with Serena would the house come alive. The parties she would host, the diamonds in her hair; the babies he would welcome with the excitement of a child at Christmas, selecting his favorite of the three – for there would be three – based only on their closest resemblance to her.

Then the difficulties of being so close to one another: of the disappointments they would suffer, on growing older. The things left undone, unsaid, the promises neither of them would keep. The years when Kit would question whether he had ever known her, or if he had imagined that delicate girl in a pink chiffon dress, whose smile had answered his every dream at twenty-one. Those horrible years when anything to do with him would seem to distress her. To the point where, on occasion, he would be sure that she felt hatred, and maybe she might find another. Perhaps, at a party, he would catch something; a glance between her and someone more understanding than he had become. And that would be enough to drag him out of his torpor, to race back and beg her to stay, to speak to her again of lilacs.

And surely old age could only be enjoyed with her, time alone to choose the best of the moments they had shared to relive. To know that death would be no parting: to hold the hand of the other as one of them went first, accepting that somewhere they would meet, once more. And all of the memories which would remain of that complex, brilliant existence as much as they could ever have asked: no room for sadness, although the pain of separation would be intolerable, but no rancor, only expectation at what they would say when they were finally reunited. Would he say as he did, after picking her up from the stage where she had fallen, "I was just thinking about you the other day. I never thought I would see you again." And would that radiant blessing of his childhood, who had turned out exactly as he wished her to, let him kiss her; as if to waken her from her slumber underneath the sweet peas where he had once left her as a girl. Yes. Of that, he had no doubt.

This is what Kit envisaged as he regarded Serena standing in the doorway of La Doucette, when he was twenty-one: the good and the bad, the mundane and the exceptional instances of life. Yet, there was so little that she really knew of him. How could Serena have guessed that her mere presence made up for everything he had been denied? It is difficult, after all, for people who have grown up with families to understand what it is to have no affection: to watch each summer pass, as he had, almost from behind a window, because children who were orphaned, like Kit, had no place to visit. The only happiness he had ever owned was during the summers he spent with Serena as a boy, and once more, as a young man returning, a Summer Visitor. Was it any wonder that he remembered her hand in his when they were children, her kindness, the perpetual flowers of her mother's gardens in the bleak world of boarding school and university until Captain Lyons generously invited him to stay? Serena was every summer of his life, the first that he can recall and the last.

The red front door was closing.

It was then that Serena smiled at him: a smile so disarming and forgiving that it has haunted him ever since. For he had not come to take her with him, he had come to say goodbye. There was nothing he could offer her anymore. His inheritance had been lost, leaving him penniless. Yet, he could not move to tell her any of this. His punishment was only to watch.

THE HOSTESS

Teddy appears in front of me on the doorstep, his arm wraps suddenly around my waist. And all the time left crowds in on me, filled with details and incomprehension and suspicion. "No, no," I say, as he pulls me backward into the party. I drink in the swirling, grotesque minutiae of everything that surrounds me: There is Lucinda, that element of doubt, emerging from Teddy's car, clutching a blue silk beaded handbag that belonged to Kit's mother. He kept the diamond hair combs in that bag; those he promised to me, the day he proposed. The day he offered me everything and, in return, I gave him everything, not leaving until the following morning.... "It's not that you left me for him, it's not..." Teddy protests, as he tries to move me away. "I've heard rumors... about Kit and Lucinda...Serena, darling, Serena, come," he cajoles; desperate to avoid the type of scene he knows I can cause. "I tried to tell you. He's not who you think he is."

I don't fight Teddy, but I'm not passive. All I am doing is daring this moment so far, to see what Kit will do, to have him choose me. I've dared like this all summer long, making similar fatalistic lunges to destroy everything that makes me happy. I did it to prove my worth to Kit, so that he would constantly reassure me of his love, despite how I believed it to be impossible. *Come to me first; make the choice,* I beg of him in my mind, as the red front door begins to close. *Don't let this be true...* Yet, Kit does not move. This is what happens when someone has offered too much and someone else has taken, I accept, my heart breaking. *Rescue me, please, Kit...* I silently plead, my arms outstretching to where he stands. *Life can only hold promise if it is almost lost...*

It is as if I am watching Kit through a telescope; his beloved figure recedes farther and farther from me as the door closes, inch by inch, between us. Yet, there is no judgment in his expression as I leave him; there is only love. And I know that I will never raise my eyes again to find such happiness as Kit inspired in me that summer; that he will hover over me in my memory as the most poignant reminder of all that I was once lucky enough to own. I know that, regardless of what I will learn, I will always love him best. So this is why I smile for him now, the way he once smiled for me.

But still Kit does not move and my tears flow freely, as I acknowledge that this is the disappointment I have sought. And all of this is last, the last of Kit. *One moment more,* I think. What Kit would say to stop me from leaving and I would always stay. But this is also a choice I'm making, the reality of loss crippling: It is part will, part acceptance, my allowing Teddy to guide me. It is his will imposed onto mine, a debt I owe because I left Teddy for Kit. *Change this,* something in me pleads, see *straight inside me and change this, make the choice for me....* "Please," I whisper, "I knew you before...." And I almost scream, I almost stop breathing, as I force myself to accept; he is not going to move. He is going to let me go.

I hear my mother's voice, so much missed, utter her crippling legacy once more: *"The summer redbirds, Serena. They only stay for a summer and then they fly away."* I think of the bird at my window, how different a girl I was mere seconds earlier. And I look to Kit again, that brightly plumed figure of my childhood, and it is as if he is rushing toward me over the fields, or waiting in the courtyard to take me sailing, or telling me, "There will be such things, Serena, such things." All of those perfect moments before that I will clutch to me forever. And all I can see is his beauty, all that I know is his love, as our eyes meet for the last time and the door fastens shut.

I cannot count the tears as Teddy turns me decidedly round and hastily wipes them from my cheeks: "I'm so sorry, Serena," he says. "I tried..." But I am not listening. All I can hear is the sound of my heart, pounding louder and louder, as the guests swarm around me. I see my father watching me at Captain Lyon's side. I look to him, searching his face for any sign of love for me, but all he does is turn away in contempt. "Serena," Captain Lyons says softly, stepping toward me. "It's better this way. Let him go. He's not worthy of you." "Let him go? Go where?" I ask.

Yet, I don't wait for his response, for it is only now that I truly understand what I've done, where my passivity has led me, as the full horror of it settles over me with uncompromising finality. Did my father and Captain Lyons know something? What were they not telling me? "No," I scream, trying to push back through the crowd to follow Kit, knowing I won't be able to live with this uncertainty: I need to ask him why. Nobody will ever tell me the truth but Kit. But I can't; the people, congratulating me and wishing me good luck, carry me deeper into the house and I'm forced to accept that there's no getting out of this. The party has consumed me whole.

And the first thing I confront after accepting this fate is that the hand of the large clock, looming over my guests, has barely moved a minute.

THE HOST

The day after her debut, Captain Lyons instructed the gardeners at La Doucette to shear the trees of the lilacs. Many considered the act to be wicked, but he has always stood by his decision. "Why do we cut the flowers in bloom, if not to savor their youth?" he has ventured, whenever asked what motivated him. "People might be surprised to learn that it is I who insists on flowers in the house. Serena thinks it vicious to cut them in their prime. I believe it merciful."

Yet, he was powerless to prevent Lucinda's visit that same day, to protest her and Kit's innocence to Serena. Lucinda's pleas invited the doubt that would torment Serena's perfectionist heart: It was one thing to believe that Kit was inconstant, easy enough to come to terms with betrayal, but quite another to learn that she may have made the wrong choice, and that it was all too late, anyway. Captain Lyons witnessed the knowledge undo her when she first noticed the barren lilac trees, immediately racing outside and falling to her knees at the sight of the shorn stumps; emblematic to her of everything she had destroyed. "They'll grow back," certain staff members tried to placate her, as she knelt there, dangerously still, unnerving everyone who loved her vivacity. But they were wrong. They never did. Not until this year, a miracle that Serena welcomed with one of her dangerously romantic pronouncements: "This summer," she said to Captain Lyons, "La Doucette has become enchanted again." While he knew that this is what Serena would choose to believe, he also resigned himself, with such sadness, to the terrible fact of the matter. It was all about to start again: He was not sure that Serena would survive another episode.

He has asked himself often if it would have helped her to watch the flowers die. What else, he has justified, did they represent to her, save for a dream of youth? In the weeks following the party, he would find her sitting by the fallen trees in the blazing sunshine, watching the road that leads to the sea, lost in her own private world. Her sole companion was the memory of Kit: Kit who had left Remsenburg immediately after the party. Considering Serena's mental state, Captain Lyons knew he could not allow her to cling so ferociously to dreams that would never come true, given what he had learned of Kit. So he rescued her. Or, at least, this is what he tells himself when the full horror of what happened overwhelms him. I cut the flowers in bloom, he insists again, watching the strange copper sky darken to black, to save them from the knowledge of what they become.

He knows that many would be astonished to find a husband as sympathetic to his wife's cloistered passions. They are hardly private, though, are they? he reasons, as the view before him fades away. I've always known that she waits for him, as equally as I accepted I would never be enough. All these years, she's believed he will come back for her; every summer Friday she appears from her bedroom, casting one regretful glance over her shoulder, at precisely one minute after she first made her entrance at her debut, to descend the staircase and greet her guests. Yet, she bears no resemblance to the joyous girl who first rushed down those steps. She still owns a profound dignity, but she's not quite with us, hovering somewhere distant in her mind where it is safe. Safe from me, I have no doubt: from the choices I have been forced to make, in order that she might live.

Captain Lyons often tries to avoid watching her make her entrance now. Time, he feels, was not particularly kind and he has long been aware that the admiration she elicits exists only for those who recall how pretty she had been. They have admired Serena, he reflects, merely for the tragedy of everything that did not come to her. They have held fast to the romantic conviction that had she married Kit, so much would be different. Yet, it's so easy to drown in the romance of lost chances, of the potential for happiness rejected by the naïve and the careless: We do so love the young, those of us who stay behind to age, who are not memorialized as war heroes taken too soon, or victims of circumstance; or else a charming young man whose destiny was decided by a red door closing, and by a damaged girl who clung to someone who would let her fall – and did – the second the audience dispersed. After all, Serena was so fragile, a tiny little soul, and fragile little souls are so easily preyed upon. I used to believe that. Now, I simply think that they allow themselves to be hunted.

He has good reason to trust this instinct, for, far more than his involvement – the decision he made that summer – what happened with Serena at the first party was a choice. On that evening, at the front door, she offered herself up as a sacrifice. Of everyone in attendance, it was Serena who possessed the most crucial information – of the things she had done that would come back to hurt her dreadfully. She had every right to run across that courtyard, to demand Kit keep his promise. Yet, Serena did not because she could not bear to see what Kit would do. How it might sully the flawless image she held of him.

But then we are all deceitful beings, despite our best intentions, Captain Lyons considers. And hostesses the most untrustworthy, for who can possibly please everyone without losing something of one's integrity? Indeed it is true that Serena – gracious, unassuming, adored – has emerged as the most duplicitous. Yet, even in spite of her ill-judged motives, Serena never set out to deceive for malicious purposes. In fact, her deception cost her everything. In second-guessing her choice that night, in turning back to try and get out once she was inside La Doucette, she invited the possibility that the fault lay with her. The door closed, nobody could see how Kit reacted; if he cavalierly walked away or else, as many have insisted he must have, ran to the door, his frantic knocking drowned out by the noise within: a fact which forced him to retreat, brokenhearted, betrayed by a vile trick and an awful truth; Serena chose Teddy. Her actions enabled Kit to be memorialized as an ideal: how she would choose to remember him, herself. Yet, how could any of her guests possibly have guessed, as they formed a bewildered procession behind her and Teddy – like a bridal march, with a blushing virgin and her beau at the helm – that they were propelling her toward her execution. In an instant her destiny had been decided for her: because she had allowed it to be.

So Captain Lyons returns to his simple question: *Why do we cut the flowers in bloom, if not to savor their youth?* In the romance of everything to do with Serena and Kit, of the story that has circulated and been swooned over by guest on guest for years past, he sees what everyone else has ignored. How Serena permitted them all to overlook the one simple, yet devastating, truth of that evening: when Serena was moved back into the party by Teddy, in the split second before the door fastened shut, Kit did not even flinch. He simply watched her go. And if one allows who they most love to be taken from them, Captain Lyons tells himself again, then there can be no complaint if someone else finds what that person has so carelessly discarded, and claims it for their own.

This is the validation he has sought, whenever the sorrow has become overwhelming. He has always found it so easy to blame Kit. Only in this way, can he excuse himself.

THE HOSTESS

There is something I did not tell you. Something that I could not bring myself to recount: those fractions of seconds when I saw Kit arrive and I turned from my window to run to the door of my bedroom. I know that I promised you the truth, but there are some portions of memory too unbearable to ever inhabit again. I cannot go there with you, even now. I can think of her only as the girl I used to be, a figment of the past. All I can do is watch her, and tell you what she sees:

She sees a memory of that morning, the only memory of her life that she will ever consider to be truly beautiful. In her mind, she returns there, to the startling sensation of dew beneath her bare feet, and the mist of early dawn shrouding The Lilac Walk of La Doucette, concealing the two of them in their hiding places. She is running away, fleeing from him, but she casts a glance over her shoulder as she hurries toward the house. And it is the sound of his voice as he calls, "We will go then, you and I, in the night" that answers her prayers.

She doesn't reply, although there is no other answer than 'Yes,' allowing herself instead the luxury of control. She relishes the heaviness of her hair tumbling down over her shoulders and the extravagant rustle of her silk petticoat, underneath her pale pink chiffon dress, the hem of which she holds gathered in her right hand to save it from trailing on the ground. Yet, at the sight of how handsome he is on waking, this person who she loves more than anyone else in the world, she falters.

I should go back to him, she thinks. Those in love should cling. No one will have missed me yet; I can stay longer... But there can't be a more perfect farewell before the party than this, everything suspended ahead of us. All that we are is each other, a choice made, a promise to be kept.

No, I don't want anything to ruin it. Let him remember me like this, she resolves. I won't see him now until tonight. But soon there will be time enough for everything. There will be so much time... She smiles before resuming her flight, imagining herself entrancing, like a nymph or a gazelle. This little performance she leaves behind for him to take with him on his travels. She knows that he will come to take her away that evening. There is no doubt.

This is what she recalls as she turns from the window at her debut. As she pivots in her perfect dress, the prettiest she will ever be, knowing that Kit has come to the party just as he promised. This party that will now be everything she ever imagined. She accepts how foolish she has been to be afraid and how wonderful this, their secret bon voyage, is going to be. It all spreads out in front of her, the hours ahead, in a whirl of gaiety and light and good fortune. She knows that her guests will delight in her, as she dances with the young man they all want and will never have. Yet, she also acknowledges, with enormous pride that, long after she and Kit have eloped – after they have run away to the many exotic places they have conjured up in their imaginations – that this party will be regarded as the most perfect there ever was; and how disappointed her guests will be when they learn that it is also to be the last. Nobody can stop her and Kit from what they are about to do – not her father, not Captain Lyons, not Teddy. All will be perfect now. Every fear she has owned is unfounded. And, in her guileless ignorance, she trusts in this as she reaches for the door handle, opens the door and enters the hall. As she rushes to be with him, she believes wholeheartedly that she will never be this happy again, careless in the pursuit of everything she considers herself to own.

Sometimes there is no moment when we stop and we think, *Yes, I am certain that I will remember this forever*, no series of things we recognize will figure as the most important events in our brief stay here. Sometimes, there is just five minutes at the end of the day, tricks of the light, the view ever shifting, the sea pouring off the edge of the horizon into forever and remnants of memories: a young man, from somewhere far away, who found me again amidst the lilacs, when I was my very best self. And the recollection of a morning before a party, turning back to smile at him as I left: the haunting sweetness of his expression, the future ahead of us. There it was, happiness in a backward glance: happiness and the certainty of hope.

The certainty of hope: Can you recall how exquisite your future was before you were disappointed, before the consoling distance of hope evolved into the sobering proximity of fact? Do you remember the beauty of your dreams and their object? Regardless of the year, there is always a Little Maid or else a love-struck girl or a guest-of-honor whose unrealizable dreams are shattered before the party even begins. Whether it is a mistake in a court-yard, or a telephone call conveying regret from the friend of the one person you wished to see, so little changes: Yet, the stain of the disappointment remains, like the tears on the breast of this dress I wear tonight. They dried, they seem invisible, but they are still there: an indelible reminder of all that was once beautiful, of all that was never to be.

So the summers die. So we move from innocence to experience, casting off our former selves. Those elongating shadows of youth that trail in our wake, swiftly disappearing as the night closes in and the lights inside the party envelop us. We arrive slightly jaded; we ask now for entertainment to help us forget what we gave up to be here. "Come in," you hear a voice say, "the party cannot start without you. Introduce yourselves; make yourselves known." So the introductions begin:

"Hello, I am The Drunkard,"

"Hello, I am The Uninvited Guest,"

"Hello, I am The Little Maid."

And the voice that speaks to you? It is mine. The life that was chosen for me was the life within the party, not the one beyond it.

I am The Hostess.

II

INTRODUCTIONS

THE PARTY, THE PARTY!

A summary glance around the room confirms, to the satisfaction of most, that anyone who should be in attendance very much is. For this last party of the season, the disparate groups that comprise The Hamptons have turned out in force. From the founding members of The Tile Club, the artists who were first drawn to the East End in the early 1900s for its fabled light; to the fabulously wealthy denizens of the early summer cottages on Gin Lane; to the newly minted who flocked to the area in the 1920s, aided by the addition of the Sunset Highway; to the members of the various clubs that occupy the rich during the summer months – the ladies' associations, the Historical and Village Improvement Societies, The Parrish Art Museum and Guild Hall Theater denizens –, everyone is accounted for.

In addition, all of Serena's dearest friends – those no party would ever be complete without – assume their ritual places: May Cook, the eighty-one year old scion of one of the original 34 founding families in East Hampton, settles in her habitual chair in the corner of the room where she can see *everything*; Helen Fitzgerald, the fabled heiress, shepherds a group of little children clutching toy boats up the staircase to an attic bedroom, behind The Little Maid running to Mrs. Lyons' room, in tears; Rupert Turner-Hume, the film star, shelters somewhere dimly lit with a pert little thing; while the immaculate Anthony Duverglas sits down in his usual spot at the end of the bar, searching for a face in the crowd. Throughout the ballroom, the game of greeting begins in earnest as all in attendance anticipate their hostess' arrival.

"Well, we all thought Serena would marry Teddy, didn't we?" chatter a group of ladies from The Garden Club, highly skilled at sewing seeds of gossip and not flora. "Especially after Kit left, but then she returns from Europe two years later married to *him*!" "Odd, if you ask me," comments an avid social climber, still seeking a culprit for being left off the 1,000 strong guest list for the opening of Guild Hall in 1932, "but then there's always somebody behind the scenes ruining it for someone else…" she sniffs, casting a dark look to her immediate vicinity. "Not to mention no children," remarks her friend, notorious for being lethal with a hoe and an uncorroborated hunch. "Well," cuts in a kinder type, who has long been at pains to stamp this type of poison out, much like the weeds in her garden. "Maybe she couldn't have any." "No, no," interrupts The Lethal One, authoritatively, "She just didn't want any with Captain Lyons. Separate bedrooms," she mouths, widening her eyes conspiratorially. "Really?" chime the women, in unison. "Surely, you're not surprised," she scoffs. "I mean you must have seen the way she used to dance with old Duverglas. Rumor has it they were having it off for years." "What rot," retorts The Social Climber. "*That* was Rupert Turner-Hume," she corrects her. "Those two were forever huddling in corners… Surprising when you think about how terribly she aged," she carps, "I mean he could have had anybody…"

"Gracious me, what a beautiful woman –" a British gentleman at their side gasps, at the emergence of Venetia Dryden from another room, impeccably soigné in a lilac dress, sundry disheveled Summer Visitors at her heels. "Irish," The Social Climber informs him, helpfully, as her friends turn cold eyes toward her. "Galway," she adds acidly, with a finality that suggests Venetia is not – and will never be – one of the Astor 400. "Trust me," she simpers, her diamond bracelet glinting winningly, "the only Blue Book you'll find her name in is her diary."

The surrounding women smirk knowingly, much to the disaffection of The Kindly One: "It's impossible to weed out malice once it has taken root," she mutters. "Indeed" replies The British Gentleman benignly. "I say, I've been reading that marvelous gossip column in *The Southampton Press* by The Eavesdropper. Such a lark! But, do tell me, why is it called The Westhampton Leisure Hour and Supper Club?" "Something to do with Teddy Worthington," tuts The Social Climber, bristling at the mention of The Eavesdropper having been mercilessly lampooned in the column on more than one occasion. "Serena always waited for him at the front door and each time Teddy arrived, he'd bow his head to kiss her hand and say, 'Dearest Sea, the eternal thrill of The Leisure Hour and you at the door.' "So will this Teddy be here tonight?" he inquires brightly. "For pity's sake," snaps The Social Climber, rolling her eyes as if to say 'not one of our own.' "What an inappropriate remark, considering. *"Who* may I ask are *you*? I've never seen you here before." "Quite," he replies, smiling with fatal benevolence. "I do apologize. I doubt we mix in the same social sphere. I'm the Duke of Windsor," he concludes, as The Social Climber, a native of Connecticut, and therefore unaccustomed to irony, almost whimpers in pain.

Yet, as The Summer Visitors stop to mix and mingle, it becomes apparent that, despite the familiar faces, this is not the usual crowd. There are strangers it seems, who on closer inspection appear frustratingly familiar. Long lost friends find themselves suddenly reunited with those who have missed them as much as they themselves have been missed. Still more realize, with a pang of horror, that the earnest interlopers at their side, are those people they once destroyed in pursuit of their own overriding successes. While for others, their chance reintroductions with ancient acquaintances mean absolutely nothing. Nobody can say that any of these new guests are the same; these long-lost faces seem somehow older, different; almost unrecognizable. All The Summer Visitors understand, without knowing why, is that they would have known them anywhere. Very few, however, are inclined to dwell on things they cannot fathom; the fortunate think better of questioning their luck lest it run out; the guilty avoid examining their consciences for fear of finding answers that won't please them; and the ambivalent return to the consoling familiarity of not thinking at all.

Soon, The Summer Visitors will meet another unlikely guest, an introduction that will be forced upon them, whether they like it or not. For somewhere beyond this house, that guest is already making the acquaintance of countless other unsuspecting souls: like the Montauk fisherman in their boats, cast far too far now out at sea, who have already accepted that they will never return to the Promised Land dock again: like the Japanese butler in Bridgehampton, who remains implacably calm, asking politely, "Will Madame take tea in the dining room or upstairs?" as the front of the house is ripped off, exposing its residents to the elements like tiny figures in a doll's house: like the woman in Westhampton swimming frantically across the Bay, accompanied only by a swarm of rats, as desperate as she not to be caught in the vice like grip of the storm's handshake: like the families in Amagansett and Georgica, who are rushing back into their houses, crumbling around them, to save what cannot be saved: like the automobile that is hurled through the front of the Willard Restaurant in Montauk, killing its driver and his wife, as the earth begins to tremor and barometers all over the East End fall to unprecedented depths. But quite unlike the blissfully oblivious Summer Visitors who, at this very moment, identify the strains of Serena Lyons' favorite song and once more willingly give themselves up to the dance...

THE HOSTESS

They hunt here, at La Doucette. They stalk the deer, those exquisite creatures. I am entirely against it. I always have been, ever since I was a child and my husband shot The Emperor.

He was everything you would expect of such a name: a thirteen-year-old red stag, he stood nearly nine-foot tall, with wild antlers and a curling mane like Charles II. Nobody had ever seen anything like him in the East End before. As children, Kit, Catherine and I used to run all over the gardens, trying to find him, but it was impossible, like trying to find the Yeti. He always hid himself so well. He was very wise, you see, The Emperor.

Do you think he wanted to die? Is that why he walked out to the middle of the lawn on that blissfully sunny day in May, when all the spring flowers were in bloom? The Emperor had never savored such freedom before, nor did he ever savor it again for Edward shot him dead: a clean shot that rung out and felled him instantly. This fantasy that he did not suffer was supposed to appease us. And, naturally, our tears were dismissed, as all hysterical children are, who cling to ideals of innocence that have nothing to with the harsh realities of nature and culling. Apparently, my husband had had The Emperor in his sights for over a decade. Worse, he was to be commended for his kill. But he deserves no such praise, because I never forgot what I saw reflected in The Emperor's eyes as he turned to his marksman: the insistent cruelty of life. He knew my husband, I am certain of this. He let Edward kill him, because he accepted that there was no escape.

For many years he was displayed in my father's study, which later became my husband's. As a child, I would sometimes go in there, to look up at The Emperor on the wall, and it was always the same: It was if we understood one another, but I had no idea why. It would only be later, after his assassin brought me back here, that I would finally comprehend our kinship.

After Edward and I returned here from our honeymoon in Europe, I was given little to do; he felt it unwise to burden me with too many responsibilities. There was only one thing that I insisted upon. I felt it was too dreadful for The Emperor to be confined to Edward's dark study, to have to watch my husband revel in his freedom as he went about his business. So, I moved The Emperor into the marble hallway where I placed him on the wall underneath the clock, facing the front door that is habitually open all summer. It is where he has lived ever since, where he can enjoy a clear view of the land over which he once ruled. Yet, I also wanted my husband to have a perpetual reminder of what he had done, every time he walked into the house. I waited for Edward the first night that I moved The Emperor, to see if he would punish me for defying him. I thought he was about to say something, but he merely noted The Emperor and myself standing beneath him and went directly to his study, where he remained for the rest of the evening.

It was then, however, that something enchanting began; something that has become one of the loveliest sights at La Doucette: After The Emperor died, the deer started to gather on the edge of the forest at the far end of the lawn, where they have a clear view straight up to the house. Before then, they had only ever strayed beyond the boundaries of the forest at night. Yet, for hours each day, I would see them there, young and old, entire families of them, and I began to kindle a notion that they had come to pay homage to him.

I placed a ban on hunting and it has been observed. Every spring and summer, I have had the pleasure to sit with The Emperor and watch as his children and his grandchildren gather together at a safe distance to pay their respects. People ridicule my conviction that they know him, but I am convinced of this. It is my opinion that they would know him anywhere, despite his altered state.

It strikes me that love is a little like hunting. You catch someone within range, pinion him with your desire, and then never let him out of your sight.

This was my mistake: I let him out of my sight. Before tonight, I have never spoken of what happened after Kit left and I followed, but I will confide it in you now. It was just like those who come to visit The Emperor:

I would have known him anywhere.

THE HOST

Heaven, I'm in heaven
And my heart beats so that I can hardly speak
And I seem to find the happiness I seek
When we're out together dancing cheek to cheek...

That song, he thinks, the music intermittently audible over the thunder and wind. It would have to be that song.

It was her favorite: how it spoke to her, Serena would insist to him, after clinging desperately to some young man, her cheek pressed up against his own, as he clumsily shuffled her around the room. Captain Lyons always thought it better that she could not see how she looked, how desperate; her white knuckled grip on the youth's slender shoulders belying her age somewhat definitively for the more astute, like himself. He winces at the recollection of how she would hesitate to let go at the song's end, clenching the victim to her, almost too long, pulling back only to search his face questioningly, before moving away, almost in defeat, at not having found there what she sought.

Yet, even in spite of her disappointment, she would always rush after such men at the party's end; "Do come again," she would call after them. "And do bring all your friends. Don't forget," she would add, too urgently, too inappropriately, but she didn't care. Some of the young men were respectful, but it ultimately became impossible for Captain Lyons to quell the rumors, especially given her blatant disregard for the respect she might have shown him, as her husband. "Serena likes them young... illegally young." These are the comments he would inadvertently hear giggled about around corners, and with it, the attendant humiliation of how little he meant to his wife.

．

Yes, were she not leaving, he would have watched her dance to this song. But he is grateful to be spared the spectacle. He has always despised the way she dances to this song.

. . .

It was years before she danced again, after Kit left. There were no more parties. Not until Captain Lyons brought her back here as his wife, almost two years after her debut. There were no more parties because she disappeared: She escaped – having sold her mother's jewelry and garnering a significant amount of money – with Teddy Worthington's help. She went to find him, but Kit could not be found so easily.

She almost ruined her reputation. For love alone she would have given up everything, then as now, when she dances with these empty boys, despite her tearful protestations, the rationale from which I have always turned away, he thinks. To save her, Captain Lyons had to tell everyone that Serena was finishing her education in France. There were some skeptics who hinted amongst themselves that there were other reasons for the trip, but it was an easy enough lie for him to manage. It was out of season. Nobody they knew would have been likely to make the voyage. Yet, every time he uttered the matter-of-fact explanation for her absence, he wished for it to be true. He wanted to imagine Serena on a boulevard in Nice or Cap d'Antibes, a guest of the Cook's, at sunset; full of excitement at what she was experiencing, the stories she would bring home with her to entertain them in their boredom. The reality, however, was far different.

Of course, he blames himself for what happened: He tried to tell her that Kit had no fortune, that she had been misled as to Kit's true intentions. Yet, whenever he broached the subject, Serena became so distressed, to the point where Captain Lyons was sure she hated him, that he was forced to keep his silence. I had no thought then that I might marry her, he recalls, although I don't think I ever loved her more than during those few months when I looked after her: She was never more beautiful to me again. But he had no real choice in the matter: Immediately after Serena's debut, her father disowned her when the familiar hallmarks of her melancholia began to emerge, still incapable of forgiving Serena's many flaws, which he considered a reflection of himself. He ceded the house to Captain Lyons; an ironic gesture, considering Captain Lyons had paid for its upkeep almost since Serena's father first built it. It was the last they ever saw of him.

Teddy visited daily, the only time her spirits lifted, which pained Captain Lyons more than he cared to admit. He permitted it, only for her sake, a decision for which he later paid dearly. His only objective, however, was to distract her from the events of the past months: the damage his bringing Kit to stay had caused. Yet, he defends himself, I have always maintained that I permitted them to love one another, as far as circumstance would allow. I cannot speak for fate, for events beyond my control. Nor can I speak for Kit. Regardless of the outcome, however unfortunate, he remained guilty of crimes that could not be forgiven, least of all, by me. He had imposed where he had no right, given that he understood the impossibility of his situation. By so doing, he forced me into a course of action, I should never have undertaken. What forced me to go against my better instincts of honesty, of truth: to salvage what was left of Serena's heart, when I found her again with the boy.

But still: I am haunted by him.

THE UNINVITED GUEST

The wind does not touch him, despite its ferocity. He is not afraid of the trees, nearly ripped with their roots from the ground. Kit seems to own strength that he never possessed before, such is his determination to see her. In barely a few steps, he will round the corner ahead and leave South Country Road behind, and then he will encounter once more what he has only dreamt of; the looming grandeur of La Doucette beyond, and Serena within it.

It seems to him now that there is no road he has ever traveled that has not ended in her, even in his mind. After the first party, he made sure to journey farther than Serena, he thought, could ever find him, unable to forgive himself for his actions. It had come down to luck; a turn of the dice and everything was gone. He had no inheritance: the birthright upon which he had hinged his proposal of marriage, thinking he would have the means to support them both. The trustees had seemingly gambled every penny on frivolous speculations, or so Captain Lyons informed Kit at the end of the summer: "You can give her nothing," he said. "I understand that you are very much taken with one another, but you must consider her position in society, her health. I fear what this information could do to her. You will certainly need to delay your plans for the time being." And it was that thought, that Kit would disappoint her as everyone else had, that pushed him into increasingly desperate acts in trying to secure their future: negotiations, transactions, assurances, choices of which he ought to have known better. Yet, scarcely had he succeeded in averting that danger, when the rug was pulled from underneath his feet in the worst way imaginable.

He had no right to what he had taken: He had selfishly trusted that all would be well and it was not. The shame he owned and the punishment he was forced to accept proved overwhelming. He had no choice, he thought then, but to agree to what was demanded: "You're a thief," he said. "As soon as you set foot here, you stole from her. She would have been happy. Maybe not as wildly in love as she has been with you, but content. The best you can do is leave the country and never see her again. She shouldn't think of you as anything other than the disgrace that you are."

He should not have gone to the party, but Kit couldn't do as he asked. He had to have one moment more of her, the future he faced so empty a reality. Yet, Serena's despair, watching her be led away by Teddy, assuming that she had been told of what he had done, of who he was, devastated him. He ran to the red front door after it closed, to beg, but all he could hear in his head were the accusatory remarks of those who he thought truly loved her, reminding him of his guilt. He almost knocked, almost. He should have, he realizes now, given what he later learned of how they were betrayed.

He left the next morning, by train from Speonk. With his back to the engine, he waited to depart, facing Remsenburg defiantly through the window. He blurred his vision to make the landscape recede to a fixed point on a vertical line, nothing more; diminishing everything he had known there to fact, not fancy. He had to forget what the view had once promised and remember it only as somewhere unremarkable, leaving nothing of himself there, lest he ever be tempted to go back and claim it.

Yet, just before the horn sounded to indicate the train's departure, he saw Lucinda. They used to meet, on occasion, as she lived near Captain Lyon's house: They would sometimes stop to talk, usually of Serena. He thought her so sad a girl, understanding of her loneliness. Lucinda loved to recall the story of their childhood when Serena played with her. Kit could only vaguely remember the day, but he found it touching that a singular act of kindness could figure as largely to her; so representative, too, of everything he adored about Serena.

Lucinda stood, tears streaming down her face, banging on the window of Kit's carriage, to capture his attention, "Don't blame Serena," she implored. "You can't know what it was like for her, after you went to school, Kit." He tried to stop her from continuing: There was nothing she could say that would change the situation, but she refused to listen, "Anything you ask of me, I'd do, but I'll always weep for the two of you. Please go back to her. People are cruel, Kit. Someone has done this to you. I am positive of it." "No," he said, touched by her compassion but resigned to owning the responsibility of what had happened: "I did it, Lucinda. It was me."

She appeared confused by his response, running alongside the train as it pulled out, still trying frantically to make him understand something that he, in his despair, could not: There was so little time left. *Hold tight,* she seemed to beseech him, gripping the handle of the train carriage, *never let go.* Poor Lucinda, that plaintive figure who stood on the same platform today and welcomed Kit home as if to say, *"You see, I was right. I never stopped waiting for you. I never stopped crying for you."*

He went first to London, where he joined the Navy. In the months that followed, Kit visited parts of the world he had learned of only in atlases; France, the countries bordering the Mediterranean and, finally, Africa, to Nairobi, but he was not a besotted groom with his bride when he first set foot on that magnificent continent's soil. Nothing was as he had imagined it would be.

He tried to convince himself that Serena would be happier without him, but the pain of her loss would not abate. He had known his fair share of lovesick men at Cambridge; been privy to their restless petulance, the toes dipped into alcoholic catharsis, the sickly pallor of disappointment that stained their cheeks, the chivvying along of their peers to try and bring them out of themselves. He had also witnessed those mornings, when they would awake suddenly restored, their troubles shrugged off, as if a race they lost or a game they weren't well enough to play. But Kit knew that he would not recover from her.

As the months progressed, having to let her go, unfastened some vital element that had held him up and who he once was, that person who is a stranger to him now, tumbled around him at his feet. The thought of her spoiled anything that followed. Other women, while lovely, figured in his mind like white cotton dresses sullied at the hems. Inevitably, the panic of estrangement set in. Kit learned what all lost lovers do; there is nothing heroic about doing what is best – separating from someone so loved – only doubt.

More and more, he found himself tormented by Lucinda's entreaties: "Someone has done this to you." What had she known? he asked. Why had she even come to the station, they were not close friends. Aspects of what had happened began to make less sense; what had once seemed a clear and honorable decision, became less certain: He had been so foolish, he realized, so consumed by everything he had done wrong, that he hadn't thought rationally about the consequences of leaving without telling Serena the reason himself. Why had he let someone else dictate his future, why had he not fought harder? To turn tale and run, as he had, was not decent, but the actions of a coward.

Ultimately, a broken promise had led to him being forced to leave. What if that promise upon which he had insisted in order to agree to do specifically that – that she would be told the truth about his departure and that he had not intended to hurt her – had also been broken? The only truth Serena would believe then is that he had callously discarded her. And what would that do to her, he worried, what would he find in her bright and broken eyes, were he to incline his head toward her, as he once loved to do at her side during their walks, should they ever meet again? Yet, still he faltered at whether he would cause her more distress by returning; always despairing of how quickly she had disappeared into the party with Teddy. Kit knew why he had not gone to her: Why had she not come to him, to ask why? Were her tears borne of incomprehension or, worse, of hatred? And it was this singular thought that would convince him against acting on his instincts: the fear that, in either scenario, she may hate him. Better, he would tell himself, not to know....

But, one afternoon, six months later, standing at a gentleman's bar in Nairobi – a drone of meaningless conversation around him, of meetings and weather patterns and who said what to someone else – it struck Kit that life is a matter of irrelevancy if we let it become so. He thought again of what Lucinda had said, "Don't blame Serena...Someone has done this to you," and the constant fear of what might have happened to her made up his mind once and for all. He had to go back and if he did, if he told Serena the truth, was not anything still possible...? But he didn't dare hope. The only thing that Kit understood was that he had let her down the worst by trusting the truth to others. Regardless of what they would do to him, he had to make sure that, at the least, Serena owned peace. He booked his passage that afternoon.

He wonders now at fate, given where he's been, what he's learned. As he emerged from the port's office, the ticket grasped in his hand, he saw her, as clearly as he ever had. It was as if she was again moving through the mist of an early morning. Yet, this time, she was not running away, but toward him, through the dust kicked up by the carriages from the road. "Serena," he called. She stopped, lowering her parasol in the brilliant heat of the mid-day, as pale and fragile a beauty as ever, her smile a blessing that absolved the pain of her absence. He could not guess at how she had found him, but he has never forgotten his elation at knowing that there would be a future for them, after all.

But it was then, as Kit stepped off the kerb to join her and looked to the road on his right that, it came to him, this future, in a way he could not have anticipated. In the split seconds that followed, Kit understood why Lucinda had beseeched him never to squander time. She was right; there was so little left.

ANTHONY DUVERGLAS

There, acknowledges Anthony Duverglas, placing an impeccably tailored elbow on the bar and surveying the general tedium of the scene around him. Yet, it is with the haunting sadness of a life involuntarily led in the singular, that he finds, within the crowd, the one face he seeks. Please, just let me look at her, he thinks, irritated by the distraction of the bartender who places a glass and a bottle of Malt 90 on the counter, which Serena used to smuggle in, especially for him. "Anthony Duverglas, you are the handsomest I've ever seen," her ritual cry, whenever he would arrive. Anthony turns his attention momentarily to the gold plaque attached to a chain that hangs around the neck of the bottle, engraved with the words: "For the immaculate Anthony Duverglas, in recognition of his refined Scottish palate," a gift from Serena on his thirty-sixth birthday that had sent the rumor mill spiraling into a near-frenzy of salacious half-truths. And now there are tears in his eyes, as he hangs his head in regret at everything that has transpired since that evening and this: Yet, the companion with whom he longs to share such memories is not at his side. Although, as if in defiance of this knowledge, he looks to her again, futilely hoping the object of his undiminished regard might cross the room to sit with him, even at this late hour. *There,* he mourns, on finding her.

It is a question of propriety, nothing more. No, he shall not go to her. No, he will not move from his vantage point at the corner of this bar to cross the room to where she stands. He will not take her hand in passing, amidst this unwitting crowd of people, as he once did as a younger man at a party so similar to the one this evening. He will not clasp her hand with an aggression he hopes might match the passion he has hidden for her; holding it just a second too long, before gripping it again and then once more before he lets go. Nor impart to her again the secret of the affection he has harbored for her and has continued to harbor over the twenty years that have since passed. No, Anthony Duverglas will do none of these things.

But, if you will permit me, if you would not mind moving aside, I would just like to look at her. It is all I have come for, all I ask. *Please,* he privately begs of no one in particular, *just let me look at her.*

Venetia Dryden stands, surrounded by a protective wall of wealth; an impenetrable invisible fence through which he could easily pass, but a sense of dignity, of decorum, prevents him. In truth, there was never a time when he could have honestly claimed her, save for three months when they first met, before she was married. While he was often tempted– and once did indeed act, that time he reached for her hand – whenever the tantalizing thought of whisking her away from her husband, Douglas, might arise, the issue would always be settled, whenever he would remind himself of the strictures of the society in which they moved and posed the inevitable question: Whatever would people think of me should I dare? How would it look? What would be whispered in those cloistered salons that reeked of belonging, within which he tried desperately to belong? And what, he asked himself, could Venetia Dryden possibly see in someone like him, when Douglas Dryden had amassed one of the largest fortunes in the Northeast. There was also no doubt, that in those days, society would not have approved of such an act. Well, decent society, at least, which is the only society Anthony cares about. He is old-fashioned, he knows, but these things still matter to him: even now, when there is so little point.

Yet, he knew from the very first that there was something he had to find out with regard to Venetia Dryden, as if she possessed some vital knowledge that would render his existence somehow necessary. Nothing has changed, despite the passing of the years, except now, because of his circumstances, it is sadly, too late for such yearning, silly almost, and yet he cannot stop himself. So many years of endless dalliances and, only with her, did he come undone: a surrender he has acknowledged with awe and gratitude, offset by how difficult it would ever be to claim her, if at all; a reality he has been forced to accept during these evenings he spends alone, thinking on why he had to find what he sought only in her.

Back in his more immaculate days, Anthony Duverglas was the one who would dance with them. This was the role he fulfilled for all of the debutantes, all of the disaffected wives. But, as he would say himself, he is of no particular note as a dancer. He is competent, but not one of these sons of fortune, who he has watched effortlessly execute the latest moves, with a confidence he never fully possessed. There are steps, he knows, that can only be learned in private schools, which, combined with an indolent grace, not bestowed upon the sons of Bridgehampton farmers, make for a dance, not quite expected and, in the end, sadly, not really good enough. His saving grace is that, despite his background, he looks the part. Or, at least, he once did.

There's an Anthony Duverglas at every party, there to provide a reliable waltz, a slow polka, an undemanding quickstep; a sigh of relief for heiresses left sitting embarrassingly alone. "Dance with Judy, won't you Anthony, darling…" grimacing mothers would cajole, nodding at the daughters who had not inherited their effervescent beauty, "Her dance card is completely empty, poor lamb…." "But, of course," he'd smile, understanding completely what it is to not quite belong. So he was the one who would dance with them if such ladies were left sitting alone: there to rescue them from callous eyes informing them on their chair by the wall, of how little they mattered. And there was a time when the more he danced, the more he believed he might be able to dance just like the best of them, if he worked hard enough. So he was grateful for his role, indebted to a society that had opened its doors and admitted him, when he should have been standing on his father's farm stand, selling English meadow wildflowers from their fields.

Yet, if there is anything he has learned over the years of attending Serena's parties, it is that, for everyone there is a time in the sun, a time when the meadow flowers bloom at one's feet more beautifully than ever before, and the trick is to recognize it once it has passed. So he sits the dances out these days. In truth, it has been a long while since anyone has considered him a dancer. But that's of no importance anymore, because there is only one dance left for Anthony Duverglas. Only one for which he will ask, should he be given the opportunity. It is just a simple waltz, but he has saved it in his heart for best.

It was the dance he should have asked for, when there was still hope, possibility. A waltz to an Irish song called "Give Me Your Hand," that Serena asked the orchestra to play when Venetia Dryden first settled here from Ireland, twenty-five years ago: one to match the soft burr of her voice and the redness of her hair that had captivated Anthony since the night she walked into La Doucette on Douglas Dryden's arm. "But it's my favorite!" she said, turning to him with her wide green eyes, and he knew then that he must ask for her hand, despite how anyone might judge him, but he was so overwhelmed by how beautiful she was, how different to everyone else, that by the time he managed to say anything, her fiancé had, rightfully, stepped in between them, and the moment was gone. Anthony watched them dance, as if he was watching the life he would not live; a situation made only worse by what Serena later told him. "Oh, Anthony," she said, "don't you realize that I had the orchestra play that, only for you. I thought it would be so lovely if you could finally dance with someone you chose." He has always considered Serena Lyons to be a great lady. It still moves him indescribably, in light of his circumstances, that someone as decent as her wanted more for him than a turn around the room.

For years, his married friends, to whom he figured as their perennial bachelor friend, did try to pair him up with practically every woman of their circle: an endless parade of the entitled and the lovely, the naïve and the cunning, but not one managed it; to turn his face south or east, like a compass, from the direction where he knew Venetia lived. In truth, such girls barely registered. Their youth bored him; he left his own behind with relief, as if casting off a cumbersome mantle that had always scratched nigglingly at his skin. He has always been something of an old soul, weary from the day he was born. Perhaps because he sensed, far more readily than anyone else, that, for everyone, there is just one great love and he would not get to keep the only one he would ever want. What his friends failed to guess was that the reason he pushed himself to become the success he was in the 1920s, amassing a fortune through investments the good people of Serena's parties were kind enough to help him with, was only to be considered good enough for Venetia Dryden, one day: because Anthony Duverglas never forgave himself that waltz.

If only Douglas would move out of the way, he would wish, if only he would find another partner... So when Douglas did begin to treat Venetia disgracefully, Anthony permitted himself to fuel that regret, of leading her away from him, with hope. And in it was in the light of that hope that one evening, twenty years ago, he found the courage to cross the room to where she stood, overcome by the possibility that life possesses; of how everything might change; of how Anthony could not blame Venetia if she should not know what he felt; to impart the truth of his regard, the secret of which he left in the palm of her hand, so that she might, in turn, offer him her own.

He credits Venetia with a wisdom he certainly did not possess during that heady instant, as she never reacted to his gesture; never offered any indication that she returned his affection. Yet, it is better, he thinks now, that she did not. Her response – that of complete silence – was utterly appropriate. Had she broken the fundamental rules of society in which they lived, and ran to him, they would have been cast out from the very places he aspired to belong within. And he would have considered it a sin for someone as refined and beautiful as Venetia to have to lower her standards, in any way. He is equally convinced that Venetia, too, understood this. Had she pursued him; had she clasped his hand in return, it is possible that his love for her would have died immediately.

These are the things he has told himself.... But the sad reality is, in that in aspiring to become worthy of her, Anthony forfeited any chance he might have had: Venetia is, to him, the perfect embodiment of how a lady should be, just as he once fulfilled the role of the perfect gentleman at these gatherings; the trusted blind date consort who would be charming to Serena's guests, suitably engaged and intrigued, who would leave without the impropriety of asking for more than they cared to give. Yet, by allowing himself to be perceived in such a fashion, he was destined never to come close to happiness. He could not reach again for her. It was not the done thing. It is still entirely inappropriate, despite how he longs for her to offer him a sign that he may do exactly that.

But, please, he begs, *just let me look at her.*

VENETIA DRYDEN

At her husband's side, the incomparable Venetia Dryden is pointedly not listening to a word he says. She is lost instead in her favorite place, in the life of her mind, her gaze fixed on Anthony Duverglas' seat at the corner of the bar on the far side of the room. *Tell me there will be a river there,* she prays, recalling her father's last words. Yet, her father was not asking God to cleanse him of his sins, but to deliver back to him his dreams. Like most working men, Venetia Dryden's father was not free to realize his grandest ambitions, but he was not bitter: "Don't you worry, my beautiful Venetia," he would say, "my dreams will keep 'til the end." For his family, however, he wished for more. When they were children, in the summertime, he would take them to a river by their house in Galway, and they would float on their backs watching the sky through the leaves of the trees above: "In the channels of the river, down to the beds below," he would tell them, "the only sound that exists is hope. Listen to your dreams, my children, this is where they are born and kept safe; the cool water is a blessing that will never tell you, No."

This is why they call her The River Girl. Not to her face – she knows they wouldn't be that brave – but close enough behind Venetia's back for her to hear. It is because the story of her romance with her husband began with a rescue. Just as Venetia's father counseled, she once floated in rivers and dreamt her dreams. The fanciful dreams of the Galway girls; of handsome suitors and whirlwind romances to grander places where the grandest people dwell. And one day, when she was all of nineteen, in late spring when the wildflowers were in bloom along the banks of the river she floated in, some of them drifting on the water beside her, her long red hair cascading around her face, Venetia was wrenched from that river by the strongest arms she had ever felt wrap around her. And she looked up to find quite the best-looking man she'd ever seen; Douglas Dryden, holding her aloft, like a conquering hero. He had mistakenly thought her drowning. And that is how an ordinary Galway girl's dream came true, and she captured the heart of an American millionaire.

The first thing Venetia learned about American millionaires is that they get their own way; Douglas courted her so intently and charmed her family so ferociously, they would never have forgiven her had she refused his proposal. The second thing she learned, however, is that an American millionaire's wife must never stand in his way by asking for anything those men do not choose to give. Forever on, she was always to be grateful for being a girl from Galway who married well.

Venetia was taught this lesson with resounding force on arriving here, when she was not welcomed, but spurned by the American girls of his acquaintance; all heiresses to some fortune or other, whereas she was the daughter of a respectable bank manager, and her idyllic life in Ireland, considered oh-so down at heel. Or so they were heard to comment after Douglas relayed the story of their meeting, failing to garner the rapt attention he sought. His disappointment was telling, – that Venetia was not going to be considered the prize he thought her – even she saw that.

Yet, in an act of chivalry of which he was never guilty again, he kept his promise to her, before swiftly drowning his sorrows in other women, who all willingly offered to pour themselves over him. There was no river then to drown the sound of the malice that echoed in her ears when she was left standing alone amidst them. But Anthony Duverglas. Anthony Duverglas was the exception. He was the only one, apart from Serena, who showed Venetia any kindness. If ever he saw me standing by myself, he would always come and sit a while. We shared an awful lot in common, she recalls fondly. He reminded me of the people from home; so nice and unassuming, no snobbery about them, just proud of what they were, what they had worked for, not inherited from the efforts of their forebears.

She never told him, but she had seen him once, before they were officially introduced, standing in a fine suit by a field of wildflowers in Bridgehampton. She was in the carriage with Douglas' sister, and couldn't help but ask: "Who is that?" "Anthony Duverglas," Douglas' sister replied, as if she owned him. "Everyone thinks him the handsomest man in the world. Penniless, regrettably," she mused. "Wonderful dancer, though…" But Venetia hadn't noticed his looks. What had struck her was how good he seemed, how genuine, how different to everyone else. Maybe it was because of the swooning that went on over Douglas. Possibly, Venetia considered, she was inured to it. After all, women who marry peacocks, quickly realize how grubby those feathers really are. They never impress the same way twice.

I think it was only a matter of course that I would fall in love with him, she thinks, as she often does at these parties, whenever she turns to his spot at the bar. I did, though, down to the depths of me. You would, though, wouldn't you, when a man as good as that keeps you company, while your husband humiliates you with every other woman in the room. But although Venetia knew that Anthony was fond of her, she always thought him destined for grander things. After he became so successful, I thought it inevitable he would marry one of the great beauties of our society. As hard as it was for me, I tried to keep those dreams at bay, but I could never quite give them up…

And then it had happened; the secret message of his regard conveyed in a room full of unsuspecting people: He had taken her hand, carrying it with him as he passed; squeezing it once, then twice, as his intent began to dawn on her, then a third time, holding it there for too long, as if he never wanted to let it go, before releasing it. Such was the passion that surged up in Venetia, she almost fainted, but what was she supposed to do? "Go to him," Serena suddenly urged at her side. "The opportunity might never present itself again." Venetia almost jumped out of her skin. But it was no surprise that Serena saw something, she remembers. Serena was always watching, everyone at her parties. And, my God, I wanted to, I wanted to run: to leave my husband and run, shamelessly, to him. Everything in me screamed, *Follow. Do it now.* And I almost did, watching Anthony walk through the crowd away from me. But as I looked around that huge room, at the foul snobs in it, the stupid social claptrap, and my rotten husband flirting with some girl, I realized that if I did, then I would be just like all of them. And the reason I loved Anthony Duverglas was because he was nothing like all of them. So I couldn't. I didn't. Instead, I locked myself in a bedroom, where

I wept, for hours. Because that is how a lady behaves, I told myself. That is how she was raised. And I wanted to believe it was the reason why Anthony liked me so much.

That was my moment, she thinks, regretfully: the one Serena was forever asking me about, but I kept it to myself. I think all miserable women, trapped in loveless marriages, yearn for something like that to happen, just once, when you're old enough to still be desirable and not too old to be desperate. Flattering, really, but nothing can come of it, not if you're a decent person, she tries to convince herself once more. Besides, I have three fine girls and there was always some beauty on Anthony's arm, everyone predicting she would be 'the One.' But, in spite of myself, I'd watch them at these parties and pray, *Don't let it last, don't let her be the one. Let it be me: Do it again. Let me know that isn't all over yet.*

But the dreams will keep, won't they, she smiles sadly, stopping herself from straying too far into what can never be, and you make peace with the disappointment. And it is true that Venetia leads a fabulous existence compared to most – because if nothing else, Douglas Dryden is a great provider. All of the parties she has hosted to impress at The Devon Yacht Club and The Maidstone; the dresses and the houses he has built, each one bigger than the last. Yet, as Venetia has often learned to her cost, the lavish jewels he showers on her are not his way of atoning for whatever affair he's conducting, although their arrival is a sure sign a new one has begun; not a sign that he loves her either. No, she knows, they're only to prove he's better than everyone else, even if his money is new... This is partly the reason why Venetia did what she did for Serena. Not to infuriate Douglas, but she reasoned that all that pain he'd caused her had to count for something. And besides that, Serena's request put her in mind of the future she might have owned, if only she had followed Anthony when he offered her the chance.

Sometimes, she dreams of him dancing: a dream she wakes from filled with hope, before she inevitably remembers: He never danced with her. And Anthony danced with everyone, she reminds herself on these mornings, when the day looms darker than most. So Venetia supposes that she may have been wrong. Because she would have settled for that: to dance with him, just once, because then she might have said, "What did you mean, that time you took my hand? Did you mean what I wanted you to mean? And can I tell you now why I cannot come with you? How you would think nothing of me, if I did: But can I tell you that it's all I want to do? To be the only one you'll ever dance with."

Venetia has often wondered what he would have said, although she'll not learn that answer now. Douglas made sure of that. Someone is always watching, after all, and it's not always good people like Serena. How ironic, Venetia has often thought, that eyes that have flitted over her in abject boredom should have spotted the one thing she wished to keep hidden. So she no longer gets to smile at Anthony Duverglas, or pass a word or two en route to the door. But still she looks, as she does this evening, to his place at the bar. Still, she dreams of that dance, despite how sad a thing it is. Maybe, she tells herself, those dreams will be returned to me, in the end. So, like my father did, when that moment comes, I pray that there will be a river there....

ANTHONY DUVERGLAS

He surveys the landscape of time that stands between them. The days and hours, the seconds and fragments of seconds, when everything might have changed, and he might not be sitting here, frozen in his longing. In private moments imagining himself a prisoner of a life that he did indeed choose but, somehow, does not seem right or fair, almost as if it has been inflicted on him as punishment for his integrity. He shuts his eyes against the sorrow he feels, and tries to think better of his heart and its whims. Yet, when he opens them, they are focused once more on Venetia Dryden's forgiving face. And, although, he can barely bring myself to accept it as truth, it is as if she is watching him, like a promise to himself he did not keep. In Venetia's eyes, in what he discerns there, he finds the courage, at last, to move, knowing that he will be welcomed.

But, in front of him, appears a young woman he once knew. She is terribly drunk, "Dance with me, Anthony, please. I've waited for you to come." "My dear girl," he protests, "I have t— " "Have to what," she slurs, "Nobody dances with me" she cries. "I never get to come to the parties anymore. Please, *please*. This is the last party. Jus' let me have one dance..." Anthony Duverglas knows he cannot refuse, considering why she has asked him. *It's just a simple waltz*, he tells himself, but it's so painful for him to effect. Yet, there is nothing to be done. "But of course. It would be my pleasure," he replies, offering his arm with customary chivalry.

They move out onto the floor, but the music ends almost as soon as it begins, a faster tune replacing the waltz, and Anthony Duverglas can barely believe his good fortune. For he is able, without being impolite, to make his excuses, to pass the young girl to a boy her own age, who knows the steps to the dance that he does not. With relief he sees that Venetia's eyes are still locked on his, as he begins to wend his way through the guests toward her: "What's got into him?" he hears the boy say, but he cannot care as he once might have, because he suddenly knows everything, as he has always known everything. And nothing will stop him as he hurries to where Venetia waits for him, as if two hands are pushing him from behind. She is still watching him and now she is faintly smiling, but it is in her eyes that he sees it: "*Yes. Come to me now.*" And it is like a clarion call to his disenchanted heart: He hears it, even though she does not speak. He hears her acknowledgment of how he loves her and he moves ever closer, and soon he will be within reach....

THE HOSTESS

He did not respond to his name when I whispered it to him:

"Christopher...Christopher..." I soothed, as I tried to make him look at me. "Kit," I said, calling him by his nickname. But then he slowly turned his head and opened his eyes. And there in the trusting innocence of his gaze, I saw the flash of recognition I had been told was impossible. "Don't worry," I reassured him, on seeing the confusion that followed, fearing him close to tears. "I'll always be with you, all that you see..."

The unwelcome sound of the nurse's voice announced what I dreaded most each evening. It was time to say goodbye. "It's 7:25, Mrs. Peel," she said. "He must sleep now."

It was the summer of 1908, the year following my debut. It had only been three days since I arrived at the hospital, but I had barely seen him. His health was so precarious that the doctors were wary of exposing him to anything that might cause more harm. I did as they asked, but the surprise and joy of being with him made me long for one moment more every time we were together. After the terrible consequences of the choice I made at the party, I vowed never to let anyone I loved out of my sight again: "Please, may I have another minute," I asked the nurse. "I just want to sit with him a little longer." I know I seemed desperate as I spoke and how dangerous it was to appear unstable, but I couldn't help myself. Each night, when the visiting hours ended, I harbored a nagging fear that somehow I would lose him. For some reason, on this particular evening, I felt more frightened than ever.

Looking back, the nurse was probably the same age as me and not yet hardened to coping with unpleasantness. Clearly unaware of the damage such indulgence could do, she relented quickly: "Alright. But just one more minute," she chastised me kindly. "I'll be back," she said, smiling as she left, but there was no mistaking the pity in her expression. We would always be perceived that way, I mourned, glancing down at him. Yet, there was nothing I could do to change how the world would judge us now.

I watched the nurse close the door on the harsh sounds of tears and anguish that rang through the corridors of that forbidding place; grateful for the privacy she had afforded us. It was late June, almost exactly a year since Kit had returned to La Doucette, and I found myself thinking of summer and how its promise lay somewhere beyond the dirty windows of the hospital, as if that idyll of our childhood was the only sunlit place in the world. Oh, to go back, I thought, to take him with me and retreat under the awning of sunny days, to belong to a society that coddled everyone in the comforting entitlement of wealth, to be pretty and welcome everywhere; a perfect girl and a perfect boy sitting on the verandah in the late afternoon, so lucky to be there. How had we ever thought we could leave? In retrospect, the decision seemed dangerously naïve. But watching his eyes, fixed on my face for survival, I knew I couldn't let him think I had sacrificed anything for him. I had done everything to myself. And he had already paid a terrible price for my mistakes.

"You never need to worry. I would do anything for you," I said. "To be here with you makes me happier than I could have ever imagined. I thought that nothing good would happen to me again, but then I found you. I know this is a miracle, even though the life we'll share won't be the same as before. That life is gone now, but I can't miss what could never include you. Please forgive me for everything I did wrong. I had no idea what I was doing at my party. I couldn't have predicted what would happen next..."

Out of nowhere, a carriage door slammed and I worried it would upset him, as other loud noises had. Yet, it was as if my voice had calmed him. He seemed engaged as I leaned over him, no more words passing between us, just the simple understanding of belonging. And I suddenly understood this to be instinct, a primal call to the soul: "I know that nothing makes sense," I said, "but I am the fixed point of your life. Wherever you go, always come back to me. I will be here waiting for you."

Why did I think of leaving when we had only just found each other? I suppose it is because I've always understood happiness to be an impermanent state. Perhaps, because I am a hostess: treasured guests sometimes find other parties they like better, despite how much you miss them. Yet, it is these last few seconds that I remember best, before he was taken from me, when I acknowledged that the responsibility for his wellbeing was the answer to who I wanted to be. I would never need to cast around for meaning, in my life; it had been given to me in his helpless form. And in his eyes that stayed locked onto mine, I found I had been forgiven and always would be, regardless of how inadequate a person I was, how undeserving of the privilege to call him mine.

I pulled the lace shawl – one of the few things from La Doucette that I had brought with me – tighter around his meager shoulders. I reached for his hand, humbled anew in the face of the future before us.

THE UNINVITED GUEST

Nairobi, 1908

He had never thought to wake to the sound of her voice again. He wanted to say something, but the words would not come. He was not yet fully conscious, adrift in the smothering haze of confusion that had become a constant of his days, but he heard her as clearly as ever. "Dearest Kit, are you better now? Can you forgive me for not saying goodbye?"

His eyes would not focus, but his head was turned toward her voice at his bedside. But I forgave you long ago, he thought. It is you who must forgive me. Forgive me, Serena. I am not the same anymore.

He wanted to touch her. It had been so many months since they had last been together at La Doucette. He tried to reach for her, but he could not move and he fought to chase the panic from his mind. He was not sure how long he had been unconscious, but almost instantly he recalled the split second of horror that had brought him there to that hospital in Nairobi, when he had collapsed in the street from the Dengue Fever he had contracted: It's fine, it's fine, he appeased the nightmare that threatened to overwhelm the loveliness of what he was experiencing, I will not try to move or speak. I won't ever ask to do that again, but please let me stay awake. I only want to be near her. Please don't take her away again.

"I am so, so sorry that you have been unwell," she said. "I have been missing you, all these months. It was my fault that you had to leave..."

But you would blame yourself, wouldn't you, Serena, he thought, sadly. It couldn't possibly have been my fault for leaving you, especially after what you had given me. How had I ever imagined that I could forget you? I thought I could convince myself it was for the best, but it was impossible.

You were always to matter to me in a way that no one else ever could. Do you know, although I cannot tell you, how much comfort I've derived from that since I lost you? Do you know that I was about to come back for you before I fell ill and was brought here...?

"The gardens are so lonely without you, Kit. I still like to walk through them thinking of our summers there...."

He struggled in his bed, as far as he could, but nothing would move, not his arms or legs or head. He tried to quell the sense of smothering frustration at not being able to reach out to her, but her hand on his shoulder quieted him. He wished she could hear what he wanted to tell her, the things he had kept secret, frightened of driving her away by appearing too eager, thinking there would be other days: Do you know I was the shadow of summer at your back, Serena? Or, the lengths I went to, to seek you out, each day? I used to ask the servants and wait for you. I was always waiting for you somewhere and you never, ever suspected how. That was part of the pleasure for me, watching it slowly dawn on you that I couldn't seem to spend a second without you at my side. "Oh, it's you," you'd say, beaming up at me and, do you remember, how quickly I would fall into time with your step, that easy, lilting rhythm of our bond; the two of us imagining brighter times, as the world loomed before us, and everything we would discover in it. When I'm well again, I will tell you this, so that what you think is real is confirmed. Tell yourself that it is as if I am hiding from you, behind a tree on one of your walks, as I used to, but only so that you can find me. I am still here, I can still hear you, but you will need to look to my eyes for the assurance you seek: It's there. It has always been there that you can find what you need to know.

"I have the poem, Kit...the one you read to me...."

"When the Shy Star Goes Forth in Heaven..." Yes, he remembered, he had read that to her.... It was the last thing he recalled about that afternoon in Nairobi, after he had bought his ticket at the port. He had seen Serena across the road and thought of how she loved to watch the stars over La Doucette, the reason why he had chosen that poem. And then, he had collapsed.... It was the book he had carried on their walks throughout the summer, the poems of James Joyce, *Chamber Music*...

When the shy star goes forth in heaven,
All maidenly, disconsolate,
Hear you amid the drowsy even
One who is singing by your gate.
His song is softer than the dew
And he is come to visit you.

Yes, Serena, you know: it's because I thought of you when first I heard it. It's why you're reading it to me, because it meant the same to you, didn't it?

"You will you be able to come home soon," she said. "If I ask my father, I am sure that you can stay with us..."

Can I, Serena? he thought. Can I now? Do you remember, my love? When we were children and one of us would tumble, how your Nanny would say, "Have you been in the wars, my darling...?" Well, I've been in the wars, my darling...

His vision remained blurred as he listened to her talk on and his greatest fear was realized; the excruciating pain, from which he had briefly escaped, overcame him again. He could not help but cry out, although he was ashamed.

"Don't cry," she soothed, "you don't need to say anything, just try to rest."

But I always will, Serena, if I can't speak to you...

"I'll get something for you," she said. "Let me help you."

No, don't go, he protested. There is so much I want to ask you: How did you find me here, so far away? Have you been so clever, far cleverer than I, as usual? What have you been doing while I have been gone, thinking of you? Have you been hosting your parties? Or have you been dancing, Serena? Have you been dancing in the lilacs? I imagine you there whenever I think of you....

But she did not answer. She was gone.

He had been dying before she arrived. He had felt himself lift somewhere, countless times, but the badgering insistence of the doctors had always brought him round. It was the pain, the unimaginable pain, which had made Kit want to give up. But what if I had, he realized. Then I would never have learned how much I mean to her. Yet, he had no idea where she had gone; all he understood is that she must come back.

· · ·

It seems to Kit now, so many years since they last met, that there is rarely the time to say enough, often not enough experience to know what to say. What will matter fifty years down the line, he asks himself, as he walks the road to her door. Is it something as simple as 'I love you,' or something more inconsequential like 'the sky is blue'? Yet, the words mean nothing, the statement is made merely so that the listener can see the speaker's expression and find there the intent that they will not forget. What lingers, what remains? What are the touchstones to those parts of our lives we wish never to forsake?

For Kit, it was her voice that afternoon, as he lay there; a destitute man in a hospital bed, in thrall to her presence; to what he had found in her. For the promise of what he would find again now that she was once more at his side.

THE HOST

He stood up from his seat outside the hospital room when the nurse emerged and pulled the door closed.

"Where is he?" Captain Lyons asked. All in a rush, it came pouring forth, what she had failed to do: "She asked for another minute with him," she protested. "I felt so sorry for her, I couldn't say no…" "But there is no hope," he replied, pulling her away from the door where Serena might hear her. "Your kindness constitutes a harm. Why make this any worse than it has to be?" "Let her have one more minute," she pleaded, "It won't mean anything in the long run."

How little you know, he thought, looking down in disapproval at her hunched figure, intimidated by how tall he appeared, everything can change. Yet, there was no point in arguing. The sacrifice had already been made. Captain Lyons pulled a fob watch from his breast pocket. "Very well then," he replied, dismissively. "One minute. I will keep the time."

Captain Lyons leaned back against the wall resolved on what he must do. He watched the nurse hovering by her station down the hall and pitied her. How he despised such optimistic souls: those who offer false hope when none exists, because they cannot bear to be accountable for the inevitable disappointment when the harsh truth emerges. Those who cower when it all goes wrong and ask not to be hated, "We were only trying to be nice," they maintain, before scurrying off and leaving the ramifications of the fall to someone else. Someone who must confirm the devastating facts: who must take away, perhaps, the one thing someone most wants to keep.

The nurse, however, could not shrink from what was to be expected of her. He would not be swayed on this point. She would be the one to go into the room and separate them. It could not be him. Nor would he give her more than a minute to compose herself. For everything, there is a price. She certainly had had one in consenting to his request.

He could not think of Kit or of what his decision would mean for Serena's future. The two of them were so weak; what had happened – the tragedies of the preceding months – had all been down to weakness. They had run wild, taunting everyone with their lack of regard for society and its strictures. The result had been predictable yet no less devastating: Neither could be saved from the other.

He watched those seconds pass on his watch, counting down to the horrifying reality of what their love had wrought and where it had inevitably led him.

THE HOSTESS

He struggled in his bed, trying to move his head, and I felt the familiar distress of not knowing how to help him. "What can I do to make you smile? Do you know where we are," I asked, trying to distract him: "We're beside the sea; a sea so blue you can see your reflection, where the boats sail in and out. One day, when you're better, you and I will board one of those ships and we will sail far, far away from here, and all of the beautiful sights in the world, you'll see, with me...."

Yet, nothing I said calmed him. He struggled more, as if he was trying to tell me something. I turned away so that he wouldn't see me cry. I had been so upset since going there, despite how selfish it was of me, but I hadn't realized how difficult our situation was going to be.

After I found out, there was no choice but to leave La Doucette. I told no one. Besides, Edward would only have stopped me, considering how much he hated Kit. All he ever did was criticize him, trying to make me admit how wrong Kit had been to mislead me. But I was certain that somebody had played a malicious game to come in-between us: the handbag was proof of this and other things I possibly didn't know about. Perhaps my father was behind it, still punishing me for Catherine. Or else a jealous rival, like Lucinda: Maybe she did want to steal Kit from me, although she furiously denied it. Sometimes, I also suspected Edward, but then he would do something so considerate that I would overlook my suspicions: Yet, he was so somber. I had no real insight into his personality, despite how he constantly shadowed me. My only other alternative was to believe the worst of Kit. These darker thoughts would prey on me whenever I was left alone, that he had not truly loved me, that he wasn't who I imagined him to be. But I could never bring myself to think badly of him. Besides, the choice had been mine.

I had enough money to live off, or so I thought. And there would always be Teddy, helping us, protecting us. The day I left La Doucette, I didn't think I would return, nor did I wish to, for it seemed poisoned in light of what had happened. All I wanted was to find Kit and beg his forgiveness for my mistakes.

Everything I had done was for him and I accepted that it would always be this way between the two of us. I would sacrifice anything for his wellbeing. It was almost as if I no longer mattered, apart from being able to look after us both. I couldn't help but touch him, he was so perfect; the softness of his cheek, the fairness of his hair, all so reminiscent of the Kit I loved. "If only you could speak," I said, "if only I could confide in you and have you understand all of the things that need to be done. Teddy hasn't come...I don't know where he is."

I regretted the words almost as soon as they left my mouth. This was not for him to hear, but I was to leave that place and take him with me: I couldn't stay much longer without Teddy's help. The fear that I intermittently experienced at what would become of us, even in spite of how far I had managed to get away, returned mercilessly as I scrabbled to make sense of what I should do. The responsibility of caring for him was so daunting. Nothing had turned out the way I thought it would. Teddy's absence only exacerbated my fears. "But how could he possibly leave us; especially now that I have you, my darling? Of course, Teddy will come," I reassured him. "Of course he will."

I was so angry with myself for worrying him when he started to cry. Already I was failing him when he needed me most. I had no idea what to say, what he would like to hear. I thought that it should be something about Kit and me, something lovely from the past that could drown out the troubles of the present. I bent down to lay my cheek against his and the instant cool of his soft skin against mine was like a gift I had never thought to receive. And it came to me then, what to tell him; something I had forgotten that we both once loved:

"I know," I said, "I know what you will like. From last summer: the poem about the stars..." He opened his eyes to look at me, and I saw they were still filled with tears, so I spoke faster, "It was our favorite...We loved it so because of all the stars at La Doucette that we would sit and watch at night, imagining the places we would go, and if the stars would be the same there. Listen, let me remember, it... let me think ... *'When the shy star goes forth in heaven/All maidenly, disconsolate/Hear you amid the drowsy even/ One who is singing by your gate/His song is softer than the dew/And he is come to visit you.'* – And oh, you like this, don't you? Please don't cry – *'O bend no more in revery/When he at eventide is calling/Nor muse: Who may this singer be/Whose song about my heart is falling'*– and are you smiling for me now? Are you smiling, my darling? Yes, it will be fine. I am going to stay and look after you – *'Know you by this, the lover's chant/'Tis I that am your visitant.'* – Yes, you know me, don't you? I told them so. And I will always sing for you, like the star in the poem, so that you do. They said it was impossible you would recognize me this soon, but they were wrong. And I will make sure that you are happy, the way that you make me happy just by being here and, later, when we go, you and I, hand in hand, when we go to –"

"It's time now, Mrs. Peel," the nurse announced, on re-entering the room, so loudly that he started crying again. "But you said a minute." I protested. "It's too soon...." "That's what it's been, one minute. It really is time." She seemed different from the cheery, sympathetic girl I had met before. "Please," I implored, trying to keep my voice low and even, "let me quiet him. I can't let him go when he's like this." I clung tighter to him, refusing to let her take him. "Mrs. Peel, there are rules here. I will get into trouble if I let him stay with you any longer. Now, please..." "But he's mine," I persisted, unable to stop the tears, his or mine, "I am his mother...."

She stopped then and drawing in a deep breath, bent over me and held out her arms. "You must, Mrs. Peel" she whispered, "for his sake. Don't think of yourself. It's what's best for him. You do understand that, don't you? I will make sure he's taken care of. Please, give him to me, now..."

It was as if she became my mother for that instant, or what I could remember of my mother before she fell ill. The nurse had the same soft tone of maternal command, when she said, "give him to me now." And so, for the sake of my son, I handed him up to her arms, like an obliging daughter. Almost as if I was giving back something that I should not have taken.

"One more thing," I said, delaying her, "let me..." And I took his tiny hand from under the loosened shawl, and asked if I may kiss it.

I should have sensed something was terribly wrong when I saw how upset she became: It wasn't too late to change everything then. But instead, I simply chose to trust her, to trust in her kind face and outstretched arms. "Of course," she said, "you are his mother." I bent my head down to kiss his tiny hand and, looking back up at her, acknowledged with the fierce devotion and pride that I never owned before and never have again, "Yes. I am."

She took my son away for the night to his crib and I watched them leave: my baby, who I named Christopher Peel after his father. I looked down at my hand and realized that I held a tiny piece of lace from his shawl that must have torn when he was lifted from my arms: "No," I tutted, clutching it to me as I lay down on the pillow, turning my face to the window. I thought of his father, Kit, lost somewhere in that vast world beyond it. In the seconds before I fell sleep, I played through every memory we had shared in my mind. I spoke to him, like always, as if he was walking once more at my side. I asked, as ever, for his forgiveness. I asked, as ever, for him to come back to me. And, like always, to every single question I put to him, he said, *"Yes."*

...

I am his mother.

I have only ever had the privilege to say that sentence once, the day I claimed my perfect baby's soul. For that one moment, it was true: I was never to have more children. The doctor told me that I would die if I tried. I was too slight, too fragile – ruined, really, as my husband has so often spat in my face. So, this memory is all I own of my son, apart from the key to my hospital room, which I tied with the torn piece of lace from his shawl. If it were not this token, I would have no proof he was ever born. As I said, they gave me so little time with him: I slept for most of the three days following his birth. All of that time when I could have held him, but I wonder now whether this wasn't for a reason: You see, I cannot imagine experiencing more pain than I did when I discovered my son was gone the next morning.

When Edward, having made it his mission to find us, arrived unexpectedly in my room, and told me he had given him up for adoption.

They etherized me, of course, to make it easier for them. Yet, they needn't have worried about my sanity, I have never grasped anything more clearly in my life. I vividly recall waking to find Edward standing at my bedside: "He is gone," he said. And somehow I knew, without being told, what he meant. Only then did I finally understand what I had witnessed in the eyes of The Emperor, that instant when Edward locked him in his rifle's crosshairs. No, there was no point in running, I conceded, as I gazed up at Edward: The sniper had a clear shot.

But I am not an Emperor. I am merely a woman who once loved someone so much nothing else mattered. And I bore his child in the most unorthodox and shameful way; breaking every rule of the society I lived in. I eluded the sniper for as long as I could, but it was easy to hunt me. There was no one on my side, beyond my conviction that I could survive. "You see, it has to be," Edward said, when I begged him to tell me where they had taken my son, "and I know you don't understand and I can't help that." And I realized then that he was the one who had betrayed Kit and me, and that he was quite mad, and that I would never get past him to the door, to run out of that building to find Christopher. It had to be, you see, and that was that. Besides, there really is nothing to say when someone takes the control from your existence and locks you into their idea of who you should be. You simply have to accept defeat.

Why didn't I insist upon my baby staying with me for the night? If I had, he might still be with me. Yet, I experienced the same fear with the nurse that prevented me from confronting Kit at my debut. All I had to do was ask a question; do you love me? But I couldn't, in case Kit didn't give me the answer I wanted to hear. So because of my cowardice, I ruined my life. And this same cowardice cost us both our son. In the hospital, I was terrified of being considered difficult, of being disliked. I was such a pleasing person then. There was also the danger of being exposed as unmarried, so I thought I was protecting our baby by doing as I was told. But I was really placing him in harm's way, because Teddy hadn't come. Teddy who had not found Kit, as he promised me he would; Teddy who was tricked into telling my future husband where we were, on returning to Remsenburg to collect some belongings: Teddy who foolishly thought Edward's offer of help was in our best interest. Teddy.

Teddy and I pretended to be husband and wife, although we took Kit's surname to protect our identities. He helped me to get away from La Doucette, housing me in a summer cottage in Port Jefferson until the birth. I was only to stay there, until Teddy found Kit and brought him to me. Because I was certain Kit would marry me, as soon as I showed him our son. But nobody came to rescue us in Port Jefferson, unless you count Edward. And I cannot bring myself to accept, even now, that what he offered was salvation.

For my own sake, I have tried to elicit some humanity from what he did. I have found none. Why allow me to keep my son for three days, why not pretend he was never born? After all, that is what I was expected to do on returning to La Doucette as Edward's wife. My husband has refused to engage me in this dogged pursuit of mine, as firmly as he has avoided any of my questions about what happened to Kit. "It was a choice he made, Serena," is all he has ever said. "I did not make him do anything."

You're wondering why I didn't kill myself. It would seem inevitable for someone with my history, especially after so unfathomable a loss. For the answer, we must look to my husband when he offered me a glimmer of hope, where there was none, on the day he proposed. He talked at length about the choices we make and how he could redeem me in the eyes of society, offer me a better life than I would have had with an inconstant young man, like Kit. He could take me on honeymoon for a year to Europe, to France, to corroborate the lie he told everybody after I ran away to Port Jefferson to have the baby. In this way, any scandal would be averted. He talked about how I could have parties and be young and carefree when we finally returned to La Doucette and how he would make sure nothing ever harmed me again.

I scratched every inch of his skin I could reach, but I barely made a mark. Except for his eyes – there was no mistaking the damage, the torment, I inflicted there. "I'll never have another party. I will never marry you," I screamed. "If I cannot have my son or Kit, I'll kill myself." He didn't react to my flailing. He merely used his great strength to pin my arms by my sides, and nodded, as if I had said something he expected to hear. "Then how will he know how to find you?" he asked quietly. And, with that, he left.

So simple a question, so dangerously hopeful an idea... Yet, this is how Edward ensured that I would return to La Doucette as his wife, as his hostess: the party was the only possible way that Kit or my son could ever find me and how I might find out what happened to them. Edward knew that I would never be able to resist this dream, that it would sustain me, and prevent me from ever leaving. So, in this way, he got to keep me, but I was not the same girl he remembered or longed for me to be. I would never be the same again.

THE UNINVITED GUEST

Nairobi, 1908

"Nurse, why is this patient not ready for the night? We must turn him. Why have you not come for me?" a ringing, commanding voice sounded in the darkness. "Move aside: Mr. Peel...Mr. Peel... Can you hear me? Can you let me know that you understand me?" He felt a rough tug on his arm. No, he thought, please no. Then, he felt a presence beside him, but it wasn't her presence anymore. Where are you, Serena? he asked. Take me with you...

"No, please call him Kit," requested the lighter voice, what sounded like Serena's voice. No, I didn't imagine her, he reassured himself, allowing the relief to wash over him; I'm not mistaken. I'm just not well... You are here, Serena, you did come. Speak to me again. And then she did, but the timbre sounded somehow different; it was not the same as Serena's voice ... "She calls him Kit in the letter."

"Letter? How could he have received a letter? We don't even know who he is," the other woman responded. But that world in which Kit thought he had found Serena was growing hazier, evolving away from him, until he could barely glimpse it. Then chairs were scraped back and movement punctuated the blissful state into which he had fallen and he was awake once more, without her.

"I found it in his bag. It was hidden in a pocket. It's from years ago. He seemed to have gone away somewhere. There's no envelope so it doesn't give his full name, but hers was Serena and there's an address. It's from America. I'm sorry, Sister. I should have come to you immediately with it, but it was the only thing that seemed to calm him down. I was reading it to him. I wanted to give him some peace."

"Fine. We'll see what we can do about finding her," the Sister relented and there was more movement and then he heard her ringing voice announce, "Mr. Peel, we have to give you another injection now and we're going to turn you. We'll turn you to the window, so that you can see the day outside, but you must be brave. We will do it on three...one...two –"

"Don't: Leave him as he is," interrupted the younger nurse. "There's no need to cause him any more pain, is there? He's so young. Can't we let him sleep? He isn't going to –"

He heard the girl make a small scream as the Sister turned furiously and gripped the girl's arm to silence her. Perhaps, the Sister thought that she was sparing him from overhearing the likely outcome of his illness, but Kit had already guessed. Yet, he didn't feel any panic or despair – that would come later. Rather, it settled on him then, the sobering awareness that comes with maturity, of what his future would hold, now that his dreams had died.

"Nurse Carter, put the letter away and...are you crying? Stop it now. Your tears are of no use to him whatsoever; they will only cause the poor man more suffering if you cannot concentrate. Now, are you ready? Wipe your nose. Now, one...two..."

Pain, pain...Yes there was so much pain, but it was no longer in his limbs or muscles or bones. It was clean and crystalline, a benevolent agony that pulled the vital air from his soul, something over which he could never triumph. In the clarity conferred by his suffering, Kit understood that he had been hallucinating again. He had imagined Serena at his bedside, as he so often did, but she had not been there. He had mistaken the nurse for Serena. Nothing of what had just happened was real, a fact far more unbearable than his discomfort. Serena had not come to him, had not spoken to him, had not appeared in the street in Nairobi before he collapsed. It had all been a beautiful illusion.

Yet, Serena was with me somehow, he knew, as those we truly love are when we are removed from them; they are the shadows at our sides; the melody we hear, in the lyric of our lives, even though others are singing the words in their stead. He had found her, in that moment, amidst the alien surroundings of his new existence, as if he was walking with her again under a briar of roses, or over the verdant grass beneath the elms at La Doucette;

ambling along together, intent on her, picking up dribs and drabs of insight into her terrified and wounded heart – so nervous of seeming lesser, of disappointing – that only he was able to understand. He felt his cheek hit the cool of the pillow as they rolled him over, like the softness of her face against his in that pink dawn of La Doucette, the last morning he was ever to spend with her. And, with that, as if it was the affirmation for which he had been waiting, Kit closed his eyes against the world beyond; to the endless winding roads and mountains and seas that had meant nothing to him in her absence, and returned to the place where he always found her: illumined amidst the stars singing forever on of everything he loved in her; as the light of all his memories, the dancer of his heart.

THE HOST

Captain Lyons shot The Emperor because The Emperor was dying. One of his legs had been cut badly and had subsequently become infected. Had Captain Lyons not put him out of his misery, he would have been crippled in short order. I have never been forgiven, he concedes, staring down at the fob watch in his hand, but this perception is, perhaps, too, my fault. I didn't tell anyone why. I simply allowed them to believe what they wanted. Life is so much easier, after all, if conducted in this fashion: Never solicit the opinions of others; they will only try to make you live the life they do not have the courage, or else the slightest inclination, to lead themselves.

The alternative was simply to let them debate his course and he knew precisely what he would have heard; "Can't you summon a vet?" "Are you absolutely certain he will be lame?" "Whose opinion are you basing this decision on because you should really speak to my man: Let me write to him and get back to you…" On and on it would have gone – everyone convinced of how right they were and how wrong he was. Yet, nothing could cancel out what had to happen. He could have waited, but the outcome would always have been the same. He had to shoot and kill The Emperor: for The Emperor's sake, not for theirs.

He has spent countless hours in somber contemplation of the choices he has made for Serena, repenting where he journeyed for her sake. There was no need for him to question what would have become of her – financed with her father's money or not – had she attempted to raise the child by herself. He understood too well the fates of such women. She was not far enough away: It was inevitable that someone would have uncovered the truth, especially with a talkative friend like Teddy, who divulged the sorry story so quickly. Yet, he

SAMANTHA BRUCE-BENJAMIN

is certain she might have loved him, had he not been forced to do what was necessary to protect her reputation and that of her child.

But not once, have I asked for her pity, he consoles himself. Even had she chosen to love me, she would soon have found that I am not a good man, nor a particularly kind one. All I can say in my defense is that I am always aware of what must be done for someone else's wellbeing, even when they do not. Yet, finally, and crucially, I did love her. Serena was the answer to the question we are born asking: Who? Who is it that will prove the enduring love of a lifetime? Even in spite of how different a man I have become, through loving her, I have never been able to see past her. I cannot even imagine it possible.

Captain Lyons has never given Serena the letter or the other personal belongings; those Kit had in his possession in the hospital in Nairobi, where Captain Lyons was summoned. A young nurse had found a letter Serena had written to him as a child, after he was sent away to boarding school, bearing the address of La Doucette, and had written looking for any members of his family who might help him. It was some seven months after the first party, by which time, Serena had disappeared: *Be with him, Serena*, Captain Lyons prayed on receiving the nurse's letter, quite in spite of himself, but it didn't seem likely. So it fell to him to follow the line back.

They told him that Kit had suffered from Dengue Fever and had hallucinated for weeks. In crippling pain, unable to move or to speak, he had been severely agitated to the point where nothing could appease him. Captain Lyons could see the young nurse was clearly more than a little taken with Kit. She had spent the greater part of her time at his bedside; moreover, her questions were slanted toward eliciting the type of information all infatuated young girls invariably aspire to learn: "Was there someone at home?" she asked, patently hoping there was not.

"She's not at home anymore." he replied, "but I suspect she's with him now, wherever he is. You have no idea where they took him?" The nurse clearly didn't understand what he meant, but it was of no real importance. "I don't," she replied too quickly, doing a poor job of checking her disappointment, "the Navy took charge. I came back off duty and he was gone. We understand that they took him to England, but he had no papers. We didn't know who he was..." she explained apologetically.

"But you can find out the ship for me?" he asked.

"Yes, we have that information."

Captain Lyons had taken a tintype of Kit to Nairobi, which upset the nurse greatly when he showed it to her. "No, he doesn't look like that anymore. I wouldn't have thought he was the same person." But you loved him anyway, he thought, at the same time as he recognized that Serena would have known Kit in a ward of 10,000 men; whether he be a wraith in his bed, whether his fair curls be darker or shorn, his eyes open or shut. The way in which, Captain Lyons understood, she would never know him because he did not live in her soul as Kit did.

He went to London, expecting to meet with the same lack of success, but there, the search ended. And not even Captain Lyons, so angered by Kit's mistreatment of Serena, could fail to feel for the tragic condition in which he found him. To his credit, he stayed true to his word, he brought Kit home: It was the only thing Kit asked for, after all. Yet, he felt it impossible to tell Serena where he was: It would surely have killed her to learn what had happened to him and, if not that, then the despair would have ruined her as it had Kit, especially after the decision Captain Lyons had to make regarding their child. So he placed him somewhere where he would be free from harm, but where she could never find him. Had the reality been different, he has reasoned, he would have let Kit keep her, and, without question, their child, but there were no choices left to him, by the time he arrived in London. All he is certain of, however, is that these decisions constituted his last moments as a decent man, before he gave in to the gnawing, relentless guilt that would plague him, at the lengths to which he had gone to protect Serena; which led to her becoming his wife, only by default.

He thinks it impossible for anyone to fathom what he experienced when he gazed into the crib at their son, accepting of what he must do. The boy was Kit's image and he recognized how Serena must have adored him on first holding him, thinking that, in some way, she had found Kit again, even in spite of her terrible fear at what they faced. Were there any other way, he has told himself, he would have taken it. But there was not. And, like Serena, he has suffered; wondering if that child is well, if the family who adopted him were kind, for the world, he knows, is full of terrible people. As he has so often acknowledged, I am one of them.

He has lived alongside her, granting her hatred free reign. He has despised himself accordingly, too, tormented by the memory of their son's perfect face, his trusting expression, as he allowed Captain Lyons to lift him from his crib, without rancor. As punishment, he has granted these questioning voices free reign in his mind as they try desperately to save what couldn't be, never more so than when he watches his wife dance to the song that plays now. Cheek to cheek she has swayed with a young man, selected according to the age her son would have been, searching for what Captain Lyons stole from her: one of the two reasons for the parties. Amidst all the people, her son might be one of them; she might hold him close once more.

How did you ever survive? Captain Lyons has often privately asked, watching her dance from a corner of the room. Might Captain Lyons have watched her dance with her son and turn to Kit, her rightful husband, at its end, contented in a way she has never been with him, had he offered to help when Kit most needed him? He has always liked this idea, despite his lack of function in their lives. I should only have been a shadow, he thinks, letting go of his grip on the handrail, knowing he can no longer avoid what he must confront inside the house. It should have been me who liked to think on her dancing from a distance, dancing for Kit. It should have been me who, although the music stops, hears it play on, longing for a woman who would always belong to someone else. But then, I suppose, that this did happen; I have only ever been a shadow, albeit one of foreboding, cast over her heart.

Life is only ever truly about the letting go of things, is it not? he reasons, wrapping his fist around the watch he still holds in his hand. This is the conclusion he has come to over his years with Serena. All must be let go off, he thinks, the sentiments, emotions and ideals we cling to when we are younger, before we learn otherwise. Just as I let fall from my grasp my own expectations; that I could make Serena forget, that she might ever love me.

And now, as ever, as he turns to the house, to where Serena waits for him in her room, he must confront again that far more unpalatable truth: the question that has plagued him over the years of their marriage, when he asks if all he did was lie to keep Serena, so that she could belong only to him. As if there was still the possibility of a moment before what he had done, when she might have been able to find something in him worthy of love.

Before Serena, he had never experienced a broken heart. Before Serena, he had never loved. But the day he returned home to find her standing beneath The Emperor in the marble hallway, his own was done for. Two souls, more beautiful than any other, who he had tried to save from pain, that were instead suspended in an agony so intense, nothing would ever appease it. He made no attempt to speak. He merely went to his study and wept: For all he could never give her, for all he would never receive.

THE HOSTESS

When I returned to La Doucette from Port Jefferson, the first thing I saw clearly was this view from my bedroom window. Everything before that was a haze; nothing was real to me anymore. "Forgive me, Serena," Edward said as he left me here, "but I must lock the door so you don't run away again." We were only to stay for a night before leaving for Europe, where we would be safe from the gossips, but I didn't object. Even so early in our marriage, I sensed that I would never be free of him. However far we might travel, he would always find the means to lock me away.

"Are you to share this room with me?" I asked. I still had no idea what he expected from me, or our marriage. "Not if you don't want me to. I am giving you the choice, Serena," he replied, moving out to the hall and closing the door, before turning the key in the lock. I almost laughed, but I stopped myself, in case he heard me and came back. I was terrified of him then. Outwardly he was still the same man, capable of random kindnesses, I had known growing up. But the deeper insights I had been granted now were too horrifying to contemplate: his shifting moods, his insidious quiet as he watched me, his softly spoken voice that would suddenly segue into shouting whenever I failed to understand him.

My choice was always to sleep alone, despite how difficult it has proved. I have slept alone from that day to this, save for the key tied with the torn piece of lace that I clutch each night beneath my pillow. It is little more than a token, insignificant to anyone else, but this key signifies everything to me: my son and the freedom I once owned.

I tell myself that he is sleeping. It is the only way to cope with his loss, if I tell myself that he sleeps, my son. He is off somewhere, you see, my happy boy. He is slumbering underneath the sweet peas or curled up in a down bed made for princes, a smile on his perfect face as he breathes the untainted air of the dream world I envisage for him; a world where I am always at his side. And, in this way, all he ever sees is kindness, and not the depravity that exists beyond the margins of my heart and its unconditional love for his flawless soul.

If I tell myself this, I can find that place in me that is somewhere higher than the depths where memory resides. I can almost rise above the agony of the truth and live somewhere exalted, up where the shy stars of heaven exist: the stars that I am equal to now as I stand here at my window. It is the one place where I might see them both again before they see me. Year after year, I have imagined Kit and my son walking toward me, arm in arm, up the road that leads to the sea: my visitants, come to visit me.

It should end here, the vigil. It is simple logic. All of the guests have arrived and the two I wish for are not amongst them. It is not likely that they will come.... And yet... my foot stirs to move; an impulse takes me to turn away, to spare myself the disappointment of waiting and not finding them for another party, but I will never observe this ritual again. And I have never afforded myself this comfort because there is always the chance that something will change when I am not looking; just as my son was taken from me in the night, just as Kit boarded a train, while I slept. If I leave now anything might happen.

So I wait patiently for these stars of mine to return, engaging in thoughts of what I will do if I see these two distant figures, coming closer into view: I will fly down the steps of the marble hall to meet them, and we will be there, us three in the courtyard, reunited. I know he may not know me, my son, but I will kiss his hand. And even if he has forgotten me, with this solitary gesture, I have convinced myself that he will remember.

My son will remember: I am his mother.

III

FESTIVITIES

THE HOSTESS

I am always grateful for a day of simple pleasures. A day that is a blissful lull of routine and ritual, where nothing remarkable happens and satisfaction is found in small triumphs: a dinner planned perfectly, china set so, monogrammed napkins placed neatly in a row. It is the type of day that offers no fresh burden to carry through the hours, where all that is required of me are the duties I know by heart: my charming cry of welcome as the front door opens to guests and we walk the well-choreographed path to the room chosen for that evening's best, an attentive smile as they settle into plumped cushions to tell me all about their journeys, a warm goodbye as the door shuts fast behind them. Yet, at this simple day's end, what I am most grateful for is to have made it through another one unscathed. And, in my submission, to have spared any bystanders the truth of what I conceal with such artistry: the secrets that would ruin me were they ever to be revealed.

Everything is about control. Everything is about making it through one minute to get to the next. This is the lesson I've learned over the years of these parties. If you must live on as part of a bribe to please a man who stole everything from you, how possible is it to maintain the illusion upon which it all hinges? How to act, to avoid being cast out to roam the streets in search of a different salvation, with no hope of ever being where those you love can find you. If your only freedom is the hosting of a party on a Friday for the eighteen weeks of summer, then how to get through the days without falling into despair. The despair over the parties already hosted that brought no word of those you loved most. And the fear about those to come that may bring the news you dread to hear, that you know will kill you.

To survive, one minute at a time, the trick is to move. You must move and not stop. Find something to do and let it occupy you. When that is done, be moving somewhere else, meeting with someone, arranging, organizing, writing mental letters of thanks – each one more courteous than the last so that those who dislike me can say, "Ugh, I cannot stand the woman, but she is so polite. I'll give her that...." This is more important than you think because negativity always breeds curiosity. Guests often come to my parties only because they've heard the worst of me and want to see if it's true. And my entire existence has depended on the fact of their attendance, for every party is a treasure hunt and every guest a star by which to navigate.

After Edward brought me back here, my only option – my only escape – was the party, for within it was the answers I sought about Kit and my son. So I had to live on, to find a way to embrace the highs and lows of the game I played with each and every one of my guests; a game my father taught me when I was a little girl, the charming way he elicited information from any stranger;

"What are the five things that make you think of the five best moments of your life?"

This game is how the pieces of the puzzle fell into place over the course of thirty years: these answers that have led me here to you, tonight. After all, you learn so much at partie—

But, wait. There's someone at the door:

Elizabeth.

THE PARTY, THE PARTY!

Every hostess avows that there is always a moment in the midst of the proceedings that determines any event's outcome, the diamond heel upon which the party pivots between success or failure. And at such a midpoint of expectation, The Summer Visitors unwittingly arrive, as a quick glance to the clock looming over them decrees that, in less than three minutes, their hostess will be with them once more.

On the dance-floor, a dandy opportunistically affects perfect jazz hands to the passing photographer from *Tatler*, only to find himself confronted by the knee-weakening figure of Anthony Duverglas, a paralytically drunk former "It" girl of the 1920s, on his arm. "Would you do me the honor? I'm afraid this is a dance I've never learned," Anthony apologizes, passing the girl to him, and hurrying off somewhere – suspiciously – beyond the dancing: "What's got into him?" quibbles The Dandy, extending a steadying arm. "Certainly not good taste," she pouts, having been 'stuck on' Mr. Duverglas ever since they'd first enjoyed a particularly jubilant Black Bottom in 1926. "Tut," both mutter in disappointment, resentfully appraising the other: these two fast friends who had badly fallen out over a romantic entanglement, yet who always seem to find themselves the last two lingering guests at parties, without partners.

"Ha, ha!" The Dandy crows, rumba-ing with devil-may-carelessness. "They don't call you the 'Last Resort' for nothing, but it looks like your erstwhile charms failed you there: Although he must be the only person on the eastern seaboard who hasn't sampled them. Why have the sailor, when the fleet will do, isn't that your motto?" he comments drily, affecting a nifty little high kick – and silently praising himself on it – in his very dapper suit. "Besides, the bloom of youth is hardly fresh upon his cheek. Isn't he a bit *beaucoup plus agé*, even for you? He must be fifty, if he's a day." "Forty-nine," snaps The Last Resort. "He's never going to partner up with you now, anyway," he sneers. "It's far too late for that: I don't know why you do this to yourself." "Aw, dry up!" snivels The Last Resort, smarting with shame at revealing her secret. "At least I still put on the Ritz. Just look at these suckers," she jeers. "Pretending to 'think poor' because of the Depression. All this threadbare gentility and gardening in pearls: All this home and hearth hoo-ha, restraint and recycling. You wanna know who I blame? *New England!* That's why there's no glamour anymore. Besides, all's I wanted was to come to the lousy party: All's I wanted was to be with him. And I'm barred from all the best parties 'cos of you, so shut up and dance with me!" she demands, determined to forget. "Was it Dotty, who said it, or was it Benchley: You might as well live? Screw it then, let's live!" she screams defiantly, twirling wildly. "Oh, what a wit you are. The closest you ever came to the Algonquin Round Table was the cat," The Dandy quips, much to the hilarity of May Cook, listening nearby.

May Cook sits clapping her hands in uneasy rhythm to the music, a sad consequence of the crippling arthritis from which she suffers. "The Leisure Hour is upon us, whatever shall we do?" she trills triumphantly. *"The party, the party…!"* she calls, waving over to The Last Resort and The Dandy. Yet, like everyone else, they pay her no attention: Something to which she has grown accustomed, and by which she is unfazed. "Ah, no matter," May clucks benignly. "The young never like to get too close. Frightened it will rub off on them." And so, with a broad and contented smile, she settles deeper into the chair's comfortable confines, against the imported French silk Serena chose especially for May, to remember of her life only what she chooses; "I shall never forget Serena and the Chinese lanterns. I used to sit beside my son, Patrick, you know. At those parties she held on the village green in Westhampton. Blue Spode of the willow pattern," she says, affectionately, "and Kit, poor boy, how he loved to watch her. Now," she avows proudly, looking over to the door *"that* was love. I wonder when he'll arrive."

All around now, the party cresting at its unwitting height, The Summer Visitors begin to make choices that will determine futures: The Little Maid disappears into Mrs. Lyon's bedroom, a priceless artifact in her fist; two blue-eyed boys, barely fourteen, accept a $100 promise from a tycoon, to go and retrieve his dog from his mansion on Dune Road; Captain Edward Lyons, soaked to his skin, re-enters the ballroom, and hurries over to his study as if there is something in there he must retrieve; alone in a corner with the Governor, Venetia Dryden catches sight of her husband surreptitiously tracing a shape on the open hand of a young blonde, hanging in limp invitation at her side, and regrets all over again the chance she did not take; at the bar, Rupert Turner-Hume loses his pert little thing for company after a dangerously suggestive comment; while in an upstairs attic bedroom, Helen Fitzgerald, surrounded by other people's children, frets about everything she has left unsaid.

Outside, the storm keeps its promise. It takes the trees. On Main Street in East Hampton, the elms, brought over by the Dutch settlers three hundred years ago, are cast back to the sea and, in gardens everywhere, poplars and oaks are abducted by the wind that abruptly changes course from the northeast to the southwest. Yet, perhaps most poignantly, The Lilac Walk, treasured by Serena Lyons, gives up its fight in a cloud of late-blooming petals that fly plaintively to the windows of La Doucette, as if begging to be remembered one final time.

And, in places closer and closer, a barometer breaks as it registers 120 miles per hour on the Vanderbilt yacht, docked in Greenport; the 187 foot tall steeple of the Whaler's Church in Sag Harbor, shaped like a sailor's spyglass, that has stood nobly observing the seas since 1834, lifts straight up off the roof, is thrown clear, and smashes to smithereens on the ground below; The Quantuck Beach Club, where so many young people here tonight race their boats, is washed away, its pavilion disintegrating on a lawn in Quiogue; the windows of The Six Corners School in Westhampton blow in and the children, gathered there for a recital, are sent out into the perilous storm to make their way home alone; the streets surrounding La Doucette – Beach Lane, Stevens Lane, Main Street, and Study Avenue – are held fast in a swirling tide of water, as roofs are ripped off and staircases collapse, first floors submerge underwater, and inhabitants are dragged out into the night, their screams silenced by the shrieking vortex of the wind; water mains fill with seawater; the St. Andrews Church crumbles as the tide begins to rise, higher and higher, until The West Bay Bathing Club on Dune Road is blown to pieces and its connecting West Bay Bridge collapses....

But these are the events happening somewhere far beyond The Summer Visitors, in a world they would not recognize were they to confront it. For all outside has faded to black now, imprisoning them within, what is to be, the last gasp of glory of The Westhampton Leisure Hour and Supper Club: a house that shines so brilliantly, it might almost be mistaken for a star.

Only now does the diamond heel pivot with exactitude, a fateful footfall that decides The Summer Visitors' respective fates, between life or death. And, as if to underscore this point, at The Patio Restaurant on Main Street in Westhampton, not yet an Emergency Headquarters, there sits an innocuous yellow notepad. On it will be written, in less than four hours, the names of the survivors. Illuminated only by candlelight, barely a handful of guests from this party will arrive to pore over it, to fruitlessly search for companions who will never again be found.

But these are the things The Summer Visitors cannot see.

THE HOSTESS

Don't be alarmed by what you just witnessed. Some things never change, as you will learn. Now that my husband has seen to it that I wear the necklace, let it be your guiding star this evening. Follow me into a party of the past, the only one that ever mattered: Let me point you in the direction of the answers you seek. But remember, everything is about perception. Anything of meaning in my life can be found in what you are about to observe.

From behind me, two hands wrap around my wrists like cuffs, pulling my arms back as if I am a figurehead on a ship. "Tell me I haven't offended you, my fine hostess…and you won't breathe a word about our…about our secret, will you?" Rupert Turner-Hume cajoles, his breath surprisingly cool on my shoulder. He hasn't loosened his grip, clearly worried that I will. "Don't worry," I say, turning slightly, before slipping my hands free, trailing my fingertips over his palms as I do. But I am already gone, somewhere removed from him in my mind. I am letting go of what he has confided because all that matters now is that I make it to the next minute. Yet, I can still hear it – what I can't ever hear – the secret that I must drown out – *"Tell me, Rupert, when you think of the five best moments of your life, what triggers the memory; a thing, a perfume, a color, what?"* And he said, *"Eton; the bulls at Benalmadena; sunset over Chateau Fleurs-de-Mer; the scent of Maria Elena the day she brushed past me at the Duomo in Firenze; England."*

Eton.

The trick is to find a fixed point somewhere far beyond everyone, like a star on the horizon, and drift toward it…. I move deeper into the crowd, intent in my every step. The silk of my dress is enervating against my skin; the hairs of my arms are shocked into static. I know Rupert is watching me leave. The trick is to drift. Otherwise you'll drown.

I pause to scan the room, praying to find the prize I seek. But he's not here. I have never seen Kit again, despite how I have searched for him. Yet, somebody knows where he is: somebody in attendance tonight. All you have to do is ask the right question when you arrive at their side....

Douglas Dryden appears in front of me and performs a few lasciviously suggestive steps of the Charleston, to entice me into joining in. I oblige, but only to maneuver him back to Venetia, who is dressed head to toe in black silk and diamonds. She is hiding behind a black ostrich fan, like a template from a magazine. "Serena," she tuts affectionately, gesturing to the images broadcast onto the white marble walls on either side of the ballroom, scenes from the new Charlie Chaplin, "to go to as much as trouble as this!"

"Venetia, what have been the five best moments of your life?" Every time I ask she flushes crimson, "Goodness, Serena! I can't tell you that, can I? It's a secret...." But I've already guessed. It's why she is my friend....

"Your necklace. Isn't it grand!" she demurs shyly, genuinely happy for me. "Wherever did you—" Then Venetia catches my warning glance and stops herself, understanding my reluctance to discuss it. The last time she asked a similar question was a day at the village fair in East Hampton; the day I met the little boy, who placed his hand in mine... But I must not do this, I chide myself; I must not venture round these corners: The day at the fair, the conversation with Rupert, *"Oh, you attended Eton, Rupert?"* I have to forget. I have to forget...

"Venetia, darling," I say, to reassure her that she's caused no offence, "you're as stunning as ever. How I envy you." She lets me know she has grasped my meaning with a slight nod that Douglas doesn't notice. And so I leave her, drifting off, further now, to safety.

At the bar, I see a new face behind the counter. What a handsome face, I think, how his mother must love him: Is he eighteen, nineteen? No, he's too young: too young to be my son – "A near miss with Dastardly Dryden there, dearest Sea. How does poor Venetia stand it," comments Teddy slyly at my side, as I ask the waiter to remove some empty glasses from a table – But might the boy be seventeen, after all? I wonder. "How old are you?" I ask him. "Twenty-two, Ma'am:" Ma'am, not Mother: No, not my son. But might you have seen him? I want to ask. Might you know him? No, don't do this to yourself.

Teddy. I have never asked for his Five Things. I know what they will be....

"I saw you talking to Rupert Turner-Hume before," he says, finishing off his Long Island Express and surreptitiously beckoning to the waiter for another, thinking I won't see. "Say you're not going to fall madly in love and run away and leave me. Is Amelia Davidson with him?" "Yes," I reply absently, taking a sip from a glass of champagne, anything to dull the knowledge I've come by. "She's back from Hollywood. Seems acting didn't work out for her. That's why Rupert's here." "Pity. Great talent," muses Teddy, "A very effective corpse, I thought, that time she played Ophelia." In spite of myself, I laugh, turning to find a humorous plea in Teddy's eyes, as he looks to see whether his joke has worked. His eyes that then melt hopelessly into the love he has for me, which he does such a poor job of concealing in public. One day it will get us into trouble.

He pulls me around a corner, where we can hide: I hold on to Teddy and rest my forehead against his. I am so grateful for him, his friendship; it's how I've managed to get through. I used to kiss you when I was young, I think, before Kit, before my husband. When I was young... "Serena," he soothes under his breath – after all, people might be listening – "come on, my girl. It's all right. I'm here. What did someone do this time, to upset you? And you so beautiful, Serena...." I can see the fine lines around his eyes and I adore them, how he has aged. We share such history, Teddy and I: the War, the end of a way of life, its rebirth, growing older. And yet, the two of us still together: the one constant thing. But I can't tell him what is wrong. Teddy cannot cope with sorrow. He might try, but to ask for his help is to destroy him. So instead I allow him the fantasy that he likes to indulge, when he reminds me that there is a way out, if I choose to take it: "I'll marry you, Serena. Say the word. We could leave here..." I smile warmly and place a kiss on each of his eyes, so that he can't see the 'No' lurking in my own. And I leave him in love with the idea of loving me because it is so much kinder this way.

"He tricked me, Serena. By the time I got to the hospital, the nurse told me you had already gone. I could kill myself for being so damn stupid...".

"Serena, where are you going?" Teddy asks, concerned. "To find the snow," I reply. He smiles nostalgically, relieved. I have made it better for him. Yet, I am gone before he can see the despair creeping up, higher and higher, threatening to overwhelm me. It is all there in front of me now, an ocean of regret: so many guests a trigger to past experiences, which is why I try to blur them into a throng of shapes, of shadows, moving through rooms. Somewhere in the back of my mind a voice confirms again; *He's not here.* No, I concede. Kit is not here.

What would Kit say if he were to learn that I have scoured the faces of the crowd at every party, looking only for his? Has he thought of me at all these past years? Do I live on in him, as he has in me, or did he forget me the instant he heard that I married another? Is this the reason why he hasn't returned? Because surely, if he had loved me, he would have sought out the road that leads back to me by now...

I think of the conviction that has brought me to this point: all you have to do is ask a simple question: *What have been the five best moments of your life...?* I know how to do this in such a way that it seems unrelated to me, so that somehow I can use what people say to turn the conversation around to Kit – to make them tell me not what is true or correct or real, but to fuel the fantasy I need to get through my dismal life. So I have felt a kindly hand placed on mine by a former schoolmate when she assured me, "I know we shouldn't talk about it and Teddy would have been a fine husband, but Kit. He was in a different league..." And I have played over endlessly the insight of a guest, who was at pains to remind me of what I prayed to be true; "Serena, I have never seen any man more in love with a woman than he was with you..." These are the dribs and drabs I feasted on, the fantasies that enabled me to make it to the next minute. But what I failed to learn is how to survive the answer you never want to hear, the one that will kill you....

"Yes, Serena, I did say Eton...Did I ever meet Kit Peel? Well, it is a small world, isn't it? Kit Peel. Yes, of course. How is it that you know him? He visited here after Cambridge? Did he, by Jove. Well, he's a dark horse. He never told me that..."

And with Rupert's words, all that stood between me and the truth was one minute in time.

But I can still escape the truth, because this party is a living, breathing entity and there are so many ways I can lose myself in it. I force myself to listen to the woman blocking my path, "Did I hear you say you live on Gin Lane? Nancy Smith. Heavenly to meet you. We're on First Neck this summer. I believe we have the Fords in common? They mentioned you when we were lunching at The Bath and Tennis…I haven't seen you there?" I exhale in relief, as if I have been swimming underwater too long. This distraction will save me.

"No," chimes the unmistakably patrician tones of Helen Fitzgerald, apologetically. Helen is nervous that she will appear to be playing a game of social one upmanship with what she's about to reveal, which her unobtrusive manner suggests would *horrify* her, "we're not members of Bath and Tennis. Bathing Corp," she concludes in her exquisitely mannered fashion. I can't help but feel sorry for Nancy. The Bathing Corporation is only for the wealthiest and most prominent families in America, but Nancy lights up like a Christmas tree at the possibility: "My, it sounds like just our kind of place…" Yet, she will never succeed in garnering this favor. The world we live in is open to anyone, but the room at the center is barred to those without history, although its magnificence is clearly on display through the glass windows. And sometimes, a door might appear slightly ajar, but it's not. There's always a servant within inches of shutting it to those who don't belong, so that the inhabitants of the glass palace can wave benignly and apologetically from inside, as if excluding others is nothing to do with them at all. "Serena!" Helen cries, sounding so clear a note of desperation that Nancy cannot possibly mistake her meaning. She excuses herself with a dark stare to me, one she'll regret later when she finds out who I am.

"You *are* a gem rescuing me like that" Helen grimaces conspiratorially, once Nancy is safely out of earshot. "But I don't want to sound churlish; she seemed pleasant enough…" she qualifies quickly. "Anyway, on a brighter note, will you be coming to the gala on Tuesday? The Ladies at the Improvement Society are hosting the annual fair and no fair would ever be complete without you...but the boat!" she suddenly exclaims, grabbing my arm, "I can't thank you enough for the little boat for Susannah—"

The boats.

"How thoughtful you are: Far too good for us, though. Well, you know what we're like! Everything upside down. How I ever came to have four boys, I'll never guess. I have no idea how their nannies cope.... But now a girl – Susannah! Serena, you have no idea how I long – But don't you look dazzling," she hastily corrects herself, as if checking herself from... What? Why couldn't she finish the sentence...? "I wanted to tell you," Helen continues, more subdued now, as if thinking better of changing the subject. "I thought the boat was just precious and what you wrote in the card, 'For the journeys she will take...' I, it was...I can't describe..." The gift for her baby: a handcrafted toy boat, my signature gift to all of the newborns on the East End. Helen is being unusually kind to me, and kindness makes me cry, and I will cry for hours and hours tonight, alone in my room. But it is Helen who is crying. "Serena, forgive me. I'm mortified, but – I'm not sure whether I'm doing the right thing, but I can't keep it from you. There's something I have to tell you.... When I had Susannah..."

But I am not paying attention. I am going somewhere in my mind where it is safe from the truth that destroys everything I hold dear. Yet, all I can think of is the child's hand that touched mine one day at The East Hampton Village Fair, and I find that I cannot escape the memory she has triggered....

East Hampton, 1921... a Saturday, a little boy who suddenly says, "You're a pretty lady. Mommy is sick. Daddy can't race. It's only for Mommies. Will you race for me?" And the shock of babyhood in that plump fist takes me back to the room and the baby – oh, my son.... No, I tell myself, shake it off and move on. Don't think about your son, don't fall to your knees and gasp for air at the pain that doesn't relent, do something: Run the race for the child.

Someone comments, "Heavens, Serena looks like she's seen a ghost". Remove your shoes; I counsel myself, feel the dampness of grass beneath your feet, worry that your stockings will ladder and they are new; a gift from the man who married you, not the husband you chose. But get to the starting line, Serena, so that you don't have to remember. Walk purposefully and focus only on the facts you see – a flag, women in pale colors, a hint of red somewhere peripheral, probably someone's tie. My skirt is too tight for running in and I pull the waist up so that the hem falls at mid-thigh – there's a hurrah from the crowd, this is scandalous. But he chose me, this child, I tell myself, as I look to see where he is...

How they admire my skirt, the other ladies. "Serena, your skirt!" says Venetia. "Are you keeping where you got this one a secret too?" In spite of myself, I let out a sob, and Venetia, worried that something is truly wrong, says, "Come and sit down." "No," I say, shaking my head violently, and she recoils in alarm. "Serena, please," she insists, but then I hear Teddy announce the start of the race; "Ready, Set, Go!" The sound of the gun goes off and I run, making it through the threat of despair because I have something to do.

It is blisteringly hot but there is an enlivening cool breeze as I dash across the grass and I am suddenly content. And I wonder if this is the joy that you feel when you have children and you do something to please them; when thoughts of yourself cease and all that counts is their happiness. Is the little boy cheering for me? I can't hear anything. I am locked in this place where I must move and it means something that I'm not doing it solely to survive. I have a purpose that has nothing to do with me. And it's nearly over and I have to race faster and I do hear people now – "Go on Serena. You're almost there" – and I'm winning and I've not won before, not anything: I always let others win so that I wouldn't be envied, but I don't care about any of that. I want to win for that little boy and I do. I run over the line first and I turn and I cannot catch my breath and my hair is everywhere, curls coming undone from the sharp pins that held the style so rigidly. But where is the boy whose Mommy is sick? Hazy images of people rushing over cloud my view, I hear a few congratulations – "Come and get your prize, Serena," calls Teddy. *It's not for me, the prize,* I want to say, as I search for him, *it's for* – and then, there he is. I see his mother, Helen Fitzgerald, and the shock of the memory she inspires – of how I lost my son – is so acute, the agony so intense, that I sink to my knees. And when they all crowd around me, I have to pretend that I fainted.

Now, in this present moment, Helen's eyes are raw from weeping and I have to leave, or I will fall to my knees again because of what she has confided. But no, I haven't heard a word, nothing to change my destiny. I can go on as before.... I can drift on and on and on and pretend that none of it ever happened. And so, I let the party take me where it will, all of the secrets trailing in my wake, where I never have to confront them. Yet, sooner or later, however hard you try to live only in the softness of the past, you will arrive at the answer that changes everything. Regardless of how often you change course, you will be washed up against the rocks of disappointment, or in the safest harbor of certitude. It is inevitable.

"You wore the necklace." My husband says.

"Yes."

And it is now that it happens. Something passes between us. Anyone might think it is passion.

...

It seems irrelevant, doesn't it, but I have not led you through one party, but all of them. Everything you witnessed is the sum total of what I learned as a hostess: Teddy, Venetia, Helen, Rupert, my husband, each of these five people possessed a secret that would come to define a moment of my life: the five defining moments that are encapsulated by *my* Five Things.

They are akin to the five points on a star, for I was once told that when we die we become stars; those by which the people we leave behind navigate. These stars contain our legacies, the essence of our souls. I must leave you all behind tonight but I have drawn a path for you to follow. From point to point, I etched a pentagram onto the marble floor of the ballroom I just crossed, a five-pointed star only you can see.

So follow now. Follow where it leads.

THE HOST

On his way through the ballroom, Captain Lyons stops dead when he realizes that the door to his study is standing open. And it is almost as if this open portal is demanding he step back into the past. For there, on the desk, he sees it; everything he hid from his wife. Everything she almost found, the only other time in his life when he left the door unlocked.

It was 1925. And there Serena was, sitting at his desk in his study, seemingly waiting for him. He stopped himself from saying her name, as he longed to. He permitted himself instead a moment just to watch her, to enjoy how beautiful she was, without fear of her turning away from him. In the vast expanse of La Doucette, they could spend days without seeing one another, and those days were a torture he could never have fathomed before he married her. Sometimes, his only reward was a glimpse in passing, through a window, around a corner, like a will o' the wisp or a ghost, almost as if he had imagined her.

But Serena was real. Captain Lyons only had to attend a party to confirm that fact. There she would be, the center of their universe, around which her guests drifted and soared, as if in a constellation of their own. But he was the sun to her, to them; an unwelcome intrusion in the nighttime world they occupied: too brilliant a reminder of the realities she would do anything to hide from; the history etched into her face every time she caught sight of her reflection. So she retreated, further and further from him, into her parties. And all of it his fault, he knew, but all of it necessary.

The parties had to continue. They were an orchestrated exercise in salvation; the meager crumbs he could offer of what was left of her life. At any time, because of what he had suggested, she believed that Kit might appear and say the words she hungered for: "*You are free.*" So they came, the guests, to the first party to find out how and why on earth she had married Captain Lyons, the second for something to do, the third and on because it amused them to find a forum where a profusion of information could be gleaned about their neighbors. And Serena learned to manipulate them, because if she failed as a hostess, they would cease to attend. And if they did not, then nor could Kit.

Despite everything, Serena seemed to embrace those early events, appearing to most as light and gay as ever before. Only Captain Lyons was aware of the dexterity, the desperation, involved in her performance. She was nothing more than an ingénue on a stage he had erected for her; a role that lasted only as long as the evening itself, when her secret quest would end in despair, without Kit discovered.

Yet, it was a platform vulnerable to pitfalls he could not have anticipated. So many times Serena veered dangerously close to revealing the truth, or invited enough suspicion to incite gossip so damaging it would certainly have destroyed her reputation, should it be allowed to go unchecked. She was too naïve, he despaired, too obvious in her eagerness to hear Kit spoken of. There were so many near scandals that he had to quash, all brought about because of her game of the five best moments of her guests' lives. For Serena, it provided nothing more than a plausible excuse to mention Kit as one of her own, to ask if anyone remembered him, where he might be. Yet, she didn't realize that there are certain questions, people with skeletons such as she had, can never ask.

And how everyone talked, the shocked mutterings of women with nothing else to do, intent on stripping Serena of whatever made her more exceptional than they, which her desperation readily allowed: "Whatever is she doing asking about Kit when she's married to Edward? She doesn't seem to want to talk about anything else...." "I heard someone say they'd seen her in Mastic that year she was supposedly in France before she married Captain Lyons...*with Kit*! Quite the scandal: hastily covered up." And, then, from those ill-informed beginnings, derived the vilest whisperings: "Oh, but he had to marry her, if you catch my meaning...." To be replaced, when she did not bear the child they expected, with.... "I heard that she was incarcerated.... Not mentally stable, like her mother, but ssshhhhh...she's over there. ...."

He hovered to save her from such malice, despite her unhappiness at his proximity. Yet, with each near-disaster averted, Captain Lyons prayed for some hint of recognition: *Evolve*, he privately begged, *see what it is that you have been spared*. But he received nothing. All Serena understood was that her life was not one she had chosen, despite how he would insist to her, "No, Serena. Everything we do is a choice, whether we consider it to be, or not."

He convinced himself that if she could only be content, he might live with his decision. In the early years of their marriage, each day he woke resolved to please her; an elaborate process that encompassed everything he observed – the slightest flicker of approval she might express over a trinket or a dress, a pair of gloves owned by someone else. He would find similar things for Serena, in the hope that she might once again say, as she did the day he gave her the hat, "I am so happy, Captain Lyons. I am so happy today." So that he could recall, once more, how her elation had touched something in him he had never thought to own; a levity, a tenderness, a notion of what he might become, if only he could share the hours with her.

Yet, all he was to inspire in Serena was the cautious graciousness of someone terrified by everything he represented: in itself, a perpetual reminder of his own fallibility as a man. So like Serena, he too came to hide away, unable to tolerate her presence in the house. The resentment he harbored at not having trusted his instinct and refused Kit his request in the beginning, came to consume him, driving him deeper into a sort of madness, fueled by jealousy and regret: a madness that impelled him to seek Serena out, solely to punish her for everything that she had done wrong.

And yet, might it have been so different, might he have heard the answer that would have changed everything for him, had he simply said, when he found her in his study in 1925; *"Turn the page, my love, turn the page."*

THE HOSTESS

What was I looking for in Edward's study, on that evening when he left the door unlocked and I sneaked inside: the ghost of my father, perhaps? Did I think to find him sitting there watching me play, as he used to when I was still beloved by him? Was I simply seeking somewhere to hide from my husband, in a place he would never think to look? Or did I suspect that Edward kept clues in there, the answers to why everything had gone so wrong for me? Is this the reason why I was drawn in to somewhere I should never have gone?

But no, it was the notion of time that so appealed, encapsulated by the minute glass that sat on Edward's desk. I wanted to watch a minute pass, to falter under the weight of every terrible memory and allow time to devour me, like glass slicing through my skin. This is why I walked to the desk to upturn it: to know that I could survive the agony. The party raged on beyond the doors, but I no longer wanted any part it.

I picked up the minute glass – was it my husband's or my father's? I had not seen it before, but I knew it was linked to sailing. Sailors used to turn them to mark the passing of time, when they suspected it was noon from the position of the sun. So much of it wasted in this marriage, I thought, where the only thing that Edward and I have is time, to drift alongside one another without curiosity, affection or respect.

After seventeen years as his wife, all that I owned was my role as a hostess, an inclination to make do, and a waning conviction that something might change. Yet, there was no sign of Kit anywhere on the horizon, my son had grown – or had he? – to be a seventeen-year-old young man who didn't even know my name, and the loathing I heaped on myself for my failings exacerbated until I grew impervious to emotion. It was as if I had spent it all in the first quarter of my life, with none left for the rest. Only the parties could rouse me from my apathy – for the control I could exert, for the confidence I derived from them. And, above all, for the news that might come from the mouth of a new guest – the singular knowledge I sought: assurance that those I loved were safe somewhere.

When we were first married, I would mark the minutes whenever I was forced to be with Edward – watching the second hand on my watch, fathoming how many steps you could take in a minute, or remembering the first sixty guests at one of my parties. I thought I could hide away in my mind for as long as it took Kit to come back for me. I did anything to drown out Edward's persistent plea, "Please try and make the best of it. I do love you, despite what you might think;" anything to escape his darker moods when he would beg me to believe that he had rescued me, poring over the past and the mistakes I made as proof of his conviction. "Did Kit not choose to leave," he would insist. On and on he would persist, until I told him what he wanted to hear: "Yes, he left me. No, he did not rescue me."

I learned to present an unreadable façade, as if Edward was staring into an empty room whenever he looked at me. I offered no insight or opinion that he could seize upon and change to suit his whim of how I must be. And in this way, I controlled him as far as I could, along with the fact that I was his wife in name only. Yet, I later realized that granting me this freedom was not an act of decency on Edward's part, but one of control: how worthless, how tainted was I, that not even he would touch me. Besides, there was no guarantee he never would: He had the key to my room.

I was allowed no authority in my home, not even as its mistress. Edward explained that he didn't want to trouble me, dismissing my father's employees as soon as we returned from France. "Each of you will now receive your duties from me, not Mrs. Lyons," I overheard him instruct them. "Consider yourselves ghosts in her presence. Which is to say, when Mrs. Lyons exists, you do not. If she is in a room and you enter to perform your duties, please leave immediately. If you are already involved in some occupation and Mrs. Lyons interrupts, you must also leave, as if you were never there. Nothing is to disturb my wife's tranquility. Bring all of your cares and concerns to me." Not even those early parties were my doing. My husband arranged them and

I followed his lead: "Attend," is all he would say. "I expect nothing more of you."

I am not aware exactly when he accepted that it was pointless to try and love me, when his plea, "Please, Serena, please. I have done everything for you…" so emasculated him that he lapsed into the callousness that has defined him. During his cruelest years, he punished me in every conceivable way, deliberately failing to defend me to the staff that complained about any given thing I did, or to his grown-up children who picked fault with me endlessly. Yet, if ever I complained about someone being unkind, his favorite line was, "No, Serena. It's not them. It's you."

How vindictive a person I became in the face of his cruelty, how shamefully I ranted and raved over the most irrelevant things. There were times when all the regrets and mistakes I had made bore down on me, pressuring my lungs until there was no breath left. Those days when I woke and acknowledged my age like a winding punch – twenty-five…thirty…thirty-five, so late, too late? The days when I convinced myself that if Edward would only tell me what had happened to Kit, I could run somewhere else before the time marched too quickly away. I could change everything and start again…. But he never would.

Sometimes Edward railed back at me and I would bask in his lack of self-possession, his manic inability to convince me of how wrong I was to misjudge him. But most of the time he boxed clever, controlling me with his silence. He would display such dignity and calm in the face of my hysteria, prizing my hands from his arms with condescending pity. "If you're so unhappy, Serena, then leave," he'd offer benignly, "You're free to do as you choose. You understand that by now, surely? I've never asked you to do anything," he'd say. "I never asked you to give the baby to the nurse or shut the door on Kit or even marry me. All of it was your choice, Serena. You did it to yourself."

"*I never asked you to.*" These are the most despicable words I've ever heard; they imply a choice, where there was none. This was his insidious brand of rhetoric, to taunt and goad me with the impossible, the idea of freedom. But I had no money. What allowance he did give me, I spent on beautiful things, anything to obscure the ugliness of his prison. I was a spendthrift, albeit one adorned with paste jewelry. No one ever guessed, but those fake necklaces were the nooses Edward placed around my neck: Yet, he held the end of the rope in his hand, ready to yank me back if I strayed too far over the doorstep.

By the time we arrived at that evening, Edward and I shared nothing beyond a mutual desire to escape from the other. This and the lesson he had inadvertently taught me: Everything in life is about control. Everything is about making it to another minute, to survive.

I fell down into the chair and rested my head on the desk. I would not cry; I had cried each tear fifty million times. There were none left by the time I was thirty-five. My tears were replaced by a smothering anxiety that often left me gasping for breath, consumed by worry and fear about what was coming next. This is why I was constantly moving: to avoid minutes like the one I was trapped within. The dreadful memories I fought so hard to keep at bay came crashing down on me, of how foolish I was to trust in such a brief romance and the horror of what can harm helpless babies when their mothers cannot protect them. I couldn't let these thoughts overwhelm me, but I had no energy left; a dangerous lack of will that might lead to places I must not go. So I took what strength I had and reached for the minute glass. I had to focus on it until the sands stopped and my grief abated.

But as I reached, something distracted me. It was a page of a letter on his desk; written in the most beautiful handwriting I had ever seen – meticulously crafted, almost calligraphic. *'The earth belongs to the living...'* I read. And something in me stopped.

Beside the letter was a ledger of some sort, open at a page. Hundreds of similar books, leather bound, lined the walls; alphabetized according to the insignias seared into the spines. I had not entered my husband's study since the day I moved The Emperor. Even so, I would not have bothered looking in them, assuming them to contain maritime details, names of ships, nothing of interest. But as I read, I recognized the ledger as a record of sorts, divided into coordinates: *'Name, Date of Birth, Place of Birth, Height, Color of Eyes, Date of Death.'* The page in front of me referred to a sailor, Robert "Bobby"

Ward; he was fifteen-years-old; five foot-five; dark haired with hazel eyes. According to the notations, he had died, on the 19th September, 1905. Yet, below the general facts of this boy's life, there were five further lines of writing under a heading that read, '*Five Things*':

> *Mother waiting for me every day, when I was a boy, in the alley behind Sunnyside Court when I came home from school.*
> *The football field in Tyne Park.*
> *The color of my sister's hair.*
> *The sparrows on the beach when we docked in Valencia.*
> *When my father hugged me after Stanley died.'*

Five Things. I turned back to the letter and re-read the first line in its entirety,

'*The earth belongs to the living and the stars to the dead.'*

Almost involuntarily I upturned the minute glass.

THE UNINVITED GUEST

He remembers a screen door, opening into the sun. A day beyond that beckoned temptingly, as days so often do. He remembers the sound of her voice as she called to him, when he was twenty-one, *"Don't leave me to go by myself. Come into the sunshine. Tell me what we'll do tomorrow and the day after that and the day after that…"*

Pools of sunlight fell around him in her father's study, but not quite reaching where he sat by the desk. At the back of the room that led outside, the sun washed over the pristine white of her summer dress, as Serena held the screen door open with the tips of her fingers: the fingers that would later be cast in marble, during her honeymoon to another man. He wanted to follow her, but there was something to be done; nothing worth remembering, until later when it mattered: a meeting with Captain Lyons. And so he watched her go, a regretful shadow cast in her wake.

"Please," she said, turning back before letting the door fall shut. And she seemed such a plaintive figure that he almost rose from his seat and rushed to the screen door before it closed; almost placed his foot on the step where the sun shone, to follow her steps wherever they might lead. But there was something to be done. "There will be other days," he told her. "Tomorrow, we will," he promised, as she disappeared from view. Yet, he had no idea if she heard him; the light was so bright through the door that he had to look away.

He turned in his chair to the enormous bay window, which offered a landscape view of the gardens ending in the sea, to see if he could catch sight of her. Where she was going? Down to the beach, or to one of her favorite places in the garden? Kit felt a sudden pang that he would not know where to find her. Yet, he kept his gaze fixed on the window to distract himself from the fact of the room's darkness, where sunlight rarely filtered in, save for the late hours of a summer's afternoon, when a haze would infiltrate, illuminating the particles of dust in the air. "Like stardust!" Serena would cry when they were children. It struck him how much the room had changed; not in furnishing, for it was exactly as he recalled, but in atmosphere. Perhaps, the heat of the day had made it feel oppressive, but it appeared darker than ever. He had forgotten this aspect; recollecting it only as the most luminous of places, Serena's father laughing as he would throw open the door around five in the afternoon, to show Serena the magic inside; the magic in which she believed, without question. As Kit was older, he understood the trickery involved, but even he came to revise what was true to how it translated in her imagination. It was always so beguiling there; how she could make the best of cheerless things.

He regretted not having followed her. It was late morning, the sky a pale blue. Yet, it was dangerous weather – blustery but hot underneath the misleading coolness of the wind – masking the heat that would burn her if she weren't careful. And Serena was, if not carefree, then careless of herself. She was the type of girl who would give up her parasol on the hottest day of the year to offer relief to someone else, despite how her delicate skin should never be exposed to the sun. She would be sorry for it later, only after the damage was done: She'll lose another hat today, he thought, her eighth so far this summer. He smiled; she thought it funny how desperate they were to be free of her.

The brilliance outside blinded him temporarily when Captain Lyons passed in front of him, blocking the light. Kit had not heard him enter. "Captain Lyons," he ventured apologetically, holding out his hand. His eyes adjusted to the dimmer light, and he found Captain Lyons engrossed in a book he held open in his hand, as he moved around to sit on the other side of the desk in Serena's father's chair. It crossed Kit's mind that he was ignoring him, but then "Kit!" he said, as if waking from sleeping, shaking his head in slight bewilderment. Kit found that he was relieved.

"You wished to see me?"

"Yes, yes…" Captain Lyons replied, as if remembering why he had invited him there, "nothing of any importance. I was merely interested in what you might do after the summer," he said, placing the open book on the desk in front of him. Kit was glad he had asked. He had been hoping, in truth, for an opportunity to tell Captain Lyons of his plans. Yet, a loud noise momentarily distracted them and they turned to the window to observe an umbrella blown inside out from the strengthening wind. Her hat… Kit thought, wincing.

"Thank heaven we are inside," Captain Lyons remarked. "You don't enjoy the summer, Captain Lyons?" Kit asked. He had rarely seen Captain Lyons outdoors, save for the early morning when he would take a walk through the gardens, before retreating into his house until suppertime. "I suppose that I've known so many sunlit days that I prefer to rest in shade. An old sea-dog, curling up to hibernate, you might say," Captain Lyons offered paternally, and Kit was pleased not to have offended him. Yet, he made no further comment, and it fell to Kit to punctuate the silence:

"What's this?" he asked, picking up an object from the desk.

"Ah, it's a minute glass. Do you know what it does?" Captain Lyons replied, immediately engaged, searching Kit's face for a response. Kit shook his head, "No." "We sailors used to use them to mark nautical knots, one minute at a time. Sailors would tie a log line, a long piece of rope, and wind it round a spool, with a triangular piece of wood attached to the loose end. At regular intervals along the rope knots were tied," He continued, tapping his finger in the air as if counting them. "The log-line was used in conjunction with a one minute glass, or with a phrase or rhyme which took one minute to recite. That was a sailor's job, to recite something or turn over the minute-glass, when instructed. Evidently, it's ancient, possibly from the time of the Tudors. I imagine it's worth a not inconsiderable amount. Priceless, probably," he continued, reaching over to take it from Kit, catching his eye slightly chastisingly, as if he was a mischievous child who shouldn't have touched it in the first place. He appeared on the verge of saying something, but instead he considered Kit for a moment, balancing the minute glass in his open palm. "Can you think of any rhymes that last a minute? What about that book you're always carrying around? What's in there?" he finally asked.

"Just poems. Joyce," Kit offered. "Actually, there is one; '*When the shy star goes forth in heaven,*' he began to recite. '*All maidenly, disconsolate…*'"

"I rather like that," Captain Lyons replied. "Go on. I'll time you. Recite it back. We'll use the minute glass. We'll see if it lasts a minute."

"No, no," Kit protested, embarrassed. "I can't remember all of it. I would disappoint you, I fear. I wouldn't be a good test study...."

Captain Lyons nodded genially at Kit's response, as if he knew it were a lie, but would make no more of it. "Very well," he replied, but Kit could tell that he was mildly irritated by his reticence and experienced the fear that befalls all visitors, invited in somewhere by the hospitableness of others, that he had outstayed his welcome. And Kit could not leave. It was what he wished to discuss with Captain Lyons.

"What's in your book, Captain Lyons, if you don't mind my asking?" he asked keenly, in an attempt to re-engage him.

"Oh, I'm not sure, you would find it interesting, Kit. It's just something I like to do," he said, reclining back in his chair, and smiling benignly, a hint of disappointment clearly discernible. Kit felt as if he had been asked to betray someone and had refused to offer up the name. And the room was cast suddenly into complete darkness as the sun flitted briefly behind a cloud.

. . .

Kit looks back now, he remembers, and this is where it was decided; all that would happen next. He could have left the room. He could have gone to Serena watching her hat spiral away to some destination of her mind, where it would live brightly on. Had I done so, he thinks. I might have owned more than a life of memory. Yet, how giving we are when young, how keen to be accepted, especially after days spent in boarding schools, their gates locked, no way out. How eagerly we grasp onto what those who live outside those gates offer, with the pitiable gratitude of a visitor who hopes always to be invited back because there are no other places to summer, and because the place that we have found, in the absence of any comparison, seems so much like Paradise.

And yet, sometimes, he remembers, pausing to observe the lights of La Doucette in the distance, we arrive at the homes of those deceptively benevolent Hosts, only to find that we must experience the summer as they prescribe. There is no other alternative, but to give in; all Summer Visitors understand the rules they must follow. And onto us, doors are shut, keys are turned, and we are locked into other rooms. Those that our Hosts wish to keep us in, so that we cannot go outside, so that we cannot live any other existence than the one they decree.

THE HOST

His immediate pleasure of finding Serena, waiting for him in his study, abated on realizing what she was reading: It was an old letter, one he had kept for years, never having sent. How much had she read? He could not tell. Captain Lyons drank in her slight frame, so thin then because she barely ate, always rushing somewhere, or fretting about arrangements for her guests. He admired, as ever, her gold and amber hair, that seemed to catch every particle of the faint evening light that filtered into the dark room and illumined where she sat, like the relief of shore sited from sea; a reminder that home is near, the journey almost over. And he felt for her terribly. She seemed so tiny, sitting there, dwarfed by the grandeur of her surroundings; It's too much for one person to suffer, he thought. *Turn the page, my love. Turn the page.* This is what he wanted to say, but the words would not come.

The log was open beside her on the desk. This is what he referred to by 'Turn the page,' not the letter. The pages of the log had clearly fallen back to an earlier entry, perhaps because of a breeze through the window, perhaps when she had first sat down there. He recognized no marking that would distinguish it as the record he had been studying. He was unsure whether to feel relief or to pity her. What she held in her hands, however, constituted an incomplete letter, missing the title and final pages. Captain Lyons could recite its contents by heart, however, for he had re-read it on so many occasions since he had first written it...

'... when I first became a Captain, we suffered a catastrophic loss in a storm off the Magellanic Strait, north of Tierra del Fuego; one hundred and thirty-two sailors drowned. Later, when I had to inform their families of the tragedy, I found myself unable to offer any real insight into their lost relatives, having learned comparatively little of the men under my command. This event had a profound effect on me; I could

not shed the guilt of how I had failed to memorialize them, despite their selfless service. As a consequence, I have become a dogged commemorator of those with whom I sail. I am, if you will, an unpaid editor of better men.

Now, whenever I welcome a new crew, I interview every shipmate before we set sail. Yet, my intent is not to elicit the mundane details of names, addresses, height and so forth. No, I only desire to be familiar with the best of them, what has defined my men and brought them to me. So, I put to them one simple question: What have been the five best moments of your life, and what inspires those memories; be it a thing or a saying or a place?

You might ask, why Five Things, why not six or twelve? For the reason, we must look to the night sky: Since ancient times, sailors have navigated by the stars, in particular the North Star, which is held to lead the lost at sea to safety. The Five Things that I ask my men to impart correspond to the five points of such a star. For when we give a sailor back to the sea, I do not believe he is kept there. Rather, I believe that he becomes a star by which we navigate, brilliantly encapsulated in the sky above, to lead us to safer shores, however turbulent the waves.

It is my conviction that the earth belongs to the living and the stars to the dead and here we must stay until it is our time to leave. So this is the reason for the log, to honor each sailor's legacy; his moments of joy recaptured, the memories that sustained him: a life in brief but yet, in those Five Things a sailor imparts to me, we find his whole life: one that exists in all its glory, despite how simple, how inexplicable, or irrelevant it might be to those who did not share in it, who might not understand that what these Five Things constitute are the essence of his soul; a star, if you will, left behind to guide forward those who will remember him best.

It is an idealized approach, I know, and not everyone has welcomed the question I pose. Many times, I have experienced difficult interviews with sailors who are irritated and bemused by my request, unwilling to offer any response. These are my saddest men and it is on these occasions that I have found recourse to privately observe them and make my own notations based on what they reveal of themselves. For all men possess souls, even if they refuse to admit their existence, and I consider it my duty to record them. Indeed, I have encountered every type of man; those so happy that they could recite one hundred things and still *more who wish constantly to change what they have confided. In these instances, I have dutifully scored out, re-written and replaced anything of which they have thought better. But then there are those men, like the person you loved, who, when asked, knew immediately what his Five Things were and told me, without hesitation. It is these that I send to you now.*

It is an incalculable gift to be able to return to you, the soul he leaves behind. Please know, that I bear the burden of his loss more keenly than you could possibly imagine. Yet, if you should find something here that you never expected, that, perhaps, even hurts you, I hope you will heed the advice I offer: Take this one day and recount these moments, live them again with him: Envisage those seas he loved, breathe the salt air at his side, make your peace, and then, forget. Forget everything about him: For the earth belongs to the living. We cannot always claim the souls of those we have loved the most...'.

Captain Lyons watched the last grains of sand fall to the base of the minute glass, as his wife reached her conclusions about what he had concealed from her. Momentarily, Serena set the letter aside and reached for the log, leafing through two or three pages. When she unexpectedly looked up at him, her eyes were filled with tears, but not, he discerned, through any discovery that might have broken her; she had not turned to the page he feared she might. Yet, Serena regarded him without enmity, clearly moved, and he dared himself to believe that they may have reached a crossroads; *Evolve, Serena,* he prayed. *Please understand me, what I have tried to do for you....*

"You wrote this letter? These logs?" she asked.

"Yes."

"Because my father used to say: Tell me the five things that make you remember the five best moments of your life...He stole the idea from you, like he stole everything else?" "Yes." Captain Lyons replied, but, in spite of the shadow cast by the mention of her father, he harbored some hope. It was the closest the two of them had come to an honest exchange since before Kit left. "He died; the person you wrote about." Serena assumed, returning to the letter without waiting for his reaction. "And you did this for all of your men who died at sea. You sent them letters like this one, comparing their souls to stars?"

He moved closer to where she sat, "I have, Serena." "It's the most beautiful thing I've ever read. A book of souls…" she said, covering her face with her hands and beginning to weep. Until that day nothing had made her cry, not even the deaths of so many of her friends during the War. Although she had hosted wake upon wake for each of the fallen, Serena had remained impassive at the functions, dutifully going through the motions; her gaze fixed somewhere else, in the middle distance.

"So it is the bereaved families who come here to see you," she said, as if finally understanding one of the mysteries of their marriage: the frequent visitors from all over the world to La Doucette, who Captain Lyons would invite into his study and sit with for as long as they required. "They often want something more than what I send to them," he replied. "And you give them that?" she asked. "I try." He was so close that he could almost touch her, standing at the arm of her chair in which she sat, but her shoulders were hunched and her head bowed so that he could not see her expression. Yet, he was surprised into taking a step back when Serena abruptly placed her hands on the desk and raised herself up. "You give them what they need; you return the soul of their husband, their brother…" she said, turning to face him – *Please, Serena, please*, he thought – "…their son."

He shut his eyes against her final words, "No, open them, Edward. I want you to look at me," she demanded sharply. "You give them the pretty stars, and it's all so touching. It must bring such consolation to return something so precious as someone's soul." "Don't say any more, Serena," he said, recognizing what the edge in her tone would precipitate, "please let us give this up now. You shouldn't have come in here." "Quite," she conceded soberly, wiping her tears away with her elegant fingers, perfunctorily. "After all, what to do with this new information? Seventeen years of keeping our secrets and this, the most amazing discovery: that you are kind. That you are a good man," she laughed, half in incredulity, half in despair. "How can that be, after what you've done, after the false hope you've offered? But maybe you think this," she considered in disgust.

"'*How will he know how to find you?*' That's how you managed to bring me back here and make me stay. It was instinct, I knew I mustn't, that I should try to find him myself, but I trusted you somehow and now it's –"

she took a deep breath as if to steel herself against what she was about to reveal. "It's too late," she enunciated, with such heavy finality that it was as if something in her had died. "He won't ever be mine. And it was all just part of your plan to keep me for yourself, wasn't it? Because you offered me the hope and then set about destroying it. The energy you've spent decrying Kit, of how badly he let me down, so that if he did show up, everything would be tarnished between us, anyway," she continued, pushing her hair back from her face with both hands, the familiar frustration of her sorrows impelling her to crueler and crueler lengths. "But you always knew it was impossible, didn't you? You've always known everything. I despise you," she shouted, starting to weep again. "I hate that you have been right."

He was no longer breathing, suspended somewhere between dread and sorrow, accepting that he must finally confront what he had prayed to avoid, given what she had evidently learned. "I meant nothing. He did, he just used me. You're right. Kit never came back. I'm not worth coming back for. Look at what I did to my poor baby. Do you have any idea what it is like to live with his loss? Sometimes, I can't even breathe," she railed, flailing against the desk and knocking its contents to the floor. "Why didn't I fight you? Why am I so afraid to act?" she cried, pulling at her dress, as if it was constricting her. "I met a friend of his tonight, Rupert Turner-Hume, and he told me that Kit has married. They went to Eton together: the daughter of some aristocrat. She's all of eighteen," she said, despairingly. "As young as I was then..." And she fell to the floor at his feet, her body wracked by convulsive sobs.

What love, he thought. To love so deeply without any proof of its return. How similar a pair we truly are; the same unflinching regard we hold toward those who have failed us completely. And yet, he considered, to be loved to that degree by someone like Serena: How lucky Kit is. It was a curious type of admiration she inspired in him as he knelt down beside her and took her in his arms, which she allowed without resistance: his wife who had been heroic in the face of unimaginable pain. Am I more fortunate than her in that I know where she is, regardless of how little she thinks of me and the impossibility of asking for anything more, he asked himself. Or is it better only to love a memory, as she does? He could not be sure.

"All I ever wanted was a house by the sea and two children, a boy and a girl, and rooms full of books for him. I have so much more instead, but none of it is what I chose, and the worst of it is, I didn't even try to change anything. I just waited and did as I was told. What does that say about me?" she said dully, exhausted now by her grief. "You're quite wrong, Serena," he soothed her, holding her tighter. "Nobody has ever tried harder than you." He had not touched her since he pinned her arms on the night he took her child; an act that made him flinch, as he recalled it.

However could we have imagined that we would end up so disgraced, he thought. Here we are, sharing the most intimate moment of our marriage, but even this, he accepted, resignedly, is overshadowed by deceit. "What was it that you wanted most? What have you dreamt of?" Serena suddenly asked. Captain Lyons leaned forward to look at her; she was a terrible mess, her hair pulled loose, her makeup smeared across her face, like one of the many floozy flappers he had seen drink too much and sing too loudly at her parties. He took his handkerchief and wiped the black stains from her cheeks, and removed the remains of the cupid's bow of red lipstick that he had loathed when first she had appeared sporting it; a fad everyone subsequently copied. He ached to say the answer that pushed insistently against the back of his lips, *You.* He had a haunting notion that she might even kiss him, if he did. It was all he desired; a single kiss, nothing more, only to know her forgiveness. Her face was tilted up to his, exactly as it had been the day of the hat in the pink and black striped box, but he could not bring himself to take anymore from her. And, besides, he knew that she would only regret it bitterly. So instead, he merely gave his wife the answer she expected, to set her on a familiar path, "I do not dream, Serena. I choose to live. It's so much less disappointing that way."

Serena's expression registered an instant of pained humiliation as she realized her mistake in trusting him, before assuming its habitual proud indifference; "That's right. *'The earth belongs to the living,'*" she said soberly, as she pulled away. "That's your big idea, isn't it? Well, I must be dead then, because my dreams are all I have." She righted herself, smoothing her hair and the creases in her dress: He had seen her transform herself before and marveled anew at how readily she accomplished the metamorphosis from hysterical to calm. There she stood, composed, unreadable; ready to meet her audience: Not a soul would ever guess at what had just transpired. In less than a minute, she could be playing the latest word game with any of the celebrated authors who ritually frequented the house: dazzling and witty, fabulously fun; the image she contrived to present to Kit, should he ever walk in again.

"'*The dead are the stars by which we navigate,*'" she said, her hand reaching up to clasp the diamond star-shaped pendant that hung from a chain on her neck. "Is that why you gave me the necklace? Because you believe it to be true, too, that I'm dead inside? Best that you don't follow me though, Edward. I'm not sure that every star leads the lost to safety," she scoffed cynically. Serena had no intention, however, of leaving and Captain Lyons braced himself for more. Sometimes she would trick him into thinking that she had calmed down, only to begin to rant again. "Won't you tell me what you did now," she asked quietly, but there was no mistaking the menace in her voice. "Will you give me that peace of mind? Tell me that you were the one who sent Kit away and that's why I've not seen him again." But Captain Lyons could not answer her.

"Why won't you give me this comfort, Edward? What have you ever wanted with me?" she entreated. "Is there a worse fate I'm to suffer at your hands? Are you jealous, depraved, a sadist? I can't know: I have no insight into you. And I don't care," she continued, shaking her head in frustration. "But, despite how you deny it, I know it was you. And you sent that handbag to Lucinda: He was your houseguest, for goodness sake; only you could have taken it from his room," she reasoned, as if it was the most logical assumption in the world. "But I didn't doubt him with her once," she insisted furiously. "He would only have been kind. You just wanted to ruin his reputation because you were so jealous that everyone adored him. And it's all for nothing, Edward, because I will never stop loving him… The way I will never love you, because you are nothing," she concluded triumphantly: a paltry triumph in the grand scheme of their marital battles. Yet, her barbs had ceased to hurt him. He had heard them a million times before. So he resigned himself to the situation and resolved not to utter a word, his usual defense against the temptation to reveal what she could never stand to hear.

"Have you ever lost anything?" she asked, glancing at him, as she gently picked up the letter from the desk. "Have you any concept of how it feels?" she wheedled, holding up the letter in front of him, before she ripped it methodically in two, letting it fall to the floor. Involuntarily, he cried out. "Agonizing isn't it," she smiled, relishing his pain, "to watch someone destroy something you set such store in. What you do for these men and their families is incomparable, so at odds with your true character, that it's a crime people think well of you. But they always will. Because only I could tell them the truth and I'm bound to silence, aren't I, you've made sure of that...." she remarked, with grudging admiration. "It's turned out quite well for you, hasn't it? I mean, Kit's not a threat anymore, is he? He's married to someone else. I can't run off with him now, can I: But I could leave you, couldn't I?" she announced pointedly. "What's to keep me here?"

"No, Serena," he protested, perturbed by the logic of her argument, "you don't understand." "But my son, Edward," she continued, ignoring his objection. "You're so clever: I can't find my son without you, can I? Not without destroying my reputation. And if I did that, then I wouldn't get to keep him anyway, and I couldn't have him know me like that. So, I continue to need you. You're the only one who knows where he was taken. Only you could bring him back to me. So will you do that for me then?" she asked, her voice catching at the thought of her child. "You see," she said, pausing to regain her composure. "I could beg you. I could claw the earth, rip my skin to shreds, but you would just ignore me, as you always do, accuse me of being unfit. I'm being calm, to show you that I can. And if you are capable of the selflessness you display in this letter – to console people in their grief – won't you console me? Please, Edward," she implored. "I want to hold him in my arms one more time before I die. Please. You don't even need to tell him I'm his mother, if he's a happy boy, but there'll be nothing else for me if I can't dream that dream."

Might my life be worth living, too, he thought, as he regarded the ripped letter, if I could honor that wish. With her son returned, might I hear her tell me, *"I am so happy today"*? He sat on the floor she had soaked with her tears, incredulous at the tragedies that had led up to that evening. What were they, he reasoned, but two actors in a marriage, concealing the truth of who they were from one another: He had thought himself selfless, but he realized then that those who caretake for others seemingly expect nothing but, in fact, demand all: gratitude, compassion, eternal devotion, no shift in mood with which they cannot deal, those who have made the sacrifice to stay and deal with what others have damaged. We should have let the broken-hearted be, he acknowledged, because there's nothing to be gained from watching them think only of the one they lost at the tables we share. It's not that they do not see us: it's that they don't see anyone at all. She's only thirty-five. I'm fifty-five, he privately mourned. Was it simply vanity, a desire to be a hero that led me to protect her? She's right. I've fenced her into an existence she can't escape from but I'm locked in this prison too...

The minute glass had been knocked to the floor beside him, but it had not shattered. He held it up to the door where Serena stood waiting for his reply and viewed her through its distorted prism: the image he found there was ugly, misshapen, Serena hunched over the handle like a scepter, bitter and desperate. What time has done, he thought: This is the true portrait; what no one else ever sees. But people would begin to, he accepted, should he deprive Serena of anything more, and he could not have her thought of as lesser. She must always be The Hostess.

"Yes," he finally consented, lowering the glass. "I will find him." At that moment, Captain Lyons thought he perceived a whisper of an expression he had first discerned that day when she was seventeen, the light in the marble hallway, a gift in her hands. From where he sat, it could have been love. As if to test his theory, he raised the glass back to his eye to look at her again. Yet, even though Serena had not moved, he could no longer see her: She had disappeared. Almost as if she was a ghost and he had imagined her.

THE UNINVITED GUEST

Captain Lyons contemplated Kit, deciding whether he was trustworthy enough in which to confide, and with a brisk nod, as if satisfied by what he discerned, said; "You are our reader, yes? Can you cast your editorial eye over these entries? Tell me what you make of them..." he hazarded, holding out the book to him.

Kit was the reader. He read Housman and Kipling and Conrad, Dickens and Thackeray and Marlow, but he had never before read what he found in that extraordinary, leather-bound book: those pages of alphabetized entries; names, dates, heights; the random insights it contained. Each line captured him; like a fragment from a poem: *'aquamarine; the taffeta dress she wore on New Year's; dandelions; that redbrick Georgian house, I'll never live in; the ribbons in her hair...I told her once, bluebells; The Buxton Arms; Tournesol, the sound of it; First light ...'*

And in those simple sentences, which appeared to make no sense, he heard the voices of Captain Lyons' men, lost during voyages at sea, recounting the best moments of their lives. Kit listened and read simultaneously, fascinated by the story that Captain Lyons elaborated upon; A romantic, he thought. Remarkable, considering how sober he appears; a difficult man, to all intents and purposes...

"For those men who have no tomorrow," Kit said, looking up.

"Yes," Captain Lyons agreed solemnly. Kit was astonished by how heavily the burden of his duty seemed to weigh on him. His hunched posture and grave expression struck Kit then almost as an expression of pain. Amidst the romance of what he had created in those pages, there existed an underlying agony, a haunting.

"It's a book of voices," Kit observed. "Fragmented lyrics of the lives of others. Lives that are unfinished, but yet, anticipate death. Almost like a hymn of departure. You can hear them, through the words, like a chorus, but each is distinct. It is an unrivaled testimony, Captain Lyons, how you captured them. I cannot imagine the solace it must bring, but, if I may ask, why Five Things?"

"The points on a nautical star, Kit. I think those dead sailors become stars that lead those they leave behind to safety. So, it is as if the contents of their soul are contained within that star."

"The dead are the stars by which we navigate," Kit said.

"Yes, that is exactly what I mean," Captain Lyons replied, but something about the way he seized upon what Kit had said, sounded a discordant note, almost of shame. It struck Kit suddenly that those men had confided in Captain Lyons, not him, never imagining their private thoughts would be broadcast. "Do they tell you willingly, your sailors?" he asked. "I should think some people might be very private with their emotions..."

"Yes, some men wouldn't say a word, or couldn't think of five. They would always affect me the most. It was as if they had no soul, a terrible thing. In those instances, I considered it more than a duty to study them and make notations based on what I perceived."

"But, if they had none, or not enough, was that not their choice? Some men might have no soul," Kit suggested. "All men have souls, Kit," Captain Lyons replied decidedly, unnerved by his insinuation. "I must commemorate the dead, Kit. That is my role. I failed in it once and I have never forgiven myself." But they weren't dead yet, Kit thought, when you asked this of them....

Considering Captain Lyons' agitation, Kit said nothing more. He turned his attention back to the book, although he was no longer reading it. You cannot know the contents of another man's soul, if he does not tell you. So, which of these are true? he asked himself. It occurred to him that behind the evocative beauty and profound solace the words within that book inspired, might lurk something darker: the imposition of Captain Lyons' will. His design on the lives of others; those, who were weak, hesitant, who couldn't conjure up Five Things, who were uncertain about what they might be, or else those who refused to bare to him, a stranger, the contents of their most private reaches. From what Kit could gather, those men had no choice but to live according to Captain Lyons' edicts.

How dangerous, Kit thought, to impose his insight onto the soul of another, to offer up as comfort what he thought he understood in them. Has he ever got it wrong? Has he ever ruined someone's life by sending their families a false soul, an edited version of how he thought their story would read best to people he has never met. And yet, how remarkable it is, if it is true, he considered. What more glorious testimony to the love we have for others, than what these men willingly offered him. At best, Kit concluded, Captain Lyons is a poet: at worst, an unreliable narrator. But Kit knew then that he must leave, as there was a hint of foreboding in that room, which began to prey on him. He looked to the screen door, and feared he would not pass through it to join Serena, if he did not excuse himself.

He handed the book back to Captain Lyons, and nodded in gratitude. "I ought to go and see where Se—" he said, making to stand up.

"Tell me yours," Captain Lyons said, reaching for Kit's hand and holding it there. Kit screwed his eyes tightly shut; it was what he had wished to avoid: It was a command; one he would have to obey, if he were to ask for the money necessary to take her away. Kit needed his inheritance to be released to him early, but Serena was ignorant of this. He had made his promises, without the means to support them.

"But I'm too young to think of death," he said. And it sounded almost like a plea.

At his side, he could sense there was light, but it was as if the entire world had dimmed to the one spot where Captain Lyons sat at that desk, pen poised to commit and render absolute, for all time, what he demanded. Kit could have lied, but it occurred to him, for the first time, that he would die: maybe that day. He might collapse of a heart attack as he stepped outside into the sunshine after their meeting, to find Serena; he might slip and tumble into the sea and drown. He might. Then what would she know of him? He had not told her everything. In fact, he had said so little. Frightened, as most young men are, of driving away those they seek to keep forever. He had smiled at her, he had clasped her hand in his, but there was nothing, he thought, that she could ever recall and consider beautiful, were something to happen to him. And it was the idea that she may never learn what he had found in her, that impelled Kit to draw that breath, and deliver a benediction for her heart that might one day grieve him; the Last Rites of a young man who had not yet died.

One, two, three, four…all the lyrics were laid bare, and, finally, *five*, but as he started to utter that singular word, the last point on the star, that said everything about his soul and what it contained, Kit found that he could not: It was too sacred a truth to share – her name, Serena. So, instead, he said something else, not as personal, not as complete, but enough. And he watched as Captain Lyon's pen faltered over the paper, as if he would not write it, as if he might even score it out, once he had. But Captain Lyons did not.

"Ah," Captain Lyons said, having ascertained the information he sought: the information he would use, to do what he felt he must. The book slammed shut, too loudly, for Kit to ignore his misgivings. But it was too late. Kit experienced a momentary impulse to seize the book back, but thought better of it; spun out more lyrics to drown out the sound of doubt, battering insistently against the windows through which he could still see out.

He thought of the screen door, the ribbons on her hat caught in a gust of wind as she stood in the doorframe, the back of her dress billowing in her wake as she moved out to the gardens; her delicate hand clutching her parasol, the hem of her pale chiffon dress as it slipped out over the step, and was gone, the door banging shut: *"Tell me what we'll do tomorrow…Please."* Things sound differently on the other side of the screen door, Kit realized, when you are left behind, when you cannot see that person so beloved. The despair is clearly audible in even the most ordinary remarks: *"Tell me what we'll do tomorrow…"*

And as Kit looked back to the desk, to find Captain Lyons holding up the minute glass to the light, he knew that he should have followed her. Kit had not seen him do so, but Captain Lyons had upturned it while Kit told him his Five Things:

"Not even a minute," Captain Lyons observed.

...

Despite the years of absence, Kit has been with Serena all along, on a shelf in her father's study, before it became Captain Lyon's. Or so Kit has heard through the screen door, where he was exiled, so that he could never follow her again. *"Open the book, Serena,"* Kit has begged, with each passing decade, *"let the stardust out."*

Yet, he asks himself, as he arrives at the top of the driveway that leads to the house, does it still seem that way to her, now that she is older. After doors have been closed? Or does it just seem like dust? That a window must be opened to ventilate the ghosts, to drive them out from where they should not hide? Who am I to her anymore? Am I simply a phantom of her romantic history, or a barely recalled lyric from a pleasant song everyone has forgotten?

He will find out soon enough, but Kit does not move just yet. Instead, he turns back to the night, to the stars above, as if, one last time, expecting to find something there.

And here, a last memory clicks into place, as he turns his face up to its flickering splendor.

Her hat...

But the sound of a car pulling up from behind distracts him from it. And so he turns away.

HELEN FITZGERALD

"Come along then," carols Helen Fitzgerald, standing in the middle of a swarm of children, running wild in an attic bedroom, "marching in a circle now and swinging your arms higher, *'Oh, the Grand Old Duke of York. He had ten'* – No, don't be frightened, it can't hurt us, it's only the stupid thunder. Let's see who can sing the loudest and drown it out – *'thousand men. He marched them up to the top of the hill and he marched them down again. And when they were up, they were up'* – come on Tommy, bang that drum with conviction! *'And when they were down, they were down'* –Don't cry, Isabella, we're safe inside, and let's finish, louder than ever: *'And when they were only halfway up they were neither up nor down.'* Hurrah!! Everyone clap! That was wondrous, truly wondrous," she enthuses breathlessly. "Who cares about a nasty storm? *'Rain, rain, go away come again another day,'* that's what my baby girl, Susannah, says. Now, let's jump up and down on the spot and when I say, 'stop!' you have to freeze like statues. Aaaand, jump! Aaaand stop! Melissa stop trying to make poor Calum twitch. No, stop poking him. It isn't fair. You wouldn't like it if he did it to—Calum! That was very, very naughty. Say sorry at once for pushing Melissa over – oh, yes, you will young man...Those big blue eyes are not going to wash with me. Well, maybe a bit, you gorgeous boy...Oh, how good of you to kiss Melissa to say sorry, that's a sweet lamb. Come and sit with me over here so there's no more trouble," Helen commands, seizing on the excuse to sit down in the nearest seat, Calum in tow. "Now, everyone, what shall we sing next...Anyone...?" she calls over her shoulder. "Why, aren't you clever, Rose – what a pretty dress – let's do Old MacDonald Had a Farm...All together, *'Old MacDonald had a farm, E-I-E-I-O and on that farm he had some geese E-I-E-I-O....'*"

Goodness, I'm exhausted, Helen thinks, slumping down into the thread-bare chair. A perfect day, yesterday. Nothing but bliss. And today a storm! Oh, it's so unfair, she could scream. All of her best-laid plans to occupy the children are in total disarray, and it had been all anyone wanted to talk about downstairs, grumbling on about the black clouds and driving rain preventing them from staying out in the marquee. Why, everyone has been so tediously out of sorts about the appalling weather this summer – this incessant rain! she frets, casting an infuriated eye toward it hammering against the windowpane. And, after that, it wasn't long before snippy asides about the children running around everywhere started: Well, they were supposed to be playing on the beach, but the weather – and now look, she chastises herself, I'm going on about it! So Helen rounded up the terrified little mites – that wind! What a howling! – and brought them up here to the attic rooms where they're out of everyone's way. She has no idea what she'll do after Old MacDonald's finished – "*and on this farm, he had some ducks...*'" she sings to the children, waving her arms like a conductor. "Excellent, sing away...!" – but by then, she prays, the storm will have passed. Or, at least, the thunder: She nearly jumps out of her skin every time it claps. And it won't do, she knows, to let on I'm terrified too, but I am! And, if this rain doesn't stop, there will surely be floods and we'll not get back to Gin Lane tonight, and I must be with Susannah....

It's incredible, Helen marvels, looking out at the black sky, that, not five hours ago, she kissed Susannah goodbye, slumbering beneath the gardenia trees where they used to swing in the hammock when she was a child. She had been so tempted to stay with her, wrapped up in that delicious late afternoon haze of warmth and comfort. Yet, her husband, Walter, made her see that she must come. He thinks it isn't healthy for her to worry as much as she does. And besides, Helen concedes, calming down a little, I would never have forgiven myself if I didn't see Serena before we leave. I suppose it has something to do with it being the last day of summer, so depressing, she considers, glumly. Oh, I know that as soon as I'm back on Fifth Avenue in the crisp weather amidst the hubbub, I'll love it as I always do, but I leave something of myself behind here, every year a bit more, because I hate to say goodbye to this extraordinary place. I linger in spirit on our street, counting the days until I can return.

Summers on Gin Lane, she sighs, contentedly, can there be anything more divine? Oh, Helen is so lucky… she knows she mustn't go on about it – people will hate her – but she has had the pleasure of living on Gin since she was born, but – and she knows this will sound selfish and spoiled, and she is, so there's no real point in protesting too much – it never struck her as paradise. Not until Susannah.

It started the summer her second husband, Walter – her first husband died, poor John… – bought them the Halcyon Lodge, not two doors away from her childhood home. "And it *is* a halcyon place," she has always insisted to anyone who will listen, "but it only became like that when my Susannah was born."

30th May, Memorial Day, 1926, that was when it happened, as it never had before. She found it, the minute they passed Susannah to her, the love – more love than Helen knew what to do with and she knew Susannah would be her favorite, and that she mustn't have one – I have four other children! she admonished herself, at the time – but she didn't care. She still doesn't. Helen wouldn't have it any other way.

Oh, those summers when Susannah was growing up, she smiles, settling back into the chair and her favorite memory. Hand in hand, every morning, they would go on an adventure, sometimes along the beach, at others up past St. Andrew's Dune Church, or Dr. Thomas' higgledy-piggledy house, which used to make Susannah laugh because it was so odd looking. Or they would go to The Meadow Club and, even though Helen knew she mustn't indulge her – Walter would simply have divorced me if he ever found out! – but she would allow Susannah to eat ice cream for breakfast. Only a spoonful or two, but her smile did it for Helen every time. And then she would give her little girl the biggest hug and kiss every inch of her little face and swell with it, from top to toe – happiness! She had never been so happy in her life.

Everyone had warned her against having another child: "You're too old, you're forty-six, you'll kill yourself," that's what they said. Even Dr. Thomas refused to reassure her, as if Helen was inexcusably irresponsible to ever have conceived Susannah. And she did almost die three times during her pregnancy, but Helen wasn't afraid, not for a smidge: She knew her baby would get here in the end. So she said nothing, and waited, knowing that something remarkable was happening, and that she would never forget the intense bliss of that time.

Everything I'd ever wished for was given to me, she remembers, and I knew I didn't deserve it because I'd led a charmed life; Oh, I adored John, I truly did, but I was so lucky to find Walter and we were wild for each other in those years, but then, to be given more! But I believe everybody gets a time, she insists to herself, watching the children, and that was mine. I didn't question it for a minute. No, I would tell anyone who would listen, my Susannah is everything to me, *everything*! And they would nod dutifully, but I could see they didn't quite understand what I meant. But Serena did, she nods, proudly: "Special" That's what Serena would always say: "A gift...." Oh, but I can't think of that now, Helen exhales heavily, covering her mouth with her hand, I'll weep and that just wouldn't do....

How things change. For the longest time, she didn't care for her. I was always, well, very put out, by the way Serena carried on, she recalls, shifting uncomfortably in her chair, however boring you understand yourself to be, you don't want someone bringing it to your attention, and that's how I always felt around Serena. Well, they had absolutely nothing in common and she struck Helen as so...oh, what's the word she's searching for...aloof: Positively unreadable. "It's impossible," she would insist to her friends, "to know where you stand with, Serena. Even when she's talking to you, it's like she's somewhere else. As if she's looking for someone more interesting and, as much as I accept that I am nowhere near as fascinating as the Rupert Turner-Hume's of this world, with his tales of Hollywood and debauchery, at least I'm honest. An out and out liar that man!

"And Edward, the way she treats him, my word," she would comment disapprovingly to her friends. "You can't guess in public there's anything amiss, but it's very true," she would confide knowingly, "that you never know what goes on behind closed doors because, one time, I did overhear them in his study: the door was slightly ajar, I was passing, I couldn't help but... 'You've given me nothing,' Serena screamed, 'all you've done is punish me because you're a pathetic excuse for a man; a cripple. You only care about your vile children who you let treat me like dirt. Well, I'm three years younger than your daughter. Think what you would do if someone treated her the way you treat me....'

"Well, naturally," Helen would proclaim to anyone within earshot, "I was appalled: Edward was injured during the War; he walked with a cane! To taunt him and to speak like that about his children – it was one thing for them not to be able to have any of their own; I can't imagine it myself – but children do not ask to be born!" As their mother had died when they were very young and Serena was twenty years younger than him, Helen didn't find it that unusual they didn't accept her. So when she heard Edward say, "It's not them. It's you." She thought, Well, yes, Edward, you've certainly put the spoiled madam in her place. "After all," as Helen was also often heard to remark, "Serena's father left her destitute: If it weren't for Captain Lyons, Lord knows what would have become of her." Again, yes, she was well aware that there were more fascinating men in the world and the common cry amongst many of her girlfriends, in Serena's defense, was; "Well, he's not Kit Peel, is he?" "No, he's not," she'd rejoin, "but Kit didn't want her. She made an absolute fool of herself over him ..."

No, Helen had no sympathy. Serena struck her as the type of woman who was never satisfied. "I mean, the jewels he buys her!" she would cry, "That diamond star pendant, for one." Yet, when Helen had complimented her on it, Serena didn't display a flicker of emotion, as if she had forgotten she was even wearing it. And then off she drifted in that languid fashion of hers to someone more entertaining, or so Helen astutely surmised.

All she was, to Helen, was a hostess – "and an exacting one at that," she frequently observed. It was rumored she didn't even address the servants, something to do with them having to leave rooms if she entered them. "Well," Helen would ask, "what type of a person could be so cold? And if you didn't arrive at the right time, and she was forced to delay the meal for a fraction of a second, like ice, all evening." But then Helen was rarely up at the house that much in those days: She was up to her ears in her committees, the church, fundraising, her children, her husband, her houses, so much to do. No time to stop and have a real conversation. When they did speak, though, Serena would inquire after the children and she would always ask about the boats.

Oh, the boats, she remembers. Whenever anyone had a baby that was the gift they received from Serena; divinely crafted little wooden boats, replete with sails and anchors and steers; hand-painted and each one unique, inscribed with the name of the child. She's ashamed now to think that she once criticized her for a lack of imagination. "Everyone, the same gift, with her full to bursting coffers. Too busy looking in the mirror and making Edward miserable," that's what she was heard to say – and she thinks Serena did hear her once – whenever anyone mentioned them.

Helen didn't keep the cards Serena wrote for her older children, but when Susannah arrived, she kept hers; *'For the journeys she will take'* is all Serena wrote. It was what she always wrote, but with Susannah, it suddenly struck Helen how profound and touching a sentiment it was. She imagined Susannah in a boat, sailing through life, and she broke down and wept for the rest of the day, her heart broken because of Serena.

Gosh, there I go, she sniffs, scrabbling in her sleeve for a handkerchief.... "No, children, I've got something in my eye," she calls out to them. "Why, thank you for that big hug, Simon. I feel so much better. What can we sing now; does anyone have any ideas? Excellent, Caroline, Wee Willie Winkie, it is! *'Wee Willie Winkie runs through ...'"*

There's truly no hope for my mascara, Helen despairs, and I don't have a tissue; I'm sure I look like a raccoon. But I can't help it. Serena should have been happy, more than anyone else, more than me. It's the secret I've kept, for years....

Pure chance: She was in Port Jefferson; Walter had docked his yacht for repair and she was eight months pregnant with Susannah and went along for the ride – well, Helen knew she would be fine, even if nobody else did – and, heavens above, her waters broke and there she was, nowhere near Dr. Thomas, and it was all so quick that she was taken to the hospital there. And then Susannah arrived, safe and sound, and Dr. Thomas finally came and Helen said, "See, I told you so," and even he, the grouchy old coot, had to agree, although he was still annoyed with her: "Now promise me, you won't be doing this again!" he barked, but she saw it, how he melted when she passed Susannah to him; the way he always would. Susannah became his favorite, and she's not making this up – it's what he wrote in her Christmas card every year – '*To my favorite little patient, Merry Christmas from Dr. Thomas*' – and he didn't ever send one to the others, so Helen emerged victorious from that particular battle, and she never stopped reminding him of that while he was alive, thank you very much: always trust a woman's intuition.

It was a blissful day outside, but it was the nurse – my, that ravaged face! she recalls. How she frightened Helen when she first saw her, and she could only have been in her thirties. Helen still can't think how it came about. She was in raptures over Susannah – so healthy and perfect – and the nurse asked her where she lived and Helen told her, "Southampton." Oh, she knew that area slightly; what street did she live on? "Gin Lane." Well, there was the usual silence after that, people tend to get awestruck, but then Helen quickly changed the subject and said something like, "Oh blow, I'm missing a party as it happens: Serena Lyons. She always has the most tremendous events during the summer. But I do have the perfect excuse, don't – "

Well.

The nurse went ashen. Helen had never seen anyone go that color before. Then the nurse's knees buckled and she fell into Susannah and Helen on the bed and Helen didn't know what to do. Should she call someone to help? What? Susannah, the angel, was entirely unperturbed and slumbered away while what Helen thought of as a comic interlude unfolded. But it wasn't funny. It was unimaginable.

The nurse had taken him: Serena's son. This is what she confessed to Helen because Edward Lyons had arranged for the child to be given up for adoption. "He arranged for his own child to be given away?" Helen asked in astonishment. "No, not his: the other gentleman's, Mr. Peel's. But he didn't come back for her... I took the baby to the orphanage, I did, but I couldn't put him in that place: She loved him so much..." And then this woman just sobbed and sobbed and Helen was left trying to make sense of what she'd told her. "The baby was Kit's," she repeated, "but he wouldn't have abandoned her. He loved her. I've never seen anyone so in – What did he look like?" "Very tall, black hair..." "Did he speak with an accent, a British accent?" "No, he was American." "And he brought her here and didn't come back and that was when Captain Lyons came...?" "Yes." "But Kit Peel was blonde," she protested, "What year was this?" Helen's mind was at sixes and sevens trying to understand her, "1908? Well, yes, Kit was gone and the only person I know who looks like how you're describing this man was Ted – Oh my God," she exclaimed, as she came to the conclusion that Teddy Worthington was the father, and the full wretchedness of it settled on her. "So where is the child now?"

. . .

From when he was tiny, all he loved was the sea; all he talked of was sailing. Helen visited Ann, the nurse, shortly after in Mattituck. Ann had had moved there from the Midwest, where she had raised Serena's son, Christopher. Helen has never forgotten what she told her: "You meet every type of mother when you're a midwife. Even after they're gone, you remember them, you worry about them: some just have babies, over and over, like a routine, no pleasure, no surprise in it; others are so bitter at the shock of such suffering that they immediately distance themselves, like they were punishing the child for causing them that much pain; but then there are those times when a child is born and you can breathe a sigh of relief because you know how much he will be loved. There was something about her – even though she was barely more than a child herself – that was special. I never saw anything like it between a mother and her child again: until you, Mrs. Fitzgerald. That was why I burst into tears because you reminded me of how she was with him. I didn't think of myself as his mother. I'd have given him back but I didn't know where she might be, until I returned here and discovered she was so famous. And that Kit Peel, I couldn't find him either. You might never understand, but he had been born to be loved and I couldn't risk that not happening. That's why I took him with me, away from here."

Helen has the lace shawl, embroidered with Serena's initial, S: It is pristine, apart from being torn at the hem. She also has a photograph of the boy taken before he left to join the Navy. That was when everything became clear to her: He was not Teddy Worthington's son; Oh, Teddy was involved, she learned, but only to betray Serena with his usual cowardice: Great for stories, Teddy, Helen has often thought, but not the type to catch you if you fall. Serena learned that the hard way, although how she could ever have forgiven him, Helen cannot imagine. But maybe, she has also reckoned, Edward did have something to do with it: She's never been sure; the only part of the story on which Ann wouldn't be drawn was him: What Helen is certain of is that Kit and Serena's son, Christopher, is unmistakably their own; it is all there in his perfect face, a map of the love that created him; a gentle grace could be said to personify this child; the grace of those who are grateful for what little they have. By the way he looked at the camera, Helen has always been able to see that he was loved: It was exactly the same expression his father wore whenever he looked at Serena, and this has offered her some comfort, whenever she has taken the photograph out of the drawer she keeps it in to look at him.

This is why she always sits with the children at the parties; sometimes, she reminds herself, mothers cannot choose the person to whom they pass the baton to care for their children. Better it be me who loves them than a hired hand only going through the motions. Children are born to be cherished, like Ann said, just as I cherish Susannah and my sons, she smiles, kissing Calum on the head and giving him a gentle pat to rejoin the others in their game.

Watching the children play at Serena's house, she thinks of Ann and the sacrifice she made; she thinks of Serena, how everything became clear, after Helen learned the truth; the poise, the distance, the eyes that only seemed to come alive when Serena would welcome the boys and girls into her home, although not playing with them, only ever watching. The day she won the race for my son, Tommy, at the fair, Helen remembers, the way she looked at me; the excruciating pain she experienced at the finish line, her child not there to thank her. She fell to her knees. Wouldn't you if you were forced to live to like that? Of course, Helen feels bitterly ashamed for how she misjudged her, but she has tried to make amends for that. Serena never had a mother, not to speak of, and this is the role Helen has tried to fulfill in recent years: She likes to think of herself as someone Serena leans on, who protects her, without ever letting her know.

Helen looks down to the handcrafted wooden boat she cradles in her lap, the only toy Serena ever gave to her son. It is very worn, played with often. This is what Ann told her; the day Helen went to collect his belongings. Those she has kept safe for Serena while she has tried to think of a way to tell her. But she never has, although she's tried to, so many times. She even broke down in tears with her once, but she couldn't: She ended up going on about some poor child with Polio from one of her charities. How could I tell her, she asks herself again, that I found her son only to learn that he was missing? Lost at sea on his first voyage out, barely seventeen. I thought I understood what it would do to her, to have loved a child so much only to lose it. I wanted to spare her what I did to myself when my precious little girl died at five-years-old: my Susannah, who I left today in the glorious sunshine underneath the gardenia trees where we buried her, and where I sit each day of summer, so that I could come here to say goodbye to Serena.

What became of them, she wonders now, all of those little boats? She still has Susannah's, a beautiful rose-colored yacht. They used to take it down to their pond by the pavilion and sail it amidst the calla lilies. It was all Helen could do not to weep for Serena on those days; her loss used to hit her so desperately hard whenever Susannah wanted to play with her Aunt Serena's boat, because Helen asked her to be her godmother. How Susannah loved that boat, she recalls, she would have sailed it in a puddle if I'd let her, but it was the only indulgence I couldn't afford her; some gifts are too special and those who give them more special still.

After Susannah died, Helen placed it in a glass box in her nursery, along with the one she has looked after for Serena, with careful instructions that they be cleaned every month. But today, Helen made a decision. When she sees Serena tonight, she is going to tell her the truth and return her son's boat, at last: She wants her to have it, you see.

For the journeys she will take.

THE HOSTESS

You learn so much at parties. There is always a guest waiting to enlighten you. A guest who will inform you that the love of your life married someone else; that your husband is not the man you thought he was; that there will be no way out of his prison, ever: So you drift on....

At any given party, there are always the secrets. They lurk around corners in the darkness of unlocked studies or behind the flyleaves of books, in the pages of unfinished letters. There are the secrets we learn about others and those they learn about us, those we keep for others and those they keep from us. There are the secrets we tell to any passing stranger because they seem so irrelevant and then those others we guard ferociously, for fear of what we might lose if they were revealed.

There were only ever two occasions when I enjoyed the incomparable thrill of thinking Kit had come to the party. Once, I spotted a man so similar to Kit he could have been his brother, standing on the farther side of a room. And another time, when I was lighting the candles in the dining room, I thought I saw him watching me through the window. His head was slightly tilted to the side. He wore the same gentle, forgiving smile as on the night when I first danced for him.

In that moment, anything I had forgotten while I was with him came flooding back and I was seventeen again. There it was between us, the righting of all wronged things into an elemental truth bound by the love we shared: a constant knowledge that could never be forsaken. How proud he was of me, as he stood there. The life he found me in was everything we had imagined together: the settings on the table, the decor of the dining room, the dress I wore, all of my interests. I had followed the dream he inspired in me to the letter, as if he was constantly at my side. "Thank you," I said, on accepting that anything beautiful I had ever known was only because of him. "Thank you, my love."

Yet, I was not disappointed when I realized that Kit was not really there. Rather, I felt lucky to recall him so vividly and embraced the vision as a sign that he *would* return for me. But it was that very evening when I was thirty-five – so late, too late – that Rupert confirmed my greatest fear and I fell into the depths of sorrow, where I remain to this day. "Can I send him a message?" Rupert asked, after he told me. "No," I replied, "no message."

What message do you send to those who have forgotten you? What could you possibly say to bring them back to where you have waited, when you are not the treasured memory, locked in a priceless box, which they are for you? When you are just a girl a boy knew once, and nothing more.... I thought back to the sight of Kit at the window as I sat with Rupert. Had Kit thought of me then, as he prepared to offer what had been mine to another and let my memory go forever? The sight of him constituted the only happiness I had experienced in years, but its aftermath did not prove bittersweet. Instead it consoled me in the certainty that I had not been wrong: It was all there in the brief space of time encompassed by that perfect summer and nothing could eradicate that fact, not even husbands, wives or time. And it seems to me now that we never truly lose sight of the one we are born to love. The mind might find another, a palliative measure, but true love lives on: the surety of what it was to know someone in every detail and to find that salvation there always, even after they have gone. I sensed that, wherever he was, Kit had wanted to ensure I felt no pain on learning the truth. I had married another and so had Kit. I understood, too, that if I were the person he thought me to be, I had to wish him well. And so I did. But I could not do as my husband had counseled in his letter – I could not forget on finding something in Kit's star that hurt me. Kit is all I have chosen to remember of my life. I can have it no other way.

And so Five Things at the end of the day: what I have written out and placed in the box on my dressing table. They are not what people will remember of me, but they are the things that I have treasured. I leave them for Edward to find after I'm gone. And I thank him for the gift of them now, although I can never tell him. The time for that has passed.

IV
LATE ARRIVALS

THE PARTY, THE PARTY!

"Thirty years and we've never found the culprit," fumes a Dreadnaught, the name bestowed upon the former mistresses of the social seas, to her cohorts. "At least Jeanette Rattray puts her name to her column in *The East Hampton Star*, but this Eavesdropper is – " "'Oh, *the party, the party...! we thrill together each Saturday morning as I tumble, like pearls into your laps*,'" interrupts a bohemian artist, who founded The Tile Club, arriving at the women's side, "'*those Tales of The Summer Visitors at The Westhampton Leisure Hour and Supper Club*.' Isn't it droll?" she concludes, inhaling artfully on her cigarette holder.

"Hardly," croaks The Dreadnaught, stepping gingerly back from The Bohemian. In 1904, The Bohemian had pounced on her in a field while she was sketching under the genteel auspices of William Merritt Chase's Summer School of Art, beseeching her to proclaim The Hamptons as the new American Barbizon, which had frayed The Dreadnaught's nerves intolerably and led to a deep-seated mistrust of non-conformity. "It makes us all look so silly. And, for the record, it was entirely misreported that I visited Jesse Woolworth Donahue's swimming club. I have never forgiven her for that wall. It destroyed the view from The Bathing Corp. I was merely inspecting the adjoining door for signs of subsidence," she protests, alluding to the red brick wall Ms. Donahue built at the foot of her garden, as revenge for being rejected for membership.

"Not everyone," The Bohemian counters, casting an appraising eye over The Dreadnaught's outfit and smiling in withering sympathy before continuing. "Only those awful arrivistes and society demons that insist on maintaining the status quo," she quips, flashing a pointed smile in her direction. "Besides, whoever it is clearly adores Serena. I once took her for a sail across Town Pond in Tom Moran's gondola, delightful little thing." "Is there any truth to the rumor," pipes up a more highly spirited mistress, thrilled to be rescued from the stultifying boredom of The Dreadnaught. "That there's a Childe Hassam painting entitled 'Serena with Daffodil' locked away some-where?" "Let's just say," The Bohemian smiles ingratiatingly, "that when Childe begged Serena to come and stand in his flower bed, she did not have to be asked twice."

"I do agree with you," The Dreadnaught almost shouts to The Bohemian, in mortal fear that The Eavesdropper might be listening, "that of all the ladies – and I do include myself in this, alongside the inestimable Mrs. Livingstone and Mrs. Vleck Jr. – who've ever tried to lay claim to the social epicenter of our society, Serena, by far, has reigned supreme." "True," demurs The Bohemian. "I suppose the last to challenge was Pauline Sabin, but what a flip-flopper. We'd roll up in the 'Twenties to Bayberry Land never knowing whether she'd be banging the drum for The Women's Christian Temperance Union or The Wet Sisterhood," she snorts, referring to Ms. Sabin's infamous volte-face from anti to pro Prohibition. "And, for the record," continues The Dreadnaught volubly," Serena has proven highly individual as a hostess, remarkable when you consider that she never had a Social Secretary. I have never found a gardener masquerading as a footman here, and she's never run La Doucette as a grand hotel like Mary Rogers' Black Point. The vulgar-ity of personal house stationery for guests and dialing downstairs for a car or lunch," she says, pulling a face: "If I wanted *that*, I'd go and visit Sara Wiborg on the Continent." "Part of the fun of coming here for me has been watching Serena," adds The Highly Spirited Mistress. "Her dresses and the jewels at her neck! For me, they've outclassed Venetia's, which have always struck me as somewhat *new-er*," she enunciates, carefully. "But it's not really fair to draw the comparison. I mean, unlike Douglas, Serena's husband has always been madly in love with h—"

"What rot!" shrieks a keen amateur dramatist, turning from a conversa-tion beside them, "they've never been able to stand each other. They don't even speak in company. Not that I can think of. And," she continues, warm-ing to her theme, "you've clearly forgotten that time when she –" "*Don't. Say. Another. Word*," The Dreadnaught commands, as if calling order at The Picnic Club, pivoting her head owl-like to make sure no one else is listening.

"I'm sorry, but I have to speak my mind. I simply must. I've never liked her," The Amateur Dramatist exhales fulsomely, her shoulders slumping, as if arriving exhausted, at a finish line of a race. "There I've said it!" The most boring woman I've ever met: nothing to say for herself. And if you want my opinion," she adds, ignoring the scandalized glare from The Dreadnaught, "I think she's brought everything on herself: She's always been a real so-and-so, if crossed. Just look at what she did to Lucinda. Besides, isn't ruthlessness key to being a hostess? Including and excluding, rewarding and denying: And for what? Why go to all the trouble if you aren't a complete megalo-maniac: to be a star in your own life, probably because you're so irrelevant in every other conceivable area."

"And I will say this, too, about Serena," The Dreadnaught almost screams, desperate to return the conversation to something innocuous. "She has never been a snob. When you come to a party of Serena's, there'll always be a surprise or two amidst the fray. I myself once had a very interesting con-versation with a Catholic and it's not often you can say that, is it?" she con-cludes, almost collapsing under the weight of the propriety she must uphold.

Meanwhile, on the dance floor, The Last Resort spies Anthony Duverglas, farther away from her than ever, and bursts into tears once more. "For God's sake, pull yourself together!" snaps The Dandy, furious to be interrupted in mid-sartorial swing. "Go and sleep it off over there," he says, pushing her toward the banquettes, lining the walls. Yet, The Last Resort's lot is not to be solitary, after all. For, as she lurches toward a nearby sofa, a rescuing hand, pulls her back upright from behind, and the charming English tones of everyone's favorite gilded idol, Rupert Turner-Hume, sounds in her ear: "Preparing for a crash landing, darling?" he inquires humorously. "You can land on me, if you like." "Butt me," she splutters, proffering a cigarette and collapsing against him. "My, that does sound intriguing," he replies wryly, helping her to stay upright. "Why don't we just light your cigarette for the time being and then let's see where the evening takes us...Now," Rupert asks, "are you feeling better, darling? I have a secret I must share with you," he whispers conspiratorially, taking her chin in his hands and turning her face up to his. "Do you swear never to tell a soul? Blink once for yes and twice for no." Always so easily led, The Last Resort feasts her glazed eyes on the form of another –slightly younger, more devilishly good looking – perennial bachelor, and, promptly forgetting all about Mr. Duverglas, blinks vigorously – twice. "As I thought," smiles Rupert. "I can see that we are going to get along famously. Now, the secret.... to the perfect screen kiss is all in the tilt. May I bend you over backwards to demonstrate? You do look a tad gymnastic, to my eye..."

And as The Summer Visitors drink and dance and gossip on, Montauk becomes an island and the telephones go dead; Lake Agawam claims Monument Square in Southampton and Sagaponack drowns; Greenport loses its shipyards, and the skies begin to fill with the remains of what once was – Anthony Duverglas' father's Bridgehampton farm, Helen Fitzgerald's beloved Gin Lane mansion, along with the calla lilies and the privets and her memories of Susannah. While just beyond the doors of La Doucette, the placid Moriches Bay begins to rise and, less than a mile away, the first body is washed ashore...

But, all of a sudden, the wind stops, the rain ceases and a glimmer of light appears on the black horizon. "The storm is over!" some of the younger people cheer, making a beeline for the marquee, "we can dance outside!" In relief, The Summer Visitors rush to the windows to confirm this revivifying false hope: the most malevolent trick that the elements will play on them tonight. That the storm is simply that and nothing will harm them after all.

THE HOSTESS

The lady lives in a cottage on Halsey Road. She is often the talk of her neighbors and how insignificant the house is compared to what she could have had, nowhere near good enough: "Why," they say, she was once so popular, so admired; "she could have lived in palaces with princes." The lady, walking home, thinks they are fools. This cottage is tiny, with two Palladian windows, an arbor of roses over the front gate and, in the rear, there is a small hut like a beekeeper's cottage. Yet, it has a turret that never fails to fascinate her, as if it belonged in a fairy tale, and a princess lived inside. Through the windows, passers-by can see the books lining the walls; the man who lives there reads all the time. Sometimes, the door is slightly ajar and then a rose patterned rug can be spied in the entranceway and a small chesterfield in the parlor. And covering every inch of the walls are pictures of far-away lands, except for the staircase; the pictures that hang there are of the family who live inside – a chronicle of time passing and beloved people growing older.

Often, a little blonde boy plays in the garden and he wears pale blue. In his hands is a wooden boat and he is thinking about supper and if his mother will allow him a piece of chocolate after it. He will ask her as soon as she comes through the garden gate and then she does and it is as if he has wished for her and she has appeared. Like magic, he thinks. And the lady, his mother, reminds herself that she must get the gate fixed, as it sticks, but she always forgets because just as she thinks of mentioning it to her husband, she sees her little boy and only wants to know about what he has been doing since she left. And as he runs to her and she scoops him up in her arms, her husband emerges from the house, a book in his hand. But he is never the same as she remembers him – in her mind, he is always young. Yet, she loves everything that has happened to him in the years that have passed, even though others comment unfavorably on how he has changed – "How dark his blond hair is," they say. "How gaunt he seems."

As he walks up to meet her, he puts on his glasses as if she were the only sight that could ever interest him. He cannot conceal his gladness that she has come home, nor would he bother to try as he used to when he was young: "Tell me everything about where you've been and what you've been thinking," he says. But what he truly means and what she hears him say is: *Look at you, what you've become. So much more than anyone might have thought.* And she replies, "I've been thinking about the gate, how we must fix the gate." He always adores the way she teases him and so he kisses her, which is what she has been waiting for, and then she says, "Oh well, I suppose it can't hurt you to know; I've been thinking of you. Is that alright?" "Yes, quite alright," he smiles, taking her arm to lead her up the path to their house, with the books and the rose patterned rug, and the beautiful little boy who loves them. None of it is good enough for her, apparently – she could have lived in palaces with princes – but all of it is what she wants, what she chose.

This is my might-have-been, what I contrived as the reward for waiting for Kit: *You see, I won't ask for much,* I coaxed whomever decides these things, *not wealth or even security, but please may I have that second chance?* And all Kit had to do was arrive – late or early – but arrive, and then it could begin, this little life of little things. I was convinced that it was so much more than what I had, even as I fastened the clasps of diamond bracelets on my wrists, or stepped into a Schiaparelli silk dress held out for me by the weary arms of a Little Maid. Some evenings, when I was foolishly tipsy on fancies, this latent impulse would resurge, sounding an instinct in me that would unhesitatingly affirm, *Yes, it could still happen, he has not forgotten you, he will come back.* And so I might confide in a trusted guest or two, this little dream of mine. Their responses would never change, always the same startled expressions, always the same horrified response: "Absurd! Why, think of the dresses you wouldn't have had, and you would certainly never have met President Harding or attended the Hampton Classic or dined with the Chinese Ambassador and think of that 18-carat diamond at your neck! Oh, Serena, how miserable you would be, watching the lives of people like

us, and not being able to join in. And, besides," they would announce leaning in, their mallet poised to sound the victory gong, "*nobody* would know
who you are and how you would hate that, being nothing more than a face
in the crowd...!"

The fate of the pleasing person would befall me then, having handed
others the deciding vote over my happiness. And the fantasy would pall, put
away until it was safe to bring it out again. Yet, the instinct would always
remain: that little cottage on Halsey Road, with the sticking gate, and its
ordinary life within. It was just down the road and all I had to do was walk
toward it. But how could I, if Kit did not come to take my hand and lead me
there; how could I, if he was married to someone else...?

...

My ritual is almost over, and soon you will be gone. Yet, might the wind
change course, or the rain cease, or the moonlight cast its light over this road
before me, illuminating the figure of a last guest? For the hope of a second
chance begins now at the eleventh hour, with the possibility of a late arrival.
Someone who might bring the promise of a dream becoming a reality, to
make up for all that was lost before it.

I know that he is coming. I don't know why, but I do.

THE UNINVITED GUEST

"No, thank you. I prefer to walk." This is what he tells him, his wife and his daughter, as they stop to offer Kit a lift on this, the final leg of his journey.

"We're incredibly late. But Annabelle *had* to come," the mother nods jubilantly to the young girl, celestial in her beauty, her white blond hair a halo, picked out with gold daisies; "It's her eighteenth birthday at midnight, and I've promised her ever since she was a babe, that one day I would bring her. Isn't that right, Annabelle?" she continues, turning in her seat to her daughter for confirmation. "So here we are! A promise is a promise and it *is* the last party. But this weather! First the rain, then the wind! We were sure we were never going to make it... Won't you change your mind?" she inquires in concern. "The wind could start again any second. Wouldn't you be safer in the–"

But then her husband places a silencing hand on her arm, as he leans across to get a closer look at Kit through the open window: "Say... didn't we know each other once? I could swear you lo—" No, don't let's talk of such things, Kit wills him in his mind; Maybe you do remember, but don't let me remind you. Let's only think of what could happen. I'm not too late. It isn't over yet... "Perhaps," Kit says, "when I was young," and he has to look to the ground because he sees the man make a vague connection to another time and place, and there is a sense, in him, almost of horror, of what he uncovers there. "But –" the man protests.

"Don't let me keep you," Kit interrupts, raising his eyes to the beautiful teenager perched excitedly in the back; her attention fixed on the blazing lights ahead, wishing only to be inside instead of talking to him. "You promised your daughter the party, remember?" "See you there, then. Don't be slow!" Annabelle calls brightly. "Daddy," she insists, prodding her father to move, smiling at Kit in gratitude, as their car roars off over the gravel.

He watches them recede into the distance; the golden girl in the back, in her matching dress, her chiffon scarf flying behind in the dark, glinting like the tail of a comet. She is desperate not to miss out on what the party has promised her, from everything she has heard. A late surprise, the revelers will part to welcome her in raptures. Yet, how sad, he thinks, that they will have so little of her. She will arrive now, only in time to say goodbye.

The sound of music beyond seems to want to drag him forward, the straggler, to enjoy the final moments of the party as it rages to its conclusion. Yet, it is a curious emotion that returning to this once loved place elicits in him, for there is no doubting the jealousy he feels. How have you lived without me? he asks, looking to the house. Why didn't you stop until I came back, as I have stopped? Something in him, despite how cruel a sentiment it is, wishes Serena had followed him, or had been forced to give up what he had, so that he might understand more of her. There is only uncertainty at the end of this road, lined by the elms, he realizes. And she is so close now, this one constant ambition he's kept. Seeing Serena again suddenly seems an insurmountable prospect, given what he has had to do to survive, the life he has not lived, the news he must bring to her.

His hand reaches to touch the iron gates, to trace the crest on their center. I could easily pull the gates shut; lock myself out, he tells himself. Nobody would be any the wiser. For he knows that if he begins to walk this road, it will be seconds before he emerges in plain sight, an invitation to whomever might see to come out and greet him. Will it be her, as I have prayed? he asks. Or is she hidden at the party's center, blind to anything beyond the faces of others? Can Serena not sense instinctively that I am here and come to the window to save me this anxiety? Tonight, I can ask for her as I failed to do when it mattered most: I can bar a closing door with my arm and insist she listen, but she may not believe me. What then, should she turn away? Where would I go, what would be left? There is nothing, though, he can do to prevent it: He can console himself only with this: One last time, she will see me. And it is all I have ever longed for in my life.

He takes his first step on to the gravel, resigned to finally learning the truth of Serena's heart. He thinks of Annabelle, of the gold daisies laced through her hair. Is she already saying her goodbyes, he wonders: So sad a thing, but then it comes to us all: There is goodbye in every step we take.

I am walking to you, Serena, he silently calls to her, as he makes his way toward the house, as I did the night of the first party. Can you hear my footfall, even from so far away? Does it sound somewhere in you, like something long forgotten that you recognize you now must do? Do you remember, Serena, the promise you made, the one you broke? Keep it now. *Meet me on the road that leads to the sea and I'll wait for you and you'll wait for me....*

This is what he has learned, the message he brings to her:

At the end, as at the beginning, everything is about the soul.

THE HOSTESS

For each of us, there comes a moment when we stand poised between one life and the next. We have a choice, where we can honor the future, by finding the courage to act, in the hope that it might lead us to a different reward. Or we can ignore the maybes and what ifs of alternate paths and return to the familiar, however timeworn and disappointing we understand its confines to be: We can stay still.

There is one more party for you to follow me into, to understand why am I leaving. Was it a choice I made or one decided by somebody else? It was only last Friday that it happened... Only last Friday that I ran sobbing from the house, the letter clutched to my chest. I ran to the midpoint of the road, halfway between the party and a new future, to keep my promise....

Meet me on the road that leads to the sea, and I'll wait for you and you'll wait for me....

I fixed my gaze on the view ahead and waited in the dying light. In the trees, on the breeze, there were the ghosts: a convocation of the living and the dead – Catherine, my mother, guests who had flitted through our world. Yet, I was not afraid. It was what I had come to last and it was all; the last expectation; the last ounce of promise; the last fork in the road, the last chance to change direction.

"Don't let me hear it yet," I whispered, "not yet." I prayed for the silence to prevail, to delay the sound of the train's horn that would signify one minute until its arrival at the station: one minute until those who chose to come late would arrive, and those who chose to leave early, would depart.

I stood with my back to the house, a last wish on my lips. But even as I uttered it, there was already no point, drowned out, as it was, by the sound of the first horn, signaling the train's intent. And before me, in that space of the mind before the final acceptance, a kaleidoscope of memory flashed past, like a performance being watched from behind a lace curtain: memories of summers lived; of soldiers returning from wars and tables laid for the dead; of tea-lights and Chinese lanterns and Willow pattern china; of inconstant hearts, of freedom and choices; of the happiest year and the sight of my beloved friend, walking up that road to meet me. All of it how I arrived there last Friday and, ultimately, here tonight with you. And before the blare of the second horn, which ended every plan and presented suddenly a new way forward, the only sound that was audible to the night, was the end of my wish:

Goodbye.

The train had arrived at the station. Too late to catch it, it would not wait for me. It was a journey for someone else to take.

. . .

Earlier that evening, I had moved through the crowd like an invisible presence. Around every corner seemed to lurk a memory, a reckoning. The front door opened to admit Edward's daughter with her family. She caught sight of me and whispered something to her fourteen-year-old girl, who immediately dissolved into laughter, her hand covering her mouth as her mirthful eyes looked me up and down. Her husband tsked and ushered them into the study, where Edward was waiting, closing the door behind him. That was their party, in there, isolated from the real one, which his daughter thought – and had loudly remarked on numerous occasions – "So completely pathetic. So completely Serena..." She always found it so amusing.

The closing door struck me as a suitable metaphor for my life at the start of that party. I was forty-eight and I had spent nearly every second of it in a house of closing doors. Those that excluded me, or else locked me away. Beyond the festivities of summer Fridays, it was a house where I sat alone in rooms, listening to the chatter and the laughter emanating from elsewhere, but was never invited to join in. Yet, despite the hours spent hoping, nothing had ever happened to force those doors to open, to allow someone in that might change my reality.

Neither Edward's son nor daughter could understand why he married me. In his one concession to my feelings, he did not tell them the truth. From the beginning, they thought me ridiculous, and found many who agreed: those ears they found at parties, to whom they lied and gossiped, standing in huddles, sneering in my direction, offering no illusion about what was being said. Yet, beyond their malice and my discomfort, it wasn't until his daughter went too far that I felt justified in my contempt; "It's shameful and ridiculous," she commented to a guest who gleefully told me. "He's so much older. I mean, can you imagine, if they have children..." And it was all I needed to hear, the one comment that I could legitimately refuse to forgive: neither her nor my husband for placing me in that situation.

It was the only time in my life when I did not try to please. But my choice backfired as such choices do when you have no control over your own life. Edward's grandchildren would frequently visit unannounced. I might be in the hall, just in time to see them running past – those beautiful children with the blonde hair and the wide eyes, who would regard me curiously, almost in fear. "Come away," their mother or father would say sharply, "come away from her...." And I would watch as my husband jovially ushered them into one of my father's rooms, before carelessly pushing the door shut on me with the back of his hand, as if I didn't exist at all.

Permitting his children to hate me was the beginning of my devolution into abject passivity; of never acting, only ever being acted upon, borne of a paralyzing terror of making mistakes that came to consume me, to the point where I dared not make a move: There was so much that I had got wrong. As the years passed, I came to recognize that I would never be able to leave, as I still prayed to, unless someone presented that choice and made it for me.

I was distracted from my thoughts when the party suddenly flared into brilliance like a Catherine Wheel, with the entrance of an uninvited bright young thing. I never learned her name, but she wore silver slippers and a silver Chanel dress and her hair was bleached platinum blonde. She was absolutely captivating; the one girl anyone would later recall and I privately wished her luck. A playwright was holding court with an ingénue, his hand lightly resting on her knee; a faded Broadway star, grubby in the flesh, a ladder in one stocking, was singing a hit song of the moment, "September

Song;" a passel of aristocrats from Britain were demonstrating the latest dance craze, "The Lambeth Walk;" and every one of the women was trying to mimic Vivien Leigh or Carole Lombard.

And it was all so new, but yet so tired: another dance fad, a different handbag – except for Lucinda – a pretty face, maybe not as memorable as the last, but decidedly fresh. Yet, it seemed suddenly a fairground, which always began and ended the same way. I had grown to dislike these newer people, nostalgic for better mannered days. I preferred to be with the Old Guard, who valued our world for its simplicity and refinement, instead of using it as a stepping-stone to things they thought more. Ultimately, however, the parties had lost their motive: They no longer constituted a holy grail; they just were, because I needed something to do to avoid the silence that was my sole companion.

"We're Off To See the Wizard" followed "September Song," which seemed to play louder and more frantically, as if to drown out the ghostly refrains of more brilliant songs that had preceded it. All around me, the new faces looked pasted, like those of paper dolls, over the old; the cuts of the dresses by the ritual designers – Vionnet, Chanel, Schiaparelli – seemed tired regurgitations of earlier styles that had suited everyone better. And underlying everything, there was the haunting murmur of more scintillating conversations drowned out by the high-pitched showboating of the newly invited: those women talking like babies and men mimicking gangsters, calling each other *Doll* and *Baby*. It was such an insipidly stupid world and I was at its centre, once more. Yet, I no longer commanded the party. It had become something else beyond my control, a new world spinning around and away from me. I was merely a circumstance that allowed younger people to revel.

My fall from grace began gradually. I noticed it first in the quizzical emptiness of young men's eyes as they flitted over me, carelessly calculating my worth to them, What does she want with me? I could see them thinking, I don't have time for this, but then she is mother's friend... Some made attempts at falsely engaging me, but should I laugh too hard at their jokes, or sound the faintest coquettish note without realizing, and those eyes would darken into startled revulsion, the message clear, Surely she doesn't think I'm interested. I'm only being polite...

How things had changed. After I learned of Kit's marriage, there were other men for me, of every variety: handsome, wealthy, impoverished, grasping, many of who did try to lure me away from Edward. Sometimes, I let them, but only up to a point. That point when talk, flirtation, and chance meetings end, when decisions must be made — of what a different future might bring, if only one can find the impetus to act. But I never could. I had shared myself once by choice and that was all. I was simply using them to torment Edward. I wanted him to watch me sidle into rooms, for a change: so that I could turn back with a smirk to close the door on him.

So many promises made in these rooms, I reflected, leaning against a pillar; how many of them were kept? Edward's promise to find my son figured in mind my like a flare shot from a ship, a possible illumination over the darkness we shared. Over the years, softened somewhat by what I discovered in his ledgers, I had even tried sometimes to understand him. Yet, being near him was always like lifting the lid on a mysterious box: Neither of us could overcome the tension that existed between us, or be sure of the other's emotions. We communicated at cross-purposes; every sentence we uttered was double-edged, so easy to misinterpret, and then there would be the unimaginable fights...Those fights when you say the most terrible things, when you are so hobbled by disappointment that every breath constricts you...Years of it inching up higher and higher, like a rising tide, anchored by society and propriety and the right and wrong things to do, until the water reaches the lips and begins to choke....

I felt myself giving way, letting go. Apathy reigned in me. I stopped seizing with a perfectionist's zeal on the many flaws I saw around me at La Doucette, allowing the gleaming edges of the world I had created for Kit to be rubbed out. So began the pall, muting what was brilliant into a state that proved underwhelming, considering the stories people had heard. But then this is what happens when second chances fail to materialize and you have to forfeit the dream that kept you waking; this is what happens when you finally realize that, even though you live with others, you'll die alone.

But then, I would tell myself; *I'm only forty-eight. I have years left, don't I? And what if, what if...* Something in me still praying that everything could be reversed, if only the right foot was placed on the right mat...and then there it was.

Sometimes, the guest you seek is already at the party. Sometimes, they were the first to arrive and you lost them in the crowd.

I considered the door of Edward's study impassively, without experiencing my usual dejection or the consuming frustration at how little changes. I had a secret, you see. It was only last Friday, but the party had assumed a different tenor because it was to be my last. My bags were sitting at Speonk station, ready for me to board the train to New York. Someone had made the decision for me, and I had finally accepted.

Yes, it was only last Friday that I stood on the road outside this window, to wait for my last guest. The train horn sounded, one minute left to arrival or departure. I clutched the letter that I had received not half an hour earlier. The letter that began, *'Dearest Sea....'*

THE HOST

It was just last Friday when the door finally closed between them, locking him in, and Serena out. No more than five days since he watched her through the windows by which it was framed. Somewhere between falling and kneeling, she lurched, sobbing, into the driveway, as if the arms she thought she might find in the mist were the only ones that could ever comfort her. It has been over one hundred and twenty hours, since she fled from him, the letter in her hand, her hair tumbling loose from the diamond hair combs Kit gave her, that Captain Lyons had thought sold or lost. Yet, how many minutes since he turned to the hunting rifles, kept in the glass cabinet, at the entrance to La Doucette? He finds he cannot count them.

My wife is leaving us tonight, he accepts, pausing momentarily at the foot of the staircase. Although, the irony is not lost on me: Only with her appearance can this last party begin: We wait for her cue, to signal the beginning, just as we did thirty-one years ago this evening. Without her, the party is nothing.

Countless times, he thinks, beginning the climb to her room, we are brought to the doors of our lives, behind which lurk the secrets: those rooms we dare not enter, for fear of what we will find within them. Isn't it better not to know? We tell ourselves. How will everything change if I should see what I suspect? So we retreat, comfortable in our ignorance, but those are safer days. Then there are those others, when we wake resolved, contemptuous of that nagging voice that says, 'No, do not enter there.' Those occasions when we find the courage to throw open such doors, and in so doing, confirm our greatest doubts – the two lovers locked in an illicit embrace; the child doing something he or she shouldn't that forever alters the unconditional regard a father once held for them; a servant stealing; the beloved wife....

And with those revelations, the terrible awareness of the decisions we made that led up to the sight before us; how what lies beyond that previously obstructed view is entirely of our own making.

I did this to her, he allows, on arriving at her bedroom door. I do not know if I have the courage for what I am about to confront. Yet, there are facts she must be told, although I cannot be certain now that she will hear them.

He stands, his hand poised to knock, but then he remembers.

It is no longer her choice whether he enters or not.

THE HOSTESS

'Dearest Sea,'

He used to call me Sea, not Serena...

'It was the garden gate. That's why I stopped tonight. I had to do something about the gate. It's still broken, even after all these years. I stopped to remember why it is broken.

Funny thing about life, you can be on your way, out the door, fully intent on your journey, and then something waylays you, something you know never should, and you stop. You stop and already it's too late. ...

Do you remember the gate, dearest Sea? Do you remember, as I do, what happened there?'

It was after the snowstorm, when I was seventeen and he, twenty-four. I was teasing him about the time it was taking him to clear the path. "As my father is often heard to say, what is of crucial importance, dearest Sea, on undertaking any given job, is to truly take the time to do it well," he replied, leaning the shovel – any excuse to stop working –against the window. "But you've been doing it for *five* hours," I protested. "True," he conceded, "but I've been busy with other affairs." "With what?" I asked, skeptically, my hands on my hips at the gate, a bower of dead roses over my head. Behind him, stood the cottage with the two Palladian windows, the shed with the beekeeper's turret.... "Oh, little things," he smiled, trudging up to meet me through the snow. "Such as?" I replied, leaning my full weight on that dangerously fragile gate. "All the little things," he continued more seriously, and I felt a surge of the nerves I tried always to keep in check, understanding what was about to happen. *Please don't,* I begged him in my mind, *please don't say it...* "that I love about you, Sea," he concluded quickly, wincing slightly under the weight of his confession as he arrived in front of me. "Oh Teddy," I said, but he failed to hear the protest.

So began the first things between us; a first deceitful kiss, wishing those lips were ones I had chosen, but I kissed him back. It was who Teddy wanted me to be.

'*...How you leaned on it after a snowstorm, so that I could kiss you for the first time? How you put your full weight on that hundred-year-old gate and we plummeted in a heap on the ground, with the sudden drop as the hinge came out of the bracket. As you know, I've never been the same since. Darned sensitive, along with my broken tooth – the tooth you broke with your kisses – to all manner of matters concerning you...*'

It was the winter I was supposed to return with my father for the season, but at the last minute there was a change in plan. I arrived down in the hall the day I was to leave, to find a note:

'*I am returning to Manhattan alone, Serena. I fear that it has been another of our difficult summers. Coming with me would unsettle and excite you, and it is vitally important that you remain calm, considering what has happened in the past. I think it would be more sensible if we do not write. We must allow the dust to settle on what you have done.*

I had hoped that we might find some common ground. Yet, I fear that when we seek to comprehend the darker hearts of others; those far removed from our field of ken, what we find there – the knowing, so to speak – can sometimes kill us. Often, it is better to remain ignorant of what these hearts contain – the duplicity, the disappointment. I pray you will be well, Serena.'

After the death of my mother and sister, my father's expansive charm diminished until all that was left of it was his smile, on those rare occasions when he could. During his infrequent visits to La Doucette, he would greet me only with a brief nod, before he retreated – much like my husband later would – to his study, closing the door behind him. He changed so much as a result of those tragedies; even his voice was barely audible above a whisper. He could not stand noise, bristling if a door slammed or a tray clattered to the floor, by accident. If we dined together, he would fix his attention on his food for the entire meal, objecting to anything frivolous I might say to try to lift his mood. If I exclaimed, "Guess who I saw?" or "I paid a visit to an enchanting house," his eyes would flit up at me, as if at some unforeseen danger, his hand reaching across to grasp my arm: "Now, let us be calm Serena," he would say. "Let us get through this, little by little."

All hostesses learn that the role is simply a game of changing masks. You study a guest briefly to find the personality that will best engage him, in order to enjoy a pleasant exchange and not to rumple feathers. You act romantic, or subdued, effervescent, or even arch. You sublimate all that you are to the one aspect that person can relate to so that they will always return. It is a temporary shift in perspective, forgotten immediately as another guest appears, and a new personality is produced from the dressing-up box. Yet, for love, we alter everything. If my father did not forgive me, I did not know what I would become. So to regain his affection, I learned to be little.

I subverted my natural inclination toward excitement, keeping my voice low and speaking only when spoken to, inching gingerly alongside him like a hunched little creature, waiting to be brought out of the cage. And piece-by-piece I chipped away at his detachment, demonstrating by my insignificance how safe it would be for him to trust me again. It started to work; my father came home more often, sometimes staying longer than he first planned. I defined myself faultlessly by his conduct, always ready to adopt any characteristic or mannerism that he required of me: "The day seems long, Serena. Do you find this to be true, too?" he might say, as he rested on a chair, gazing somewhere undetermined. "As long as I have known it to be, Father," I would agree, emulating the inflection of his voice but barely moving a muscle, as if caught in the same trance-like state as he.

It was a life of little things; a life of placing salt dishes back on the exact spot they were taken from; or precisely setting keys down on a table, making sure not to make a sound with them; or closing all of the doors the same way, by leaving them exactly so much ajar. "We must not upset the balance of them, Serena. We must strive for harmony," my father would say. And the marking of time: My father would religiously observe the chimes of the clock on the hour in the hallway, like he was being called to prayer, before retreating back to wherever he was hiding. But whether it was from me or from himself, I never guessed.

It was years before I earned his respect, but I committed myself to the role, in place of any real learning. Besides, I was hardly a scholar. It was only later, with Kit, that I would understand how a word could cup beauty and hold it there to be admired, like looking into a teacup with a jasmine flower blooming at its base. I barely read at all when I was young, unless you count people. In them, I could always find whatever I needed to know; whether it was the precise shade of beige to paint a kitchen wall, or how to flavor meringue with lavender, or the minutiae of an accelerating crises in some far-flung war to which I later lost my friends, people often said that talking with me was like sitting an exam in whatever subject I consider them an expert. Given my encyclopedic knowledge of things, I am considered intelligent, but it is merely a surface glory. My sole talent is in knowing how best to deceive, filling in time between vacancies.

Finally, I was rewarded with the promise my father made, the summer before my seventeenth birthday; "Serena," he said. "I think you might accompany me to Manhattan this autumn." I was so elated that I almost forgot myself. Yet, nothing in my tone betrayed my emotions. "Thank you," I replied, displaying a rigid restraint; my head bowed, hands folded in my lap: "Very well," he said. "I will collect you in September." When I briefly glanced up, I thought I discerned the vaguest flicker of approval in his eyes. But backward glances can often prove romantic. Approval is what I wanted to find in my father's eyes. With the benefit of hindsight, I wonder now if what I witnessed there was malice.

It was the first and last promise my father made to me and kept. I looked up one hazy August afternoon, to find him unexpectedly standing at the low-slung fence bordering Remsenburg Park. He had come home early. I was rushing around, squealing in excitement, being chased by Douglas Dryden's Afghan dog. I was so pretty and popular in my shirt-waisted dress and wide-brimmed hat, my hair styled like a Gibson Girl: I was wearing a pair of purple shoes, my one concession to individuality. It was the year I was finally invited to every picnic, boating trip, horse show, tennis game, clambake and tea party. My new friends and I had met that day to play in the park, full of what we would do in Manhattan in the Fall: "I'm coming too," I told anyone who would listen, metamorphosing into someone other than the girl they were only friendly with from May to September.

High spirits, the boundless optimism of things changing for the better, that's all it was. I was just a girl in a perfect dress on a perfect day; with a perfect self selected from my wardrobe of personalities to please those who had invited me into their world. The *no* started somewhere underneath my breath, as I caught sight of my father; as I grew aware of the mistake committed, that would never be forgiven by him: The *no* that elongated with more intensity, wrapping itself around my heart to wring the wistful fancies out, as I stopped dead in front of him. "Who are you, Serena?" he asked, making no secret of his contempt. I started to cry, caught in the middle of another performance; what I needed to be for my friends, so that I would not be left alone, when he was gone. "I am a liar," I replied. "Yes," he agreed, and walked away.

'...*Odd, isn't it. How things work out. That I would live in the cottage where you once did, dearest Sea, that Fall you were alarmingly sick – your poor nerves – after your father didn't take you to Manhattan. When they brought you to my mother's estate – Remember how grand we were then, before it was sold off to make ends meet...? — Nobody had any idea what to do with you, you were overwrought, but all you wanted was that cottage in the grounds: "It is something little, you see. I think that's best for someone like me." "But it's not nearly good enough for someone as pretty as you," I tried to convince you. "Why the roof leaks and the floors squeak. And Sea – trust me – there are little things in there you don't ever want to see.... Suppose you just stay here in the big house." But, no: You drank in how enormous a palace it was, and that's when you broke down, prompting words like hysteria and medicine, incarceration, to be bandied about. So, to put an end to it, I agreed: the cottage it would be.*

I could feel your bones jutting out, even through your heavy coat as I carried you up the path to your new home, – you'd been starving yourself, hadn't you...? – where we placed you in a bed by the front window. You'd seen it in *the summer and had been — now, what's one of the words you'd use — oh, yes, <u>enchanted</u> by it, as only you could be by things impossible to repair that once held a certain charm; things like my tooth... "That poor girl," Mother fretted as we left you in the care of some staff: "Now, you be good to her, Teddy. I would stay but I have to go back to Manhattan for the Governor's Ball at the Metropolitan. I mean it: I'm <u>trusting</u> you with this..." she concluded with the habitual empty menace of a mother whose child had been expelled from every exclusive boarding school in the Northeast, having never found the discipline to prevent it. There was no choice then, Sea, when it came to you. Couldn't say no to anything, not after what you'd been through. And do you remember, Sea, how that first day, I took your hand as I was leaving, and I said...'*

"Goodbye then, Sea," he said, shortening my name without permission, but I didn't object because there was something wonderfully kind about Teddy. "I'll come for a visit tomorrow," he smiled, "and we can talk of little things...." And I looked up at his humorous eyes that never mocked but rather consoled, and I thought that I would be safe with him in that tiny doll's house. You see, all that is left to exhausted minds, which have tried so hard to please and failed, are the little things. And my darling friend, Teddy, was the first person who ever understood that about me, without needing to be told.

'...That was the year you loved me. I kept you for a year.
But I'm not getting to the point, am I? I'm just remembering who we were before: before wars and marriages and late promises. So, back to the gate...'

As he left me that first day, Teddy didn't close the gate behind him; it stayed open until he returned. It wasn't broken yet, but his first promise to me was: Teddy didn't come the next day. Teddy didn't come for weeks, despite how I waited for him. Until, one afternoon, there he was, jovially marching up the path, with all of the staff from the main house behind him, carrying silver platters high above their heads. "Dearest Sea," he announced through the open window I was sitting beside, " The Leisure Hour is upon us, so I thought I'd visit with you. You don't mind, do you? I do hope I'm not interrupting anything, but I am in a quandary, Sea, and I'm hoping you can help," he continued earnestly, breaking into the brightest of smiles. And, as I always would, I forgot about how long I had waited for him, and gave myself up to the joy Teddy brought with him wherever he went.

"See you anon, Peter," Teddy called, turning and waving somewhere far off down the street where I could not see. "Who's Peter?" I asked. "Peter, Sea?" Teddy reiterated benignly, "Why, Peter's my best friend. Great fellow, you'll adore him. Always getting himself into scrapes, though. Personally, I blame the pygmies," he remarked ruefully, shaking his head. "Pygmies, Teddy?" "Mmm, he's got several... They cling to him like limpets, the little devils. Peter spent some time in New Guinea. Never mention it, though. Rather dark period," he confided conspiratorially. "Awful show-offs Pygmies, did you know that? He's completely at their mercy, forever running around trying to please them and now he's in a real bind. They're urging him to write a play in Karam-lish. Do you speak Karam-lish, Sea?" he talked on, barely pausing for breath. I shook my head, all cares forgotten. "Not to be confused with Bantu – Please don't ever make that mistake, as I did, at dinner with them the other night. It caused something of an international incident, I'm afraid. In the end, we had to call in some nuns from the convent in Water Mill to smooth ruffled feathers – obviously, we were thinking of missionaries. They seem to respond well to them in their native habitat – forgetting that they're always entirely nude save for their little grass helmets, which again caused somewhat more controversy when the good ladies arrived. Good Heavens, what an outcry. Thank God I didn't confuse them with the Mbutu. Now that," he observed soberly, lighting a cigarette, "truly would have been *The End*. Frankly, Sea, the time you spend at this window, hiding away, I'm amazed you haven't spotted them."

"Shall we set up in the kitchen, Mr. Worthington?" his mother's butler interrupted. "Thank you, yes, Mr. Forbes. That would be perfect," he replied, and returning his attention to me he said: "Anyway, Sea, we're in a pickle, Peter and I, and that's why we need you. Thing is, they're eating him out of house and home and they're becoming so large they're in danger of being mistaken for bowling balls. The other day, they had a narrow escape, and Peter's quite beside himself. Also, they're constantly interfering with our supper club: Bit of a gourmand, Peter, delicate palate. In fact, he was just saying, 'Nothing says summer more to me than a barefoot pygmy holding aloft a platter of sweet sopressata and depositing it with artful decorum beside a freshly crumbled Roquefort from Occitania...' and who can argue with that, Sea?" Teddy asked, drawing somewhat shiftily on his cigarette, "He's grown quite attached to them, despite his complaints. I, on the other hand, have been starving to death, so would you mind if we hold our little supper club here, with you? Peter'll be along next week. He's agog at the prospect of meeting you. He's always asking when you'll be coming out to play...?" he concluded, dropping the cigarette to his feet, and stamping it out on the ground. "My," he shuddered, turning his face up to the sky and exhaling a plume of mist, "Bracing weather, isn't it? Can I come in now, Sea?"

"What are their names," I asked skeptically, as he proceeded to walk toward the door. "Their names, Sea?" he replied walking backward to the window, placing a hand to his ear as if he were hard of hearing, "Well," he considered momentarily, inhaling deeply, "there's Llewellyn – pronounced in the Welsh Th-le-weth-lyn fashion," he enunciated perfectly. "Not entirely trustworthy, it must be said, but you know how the Welsh can be. Then there's Roldofo, a passionate Latin, and finally, a very-giving Portuguese, Ermenegildo," he concluded matter-of-factly. "Teddy," I said, studying his meaningfully composed expression. "I don't believe you." "No, all true, Sea," Teddy assured me, smiling genially, "All true. And now, if you will permit, can I come in? Something will distinctly drop off if I stand here any longer." And the sudden twinkle in his eye made me forget every care and compelled me to forgive the inconstancy at the heart of the man who would become my most beloved friend: Teddy, the patron of The Leisure Hour and Supper Club, which he created that day, in my honor. "Would you mind if we stored some of the food here? As you're not eating..." he observed innocently, arriving in the parlor and settling down beside me on the rose-covered armchair, "it seems the safest place...Hmm?" he nodded, catching my eye in sympathy, as he raised my hand to his lips to kiss it.

The Leisure Hour and Supper Club: the story Teddy invented to make me eat. But he would never admit it, spinning out the fantasy for months to come, disappearing for weeks on end and then returning with sumptuous delicacies he claimed to have brought back from every corner of the world. A lie that I later learned caused his mother to cut off his allowance, as punishment for running up the most astronomical food bill she had ever received. In those days, most of the food was grown on the farmland attached to our houses. Teddy had been sending to Manhattan for hampers from Bergdorf's. "Nonsense, dearest Sea," he protested, when I confronted him. "I don't care whether you eat or not. But now that you mention it, are you sure I can't tempt you to a sliver of Brie? It's Peter's favorite...Oh look, there he is," he exclaimed. "Quick, Sea, quick, you'll miss him. No, too late," he commiserated, after I'd jumped out of bed to get to the window. "I'm off to Paris next week. What a shame you're still not well. I tell you what; I'll bring you back some Parisian macaroons from Ladurée in the Rue de Royale. Marie Antoinette's favorite, you know. And Peter, too, is often partial to a nibble on something dainty. Would you like that...? I'll only be gone a few days...."

From the beginning, there was never a promise he kept: an assurance to come in a few days would turn into weeks. Yet, he would brush his disappearance under the carpet when he did arrive, some wild story on his lips. "Whatever happened to you, Teddy? You look cooked through," I asked, when he appeared one afternoon in November, a victim of horrific sunburn, after going missing for two weeks. "If you don't mind, Sea, I prefer cured like a fine Italian meat. Well," he sighed stoically, "It was Roldolfo this time. Attached himself to Captain Lyon's leg and would not let go until Bermuda. Became besotted with a mermaid once he got there. And, well, that's a longer story involving a hastily arranged marriage and a fair amount of bitter disappointment. So that's where I've been, Sea. Have you missed me...? May I say how good it is to see you out of bed and what a lovely dress," he remarked, changing the subject and bowing down to kiss my hand. And I found myself replying, "I've you missed you terribly. Don't go away again." But he would and when he returned there was another story. As the months evolved, that sparkling moment when I first met Teddy and he invented The Leisure Hour and Supper Club withered into disappointment, to the point where I wasn't truly listening to him anymore. "Where have you been? You've been gone a month. You said a day or two," I'd insist. "Did I, Sea?

What a superb memory you have. I'm awfully pleased I have you to keep me right." But I offered no hand for him to kiss this time and so he tried harder, staying for longer, and going to greater lengths to appear sober. For even then Teddy drank, far too much. And in this way, I learned how to keep Teddy near, but only for a short time before he would need to be off, unable to keep up the pretense. Yet, I owed him my health; his fantasy had given me reason enough to forget to die.

'...*Tonight, on my way to you, I stopped at the gate, to remember why it was broken, and then I found myself thinking of the Chinese lanterns. When I came home from the War and you resurrected the supper club, Lyons away with the Navy. How you found the lanterns in your mother's old bedroom, one day, and announced, almost the way you used to be – so sad when you thought others weren't looking – "wouldn't these look exquisite hanging on the boughs of trees?" And, pulling out one of the blue and turquoise white concertinas to hold it up to the morning light, you said, "Teddy, my love, I think you deserve a homecoming...."*

Teddy, my love.

1917: Ten years after Kit, after your baby, after you were forced into that horrific marriage I like to pretend never happened. The new beginning of The Leisure Hour and Supper Club for the people left behind, or those returning home first, while braver men fought on. Men like me.

Wasn't much of a soldier, which didn't surprise you: "Predictable," you sniffed, when I came to see you, standing in the immense doorframe of La Doucette, perpetual cigarette lit – probably your 50th of the day, if I know anything about you... – But then two porcelain hands on either side of my face, a kiss on both my eyes and you said; "You're too beautiful to fight." And everything was fine again. I couldn't believe it – that second chance – but we would have another year...'

As I promised, I gave Teddy a homecoming. "I always keep my promises, Teddy," I teased him, "*unlike you....*" But then, on realizing how he would interpret it, I protested, "No, I didn't mean it like that. I'm so sorry. You couldn't possibly have done anything about it. It's not your fault. Don't hate me, Teddy, don't hate me...Still be my friend," I begged, pawing frantically at his hand, as if I was frightened he'd run away. Like he had done before? But let's not think of that... I took the lanterns to the village green in Westhampton, off Main Street, and strung them over the boughs of the blossom trees to welcome him home, to help him cope. His hair had turned completely white from shock and I sensed that if I didn't do something, Teddy would immediately fall into his usual bad habits – the drinking and gambling I had never once acknowledged to him. So, I had the staff bring the dining room table from La Doucette, all of the Irish linens in the house, every candle stick we owned, and –

'...I never forgot this because it was so important to you, blue Spode China in the Willow pattern. And pausing to think, a finger to your lips and one hand on your hip in your dining room on a Tuesday morning, me at the head of the table, watching, you said, "we must have the Stieff Rose silver, not the Gorham, that's crucial, and...." – and here you lit up in excitement on arriving at another grand idea – "let's just have tealights everywhere, to light the road down to the park! What do you think, Teddy? Tell me you adore it. It's all for you, after all...?"'

They were the only parties that were ever truly mine. I resurrected The Leisure Hour and Supper Club to give Teddy somewhere he would be welcomed just when he feared being excluded. It was the happiest year of my life. I was constantly at Teddy's estate where we'd take tea in the cottage, while he recuperated from his injuries. Those injuries he would not discuss and I pretended did not exist, just like old times. And every month, boxes of books from all over the world arrived at La Doucette. The books I ordered to make up for the years I had spent trying to please my father and not learning a thing about anything else. I would stand in the courtyard and sift through them, with all of the doors and windows flung open throughout the house, bathing The Emperor in sunlight and inviting the perfume of flowers in, as if the house and the garden were one and the same thing. It was the most freedom I had ever known.

It was unheard of, but I invited everyone; using the War as an excuse to collapse the hierarchy we were imprisoned within before it: Helen Fitzgerald, May Cook, Sara Wiborg, the vicar, the butcher, Beulah the bartender at The Westhampton Bath and Tennis Club, who I adored because he sang spirituals from the South to me whenever I was taken there: "Come, come to dinner for Teddy," I begged, rushing around town, like a child who had been told I could have whomever I wanted to my party. Yet, Beulah would not sit at the table, despite how I pleaded with him: "No Ma'am. There are places I belong and places I don't, but I will happily serve you, Ms. Serena." I did not insist. It would only have insulted him to do so, but he taught me a lesson I've never forgotten; we can belong and not belong in exactly the same space, it is all just a choice. So I created an environment where my guests could be free: where we could present ourselves in any fashion we liked and nobody would judge us for it.

'...*Word got out. Quickly. Serena's party, a new club – The Leisure Hour and Supper Club – Friday evening, starts at 7pm, on the village green in Westhampton. There'll be an orchestra...* "An orchestra," *exclaimed May Cook, taking tea with me in Georgica,* "My, that girl. She thinks of such stupendous things. I shall most definitely be in attendance. We must honor your contribution, Teddy, as well as those other brave soldiers who are still fight-ing,*" *she insisted, sipping her tea and looking benignly away to the sea beyond the privets. Her son was never to have a homecoming, although you would always set places for those who died. By the end of that summer, there were five tables of their names. We sat shoulder to shoulder with the dead.* "I will sit beside Patrick," *May would announce, heaving her not insubstantial frame into a chair beside his empty place, as if it was the most natural thing in the world. But that was later. The first party was for me.*

We settled down to dinner that Friday. "Isn't it enchanting, Teddy?" *you trilled in your white muslin dress, ghostly white against the night, twenty-seven but could have passed for nineteen, fine-boned and pale like a moth with your enormous eyes, the bluest blue, after I had walked up the road to La Doucette to collect you. That was the beginning of it, our tradition of that year:*

"Meet me on the road that leads to the sea. And I'll wait for you and you'll wait for me...."

My favorite memory, did I ever tell you that? No, I wouldn't have. Far more than the garden gate, actually. Meeting you on that road, the way you speak, Sea, like a song, this is what I loved: half-light, sea-air, being young with you. That gray light, Sea, you know what I mean. Only those of us who have been a part of this landscape understand it: nothing like it, anywhere else. We were lucky people then, Sea, your arm in mine, our walks toward the park through the tealights. All men should be as lucky, coming home from wars.

There were blossoms and an orchestra playing Mozart and Chinese lanterns and a ghostly glow cast by the candles you lit everywhere in this perfectly themed world of your creation: "All for you, Teddy." And I believed you; I took my seat at the head of the table. It seemed so right for me to sit there, where I was always supposed to have been, watching you. And if I fixed my attention on you, dearest Sea, I didn't need to think of wars; the way a bomb explodes on another man in front of you, the one you let run ahead.... It was almost the way it was before Kit; everything where it should be, time settling scores. As if none of it had happened – bad memories. Those you need other people to paint pictures over, to forget what came after.

Funny, I thought, how things work out, as you stood up to toast me. After the bad decisions, the surviving we both did of our different wars, it was as if we'd never parted. I hadn't loitered at that garden gate that night, Sea; I'd rushed straight through. To get to you...'

All those Friday evenings of spring and summer in 1917, I waited for Teddy on the road that leads to the sea. In the gathering coastal mist, I would close my eyes on hearing his footsteps and imagine he was Kit coming back for me, somehow. Just for a moment, I would pretend that somewhere far away Kit had heard I was free, so I could finally say to him: "Look, my love, I can go anywhere, do anything now. Forgive me...." It was all part of the fantasy, the masquerade, inherent within The Westhampton Leisure Hour and Supper Club: We were all pretending to be something other than who we truly were, as if nothing had ever changed. But it was always Teddy who appeared at my side, although he was not the same as I remembered and nor was I. So I would paste another face over his and he would paste one over mine; the face of that girl he believed loved him before Kit. The girl he saved from dying, before he suffered the bitter disappointment liars wreak on those who trust them. And I would envisage the Teddy of that year too, the kind but degenerate young man who drank and gambled and smoked too much.

The Teddy who found a purpose in helping someone as much of an outcast from society as he, who in turn helped him to believe he was a hero. Not the damagingly inconstant Teddy who broke his promise on a later evening in a Port Jefferson hospital; who did not marry me, when he couldn't find Kit, or let me live in the cottage on Halsey Road, with a little boy dressed in blue. *It was too late, Sea, by the time I got back to the hospital; Lyons had already taken you.* "Yes, but Teddy, why weren't you early? What made you late?" The questions I never asked him, to avoid the devastation the answers would bring.

We were two little tricksters; gliding off, arm in arm, to a twilit daydream that provided us both with a reason to live, despite the awful hidden things between us. But this is what disappointed people will do for one another: those of us who are left behind to deal with the little things, after the grander dreams have died. We pick and choose whom we will forgive, or whom we will blame, only to make it easy for ourselves. Yet, underlying every exchange is the certainty that the friend on our arm will not catch us, should we fall. We know it is all artifice; a pretend life created for pretend people too damaged to try any harder, or too frightened because of the history that exists to dare. And sometimes the masks slip and we see the truth.

Meet me on the road that leads to the sea and I'll wait for you and you'll wait for me.... It was a borrowed line, something Kit had said to me when we were children, the day I found the Chinese lanterns in a box in my mother's bedroom. My father had brought them back for her from Peking, shortly before Catherine died. We strung those lanterns over the trees of The Lilac Walk that night and picnicked outside, all of us together; mother, father, Catherine, Kit... And the parties of 1917 were inspired not by Teddy but by memories of Kit and the summer we shared: the memory of a day in late August, his arm in mine, as we walked under the elms. I remember the shadow on the white linen of his suit cast by my parasol, when he said, "After we marry, Serena, you'll always give parties, so that I can watch you in them." And all I heard was the exhilarating ascension of '*after we marry*;' a statement that only augured more, the more I could barely imagine, the more I was going to receive... "No, you can't watch," I chastised him. "You have to be the Host, remember: A Hostess is nothing without a Host. I know!

We'll do it together. We'll have tealight votives." "Because I first kissed you amidst the tealights…" he interrupted. "Because you first kissed me…yes," I replied, with a smile, "but I will choose the decoration; lace tablecloths, Stieff silver and all of them will be outside on a Friday in summer, wherever we might live…." Beneath my eyelashes, I caught a glimpse of the soft waves of his fair hair, and in the gentle nod he gave me, a hint of delight that I held the same view of our future, as he did. "Yes," he agreed, "and I think we must live by the sea, because we met each other by the sea." These were the promises that passed between us, as his arm slipped from mine to take my hand, to raise it to his cheek and hold it there, because there were tomorrows for us then…. "And we will live in a little cottage with Palladian windows and an arbor over the gate, and a shed with a beekeeper's turret at the back, with hundreds of books for you, and a rose-patterned rug…" I continued. "You seem like you know this place," he replied, intrigued. "It is real," I assured him, "I can take you there, tomorrow." "Then, tomorrow we will go and see it," he said, inclining his head to smile at me. "Yes," I replied, safe in his assurance that we would. "Tomorrow, we will."

I was as guilty as Teddy: I stole his dream of me, by replacing him with Kit. And my parties of 1917 offered nothing more than an excuse to live in the past. It was the old faces beneath the new masks that we lived to catch sight of: Teddy looking for who I was before I left him; me for my old friend, for Kit; May Cook wishing for her dead son; Venetia Dryden chatting to wounded soldiers, every one of them Anthony Duverglas in her heart. Those parties allowed us to live within the worlds of our imaginations without retribution, albeit with empty chairs, or new actors in the places of those who would never return. They granted us the freedom to remember how good we once were; the lives we had longed for trailing behind in our wake, like shadows cast by the disappointment of all we did not become. Every time we arrived, we could forget the truth for a time.

'…Your toast to me: "In honor of Teddy's homecoming and how beautifully this garden blooms – don't you love the daffodils," you asked gaily, but I saw something then, reflected off the crystal on the table. Only a glance, but I recognized it from before, and I felt a creeping sense of dread, at what might *follow.* "*It makes me think of a poem by Mr. Wordsworth, about spring and meadows and splendor in the grass like we are enjoying here tonight. I should like to recite it for Teddy and for all those other fearless soldiers who fight on, who we may never see again. Those sons born to bless the earth over which they run in our defense, who we long to cradle still in our arms, but who are torn from them by the savagery and weakness of others; and for whom we will never stop waiting; and for whom there will always be places set at this table...*" *A deep breath then, as if to steady yourself and stop the tears I knew had pooled in the depths of your eyes, as you started to recite the poem:*

> *What though the radiance which was once so bright*
> *Be now forever taken from my sight,*
> *Though nothing can bring back the hour*
> *Of splendour in the grass, of glory in the flower;*
> *We will grieve not, rather find*
> *Strength in what remains behind*

And then you looked at me...'

And then I looked at Teddy and raised my glass in a silent toast that only he and I could hear: *Yes, this is what it feels like, Teddy: to expect something, to hinge everything on it, and then to have it taken from you. Haven't we both been punished now?* Yet, the regret set in as soon as the words left my mouth. I crucified myself for being so cruel when Teddy's mask momentarily slipped and I saw him as he really was.

'*...It was just an idyll, our little club, Sea, wasn't it? Where we could disappear and in each other find a receptive heart, a welcoming ear. Two broken people — you by the actions of others, me by bad genes, I think: an inability to focus on the task at hand, a tendency toward flight. Yet, as I realized that evening, sooner or later, truth filters into fantasy. The longer we knew one another, the more we were disappointed and what started as a place to hide became a prison because I was trapped there in a lie with you: everything I never told you. That I was as responsible for what had happened to you and your son as that demon you married. Yet, somehow, you could* *forgive me in a way you never could him. Maybe because I was weak and weak people don't act because they have no courage whereas ruthless people do: Or maybe, because you pitied me. But something changed. As soon as you finished that speech, you burst into tears and came and sat beside me, and, as ever, I was forgiven. Just as I'm sure you might try to forgive me now for what I am about to tell you. But I can't have you do that.*

I'm not coming for you, Sea. I expect you've guessed this already...'

THE HOST

It had started, his fear, at the start of this season, when she announced, "This summer, my house has become enchanted again." Enchanted because of the lilacs blooming on the trees and not dying, as if in reverence to the memories they had bestowed upon her, the like of which she had never experienced since: It was one of the few occasions she had spoken directly to him in recent years. Captain Lyons had grown accustomed to receiving nothing more than a passive acknowledgment of his presence. Sometimes, she might look at him, in her sad and contemplative fashion, when she replied to a question. Yet, the answers were spoken so softly he had to strain to hear them, as if the sound in Serena had been diminished, almost to a whisper, by the weight of the grief that bore down on her.

Yet, something in Serena finally enabled her to consider him as someone other than a monster. Thirty summers as man and wife, he thinks, turning the handle to her room, and yet, only this last, did we appear to share ourselves with one another, instead of experiencing it from our separate corners. Had I been a younger man, might I have thrown this late concession back at her? Is it because I am old and fearful of loneliness that I grasped onto her slight regard with a conviction I have felt for nothing else, not even the affection of my children? Or is it simply because I sensed she was leaving me, as I always suspected she would, that I wanted to savor these last things between us. I would like to think on these past months as the summer she forgave me, but my punishment is only to be scrupulously honest with myself. This was not the summer she forgave me. It was our summer of last things.

She would allow him to sit with her, on the lawn, where he would join her every afternoon. Often she was quiet, somnolent, as if drunk on the pleasures of the season. He almost felt as if he was the last guest left at the party:

someone to whom she felt indebted, entirely aware that he had been over-looked in favor of more insistent, or else, more intriguing guests. Yet, her ineffable dignity meant she could not ignore him, almost as if she harbored a bemused admiration toward him for hanging on to the very end.

For the first time since she was a child, he found himself the recipient of her charm. The interests she would draw out, the sing-song way she spoke, the rise and fall of her lilting voice, like a chiming clock that did not augur hurry but leisure; *Stay,* it soothed arrestingly, *sit with me. There is so much time, and it is yours for as long as you need it...* He learned that Serena's gift was only to listen; she would take him so far down a path, segueing in and out of thoughts until something struck a chord. Then she would fall silent, a pleasant smile on her face, her attention engaged somewhere beyond, nodding, on occasion, to show that she was still listening, like a swan bowing its head to the water.

He told her of the places he had visited, places he had never taken her, because, after their honeymoon, she would never travel. Together, they circumnavigated the globe and, along the way, there were insights she elicited, aspects of a husband of which any wife should be aware, but she was not; his favorite food, *gambas a la plancha* – "I'm not sure I want to know what that is..." she had teased; how mesmerized he had been by the way the sun set in Japan, exactly as he had once read it described in a book – "Extraordinary," she had agreed; the comedy that had ensued on bumping unexpectedly into May Cook in Firenze – "Now, I like May," she had chastised; how one of his favorite afternoons was spent riding a bike in Formentor, a Balearic island – "A bike!" she had exclaimed, "Goodness..."— how free he had felt, barely twenty-two; how he had almost pitched a tent on that Moorish island, of white beaches and clear seas, and stayed there forever. "Yes, how wonderful it must be to know such freedom..." she had replied. And not even Captain Lyons, so foolishly, so pitifully grateful for her time, could fail to detect the discordant note of despair that cruelly sounded between them.

There it would be, the shadow that perpetually loitered at their backs; those conversational corners, around which he would have preferred never to venture; a mention of the silk slippers he had found in Mandalay –"Yes," she said, "I owned a pair before that. I wore them for my debut..."; a favored poem, by John Donne, which she placed a hand on his to stop him from reciting, the first time she had touched him in years, "Thank you, but I have my own poems…"; or the sudden excitement that might seize him if their conversation grew more relaxed, "I remember when your father…" and the words were out before he could stop them, and all she said was, "Yes," but there was no mistaking the chime in her voice that augured an ending, whenever reminded, however unintentionally by him, of what she had suffered at her father's hands, at his. Yet, it was unavoidable. There was no escaping the facts of their marriage.

Even so, in the beginning, he blithely savored his good fortune, that Serena had accepted him at her side, however briefly. He deliberately ignored the platitudinous ring to every comment she made. He even inched toward a ludicrously tempting fancy; simply that something had enabled her to understand there was no other option available to him, in the past. But as the weeks progressed, it became impossible to avoid the signs: of the harm he had caused to a woman he had once professed to love, yet had only destroyed. He was distracted, however, from acting on his concerns, when she suddenly asked, one afternoon, a question so touching, he deliberately went blind to the truth of what he witnessed daily in her: "Would you read to me from the Book of Souls," she asked, referring to those logs of lost sailors that he kept in the study. "I'd like to hear about the 'Five Things,'" she said.

Each day Captain Lyons would bring a new log – As, Bs, Cs, and so forth. And he would read aloud the fragments of those men's souls that he had compiled, as Serena watched the lilacs in the Walk, where she had once danced as a girl:

'The sound of the sea after a storm…When I won the prize for the best kite when I was six…Flatlands…A rain of blossoms in Rome…A place where there is no sea that would take me away from home…Paella…Hawthorn's Bend…Football on the beach in Egypt, that afternoon with Bill and Mike… The first time I took her to the races…Dendrobiums…Salinas in the late afternoon, the pine needles beneath my feet, the cool of shaded sand when you walk on it…Stewart…'

"How old was he?" she would ask, each time he finished reading an entry, and Captain Lyons would dutifully tell her the names, the ages, the dates of birth of every man, the years he had lived, the year he had died. Serena would listen, enthralled by the poetry within those pages, a sad smile on her lips, nodding in recognition of the happiest memories of those men who had died at sea. Yet, he noted that it was always the singular names that appeared to touch her most; *Alexandra; Ruth; Linda; Barbara; Alice; Winifred; Hilda; Susan; Juliet; Jennifer; Emma; Kirstie; Katie; Romy; Adele.* "Oh, how beautiful," she would remark, "to be part of someone's soul. Those women must have taken such consolation from this, despite their sorrow." "Yes," he would reply, "I hope." And then, one afternoon, after he had finished reading the Five Things of James Hume, who had drowned at seventeen – '*Music... Dancing with my sister at the Pally on a Saturday night...The smell of the dockyards...Warm stones Mum gave me to put in my pocket on a winter's day to keep my hands warm...When I see Dad at the table through the front window, knowing he's back safe from sea....*' – Serena reached across to where the book lay open on his lap, and closed it. "That's enough now, I think, Edward. Thank you," and she gathered up her few belongings, and the small vase of sweet peas The Little Maid would ritually place on her tea tray, and walked slowly back to the house. He watched her go, little realizing that it would be the last time he would ever watch her walk across the lawn; the last time he would ever wince in pain at how beautiful she had been and would always remain whenever he thought of her; the last time he heard the song in her voice when she would remark, "Lilacs, so late. How lucky I am to see this after all these years..."

So many times he almost told her, as he witnessed everything she did not become, how mercilessly time ravaged her: no amount of make-up could conceal how difficult her life had been, however charmed. He accepted the opprobrium of her peers, without rancor. He had indeed ruined her, in his fashion, but had Kit not got there first, he would argue with himself. Yet, he knew it meant so little now. All that was of any significance was the act he had instigated, what he had refused: a choice which led to him sitting, a stranger at her side, on a deck chair in her father's garden, where he had imposed himself as Master. Where he sat beside her, watching flowers that did not exist, reading aloud from a book of souls, the best moments of the lives of others.

The lilacs were not in bloom, as Serena told anyone who would listen. They never flowered again after he sheared them of their branches. It was nothing more than a hallucination conjured up by her heartbroken mind. Perhaps, Captain Lyons told himself, this is what happens to those who live in the past. They begin to imagine only what they once loved in the bleak course of any given day, in order to survive it. He thought it was doubtless more appealing than the reality of what Serena faced each week, how she was almost invisible at her parties, despite how hard she still tried to rise to the occasion. Until one evening, about a month and a half ago, when she stood up from a table at which she was seated, surrounded by people she had never met and who clearly did not care to know her, and ascended the staircase to her room, where she remained until the next morning.

Captain Lyons followed her, concerned as ever, noting the too-familiar signs of her illness. She had left the door ajar, careless now with her secrets of what she did in there. She stood at her window, in one of her pale pink dresses, frozen like a statue, her gaze fixed on a point outside; waiting, he knew, for the guests who, in thirty years, had never arrived.

It is this image that he will keep of his wife; her back to him, hair bobbed according to the fashion, the haunting nobility of her stature, as if she had triumphed over untold humiliations and would hold her head up until the end, despite the fact that she was merely a lost girl at her window, confined to her nursery, just as Kit was a lost boy beyond hers. He thinks it curiously appropriate for her to leave him only with this. He wants to believe that she found an incomparable solace in her retreat, for nothing was asked or expected of her while she stood there. This past summer, he has convinced himself, the life she has led has finally been one of her choosing.

But it is only now that he thinks this. Last Friday, Captain Lyons thought differently: After Serena told him she was leaving and closed the red front door on him, in an attempt to separate them forever. For it was then that those fondly recalled summer afternoons he had spent with his beloved, if unknowable, wife, which had glistened with the unbiddable promise of more to come, segued momentarily into something other, something so dangerous.

No, he thought last Friday, what they had shared were not exchanges forged by affection or even fatigue, a recognition of their years together, but an appeasing game; a trick, a lull in the recriminations to offer false hope, that Serena understood – because of what she had been doing with Teddy – would leave him alone, without her. As terrible as that awareness was, even that was more tolerable than what he was also forced to face up to: the letter from Teddy, delivered in the middle of the party, telling Serena about Kit. Captain Lyons could not know the extent of what Serena had learned, or how Teddy could even have found out what he had done. Regardless, whatever Teddy had said, had turned Serena irrevocably against him.

Through the window that framed the entrance, he studied her broken figure in the distance: his wife, standing again in full view of every person they had ever met, waiting for someone she had never forgotten to take her away from him. *There's no hope,* he wanted to cry, *none. If you had seen what I had, you would have done the same thing. It was impossible for me to bring him back here.* He almost went to her, to spare her the disappointment she would surely suffer when everything became clear. But then. But then....

He could stand it no longer. When he saw that apparition from the past appear, Captain Lyons knew it had to end, once and for all. Kit could not claim anymore of Serena. It would have been too cruel, considering. And so he reached for the gun.

...

There is no time left for us. It has all come down to this, he accepts, pushing the door to Serena's bedroom open. I cannot tell her any more lies.

Just as he cannot tell the guests how very wrong they are. The worst of the weather is not over. What is happening now is not a second chance at a clear sky, but a false reprieve; like the forgiveness of a woman who offers it only so that her husband will turn a blind eye to her duplicity, who closes doors on him with a smirk as she plays with other men. This storm has turned the key to lock us in, he acknowledges, looking out to the guests as he pushes the door closed. This, now, what is happening: It is not a lull. It is the eye.

She has become a hurricane.

THE HOSTESS

I convinced Teddy to run away with me, by stirring up all the old memories. "What's keeping us here?" I beseeched him. "Haven't we all made mistakes; perhaps we can salvage something from what's left for us. Couldn't we go to these places we've imagined and actually live in them, instead of just thinking about it...?" I knew how easily he would tumble into the dream of escape because he needed the money that I would bring with me. The money I would garner from the sale of this star-shaped diamond pendant I am wearing tonight. It isn't the one made of paste that my husband gave me, but the copy Douglas Dryden had made for Venetia, to outclass mine. The necklace Venetia gave to me, after I confided my plans: "Follow your dreams, Serena," she told me, placing it around my neck. "Don't keep them for the end."

I never believed Teddy would actually go through with it: I simply needed him to make arrangements, to buy tickets, to make every choice for me. It's like I told you earlier; I can't act – I don't, so that I will never make a mistake. And I can spin such beguiling stories. I can be whoever you want to be. I can play into the fantasy of what rescuing someone would inspire in a man who could barely dare to place his foot outside his door, except to gamble what meager allowance he had. I knew that I could count on Teddy to take me far enough away, before he would inevitably turn and flee from the reality. My inconstant, Teddy, who ran and hid when times were hard, who projected onto me the dreams he would never realize. Yet, he needed them in order to carry on and it was so little to give. Do not ever think that I did not love Teddy. We were a pair, he and I. I loved him to the depths of my soul for everything he was, everything he couldn't be. And he loved me for pretending not to see.

But aren't you wondering why? Why, at this late age, did I make a break for freedom? *It is the knowing, so often, that kills us....* Do you recall that parting gift from my father? But he was wrong: the truth did not kill me, the reason why I could finally leave La Doucette. You see, I found something that I thought was lost forever. It was in the garden, at the start of June...

I sat on the lawn in a chair I was given by a British acquaintance, a million parties earlier —"Thank you very much for the invitation," he said genially on the night we first met, and I felt myself involuntarily melt on hearing his accent: He reminded me of Kit, naturally. Although he was portly and bald, he displayed the same poised and considerate attention: unwavering, genuine and kind all at the same time. Unexpectedly, from behind his back, as if he was a magician presenting a fake bouquet of flowers, he produced what looked like two pieces of wood, with blue and white striped fabric folded haphazardly in-between. It will all be creased, whatever it is, I thought, as I affected surprise. "I understand your mother was British, Mrs. Lyons. I thought this might be appropriate," he explained, offering me his gift. "My wife used to adore sitting on Margate Sands, on something like this. I don't believe you have them here...."

I barely had time to thank him because Lucinda collapsed drunk in the hallway and I had to hurry over so that her husband did not drag her into another room and... well, those things we can't conceive of that other people suffer. We hadn't spoken in years. I could never bear to look at Lucinda, averting my gaze as soon as she would appear, more beaten than the last occasion I had seen her. Yet, our faces were inches from one another as I crouched down to help her, we two supposed former rivals, the unresolved mystery of the handbag still hanging over us.

Who won here, I asked myself, as I struggled to pull down her skirt and get her to her feet, everyone watching in disgust. *Oh, but it could happen to you,* I wanted to scream at their aghast faces, frozen into impeccably made-up portraits of appropriately scandalized horror; *you have no idea how quickly....* What a scene it was in the midst of the elegance; two older ladies destroyed by disappointment, clinging to a remnant of the past in order to get through the hours: Lucinda to a handbag and me to a party. Who was I to suggest Kit hadn't sent it to her, I realized, what if he had? What possible difference would his compassion for a neglected young girl, forced to cancel her party so that I could have mine, have made to his love for me? "Sheee, sheee, Shareena," she slurred, clinging to my arms. "I did... after...shee." But I couldn't understand a word she said and I almost gave up helping her because she kept trying to force me to take the handbag.

It was in perfect condition, unlike us; it spoke of all we could have been, all we were not. What might have become of her, I thought, had she never received it? Had I not turned my back on her, might Lucinda have been my friend, after all? Would her brown hair have curled prettily, instead of hanging dull and unkempt, pinned off to the side with a hair grip, her face a mess of burst blood vessels, and badly healed broken bones? Could she have married James Bentley, who was too shy to say he liked her, instead of her brutish husband who tricked everyone into believing he was the prize: This was the real reason why I couldn't bear to look at Lucinda. For, in a way, every blow she had ever suffered was my fault.

I couldn't get her up. So, I fell with her, down onto the floor. *This will be over soon....* I said to myself, watching Teddy hurriedly leave the bar to come and help us. *This will be over soon...* But then Lucinda said something I shall never forget. Over the many parties in this house, I have been privileged to hear kind words said about me, amidst the sporadic outbursts of spite, and I have been grateful for each and every one. But the most poignant words I ever heard was that evening on the floor with Lucinda, when she suddenly said, as clear as day, "There, there," she soothed, moving her hand onto mine. "There, there..."

Teddy thought I wept because of the memory she inspired, but I wept for her pity. She was the only person who had ever consoled me, despite what my actions had cost her. I realized then that I had always envied Lucinda, first because Kit might have loved her, but ultimately because Lucinda was free. Her escape was her drunkenness, her courage not to care, to disappear somewhere others could not reach into, where all that mattered was what she chose to remember. I did not have the strength for that fate. My actions had condemned me to a perpetually wakeful state, wide-eyed and searching; terrified a clue might flit past me in the crowd. Yet, too much time had gone by to offer Lucinda anything more than what I did: I had her husband beaten to within an inch of his life. I'd like to think that he has never touched her since: I made sure those men, who pulled him over at the side of the road, were frequently at my parties. But with the vicious, and the angry, there is no guarantee. After that evening, Lucinda and I never spoke again, although I did try. Her drunkenness exacerbated to the point where she was unintelligible. The only person who would sit with her was Teddy: But then Teddy was always so good that way.

It seemed Lucinda was destined to always come in-between some charming British gentleman and me. After I was distracted by her, we drifted apart and I learned nothing more about him; nothing of sandy beaches, or who he might have known, schools he might have attended – *"A pleasure to meet you, Sir. Yes, I'm visiting from Berkshire. It seems funny to be here, at long last. Many years ago, I had a friend at Eton. Poor chap would tell me stories about...."* The things you miss, happening in farther corners of farther rooms....

Yet, guests, who make an impression, often return to haunt hostesses. Some time later, I heard a line from a poem by T.S. Eliot, *'On Margate Sands, I can connect....'* A posturing academic was luxuriating in the sound of his own voice as he decried its genius, but all I could think of was that British gentleman, and I had one of the maids find the deckchair. I have used it ever since. It is my summer chair, which is always placed on the grass in front of The Lilac Walk. I have no idea where Margate Sands is – unusually, I didn't bother to look it up – but the sentimentality of his gesture moved me. He was a man so in love with his wife that he could not even offer a present to an unknown hostess, without including her ghost. I honor that in others. I suppose because I have devoted my own life to memory. I could never sit in that chair without thinking how lucky he was to have loved her so well.

In the garden, I wore a summer picture hat and one of my old white muslin dresses, for comfort. From that easy chair, I drank in the miracles of nature surrounding me, arriving at conclusions in the clarity of the sunlight that seemed to shine on the habitual planes and corners of my universe. I learned that I was my mother's daughter, after all. It was true that I had inherited her instability, the debilitating sadness that I controlled by filling my minutes with occupation. Yet, I had also inherited her love for the flowers. Nothing compared to my admiration for them as they fought to live; returning year on year, as resplendent and proud as ever, perpetually suspended in their prime.

"Wouldn't it be lovely to be a flower, Elizabeth," I said, as she arrived to collect my tea tray that I always requested be set with the Willow pattern Spode; a nod to that year I was free. "Wouldn't you like that; to bloom every year, sometimes more beautifully than the last?"

Elizabeth picked up the tray and turned to consider the roses and the rhododendrons, the fuchsia; "Your garden is the nicest I've seen, Mrs. Lyons," she said, politely. Since she arrived, Elizabeth had refused to join in with the games of the other maids, instead slipping unobtrusively in and out of rooms where I sat; never giggling or too-forcefully closing doors behind her so that the curtains around the open windows would snap and billow, shattering the peace, or letting tin cans full of cleaning fluid suddenly clatter to the floor. The rest of my staff display the inherent lack of respect so many do when they find themselves in control of someone they should answer to, but do not: They are surly and resentful, having believed the stories they were told about me, regardless of whether they were true. Yet, from the beginning, Elizabeth was different.

"Have you ever seen lilacs this late, Elizabeth? They should be dead by now. It's June. Did you have a garden at your house, growing up?"

She had taken a few steps to leave and seemed surprised by my detaining her. I almost thought she felt sorry for me. There was something in her expression – empathy, I think – that caused her to hesitate before answering: "No, Mrs. Lyons, not this late. I think they must be blooming for you. Maybe..." Elizabeth glanced anxiously up at the house behind me before continuing, "maybe, because you love them so much, Mrs. Lyons. I don't think I've ever seen anyone love a garden more."

I have loved a garden. I have loved a view from a window. I have loved a memory. I have loved possibility, but my arms have remained empty....

"Tell me, Elizabeth, what do you love?" I asked. "I'd like to know more about you."

"What do I love, Mrs. Lyons?" she repeated, clearly flattered by my interest, "Oh, yes, I do. I do love, Mrs. Lyons."

"What then?" I pressed, reaching for her slender arm and forcing her to lay the tray back down on the table so that she could crouch beside me.

"I love it here, Mrs. Lyons, with you. I love your house," she enthused shyly. "I love to look at the trays of your jewelry and imagine you wearing them; the ornaments and figurines, and carpets. It's real nice here. Because of the way you've made it."

"How lovely of you to s—" I said, but we were distracted by a cabbage butterfly that suddenly landed on the breast of my dress.

"Look, Mrs. Lyons," she whispered in excitement, "I love these butter-flies, their white wings. They're summer butterflies. Do you know what it means when they land on you?"

It's the soul of a dead child, I know, Helen Fitzgerald told me this, once.

"It's supposed to be the soul of a dead child, Mrs. Lyons. Look he chose you," she said softly.

"Or she." I added, thinking of Susannah. I remembered Helen carrying her everywhere: I would walk out to meet them in the driveway and there Helen would be, the baby on her hip; "Look, who I've brought to see her godmother!" Helen would exclaim, her rosy cheeks and joyous mood making her seem somehow young again. "Let me kiss you everywhere!" she'd cry, smothering Susannah with kisses as she lay in her Moses basket, as the three of us sat outside in the garden. Helen was always so concerned about whether she had done the right thing in asking me to be Susannah's godmother. "I wasn't sure," she would say, furrowing her brow, "but I can't think of anyone more perfect. If anything were to happen to me...She is so –" "Special," I'd agree, "a gift. Yes, you were right to ask me. You have no idea..." I almost told her the truth about my own baby, once or twice; her expression seemed to invite confidences, but I couldn't. I simply adored her child instead.

"I loved my brother, the one I told you about," Elizabeth continued, distracting me from my thoughts. She was sitting at my side, but facing the house and gazing up at it, almost in defiance. "The one who loved to read, who went to sea. He was much older than me, but Ma – my mother," she hastily corrected herself, her face coloring at her faux pas, "My *mother*, used to tell me stories about him. I guess that's what you do with last-borns, like me," she laughed nervously, "entertain 'em – *them* – with stories of brothers and sisters because the hand-me-down toys are ruined from years of wear and tear, so there's nothing to play with." I winced privately as she tried to joke about how little she owned, clearly embarrassed for me to learn of it. I smiled at her to go on.

Since Elizabeth arrived some months earlier, we had shared similar one-sided conversations. Curiously, I often found myself worrying over how the other staff members might treat her. When I learned her mother had died, I told myself this was the reason for my protectiveness. Yet, it was also because when I asked her why she had wanted to come to La Doucette, she simply replied, "Since I was real small, I wanted to work here. I always heard about the parties at the orphanage. I had to see it for myself. I wouldn't have got here any other way. And," she added, her eyes sparkling, "I heard Rupert Turner-Hume comes here. Is that really true? He's my favorite. I seen every film of his, at least three times. I got every magazine, too, with his picture in…I'd surely faint if I ever met him. Does he really come, Mrs. Lyons…?"

It was the fancy of a simple girl, placed immediately out of her grasp because of the town and the house where she was born. Elizabeth would never be invited, despite the reach of my parties, but she accepted this without rancor. Nothing about her – her hair, her vaguely hunched posture when confronted by a society that would forever belittle her, her slight features that would grow more pinched and worn by work, not pleasure – belied her working-class origins. Dressed in ermine and diamonds, she would always be a Little Maid, albeit one gussied up for the evening. I admired her, for her courage to dream only so far: It would be a nice memory to tell her children about, one day – how she worked for Mrs. Lyons at La Doucette. But this was before the young heir and the expansion of her modest ambition to encompass something unattainable. Before whatever he said – that empty lie – prompted her to ask, "Why not me? It happens to other people. I read about it once in a magazine…."

"You like sweet peas, Mrs. Lyons," she said, but there was something pointed in her expression as she looked at me. "That's like my brother, see. When he was small, my *mother*," she enunciated, proud now of not making the same mistake twice, "told me that my brother fell asleep next to a jar of sweet peas on the kitchen table: He loved the smell of them, see. He was only four. He'd climb up – he wasn't s'posed to – and lay his head on the table to look at the colors; he liked the pictures the light made through the petals. Seeing you here, how you always ask for the sweet peas in the jar on the tray, it reminds me of him. He's like you, in a way."

"How old is your brother?" I asked.

She squinted against the sun, and I saw her fasten her grip tighter on the edge of the table at my side to steady herself, "He would have been thirty, if…"

No, how sad, I thought. It's too blissful a day to contemplate the 'ifs' of the world. How cruel a word it truly is, denying things as is its wont, even while it offers the possibility that it will not; I can love you, *if*…. I will come for you in Port Jefferson, *if*…I will find your son, *if*…. Even before Elizabeth completed the sentence, I felt for her indescribably. She often spoke of her brother. Yet, I had not even guessed at the truth; he was so alive to her.

"He was lost at sea. He was in the Navy," she said, sadly.

"He was much older than you, Elizabeth?" I asked, careful not to push her into saying more than she could. "It's funny, I know everything about him," she replied. "But I don't remember him. He was lost at seventeen, his first trip out, somewhere off the coast of New England. There was a bad storm and the boat was wrecked and not a soul was found. I was only little, when it happened, so I don't go– *have* any memories, to speak of. Those I do are what my mother told me, and that other lady who'd visit, sometimes. All they'd do is talk about him. How he loved the sea, Mrs. Lyons. Gosh, I can't even begin to tell you how much. Ma always said he'd be a sailor. The only toy he ever played with when he was small was a boat, a wooden boat. He'd had it since he was born. It was real special. It had been made in Eastport and it had tiny sa –"

"Goodness," I said, in surprise, "Yes, they make them in Eastport, Elizabeth! Handcrafted wooden boats, with tiny sails and with the name of the child written on the side; I used to give them as gifts to all the babies out here. What a coincidence that he had one too. I know so many children who loved them…" I continued; my eyes fixed on the lilacs. I thought of poor Helen. *"Susannah! Susannah!"* she would cry in ecstasy, every time her little girl woke from sleeping.

"Yeah, the same thing," she cried, clearly thrilled that we had something in common. Precious child, I thought. But then, all in a rush, there was more...

"His was called Christopher, but my mother called him Kit. It's a nickname. I never knew that. British, she said...." But she was interrupted from finishing what she had to say by Edward suddenly calling for her from his study. "I got to get back," she said apologetically, but she paused before leaving, "Look, Mrs. Lyons he hasn't moved," she observed of the butterfly. "Do you think there's something wrong...?"

I looked down to the white butterfly, still resting on my heart. The words escaped me, although I could not feel myself articulate them, because of the pain that eclipsed everything:

"No," I said, "He's just sleeping."

THE UNINVITED GUEST

It was many years before he found him, but he did find him.

In his defense, Kit did not know, until the very end, when Anthony arrived one day, and placing his hand on Kit's shoulder said, "You must come outside now." And there, in a place Kit never ventured, he confronted the truth of the marks he had left behind; the stains that lovers make on those who love them best.

He would have known him anywhere.

Kit watched them gather around him, the boy. He followed, a spectator in that cheering crowd.

And he thought of lilacs.

RUPERT TURNER-HUME

"Ah well, the jig is up, but what a jig it was," sighs Rupert Turner-Hume, glancing wearily around the room. "The last party, the last magnum of champagne, the last cigarette: It's all down hill from hereon in, as you and I both know," he insinuates knowingly to The Last Resort on his arm. "Anyway, a toast, 'To rosebuds....' Come on," he cajoles, "you say it, like a good girl. No, no, on second thoughts, please stop talking," he interrupts, placing a silencing finger on her lips. "Darling, that was not English that just came out of your mouth; perhaps some version of Swahili I'm not acquainted with or else you were speaking in tongues... But you really are far too gorgeous to be so drunk," he says, considering her admiringly. "Well, as it happens, so am I: We're a pair! Now, if you're not careful you're going to fall over," he warns her. "Hang on to my arm and let's sit down...Oops, nearly..." he says, shuffling her over to a banquette in a dimly lit corner. "Here we are. Now, on three, descend – as I once said to a particularly comely Swedish girl. But I digress...One...two...three...

"There we are, smashing," he says, settling into the plush velvet confines of the banquette. "Comfortable? Right we are then, let me take a look at you, Mabel," he says, as The Last Resort attempts to protest a response. "Yes, you rather pert little thing, I do know your real name. I was an intimate of your charming mother for many a moon. And your father – let me see, if memory serves, he is the President of the United States? No, but I'm teasing...the President of the Mercantile Bank, isn't it? It did always sound very important whenever he frequently announced it..." he continues, raising a sardonic eyebrow. "Yes, he's good old Edward Lyons' cousin, God help him. I see he's back inside now," he says, craning his neck to catch sight of Captain Lyons disappearing inside Serena's room. "What did he think he was playing at, staying out in this weather? I don't know about you, darling, but I've often thought it extraordinary to find a head that large on any human body. It's a wonder he doesn't topple over with the sheer weight of it. What Serena ever saw in him...But I'm being horrid, aren't I," he admits with faux contrition, returning his attention to her, "and we really shouldn't be waspish this evening.... Cigarette?" he asks, pulling a gleaming gold case from his breast pocket.

"What a beautifully tailored dress," he compliments her, offering her a cigarette, before lighting his own. "From Monsieur Dior? Fits you like a glove. And what are you? All of nineteen, I'd say...what's that? Twenty-one? Fine then, Mabel, let's pretend you're twenty-one. I won't tell a soul...Ooh, don't pout and do try not to drool. Here, rest your head on my shoulder," he says, pulling her towards him, "let's see if that makes any difference.... Sorry?" he furrows his brow charmingly. "I'm having some difficulty understanding you, it's that old Swahili coming through again.... You say you've heard about me? My, that sounds very intriguing, and what is it that you've heard? Hmmm? Yes, that's true," he replies, nodding in amusement. "I am a very old man – forty-five; much, much too old for you...although, arguably, I could teach you rather a lot....

"How observant, Mabel: Yes, I am British. You like the accent? Shall I charm you with it, my sweet? Will that help you to get over being humiliated by one Mr. Anthony Duverglas?" he teases, much to Mabel's distaste, but she's far too drunk to make much sense now. "I was watching you on the dance floor when he rather unceremoniously passed you to your young friend there, not that you noticed me, which I find shocking and unbelievable, enough to cause a revolt in some South American country.... Besides, he didn't intend to be rude, but I hope you've learned your lesson now. Never chase a man, darling. People will think you're Russian.

"God, please, no," Rupert exclaims in horror as Mabel collapses into uncontrollable sobs in his lap. "I have a reputation to consider. Besides, I had higher hopes for you, Mabel. You're surely not in love with old Droopy Duverglas: All those years mooning over Venetia Dryden. Poor old bugger; he should have got her when he had the chance, but he dilly-dallied and now look," he continues, wagging an admonishing finger. "Always act, Mabel, that's my motto – but it only applies to gentleman, not to beauties like you. Curious to see him here tonight, though," Rupert remarks, casting an inquisitive glance over at Anthony pushing his way through the dancers on the floor, "haven't seen him in fifteen years. He can't possibly still have her in his sights," he considers, an idea dawning on him, "but how very romantic nonetheless.... I'd forgotten about him, actually, but when the champagne flows as freely as it does at Serena's, it's very easy to forget, which is just the way I like it. Let's forget; why don't you try it? Come on, turn over on my lap and let me see that pretty face. That's a good girl," he smiles down at Mabel as she obliges him. "Now, forget Anthony and think of me. It should be easy enough. I can be terribly memorable. In the right hands...And, clearly, if your misspent passion for Mr. Duverglas is anything to go by, you do have an excellent, if more mature, palate," he says, tapping her gently on the nose, as if she is a naughty puppy.

"So," he announces, with good-humored entitlement, "now that we're acquainted, Mabel, may I have this kiss? It would be something of an honor, not just for me, but also for you, I suspect. I have kissed some of the finest lips in Hollywood. And, despite everything, I'm still rather famous for it. You look skeptical. Shall I tilt you over backwards to demonstrate? It's all in the tilt, my darling. And I do have exceptionally strong arms. We could start there and then work our way in any other direction you might prefer. Bette always liked to begin that way, especially when she was your age. As she grew older – yes, I do mean Bette Davis," he agrees, lowering his head to try and comprehend what Mabel is trying to say, "Your favorite actress? Yes, I can see how many of the characters she has played would strike a chord, particularly that last one, what was it again. Ah, yes, *Jezebel*.... Ow, I'm only teasing, Mabel," he cries, as Mabel's fist suddenly surges up to hit his head.

"I stand corrected," he concedes, raising forestalling hands to prevent her from hitting him again. "I think *Of Human Bondage* may be a better fit, for someone of your qualities..." he considers, pausing for a similar reaction, but this joke is fortuitously lost on Mabel. "Lips like ermine," he continues, the threat of further head trauma having passed. "Blasted nuisance getting the lipstick off though, but not as bad as Joanie: an eager type, very keen, I'll give her that, but dear me, like being attached to a suction cup. And then to find so few teeth in there, to boot...." He grimaces. "Not pleasurable in any sense of the word: I don't know how Clark coped, but perhaps it was a virtue in other areas... Not that I expect you to know anything about that..." he remonstrates paternally.

"Yet, to talk of teeth that glistened perfectly evenly, a delicious invitation to press my lips against, Clara, Clara Bow," he sighs, rapturously. "My first film. Then Lulu Brooks, how that Cupid's bow mouth glistened with gloss so temptingly: like ice though when touched, enough to give you frostbite. Very disappointing, but then those lips had pressed against very many others, hardly a victory for me. But Garbo...ah, Garbo, who Lulu and I shared, at one point, along with Mr. Chaplin –an epic tale: one for the fire on a rainy evening – was the most memorable of the lot. If I had but one wish, Mabel, it would be to kiss her all over again in Sweden, on a white night, because that way it would never end. I think she felt the same, I don't believe she ever entertained another man, after me. And, if you can keep a secret, which, of course, you can't...She kept her eyes open. Throughout.

"What enticing lips you have," he observes appraisingly. "And you'd let me seduce you, wouldn't you," Rupert continues knowingly, "desperate to be in love with someone who knows what he's doing. You're young enough to fall for it, too, my particular brand of matinee idol charm; well what used to be, before I aged too much, amongst other details.... But the jig is up, darling, as you well know. There's no doubt that I need, now more than ever, a gorgeous young lady like you to make me feel better about the whole shebang, but I wouldn't be up to much, not considering," he admits, stroking her hair. "A few years ago, it would have been different: you'd have been on that plane back to Hollywood quicker than you could blink. And I could have shown you it all, tennis with Mayer, drinks at the Copacabana, swimming in Tracy's pool, lunches on the studio lot, great times. But I would only have ended up disappointing you. I would have lived through you for a while, deluding myself in the mirror, but then you would have started to notice how old I really was, after the parts dried up and the invitations didn't drop on the mat as frequently. That's when it would have been smashed to bits," he says, regretfully, "when you would have started to wonder what it was that you might be missing elsewhere. Besides, I probably wouldn't have been very nice to you, despite my charming reputation: I have my ghosts, Mabel: a bit ironic, considering. They haunt me, especially when I think of the lips that started it all. So, don't look at me like that," he chastises her. "I'm a better man now than I used to be. Let's have another drink instead and a toast. 'To rosebuds...'" he announces, a hint of sadness in his eyes as he raises the glass to his lips. "And down the proverbial hatch it goes...

"Anyway," he says, attempting to lighten the mood, "it's far too sad to think of those bygone kisses; Bette, Joanie, Mae, Vivien – oh Vivien, what a lucky boy Larry is – Olivia, her sister... the list goes on and on; those Hollywood days in the sun, me on the cover of every magazine, a screen goddess in my arms, locked in an embrace..." he continues, slower now, the memories heavier than he might wish. He looks out over the sea of people and steels himself against continuing down this particular avenue of memory: It is too sad, as he knows far too well. "Heavens, I think I've drunk more than I thought, can't seem to keep my stiff upper lip stiff..." he tries to joke, shaking his head as if to cancel out the bad thoughts. "Never look back, Mabel," Rupert counsels stoically: "It's a dark and murky place, the past. Always move forward and never get a tipsy matinee idol onto sentimental subjects, we can metamorphose from clown to tragic martyr quicker than you say, *Darling, you're marvelous*. And so often, we really rather are...

"Back to you then," he says, brighter now. "Make an old man happy with your chatter. Tell me of the deliciousness you get up to. Mabel? Mabel! Are you sleeping?" he asks in astonishment. "Well, of all the bloody nerve. Out like a light. I know I've been badly reviewed for my one-dimensional acting skills but I must say, I didn't think I was so wooden as to bore you to sleep... No, come on Mabel, wake up," he cajoles, giving her arm a gentle shake. "You really must," he insists. "Tell me anything you like, but don't leave me to sit here by myself.... No, it's not going to work, is it?" he perceives, noting that Mabel is literally dead to the world. "Maybe it's better this way," he says, more seriously. "You might not wake up until it's over. You're far too young anyway, but there's no getting around it. We're all here for a reason, after all..." he acknowledges, with a heavy sigh.

"In any event," he carries on, as if she is still awake and listening, "please accept my unreserved apologies. If my mother were still alive and had heard the suggestive way I've been speaking to you, she would have knocked me from here to next week, deservedly. It's a mask, Mabel, that of the ageing roué, scandalously indiscreet, it's why I was always invited, to play that part; everyone coming to me for the good old gossip and I never let them down, but I think I might take a break as we've turned this rather maudlin corner.... Nothing for it then, I suppose, but to polish off this champagne myself and sit here until you wake up.... 'To Serena...'" he announces, raising his glass. "Now there," he says admiringly, "were some lips I would have loved to have brushed against....

"Serena," he repeats, sadly. "I'll never forgive myself for that one. Why I said anything.... But that's the problem with us ac-*tores*, we do so love to run on, especially when the audience is as captive as she was that evening – '*What have been the five best moments of your life?*' First time we ever met. I was so taken aback by the question, I didn't stop to think; I seized on the opportunity and poured forth. Had snagged an invitation, somehow, doesn't really matter – Ah, yes, Amelia Davidson, lips like cotton wool, not very memorable.... Well, the well was overflowing by the time I'd finished and it was too late to take it back, and there I was, stuck in a lie – God, 'Five Things...' it was twenty years ago...

"Eton

The bulls at Benalmadena

Sunset over Chateau Fleurs-de-Mer

The scent of Maria Elena the day she brushed past me at the Duomo in Firenze

England

"Rather a performance, all of which I elaborated on with gusto. 'Yes, the glorious years at Eton, Serena – may I call you, Serena? Thank you... No, I was never so content as when I was sent up from Summer Fields, the preparatory school that every generation of my family had attended. The friends I made (cue names, nostalgic smile, winsome eyes), the best of men — too many lost in the War (hint of misty-eyed regret); (change of tempo, making do after the onslaughts of battle, presentation of self as world traveler) and then running with the bulls at the *castillo* my family owned in Benalmadena where we summered (threw that in so that she knew I was of similar background); and then *Chateau Fleurs-de-Mer*, a property I bought with my inheritance, which regrettably went to death duties (affect remorseful expression, followed by quivering stoicism); that sensuous beauty who I would have married had she not been killed in a fire while I was buying an emerald in Paris because it signified jealousy and I wanted always to be jealous of any other man who might steal her from me (force a tear); and, finally, England, forever England, my home, my kingdom, the worthiest of lands (cue pride of a fallen man, a broken man, but a British man).... (Eyes appropriately misting up: Exeunt).' Bravo!

"And Serena, poor, poor, Serena, said, 'Did you say Eton?' And I said, 'Yes, Eton...' And she said, 'Did you ever meet Kit Peel,' And I replied, 'Well, good lord, you knew him too...?'

"Not one word of it true. Never met him before in my life.

"Said he was married," Rupert continues, focusing on his champagne glass somberly. "Incredible now that I think of it. No idea that he was the love of her life. I'm not a good type," he admits with a silent guffaw, "I have no illusions on that score, but when it comes to love, I would never try to spoil that for anyone else. But I did. I'd like to get a minute with her before she goes," he says, looking up to Serena's bedroom on the mezzanine, "to tell her, if I can. But I'm not sure there will be time now. But then, there never is, is there..." he observes, with timeworn disappointment.

"I didn't have five favorite things," he remarks, quietly. "Only one.

"'*Ta-ta, Love. Ta-ta.*'

"It was what she said to me, standing in the doorway, the day I left for the War. My first wife, Jane: the original rosebud. Oh, my dear and darling wife.

"Now, if you were awake, Mabel," he says, "and paying attention, you'd find the accent has changed. That's Yorkshire, my wife's accent, my original

accent, before I adopted the dulcet tones of the well-bred Englishman…
'*Ta-ta. Love. Ta-ta*…' the last I ever heard from those rosebud lips… When
I was a young man, I used to kiss her and forget about breathing; the most
beautiful of the most beautiful girls I've ever seen. The best there was where
I grew up and she was mine. Jane surprised me though, jumped up no mark
that I was: She was more than a triumph, the envy of the other lads; she set
me at a disadvantage from the first date I ever took her on. I didn't expect to
love her, you see: I only wanted to win the bet. Who could land the prettiest
girl on the working class street? Well, clearly it had to be me, everyone said
so: the best-looking boy on the working class street, the one with the swag-
ger, destined for bigger things: And I had my dreams, I made no bones about
them, my bags were always sitting packed. I was going to be off, to tread the
boards, become a great actor, once I knew I'd won her. I was eighteen: It was
time. I'd waited my whole life to get on that train to London.

"But I didn't go. Because with Jane, I didn't need to: Because I was
already a star to her. When we first met, I used to talk to her about those
plans. She never deterred me, she'd say: 'You will, you. I'll be able to say you
courted me once upon a time,' and then everything suddenly seemed very
foolish under the weight of those eyes watching me; her every faith that I'd
succeed; her assumption that I'd not be taking her with me, when I did.
How could you be so callous to someone that beautiful, I'd kick myself after
walking her home? Why would you go off somewhere she wouldn't be? Who
needs London, I'd tell myself, Jane and I could be the most famous couple on
our street; the best-looking, the best-off because I'd work hard to provide for
us both, and I could rise up, I could get promoted and then we could buy a
bigger house, a newer house…And then it didn't seem such a come-down to
imagine a life with someone like Jane, as enviable as any actress on any stage,
because that was back before films started. 'Never mind,' I'd tell her when
she'd ask me when I was leaving, pinning up the washing in her mother's
backyard, too menial a job for someone that special. 'None of it could possibly be better than you,' I'd say and I meant every word. Everything I ever
wanted, I found in Jane. Too dull a name for someone that rare. So, I married
her. The happiest two years I have ever lived; those rosebud years. But then
came the War, Mabel," he winces. "What you see, what you forget, what you

give up for more tempting prospects: Particularly, when that person who used to change your mind isn't around to convince you otherwise.

"I didn't forget all about her," Rupert confesses, more quietly now, "but I was *distracted*, shall we say. As soon as I arrived in front of those Corporals and Lieutenants, old Etonians and aristocrats, leading us into battle, I crumbled under the weight of my own inadequacies. Out came the accent in flawless imitation of their own, because I'm good at accents, me," he nods cynically. "And they fell for it; believed the tall tale that I'd been educated at Fettes, aristocratic family fallen on hard times, that kind of thing. I held them rapt for hours with my lies, but what a talent I had, I realized, a brilliant raconteur – or so the critics later praised me.

"I wonder now if those soldiers were too shell-shocked to question me, but you meet people that way, Mabel, when you're sent home on leave and you have the choice of visiting London salons, where the well-bred, who you amuse, can make the right introductions for you. It's either that or go back to the working class street, just another soldier, to join the job queue to work down the mine; an honest, solid existence, tea on the table at five, slippers by the fire, a pipe already stuffed with tobacco waiting for you, and the attractive wife who grows more coarse as she ages, with the children she frequently has, waiting, telling everyone, 'any minute now, he'll walk through the door, my Charlie!:' Because that was my name then, Charlie Munn – not exactly double-barreled. Not the type of name to take you places.

"So I never walked through the door again, where she waved me off – '*Ta-ta, Love. Ta-ta.*' That day I went off to war, promising to come back safe and soon. And then she died, that beautiful girl with the rosebud lips. Cancer. She found out before I left, but didn't want to worry me, I was later told. Six years she waited – she thought I was missing. It was the story the families made up, so as not to break her heart: It was a miracle, apparently, that she lasted that long, considering how ill she was. But then one day, she picked up a London theater magazine, and saw my picture; my first starring role, and that's when she discovered that I was alive and well and simply hadn't bothered coming home. She died that very night.

"'Forgive him. He was always meant for better.' Those were her last words," Rupert remembers, his voice breaking. "That was my Jane, understanding my dreams and forgiving them, even when they didn't include her. I learned this from my mother, years later. I found her one night, waiting for me at the stage door... 'You're no good, you. You never were,' she said. 'And what did you gain; prancing around pretending to be other people, famous for loose women smearing their cheap lipstick all over your face.' She never forgave me, the shame I brought on the family. They wouldn't even let me go to her grave, not that I deserved to. And I never went home again. Couldn't ever walk up that street knowing she wasn't there.... But since then, I've searched the world for those rosebud lips. Because you never forget your first kiss, Mabel, not when they were as perfect as my dear and darling wife's. So one thing, that's all there is in my life, when I think of the best moments; that day in the doorway, her rosebud lips, 'Ta-ta Love. Ta-ta....'" he smiles fondly, closing his matinee idol eyes to stop his tears from falling.

"Good Lord! I have been going on," he inhales deeply, upon opening his eyes and realizing that something of an audience has gathered round. "It's a minute to seven. I'm afraid I can't dilly dally here with you much longer, despite how captive an audience you've been," he says, forcing a laugh and struggling to quickly pull himself together. "Forgive me, but here comes your friend, now, Mabel," he says, noting a face in the crowd. "Quite a dandy, from what I've seen. I think I'll pass you over to him," Rupert says, sliding out from underneath Mabel and placing her head gently on the banquette. "You'll be leaving together, if history is anything to go by..." Rupert winks down at her knowingly.

"Time to fulfill my obligation, you see. I suppose it won't hurt to tell you my real secret," he says, bending down to whisper in her ear. "I'm here for her: the girl on the staircase, watching the party. The one some over-privileged young man has been making rather a fool of this summer. Never been kissed, or so she told me at the start of this summer, the first party she'd ever attended. And who am I to resist a challenge like that, darling Mabel?"

he asks. "So, if will you excuse me, rosebuds await me.... First, though, there's still time, I think," he remarks, turning to consider the large clock overlooking the marble hallway. "I might try to get to Serena, to tell her the truth. I owe her at least that much...But before I go," he says, turning back to place an affectionate kiss on Mabel's forehead: "Night-night, darling: See you on the other side...."

THE HOSTESS

"Read to me from the Book of Souls," I said. Let me hear the happiest moments of those boys who did not get to live with us, who are lost somewhere, in the seas that surround us. "How old was he," I would ask, after each entry and Edward never guessed why. How old was the boy that the sea claimed? Twenty-five; thirty-one; twenty-six; nineteen; fifteen; twenty-three; eighteen; fourteen; seventeen: *Seventeen.*

I listened for my son in those books, but I did not find him. So this is why I do not believe him lost, but sleeping. Does he drift, his hands a pillow for his cheeks, on the South China Sea, or else does the Tyrrhenian cradle him like a crib, beneath the Gods who safeguard his beauty? Or has he been washed ashore onto a white beach, a beach so white, it would blind me were I ever to have set foot upon its sands? A beach in the Mediterranean, perhaps, that island called Ibiza that Kit once told me of; an idyll of Moorish splendor, where the olive trees grow and the pine walks stretch for miles and the water is the color of aquamarine. Does he rest there, a blonde boy, on the sands; does he dream and in those dreams laugh the laughter of the ancients. I do not know. But I wanted to find him, after what I learned; I wanted to leave La Doucette, to sail away to that white beach where he might be; to watch his eyes open as I woke him from his slumber. And in his beautiful smile, the smile I have never seen, find a safe haven for the rest of my days.

How could I carry on here, considering? Or confront Edward or Teddy; what would have been the point of any of it? Teddy would simply have disappeared again until it was safe to return, just as it had taken him a year to visit when Edward brought me back to La Doucette as his wife. And Edward, as ever, would have said nothing at all.

I had all the money I needed to live. So I could leave. I was going to slip out in the middle of the party to go to the station and board the train; to try and find another life before it was too late, even if it was only one of memory. But then, every time I act, I err. I only expected Teddy to come and tell me he couldn't take me. I didn't expect him to write....

'...You won't believe me, but, this evening, I <u>was</u> coming for you, placing one foot in front of the other: an older man now, braver than I'd ever been. But then, I wonder if there's a problem with second chances, Sea. You already know what went wrong the first time; maybe you anticipate it, the second; invite the problem. I got right up to the gate and then I remembered, the second I reached to push it open, what I usually do absolutely anything to forget.

It was me, Sea. I was the one who did this to you. Kit was disinherited somehow, the money gone. Your husband told him at the end of the summer. I met him, after he'd had that meeting. He'd asked to borrow money and Lyons had refused. He was beside himself, couldn't stand to let you down; didn't know what to do. But, not to worry, I had a solution. I had a man.

Let's remember the first party, Sea: Lucinda in the courtyard with that silk purse which had held the diamond hair combs Kit once promised to you: the assumption you made that Kit had been dallying with her behind your back, because of the rumors I'd started; me, your ever constant Teddy, steering you into the house as if to protect you....

The combs were the only piece of his mother he had ever owned because she died when he was a baby, he told me, but for you, Sea...."Yes, you're quite right, Teddy," he agreed. "Jewels are meaningless. What is important is that I have the money to support her. You have a man? You could sell them for me and then we could still leave here?" "Sure, I'll help you, Kit," I assured him. "I'll get the best price for them and you can stick to your plan: I'll go to NY, three days before the party. It'll work out fine. I won't breathe a word of it to anyone..."

I told him I was mugged and they took the combs, but as you hold them in your hand now, you know that's not true. They are a symbol of the life I stole from him, as revenge for what he stole from me: You, my dearest Sea.

He didn't go without a fight: It took some time to convince him. Nor did I spare him; I was merciless. " Do the honorable thing, man," that's what I said: "You have no fortune. You've almost destroyed her reputation..." Good God, his grief.... A singular act of jealousy, but I defended it, at the time: I could give you more. And anyway, you were mine, first, and he was barely more than a stranger to us. "Let me say goodbye to her," he begged. "Why make it any worse" I asked "I can marry her; if you tell her the truth, then she won't be able to love me because she'll constantly hanker after you. Would you wish that on her? Your situation is hopeless. Please, for God's sake..." But no: He only agreed to leave if I swore to tell you why and, as you know, Sea, until this letter, I never have.

I sent the purse to Lucinda, with a note supposedly from Kit. To cause suspicion, in case you might ever be tempted to doubt the choice I was about to lead you into, because I suspected Kit would show up at the party, regardless. Another juvenile lie, I rationalized, but it ended up destroying you and Lucinda. So that was the reason why he didn't move toward you in the courtyard — that lone fact that has caused you such terrible anguish ever since: It wasn't because he didn't care for you, but because he did — more than anything. He couldn't bear to let you go. He clearly wanted to see what you would do, after I'd told you the truth.

Maybe he thought you might forgive him, abandon society. Yet, when he saw you go into the house with me, he would have assumed that you had chosen to leave him, chosen me. So, you see, I broke his heart for you, so that you could be mine. And you have been mine, haven't you, these years. I got to keep you, keep the party, but you were never the same girl again who had sat in the window of Halsey Road; nor was the party ever the same either, because you weren't waiting for me anymore, but him. How was I to know that you were expecting his child? Even then, you wouldn't marry me. You would sooner have been ruined than give up the chance of being with him. But I was the one who ruined you by forcing you to stay here.

I'm not beautiful, as we are well aware. Not Kit. I shouldn't have let you back in, but I've never been sensible when it comes to you, Sea. It's an awful awareness to know what it is you want, to find yourself within its grasp, but to understand that that person you love so much will only be settling for second-best. It's humbling. Gives a man pause. Stops a fellow from acting on a desire, remembering what happens after the rejection. Makes you stop at the garden gate when you should stroll straight through it on your way to what you want. Even if, the person you still love changes their mind back to you later, when every variety of excuse can be made for why you didn't stay the first choice, the scar remains.

Did you think I ever considered myself good enough for you, Sea? That's the real reason why I didn't visit, at first, when you were sick, the year you lived in the cottage. I often think of you at the window where I sit now, writing this letter, that someone else will deliver. I think of me, too, who I was then. Every day, I'd dare myself a little further up the road to the gate, because, like most men, Sea, I was smitten with you. I made so many bargains with myself that year: If you would only smile at me…if I could make you laugh…if I could only have a year, one year where I could call you mine, that would be enough. Why a year, I cannot guess. Maybe I thought that's all I'd get.

I tried everything to make sure you wouldn't tire and go off with someone else; to be nicer, more accountable, more sober, funnier, but those tricks don't work, do they? Not when that type of person appears and you see it; what true love really is. The day you lost your hat, when I came across you two that evening after your recital, dancing in the gardens, I saw it, what we didn't share; even though I had a ring for you in my pocket. Yes, Sea, I had dallied at the gate, trying to summon the courage and, by the time I arrived, it was too late: You had found one another. Indescribable, but there's an almost immediate resignation as it happens in front of you; a performance you can't participate in, merely watch with envy and admiration. It happened to you both, in a way that it didn't for us. And there lies the awful sadness of coming second, when, in fact, you got there first.

You would have stayed with me, to be kind, but I wanted all of you. So I tried to hate you for a while, even though you thought I was still your friend. Remember how hot and cold I blew, how nasty I could be sometimes. The problem being that you always forgave me, whenever I let you down – and I always have, whenever you've asked anything of me, despite my best intentions. I have let myself loiter at the gate, instead of rushing off to catch a train or walking up the road to take you away from the site of all your misery. "Best not," I'd deduce, returning to the parlor, but never flippantly, instead understanding myself to be infinitely less of a man than even I suspected.

You see, women like you, Sea, you hold up a mirror to someone's true self; it's almost like a dare. Can you be whom I will need? Can you carry me along because I cannot walk, despite how strong I appear? The gate signals to me the reason why everything did not happen as it should have; it opens to set you free, it shuts to fence you in. Mine sits ajar; it's undecided: much as I have been. It serves as a constant reminder of how I have failed in the promises I once made to myself and to you, the very few that were ever accorded to me to oversee.

You have been my greatest love, Sea, but I've always known, deep down, fundamentally, that, regardless of how often I could have claimed you, called you mine, I never once had the courage for you. And, as such, I have hesitated in my life, a moment too long every time. It was how Edward found you in Port Jefferson; I came home to collect some belongings.... I thought he wanted to help you. At least, that's how he explained it to me and then, what happened, happened....

Why am I returning the combs now, Sea? Doing the right thing by you at last? I'm giving back the life I stole from Kit, me masquerading at your side in his place. I've only made it this far because of you, because of The Leisure Hour and Supper Club; the certainty that you'll be waiting for me at the door and, for that brief while, we could pretend that anything could happen, every time we turned to survey the beating heart of the room. The thought that, maybe, we might find some meager prize within those walls, redeem ourselves, be reunited; our flaws overlooked in that world of little things you created. But, without it, Sea, without its comfort and security, I won't survive: especially when I see what I am reflected in the eyes of others. If I were to come with you as we'd planned, I wouldn't be able to protect you. I never have.

Besides, I couldn't take you away from the one place where Kit might find you. It's funny, but I almost feel like I've been waiting for him, too. I'm certain he's not forgotten you, though; married or not, I know he'll come here, someday. Or why you don't take that train ticket, sell the combs as Kit planned and find him, if only to ease your sadness? He'll forgive you, when you tell him what I did. I pray for that for you, Sea. But, whatever else you do, get away from that husband of yours. Get away from him.

There are those people you hinge the memories upon, as I have with you: the left or right of the direction any given life might take; those memories that are too heavy for some garden gates; of our first kiss, the snow, who I was then, who I wanted to be, the joy of those early parties. I look at the gate now and how I wish I could have been better, Sea, because I remember how good it all was because of you.

I could have told you this myself, but it won't surprise you that I wrote a letter instead. It's selfish, I know, but I want to remember only how you loved me, once: It was just yesterday that you came to the gate, the roses in bloom over the arbor. I kissed you, knowing it would be the last time, and told you that you would have my heart forever. It's true: I'll always be waiting here for you in some fashion, Sea: I hope one day, I'll look up and see you standing in front of this window, full of the news that you've found him, full of joy. Almost like when we were young, those Friday nights of summer in 1917, when I was first back from the War, so different a man to the one who left to fight. The memory of you standing on the road that leads to the sea, waiting for me, The Leisure Hour ahead of us: "Teddy!" you'd cry, taking my face in your porcelain hands, and placing a kiss upon both my eyes. Forgiving me for how I had failed you, for how I always would.

Until the snow then, my dearest Sea.

Forever yours,

Teddy

THE HOST

"There's a child."

This is what Teddy said in 1908, after Captain Lyons pushed him back into the cottage where he had been hiding, demanding Teddy tell him where Serena was, after she ran away: Teddy, that once bright child who he had watched grow. How they had adored him when he was a little boy, the hapless, exuberant naughtiness that inspired his every move: the tall tales of why things were broken, spilt, vanished, the big blue eyes cast up at soft-hearted nannies who would never reprimand him because about Teddy there hovered, always, a sort of sadness: indefinable, but distinctly there. The type of sadness that forever mists around the shoulders of men destined to never keep a promise. As if, from the day he was born, he understood his inherent weakness.

Look at him now, Captain Lyons thought half in contempt and half in pity, watching Teddy cower in the corner, saying anything to get away with it: "I was going to marry her, I promise you, but Serena wouldn't hear of it – all she wants is Kit – Captain Lyons, I don't have any money, please, please," Teddy begged, weeping.

It would have been fine, Captain Lyons has told himself. After Teddy revealed where Serena was and promised never to see her again. After Captain Lyons paid off Teddy's gambling debts in return, holding off the men who would have killed him. Yes, it would have been fine, he has told himself: He could have provided the balance Serena needed; they could have led a life of comfort and, he thinks, mutual respect. He would have told her, too, about Kit, were it not for the one sentence he still prays he had never heard. As vicious a parting shot as the letter Teddy later wrote to her: Teddy calling after him as he departed for Port Jefferson:

"There's a child."

Captain Lyons didn't stop long at the door on hearing the words, but he remembers every facet of those moments; the quiver of the leaves, the unhinged gate, the dried out flowers lining the path, the sound of Teddy's sobs behind him. He had a sudden fancy that Teddy's tears would pull them under and then they would be gone, exonerated from Serena's hatred, unable to act. He watched the day, which had turned on its heel from sun-filled to twilit, and felt it plummet in him. That reserve of hope that he might just draw enough from life to be content, to carry on without bitter regret at things done and not done; that he may look back, at some further point, and say, "I was a decent man." He might as well have tied a rock on my back, he thought that day, for here it is, the end of hope for me. How could she ever forgive me for what I will have to do: Who could possibly expect her to?

There was no choice. As Teddy had been seen in Remsenburg after Serena disappeared, while Captain Lyons was in Nairobi, everyone knew Teddy had not eloped with her. Were Captain Lyons to claim paternity, the child would always be presumed illegitimate, whether Serena agreed to marry him or not. Moreover, if he had given Teddy the money to marry her and they were to live elsewhere, isolated from society, Teddy would only have dissipated it: Captain Lyons thought Serena's life would be a misery if he could not watch over her. Too much time had passed to change anything. Months. All of those minutes, he mourned, when anything might have changed, but nothing did. So Captain Lyons found himself beside a baby's crib – such an innocent soul, so loved, so unsuspecting of what would follow – born to be given away in the most evil act imaginable for any man to have to effect. And effect it he did, although he questioned the point. Either way Serena's life would be ruined. The only difference was that by acting as the perpetrator, in one scenario she could hate him, and in the other, if he told her what he had learned, she would have died.

. . .

We tell stories, those of us who are left behind, he thinks, as he crosses Serena's room to where she waits for him. We create a truth we can bear.

Sinners become Saints; the cruel, decent; the ordinary, in some fashion, re-markable. This I have refused to do for anyone else, save for Serena: only to give her a reason to live. Yet, countless times I have been forced to concede that maybe all I wanted was to eradicate any trace of what had happened – of Kit and her child: an act of palimpsest, to write over her true story to create a reality I could endure, where nothing I had done had ever harmed her.

He understood nothing would be gained from separating Teddy and Serena, despite how he has resented their friendship. And so he has watched them laugh and console one another, the affection he craved lavished on someone who sold her for the sake of his own skin. On numerous occasions he has been sorely tempted to throw Teddy's betrayal in her face, as Serena rails against him for the unaccountable sins of which she believes him guilty, but Captain Lyons can never do so. For all he sees when he looks at Serena, as he does now, is that innocent and kind seventeen-year-old-girl, poised at the top of a staircase, who had never hurt a soul and who never would, who was within seconds of the type of happiness for which many pray and rarely ever receive. He makes himself think of her there whenever he is tempted to hurt her more; when the terrible tragedy of what he did torments him so that all he can wish for is death: He is as in awe of that one moment of joy as she once was, when all she owned was hope: the one moment before.

One moment before: There is always this, before every act. Until Teddy sent the letter to Serena, Captain Lyons had never suspected that Teddy was responsible for Kit's departure. It was true, that Captain Lyons had informed Kit about his loss of wealth, without offering any remedy to the situation. Annoyed at himself, at Kit, for not having trusted his instincts: Serena would be upset, just when she seemed to be well again. He thought to teach Kit a lesson about impetuosity, to make him think about her health. But he was ultimately going to help him, or so Captain Lyons has assured himself in the years since. He merely wanted Kit to consider his actions for a few days. He had planned to take Kit aside at the party, to discuss what he could do for them both, but then came Teddy: what Captain Lyons could never have known until he picked the letter up from the ground, where Serena had let it fall, last Friday, and discovered the truth.

He's berated the boy for years, to Serena, to himself, despite how hideous a thing that was to do, he has realized over this past week: Of all of us, he thinks, staring down at Serena, he was the only one who genuinely loved her: He gave her up to guarantee her future happiness, with no thought for himself. And all because of that one moment before when I thought to play God: to protect Serena, when, in fact, what I did was set in motion a catalytic series of events that would destroy everyone involved.

All I owned in defense of my conduct, until now, was that I believed Kit had fled from his responsibility, and I despised him for his cowardice. Always, there was that whenever the guilt became intolerable. What led to the decision I made, after Nairobi, to lock him away, to never tell her, so that she would not suffer more than she already had. This is why I have allowed The Westhampton Leisure Hour and Supper Club, as they call it. Only for Serena: So that she might live in a moment before, to own a hope that does not exist.

THE HOSTESS

I ran, sobbing, the letter clutched to my chest, one last wish on my lips.

From behind me, I heard Edward calling my name:

"Serena...Serena! What are you doing, come inside!"

I turned and caught my reflection in the glass of the Pavilion: a tortured face, well past its prime, stared back. *It's the light*, an internal voice cajoled me to believe. But it wasn't the light or the angle of the glass, it was simply me: *Yes*, I nodded to my true reflection. *It is all too late now.* "Serena!" Edward called again, a familiar, needling insistence in his voice.

I wiped my tears with the flat of my hand, resigned to what I must do. I gathered up the hem of my dress – not a pink chiffon dress anymore, but the fluid silk of a late forty-something year old woman's appropriate attire – and walked the half road back to the house, marking the familiar pattern of minutes to endure the time left. *Sixty steps, sixty breaths, sixty tears never to be cried....* I climbed the steps to where my husband waited for me at the red front door. He surveyed me darkly and took a step back, deeper inside, to allow me to pass through.

I observed the eddying vibrancy behind him, the life within La Doucette, – all of the people, the flitting shadows, the loud hurrahs, the stifled sobs, the carping gossip, the boring segues in conversation to something even more tedious, the romantic murmurings – and I tried to fathom what I should do. Should I confront Edward with his lies and beg him to tell me the truth, knowing he probably never would? Or say nothing and simply return to a life of little things? If I immersed myself once more in the minutiae of days leading up to the weekly party, I could rescue it from the brink of its failings – clean the rugs, fix the cabinets, buff everything to a new luster. If I was no longer an object of desire, I could become something else: Perhaps, a clown or a gossip, or else someone venerable who could insistently impose my will upon my guests. I was only forty-eight. There was so much time left to make everything perfect again. All I had to do was carry on as if I never received Teddy's letter...

I could spend an eternity adorning myself in paste jewelry. And the books from all over the world, in all languages... Yes, I could resurrect the tradition of those Friday mornings, once a month. Those mornings when I used to pretend that Kit lived in this house with me: My beloved Kit, who once told me stories of what he loved in those books. I could indulge again the fantasy of myself as his wife, imagining him in the courtyard, waiting for their arrival. I could resume the treasure hunt with renewed vigor, when I searched the face of every guest for his. I could even throw caution to the wind – Edward be damned – and ask every guest if they had ever seen him. Or even try and find him, just like Teddy suggested, and travel to the many places I'd never seen. I could do all of those things, but there was so little point. Nothing would change. Nothing ever had.

Kit wasn't coming. And the secret that Teddy confided was not a blessing, but a curse. For I would not think of Kit again or anything we shared, without it being tainted by the truth of what really happened. Teddy's letter destroyed my hope once and for all. Decades had passed, times had changed, and yet Kit had never come back to explain or apologize. So either Kit hated me or I had not meant that much, in the first place. The truth was that nobody had kept him from me: Kit had merely forgotten me long before and I was just a foolish woman, clinging to a singular moment in the past that I had been unwilling to move beyond. But no one had forced me to accept this reality until last Friday when my day of reckoning finally arrived: So I stood in front of my husband on the doorstep and confronted mine at last.

Edward smiled at me, a haunting smile full of anguish. He suddenly appeared somewhat courageous, waiting there, humiliated, wholly aware he wasn't enough. He embodied a similar valor as that of an ageing woman waiting on a road and realizing that no one would ever walk up it to meet me again.

"Won't you come in, Serena?" he implored. "I can't leave you out here in the cold. Don't you feel it? The summer is almost over."

I might have, were it not for Teddy's letter. Yet, for the first time, I saw Edward exactly as he was, despite his beautiful words written in lonely rooms. It was as if he was willing me back into a marquee where he was the ringmaster. And it all looked so gay and exotic behind him, but I knew how it felt once you were confined within it, how the light darkens to something sinister, infinitely more dangerous.

How pretty a prison it is, through this door, I thought, my feet suddenly cold inside my shoes, on the gray stone step, But you'll lock the door on me again, won't you? You'll paint a smiling face on me and instruct me on the day. You'll prop me up, like a rag doll, a beautifully clothed Little Orphan Annie, waving my limpid arm up and down at the guests as they arrive. Like a ventriloquist, you'll speak for me, making sure it's only what you want me to say. Won't you, Edward?

It was as if I was the last guest to arrive at my own party. A freedom was conferred upon me that I had offered to every guest: to come or not to come, to be early or stay late, to drink all night, to dance until it was impossible to dance anymore, to make any decision and never to be judged for it. I finally understood what I had given them: Love. Because love is freedom; to make a choice, regardless of the consequences to oneself; to forgive, even those actions that had silently forced me to my knees; to wait, convinced that waiting was the right choice because I had trusted the instinct within me that pulsed with conviction whenever I faltered, borne down by the weight of fact and circumstance; *No, it was then, it was there, with him, with Kit; that was the love you were born to give and receive.... Wait for him still.* So, I made my choice.

Every party becomes a ghost of its former self, just as life cannot replicate its flawless beginnings. There are the guests you wish would always come, but who never do. There is ever the backward glance toward the door; the body poised to turn and grasp the fleeting splendor of what once was that might arrive in the shape of someone long lost. Yet, there is, too, the danger of staying too long, of never finding a new partner, of only waiting for an old one to reappear. In the constellation of any party, the guests inevitably begin to burn less brightly, evolving into specters of who they once aspired to be. They no longer say, I am; they say, I was. *I was The Gibson Girl, I was*

The Perfect Gentleman, I was The Woman Who Loved Him From Across the Room. And the chances slip past them on the heels of the latest dance craze, the one it is too late to learn.

The only way to prevent it is to leave before the goodbyes. To reach for the front door, as I did last Friday, pulling it toward me. I willed it to close, inch by inch, not on a beloved boy, but on that unpaid editor of better men, my husband.

When Edward first brought me back to La Doucette, I naïvely pranced into the cage, thinking I could cope, if only visitors kept me company. Yet, for every hostess, another attraction in another gilded cage comes along to amuse sooner or later. So the line shuffles past, onto a different spectacle. The party was dying for me; I was an old fixture, a forgotten trend. I understood how it would end; the guests would stop coming, one by one, felled by death or ambivalence. Soon Edward and I would be the only two left, with no other distractions to keep us from one another.

"Do you remember what you asked me once?" I asked him. "You said, it was so brief, what Kit and I shared. You said: How could it have been enough?"

"Yes," Edward replied. "You didn't answer me."

"We all have an ideal, Edward, what we would wish would happen, and, most of the time, it doesn't. We mark the days, we watch the minutes pass. Sometimes being disappointed, sometimes not, but ultimately, we're forced to give up those dreams that disintegrate in the face of reality. So we find ourselves leading the life of some stranger, entirely at odds with everything we secretly desire. We don't recognize this person, we try to ignore what is happening, but yet, one day, we are confronted by a mirror held up to us, and a mere glance confirms: This is who I am, and all the time is gone now and I cannot change a thing.

"Edward, I had a dream of what I wanted my life to be, and it didn't come true. I loved Kit so much and, as the years went by, I knew he wasn't coming back, but the memory was all I had. He and my son are the most precious things that ever happened to me but there's nowhere I can go where I can speak honestly of them, except for in my heart. So I've lived the life I longed for in my heart. And that is how I have survived this, what you have done to me, what Teddy has done to me."

"I don't understand what you're talking about. Come inside. Let's discuss this," he pleaded, his hand moving to stop the door from closing on him. "No, Edward," I said, pulling harder on the handle, "Teddy told me everything in this letter. It was you who betrayed us. You didn't give Kit the money. And that is why my son..." But I couldn't say the words.

The red front door was closing...

"You made me pay so dearly for the mistake I made on this doorstep," I said. "I don't mean by letting Kit go, but by ever loving him in the first place. You thought I should only love you and when I didn't, you re-wrote my future: you edited me into a life I wasn't born to lead.

"All we've ever appeared to share are the parties, but they aren't really for me, are they? They're for you. That's why you've never stopped them. They're something dazzling and privileged and enviable, so that you can impose yourself, even despite your silence, as someone of consequence because you're married to this woman everyone needs. How else would you be invited otherwise? I've been nothing more than a marionette of your creation, performing for you, but only in the fashion you chose. Anytime I've challenged you, you've punished me beyond words until I've become this stricken being, my entire identity and worth wrapped up in how others perceive me, changing my personality at whim so that I won't be left alone. And I've never dared to act to change anything until now because of what I've let you to do to me. I have hated my years with you, but they are safe, they demand nothing, except my tears and my unhappiness: what I believe I deserve to suffer because of the mistakes I've made. I am someone who handed over my freedom to you, without a fight. I am someone who waited, this evening, for a man who I already knew wouldn't come, to feel worse, again, about who I am, where I've been.

"But here, at the end, I accept that I did it all to myself: I let you, because it was easier this way. You were right: nobody asked me to do any of it. I could have refused the parties and stayed in my room, but something in me wanted to star; maybe that's why I turned away from Kit, the allure of the party was too intoxicating, I don't know. All I do know is that I must go somewhere where I can say with pride who I am, instead of remaining an actress on your stage. I have amounted to very little, despite my privileges, but all that means anything is that I was a mother once and that I loved the rightful father of my child more than anyone else in the world and that I still do. That is why it was enough: it didn't matter long how it lasted. What mattered is what it bore: the son I once held in my arms. I don't choose to deny the truth any longer to suit you, Edward. Because all the time is gone now," I said, my voice breaking, "and it really is too late to change a thing."

"But I tried to find your son, Serena," he protested. "I tried desperately hard, but I couldn't."

"No," I said, unable to stop the tears. "You couldn't find my son."

Our eyes met in a final reckoning as the door inched further shut between us. Yet, all Edward could do was watch until it clicked resoundingly closed; locking Edward into his party and me, the first guest brave enough to leave, into the outside world of the dusk, where no such party would ever exist again.

I walked to the midpoint of the road. I wanted to be there when the horn sounded for the 8:16pm train, somewhere beyond in Speonk: the train horn that always alerted passengers to its arrival one minute before it reached the station.... It was the train I was to board, the one I never would because I had to stand on that road one last time, with a last wish on my lips. The wish I uttered to the night when I heard the first horn....

"Meet me on the road that leads to the sea, and I'll wait for you and you'll wait for me..."

I closed my eyes, tipped back my head, and extended my arms out to the sides as if I could touch the ghosts arriving to haunt the night. The ghosts of those glamorous young girls from the legions of parties I had hosted. Girls like I had been once, for whom chances still existed. I sensed them dash and flit teasingly past my fingers reach in two lines on either side of me, jerking their silk dresses away, just as I thought them close enough to catch. But they were too light, too limber, too quick. Youth trailing at their heels, they rushed past me into the party, leaving me alone in the gray light of a Hamptons evening: the splendor muted, the brilliance diminished, too late in the day to beguile anyone outside.

I opened my eyes and looked at the empty road ahead. All I would ever find there would be ghosts, those inconstant souls in whom I had once placed every faith. As I lingered in that defining moment, I realized that however hard you try to replicate the love you once experienced, it doesn't happen twice. You clutch at the prayer that something can be salvaged from the rubble of broken promises, but all that exists is dust; an impermeable stain on the fingertips that never washes off. It was my last gasp, my what-if-it-isn't-too-late moment, that somebody thought better of. Nobody was coming. Nobody ever would again.

The tears spilled down my face as freely and desperately as the night of my first party, staining the dress of my gown. Everything had come full circle. I felt like I was watching myself from a distance. The figure I cut was vaguely proud, a little noble, a confirmed icon of defeat now. Watch through the windows, pretty girls, I thought. This is what happens when you let the chances slip. Sometimes, there is only one person who waits for you. The greatest gift you can ever give yourself is to go with him, when he asks. Run across a courtyard and ask him to take you with him …

I dared myself to stay there and allow the nothingness to filter in. All that was left to me was memory: A place where I could hide from the harsh realities of my many failures, where all that mattered was the handful of moments in my life that I chose to relive in the absence of anything else. And for the first time, since I last raced over the endless lawns of summer hand in hand with my friend, Kit, and my sister, Catherine, I felt joy.

Suddenly, I saw a plume of fire engine red streak across the gray sky overhead: a sight that seemed to confirm my choice, bearing me back to the only beginning there ever was and should have been. It was a summer redbird, the first I had seen since I was seventeen.

"Have you come to say goodbye?" I asked, turning my face up toward it in delight. "Or are you a hostess, too? Have you come to lead me out, the last guest of summer? Have you come to take me to where the summer redbirds go?"

But then, from behind me, I heard a sound that drowned out every whim, wish and plea in me: a savage yet crystalline sound, a clean slice of noise through the ebbing light. It was an echo to the ear not of what might have been, but of what truly was: the sound of life continuing, even as it ended.

All around, the haar filtered through the sky like a sea-gnarled gray shroud that fell softly and soundlessly over me. I stood, for the last time, and savored the resigned and fleeting beauty of the dying day as the colors of my once fabled existence faded serenely away: I watched the summer redbird fly on to a place where I would never follow. I turned my eyes to the road that leads to the sea, and let the last word leave my lips…

"*Goodbye….*"

And then it was night and all I could see was the stars. The stars that confirmed the only truth left to me as I navigated my way through them:

I was The Hostess.

V.

FAREWELLS

THE PARTY, THE PARTY!

As The Summer Visitors begin to speculate over how quickly they can leave once Serena arrives, in order to return safely home, they are distracted from their concerns by the late arrival of Rosemary Adams with her sublimely beautiful daughter, Annabelle. Dressed in a Vionnet lame gown that clings to her limpid frame as if she has been dipped in gold, Annabelle arrives in the hallway to find she is the center of attention, The Summer Visitors transfixed by the allure of everything she might bring to the party.

"Why, I never even imagined we'd get here!" she says, excitedly, as the guests crowd around, her parents distracted by their friends elsewhere, "we were positively quaking in the car because of the wind– it almost turned into a ditch. Mother was beside herself with nerves. Thankfully, she had a vial of her special medicine and that soon calmed her down, much to Father's relief. My, thank you," she replies charmingly, to a gentleman at her side, "it's a Vionnet. I know, I'm a very lucky girl, but it is my debut. I'm going to be eighteen when the clock strikes midnight. And to think I feared we would be celebrating it in a car in the driving rain. Why, it's enough to make one positively giddy with relief. Not to mention, meeting someone as kind as you as soon as I walked through the door. Yes, please," she says to him. "I think I would like some champagne, thank you. No, I don't smoke, but… yes, well, you're right, I am big girl now – well, at least, come midnight, so I think I will try one.

"Oh, did Mother mention it? Yes, I'm going to be modeling as a mannequin in Manhattan this Fall. I'm staying at The Barbizon. Oh, how splendid of you to say; yes, I would love to be an actress. I went to Sacred Heart and I played a lot of roles, to some very nice notices. It's why I've cut my hair – Father went through the roof when he saw it, but I like it blonde.

No, I have awful red hair, and it's far too curly and I hate it. Sadly, there's nothing I can do about my freckles," she laments, placing her hands on her cheeks and guilelessly drawing attention to her perfect retroussé nose, of which, in private moments, she is also somewhat critical. "Why, you're very kind Mr. Dryden —I couldn't possibly call you, Douglas. Why, we're barely acquainted…well, only if you promise not to tell Mother I was so forward on my debut," she blushes, lowering her eyes to consider the champagne she has not yet sipped.

"I simply cannot believe I'm here at last!" she says, awed by the thrill of it all. "See, I grew up reading the stories about these parties in The Eavesdropper's column every Saturday morning and, of course, my parents were invited an awful lot, too. Oh, Mother's dresses, you've never seen gowns as splendid! But she always used to come back and tell me all about Mrs. Lyons and what she was wearing and whom Mrs. Lyons had invited, and anything else she did. My, to grow up and be like her, I would think, so famous and adored. And my parents were always very merry when they came home and, sometimes, they'd let me stay up to wait for them. Do you know that there have been some very, very famous people here, including President Coolidge, can you imagine? Film stars like Rupert Turner-Hume and Valentino, so exciting! No," she says, her every dream coming true, "all I ever wanted was to come to one of these parties and now I'm finally here! Mother did tell me it would be sublime, but I had no idea it would be as sublime as all this… Why, it's grander than I ever dreamt! And just look at the fountains of champagne and that surely cannot be, but yes it is! That is Errol Flynn as I live and breathe!" she marvels, placing her lovely hand on her youthful heart.

The surrounding Summer Visitors forgive Annabelle Adams her error: the gentleman in question is not Errol Flynn, but a waiter from Shirley, with similar facial hair. "Charming child, if a bit short sighted," they smile approvingly.

May Cook smiles sadly as Annabelle enthuses on. Her gaze flits to the imposing clock that has diligently marked nearly every minute of the life of a girl once so similar, Serena Lyons. "One minute to seven o' clock," she says, drawing in a deep breath. She thinks of Serena, upstairs, waiting for

Kit, and hopes she is not mistaken. She is old, she knows, but she had been so certain that he would come. "Still, there's time," she assures herself, a tear trickling down her cheek which she hastily brushes away as she looks back to Annabelle Adams, the brightest new star ever to be born at The Westhampton Leisure Hour and Supper Club. While, at the top of the staircase, another young girl, who will never be admired by anyone, The Little Maid, pauses to watch the beautiful people below, and weeps even harder at what she just found in Mrs. Lyons' bedroom.

An ambivalent heiress, married to an apathetic heir, to create a surname vituperatively envied by everyone below them on the social register, contemplates the room with a sigh. "The endless tedium of The Leisure Hour. It never seems to end," she mutters. It's not that she doesn't want to be here. She has no idea where she wants to be. What she is certain of, however, is her distinct lack of interest in Annabelle Adams, having seen more than a few of her kind pass through similar mansions since her own coming-out, a decade prior: She'll last a season and then marry some stockbroker, from one of the newer families, The Heiress deduces, wallowing in the tedious inevitability of the girl's fate. Perhaps their paths will cross at The Metropolitan Club and they'll nod in perfect comprehension of the pecking order: one superior: one almost, but not quite. Something to look forward to, she muses more cheerily, turning her attention to the window by the front door to see what the weather is doing. Yet, in the sudden illumination cast by the clear skies, The Heiress catches sight of a young man so handsome walking toward The Lilac Walk, that she almost stops breathing.

With a passion she has never before experienced, The Heiress tumbles into love with Life. She thinks of mansions and beaches and sea; tennis courts and dresses and laughter; teacups chinking off priceless porcelain and freshly cut flowers perfuming the rooms in which she sleeps and her children, so dark and bonny, the curious things they say; she thinks of never worrying for an instant and the lack of sadness she has known of the tragic surprises that can arrive in the midst of the monotony: What an incredible thing it is, she enthuses, gulping down air, as if for the first time. How lucky she feels to be standing here, watching him. How wonderful it has always been, and I didn't even know it, she realizes, overawed by the beauty that streams past her of everything she has been fortunate to receive. But the feeling is interrupted when the front door swings wide open and The Stationmaster from the railway, looking as if he had been dragged over a dirt track all the way to the party, rushes inside and announces to The Summer Visitors:

"Lucinda, dead on the train tracks. The wind blew her back into the path of the –" "Yuck, she drinks, you know," someone squeals, "and she reeks to high heaven." "Please," says The Stationmaster, turning to her in disgust, "say no more. Please."

And, almost as if at his command, The Summer Visitors fall silent, and try desperately to turn their thoughts away from Death.

THE UNINVITED GUEST

It flew away, that last hat. It was plucked off her head by a sudden gust of wind and buoyed toward the Atlantic Ocean, from the balcony where they sat, at The Maidstone Club. "Don't you want to join your friends on the beach," he had asked, gesturing toward some acquaintances, hosting an elaborate picnic on the sands, with tents and an Arabian horse. "They camped there overnight, you know," Serena whispered conspiratorially, widening her eyes, "Gerald and Sa—" and then, a gust of wind, and off went her hat...

It was wide-brimmed, and the chiffon attached to it ought to have been tied underneath her chin, but she had let it fall loose, like a veil over her shoulders. "You look like a beekeeper," he had teased, as they settled down to lunch. "I like bees," she had countered. "You know I do. It's like that cottage I adore in the grounds of Teddy's estate, the one I showed you, with the turret. I think it's the prettiest house in America." "Not La Doucette?" "No," she shook her head, and Kit watched a different veil from that of her hat fall over her eyes, an affect of brightness over something sad.

"They don't really look after it, but I would. It's such an easy place to manage; you could make everything perfect in a tiny house like that. At La Doucette, there's always a chipped molding or a broken door and it goes on and on. As soon as something is fixed, something else needs to be repaired.... But *there*," she continued, more animatedly, the sadness gone now, as she imagined living within its rooms, "you could have bookcases and pictures on the walls and you wouldn't need to walk for miles, or peek into a million rooms to find people, it would all be right at your fingertips; family..." Her voice trailed off as she spun out the rest of her dream and she seemed to Kit so much like a little girl who couldn't find her mother. Almost as if she sensed, even then, that her dream would never be anything more than that.

"And you could make delicious dinners in the kitchen, and neighbors would come in and out of the screen door, and you could grow an English country garden in the back and the front garden is where children would come and play, and you would be friends with everyone on the street..."

Kit smiled and said nothing as she talked on, despite how sorry he felt for her: Serena and her obsession with little things, he thought, sadly. The ordered meticulousness of her existence, dedicated only to pleasing others. Even her daydreams only seek to include.

In her room, on her desk, sat neat rows of colored notebooks filled with memos written about anyone she had ever met: all of their names, alphabetized, the dates of their meeting, likes and dislikes, and messages to herself; an instructional guide to instigating friendships from the pen of the loneliest girl: *'Talk to Sophie about Cocker Spaniels; Find out more about lacrosse, so Peter will visit, which will make Margaret happy; Never correct Violet, she is always right, and it would be dreadful if she turned Lily against me; Genevra will only gossip, so pretend to be intrigued, but don't listen....'* Then too, were her insights, within those notes; *'Don't forget to compliment Brooks on his manners, they are all he has, and he is so sensitive; Make sure William sits next to Violet; Lavish attention on Sarah, during her dark moods. She only has them to draw attention to herself; Remember to include Lucinda. Look for where she is hiding and bring her in...'* And one that he looked up, one afternoon in her bedroom, where he ought not have been and she did not know he hid; *'Always love Kit. He has no one else.'*

'How To Keep Friends:' the title page of the notebook, as if the very idea implied that she had none, or that the act of people liking her would require some effort on her behalf – a bargain or a Faustian pact. Serena never questioned the role she felt she must play for her friends, not even with him. Serena always tried so hard.

So her hats.

Despite the fact that they were her pride and joy, Serena's hats had not been pinned on since he had first arrived. On those mornings when Kit would collect her, she would tiptoe out into the courtyard, her head bowed so that the brim of her new one concealed her face, and then, she would look up, "Do you like it?" she'd ask, expectantly. All part of the ruse, he came to discover, but not one of vanity: Serena was not in search of praise. She did not consider herself pretty, which was inconceivable to him. She avoided mirrors, whenever she could: "I don't like what I find there," she'd say, and no amount of compliments or bemused protestations at how mistaken she was, could change her mind.

Wherever they walked together, she lost those hats to the wind, and Kit would chase them down country lanes, ripping his suit clambering over privets, or performing rugby tackles on perfectly manicured lawns to try and catch one as it made its bolt for freedom, Serena laughing at his back. "Never mind," she'd call, thrilled at his efforts on her behalf, "never mind, Kit. Let it go, let it go. It clearly wants to live on someone else's head." She failed to mourn a single one; Serena seemed happier after they were lost than before: carefree or careless? He could not be sure.

"Tell me where it's going," she would say, as he collapsed breathless, vanquished, onto the grass at her feet. Together, they would sit and watch its flight, the dip and soar of pale pink ribbons and ostrich plumes and wreaths of flowers on straw beds. And he would tell her stories of each and every one, the reason for its departure, its final destination. But he did not run to catch that last hat, a few days before the first party. He let it fly away, too concerned about the loss of his inheritance and what he could do to rectify the situation. "I think this one's bound for France, Serena," he said matter-of-factly, as if he was no longer shocked by the fact of its escape. "Really, how so?" she replied, her head tilted to the side, watching the sky. And only now can he hear the tears in her voice...

"The Pompadour frame, after one Madame de Pompadour," he pointed out, watching it soar over the beach in leaping arcs. "I suspect her head was chopped off in the French Revolution after the French wasted all that money securing your Independence and now your hat is looking for its original inspiration to perch upon again." "Impossible, my dear friend," she parried charmingly, affecting a similar tone. "My hat is bound for her grave, to pay homage to a greater head than mine, still very much attached to her. She died of tuberculosis, tragically young. Did you not pay any attention during History?" "Not a jot, Serena. I was thinking of you..." he replied, taking her hand, as she contemplated him from behind one of her dazzling smiles, "and there is no greater head than yours, in my opinion. But you will need to forfeit your Republican leanings when you make England your home: That's absolutely no way to discuss a country that will prove so hospitable to you." "Why, am I going to live there?" she replied, as if she didn't believe him, tilting back her lace parasol, a humorous query in her eyes, like she was kindly appeasing a child. "Indeed you are," he said, leaning in closer, "and although I will be able to provide no crown, I will buy you every hat in the country." "Well," she replied, and he remembers the shadow her golden eyelashes cast over her cheeks, as if she were a porcelain doll and they had been painted on by a creator more in love with her than anyone real, "in that case, I think you might kiss me."

"Without a hat, outside, in the mid-afternoon? Whatever will people say, Serena?" he said, in mock horror. "It could ruin you." "Ruin me then," she replied, underneath her breath, opening her eyes as he placed his lips on her own. And he can still feel her tears, hot against his face when she rested her forehead against his lips and how her fingers clenched his arms, almost painfully, despite her fragility. "Why these tears," he coaxed, confused by her sudden sadness. "Silliness," she said, before turning back to the view beyond, affecting the poised and captivated attention of a spectator at a game, to catch the last glimpse of her hat, spiraling over the sea, nothing more than a speck on a far horizon: "I just particularly loved that one."

In the face of her quiet disappointment, he almost leapt out of his seat in a futile attempt to make an effort, but it was too late. The moment was gone. Besides, he was further distracted from his thoughts by Serena, when she changed the subject to something else: "Gerald and Sara camped here together on the beach last night..." she said, gesturing to where they played on the sands below.

But her eyes no longer widened in scandalized conspiracy, they fastened onto his, and all he sees in them now, is a plea he was too young to understand. It was only later that Kit realized there are girls who lose hats because they are careless. Or those who own so many, another will never be missed. But Serena lost her hats on purpose, not to watch them fly away, but to see if he would save them: For Serena associated effort with love, because no one ever tried for her. And on that one occasion when he was too preoccupied to chase it, she interpreted it as a sign that he didn't love her anymore, and so offered the one thing left that he had not yet taken. Perhaps had he searched her room, he would have found another list; *'How To Never Lose Kit...'* And it's so sad to Kit to realize that, even with him, she had to go to those lengths. He would have sat next to her in silence, every year of his life, only to be near. In many ways, he has. He has kept the memory of her beside him, turning to it when he can bear, to catch a glimpse of that last summer: to relive her happiness whenever he fell breathless and defeated at her feet, her hat lost to the wind.

...

He arrives now at the end: The Lilac Walk, where everything began between them.

It is a bittersweet reunion of time and place and remembrance, because he can still hear her words, *"Ruin me,"* echoing in his ears, knowing that, ultimately, he did.

He ruined her amidst the lilacs. He left a mark that could never be erased. Something that was synonymous with shame; that deprived Serena of every ounce of happiness he wished for her to own.

But he is here to ask for her forgiveness, to bring her news of what they lost: those happy boys he has sometimes found in crowds.

THE HOSTESS

Our time together is nearly over. Stay with me, won't you, until the end. Let us savor the last seconds we will ever share. Soon we will all be shades and this evening nothing more than something past. For we all become ghosts when we become a memory, even while we still live. When we are only recalled in the minds of those we once meant something to, we haunt the margins of the parties they wish we could still attend.

We who remember are forever searching for those spectral stars. So we are drawn to the windows of our lives through which we perceive our histories, as I have this evening, with you. Here, we have watched a procession of the people I passed through and among, some of who altered my destiny irrevocably. I have been lost in a reverie of all that was and could have been, to honor the ghost of a boy, so fair and delicate: a boy who once smiled kindly, in perfect comprehension of my pain. And his compassion is stained with immortality, because it only happened once.

I do not know if he loved me or if he has ever thought of me again. But in farther rooms that I have never known, I have placed his son amidst the playthings of other children, on the floors of the houses in which I imagined we lived; I have stood on balconies and surveyed that endless sea he once sailed across to come to me; I have dreamed of English fields and books of poems he might have read; I have watched his receding figure chase my hats as they flew away, and I have been grateful for the gift of having known such kindness, even if it was not mine to keep. Some might think my years wasted, sorrowful, but they have not been empty. I have lived the life I longed for in my heart. And it is beautiful there.

Sometimes we are written down in books. Or, someone tells a story in which our name figures. And so we live on, through someone else's voice...

These are the indelible marks others make of us, like the watermarks of high tides, names carved into barks, or stamps branded onto belongings. For what else is history but the collected voices of others, who sing a chorus of what once was. It is not words but voices that are the inscriptions seared onto pages, into minds, of the fragments others glean, as we live our lives in passing. Flitting and fleeting, we rub off as we move through, and in our wake is cast the dust of the stars that we become. And sometimes it is caught on the fingers of others, and they press that gold to their lips, where it glistens, an eternal testimony to the fact that they adored us: So we, those of us who remember, we grow more golden as we age, as if cast into statues that commemorate the splendor of those who loved us, and those we were privileged to love.

Wait with me now, wait for the stars. For only with their arrival can I go. As I told you at the start of this evening, I am leaving in the night, but not with Kit. Where I am going is a place I have never seen, that I must journey to alone. And in this, the fading light of a life less lived, all I ask is that what we once shared has meant something to him, and that he will be the last guest to appear on this road before me. So that I can know that he did return for me, in the end: if only to say goodbye.

Soon, soon, we shall see the first star. Please let it be his. Please let it b—

No.

. . .

There are those keepers of time, whose ticking timepieces do not match the rhythm of our own. Sometimes the minutes are yet to elapse; sometimes they already have. We have been living in a moment that has already transpired, its outcome determined. It is seven o'clock by someone else's watch: the only watch that matters – Edward's.

There is no need to hide. He will not see you. You only exist to me.

I could beg, I could plead: *One more minute: Please one more... Don't make me turn away. Please let me see if he will arrive in the dying light of this, my final hope.* But he will be deaf to all my pleadings: For we are leaving now. We are all leaving in our ways.

I am a prisoner, trapped like everyone else in this house, by this storm. I can only do as he says. I cannot move. I have no voice: He was the one who placed me here. Don't you recall what I told you? *We all become ghosts when we become a memory...*

I am nothing more than a ghost at a window.

Edward has come to lock me away.

But look, he has brought me lilacs.

THE UNINVITED GUEST

This road to her is not new but ancient, one that merges past and present. As if life here at the end has arched back to touch its beginnings, complete at last, and all that was in-between is not meaningless, but everything. For contained within it was the thought of what could be again, if only the path back to where it started could be found. He is walking to her now, to where he will find her, the heart's objective the same. Beneath his feet are the lilacs; sodden with remorse, pulled from their branches, and he hears Serena say,

"Ruin me."

And this is the beginning Kit has sought, as he has waited for her these years. Another night so long ago: the night before the first party…

That evening, the lavender brushed heavily against the sides of his legs as he passed under the bower of roses, that seemed to drift like lace overhead for miles. Between their thorns and leaves, he could glimpse the sky diminishing to pale yellow as dusk approached; the light seemed so different in September, edged in gold, after the white brilliance of August. The summer was dying, there would never be another the same, and as if in recognition of what they did not know then, there would be a party to commemorate its death: Yet, all of it was still to come, in the minutes and hours that would follow. But, first, there was the promise they had made: "Meet me at The Lilac *Walk.*" She was waiting for him there.

There was purpose in every step they took toward each other: the fatalistic intent of lovers who understand the danger of the game; who will love to consume, by embarking on its course, daring it to be taken away by some mis-step, a flaw, a lie the heart might make, culminating in ruin. For those who love truly, wish only to be destroyed: *Mark me, sear something onto my flesh…* This is what they beg, before the fall. Then, as now, he walked a deliberate path to her, for what existed between them, would end, with what they were about to do; that promise to one another they would not break. And if tonight, another promise is kept, everything will end again. This is what Kit prays.

They leaned, deeper and deeper, toward that floor of petals, Kit's arms locked at her back, afflicted by a disease that stops the heart at its fullest. They were resigned not determined on desire; already the agonizing regret of loss punctuated every intake of breath. There could be no avoiding their fate. Their limbs wrapped like the coiling branches of the trees that wept their petals over them. Her hair, fanned out like sand, tumbling into spirals beneath them as they inched closer and closer to that white and lilac floor. And there, in that moment of suspension between standing and falling, it passed between them, the fusion of souls. The fusion that would ensure they would be forever branded by that promise, by what they would find in the memory every time they turned back to acknowledge it: Death. For as soon as the soul is joined to another and then lost, there is no point in anything afterward.

We were ruined, amidst the lilacs, as all lovers are wont to do, Kit accepts, looking back to the trees. Lovers ruin other lovers; so no one else can ever trespass there.

. . .

They are unlucky, the lilacs. If you take them from where they should not be. The myth says that Death arrives, if they are shorn from their branches and displayed inside houses. Or worse, that the fairies lock the lover in with the dying flowers, away from who they love most, who is then condemned never to return.

He remembers that Serena took the lilac with her when she left. The following morning, Kit watched her run from him into that pink mist, petals and twigs clinging to every inch of her hair and dress. Yet, how could he have foreseen that she had been devoured whole by desire, that the flowers would ensure she was punished and he with her. They were stained by their violet ink, their perfume, a poison smeared over their skin that aged and withered their hopes and dreams, like their petals curling into ugliness, after they were plucked from where they grew and should have remained. Serena was locked into her house, and Kit imprisoned from where there was no escape, except in his imagination.

And yet, all there has been for Kit is this memory of her amidst the lilacs, that last glance between them, as she turned back to him that morning, the defining moment of who they were – and would always be – to one another. For contained within it was the creation of a child; a son that neither of them would know.

How many last glances are there in a life? Kit asks, as he approaches the courtyard. If we could recognize those minutes, as they arrived, and accept them as the last of all we have loved, could we find the courage to turn back at that final moment, without fear or expectation? Or would we still look away, unable to confront what we would lose. In his memory, Kit has buried his face in the ground he slept upon than watch her leave him. He has been haunted by her smile, by the contentment and gratitude of that lonely girl, who gave up everything to please him, who had such faith that he would never fail her.

Was it this act, the places where they trespassed, or Teddy's betrayal, or the secret Captain Lyons kept that destroyed them both? Was it the sprig of lilac, pressed between the pages of a book that separated them when Captain Lyons locked it into a study, and Kit's soul with it? Kit does not know. All I am certain of, he thinks, is that we are passed into arms when we are born and sometimes we are held for far longer than is our right. Yet, those arms seek only to pass us to those of another, who waits somewhere, where we ask to be embraced, cradled in comfort and remorse and pain and privilege until we die. Serena was right, all those years ago. Those in love should always cling, with a strength previously unrecognized, with the force of life exulting and continuing, claiming what it is their right to own. And at the end, after we have turned away in our foolishness, we search for those arms once more, because only within their embrace can we find peace.

I have come to tell her that our son was held by other arms who loved him, because our own could not. I have come to tell her that once, many years ago, in a place I would have hoped never to find him so young, into my arms he came.

THE HOST

"Serena, my dear, do not be afraid," he says softly, sitting at her side and reaching for her hand. "I have not come to hurt you. If I could simply sit with you a while, for the time that is left to us, that is all I ask. I would like to say goodbye, and to give you something I have kept, something from a summer long ago.

"I know that you can offer me no sign to tell me yes or no. I can guess, too, at your despair, that I should be the last face you will ever see. I know how you have prayed for someone other all these years. You have waited in this room, for him to return; a private ritual before these parties that I have orchestrated for you, the consummate hostess. Yet, I have something that I must tell you, Serena. So again I must impose myself; to insist that you listen, in the absence of the person you loved most. And I know it should be him with you, here. It should be his hand that holds your own and weeps for you.

"But Serena, my beloved wife, Kit is not the same as you remember. And so it falls to me to tell you why.

"I should not have chosen this dress for you," he says, touching the chiffon of the fabric. "The contrast between the first party and this last is too marked, too unkind. Yet, I wanted your guests to remember you as you once were, not how you are now. Because that is the memory I shall always treasure of you, Serena, after this final door closes between us: of the first party, your golden russet hair starlit, the silk slippers on your feet, your fabled lilacs still in bloom.

"I have brought some for you. I know you think it cruel to cut them, but you will understand when I give you what I hold in my hand, why I wish for you to have these. They are dried, not real, for you to keep where you will go now.

"Forgive me, Serena. I would not have you see me weep, but I am powerless to stop. I cannot stand for you to leave, but it is far too late for regret, for second chances. I have asked myself, this past week, how it will be between us, after they take you. When I can no longer come and sit with you, as I do this evening, when I can no longer reach for you. What shall I do when I cannot share all I have seen; the stories from beyond this room, where I have kept you in front of this window, of these people you have loved? I shall visit, if you will let me. But it will never be the same. You will be locked away, where you will be safe. Yet, how might it have been different had I simply said: *Turn the page:* Might I have spared you this? Or is this, even now, preferable to anything you have ever shared with me?

"I know that you wished for your guests to see you, as you descend the staircase, one final time, to arrive at this, the last party I can host for you. I promised you this, last Friday, when I held you in my arms on the road outside the house... After what happened when you closed the door on me, to go to where I could not find you: But, this, what I have done to you, must not be the last thing that your guests see. It is better this way, Serena, for they will only remember your grace, and it is like I told you once; there is nothing more sacred than memory: We are only as good as we are remembered. I hear these words again, Serena, as I place in your hands something that belongs only to you. Forgive me, my love, for having kept it so long.

"I gave you the party. It was all I could give until today, the hope that the red front door would open and he would come back to you. There is only ever one guest at any party of the heart: I have learned this better than anyone. For me, it has been you. For you, Kit. I say this without rancor, for I have guarded the love you owned, keeping it alive, as best I could, in this house where it was first taken from you. I did this for you, Serena, so that you might live as you once dreamed, Kit at your side, despite how far he was. This is also how it will be for me, when I cannot see you anymore and all I can do is remember. I will live the life I wished we could have led, safe from disappointment and truth, where I can pretend that you chose it, where I can pretend that you chose me. I will sit at your side and speak to you of the souls of better men; I will walk amongst the stars to find you the brightest amongst them."

Captain Lyons watches as the last of the light falls over Serena's perfect face, and, for a moment, although he knows it is impossible, because of the years in-between, she seems suddenly so young; "You are far too young to be leaving," he says, "but we cannot dictate the hour we will depart, or the minute when someone, like me, sends us on our way, as I do with you now.

"My only solace," he says, drawing down the door of the coffin over Serena, "is that in this place where you lie, I can keep you as you were; a seventeen-year-old girl, so full of promise. And it is like drawing down the lid on a ballerina in a music box, to safeguard all of the beauty contained within: the beauty that will never spoil, that will remain forever on in my heart as the most exquisite sight my eyes ever stilled to watch.

Goodbye, my beloved Serena."

THE PARTY, THE PARTY!

The only detail on which The Summer Visitors can agree is that the two shots sounded at exactly the same moment: the shot that killed Serena Lyons and the shot, through the back of the head, which killed her oldest and dearest friend, Teddy Worthington.

"Soul mates," some swear. "Nonsense," counter others, "have you forgotten Kit and what of Captain Lyons?" "What of Captain Lyons," still others rejoin, "he had a rifle in his hand!" "He never shot it," the more considerate hiss: "It was an accident. He said he was only trying to shoot a bir—" "A bird, in the middle of a party, in the fog? You cannot expect anyone to believe that, can you? " "How cruel, to shoot a bird," others protest, "but then, he is known for hunting, isn't he," they concede, acknowledging The Emperor. "It is not the same thing," interrupt the exacting. "You're all being overdramatic. Serena had a heart attack because of the firework that exploded over her head. In any case, does it matter? She's dead now..."

Yes, their incomparable Hostess is dead. And The Summer Visitors have come to mourn her passing, just as they mourned her dearest friend Teddy Worthington, not four days ago. Yet, the two occasions could not have proven more distinct. Without Serena to help him, Teddy was lowered into a pauper's grave, his family estate mired in the debt he committed his life to accumulating. Not a soul, not even their Host, inconsolable at what he had learned, volunteered the funds necessary for a headstone: a decision May Cook understood but could not support. She had never approved of how Teddy treated Serena, but out of respect for her and how she always looked after him, she saw to it that one be placed by his grave in the Remsenburg cemetery. It reads simply, *Theodore Charles Worthington, 1883-1938. Lover of*

Snow. "I think Serena will like that," she explained at the funeral. "I must remember to tell her, when we meet again…"

"Will you stand for her?" A very proper gentleman from New England, asks rhetorically of his companions, assembled around a table at the French doors – "Refreshing breeze through these doors. So hot in here," the ladies agree, rolling the pearls of their single strand necklaces between their fingers, and nodding their grey-haired bobs in unison – "I think we must," he insists earnestly, pointedly, casting his eyes around the five members of his group for the affirmation he does not seek, because it will be done his way, whether they like it or not; "Everyone," he announces pointlessly to his immediate environment, "We must stand for Serena, when they bring her down. There's a hymn: '"For Those in Peril on the Sea.' She cho – "

"'For Those in Peril On the Sea?' Echoes a passing churchgoer in contempt. "Why in the world would she choose that one? I don't really think a hymn is appropriate considering her conduct before she died." "Now, now," chastens The Proper Gentleman, recognizing that the conversation might dangerously sidle into totally inappropriate areas, considering that it is Serena Lyon's wake. "Perhaps it was *his* favorite," insinuates his friend's wife slyly. "How so," questions someone else, instantly interested, "do you mean because…?" "Yes, I do"…she replies, with gusto, before lowering her voice conspiratorially, in grudging deference to her husband's appalled expression. "He left the house to her." "The house! That derelict cottage!" reiterates her partner, aghast. "What would she want with somewhere like that? I ask of you, the Grand Dame, Serena Lyons in that ramshackle old hut, makes no sense." "But didn't you hear?" cuts in a wildly attractive starlet, "It had a se-nt-i-m-ent-al value…." "You don't mean…." the women insinuate. "Yes. I. Do. Word is, she was leaving with him. With Teddy Worthington."

"But he only had one eye," exclaims The Proper Gentleman's wife. "Now, that really is it! I forbid you to say anymore," her husband admonishes. "How could you be so unfeeling? He was injured in the War: He was only there a month. Sometimes I think I've never known you." "Highly probable," his wife retorts sharply, the pent up loathing and resentment of decades causing her to tug violently on her cashmere shrug. "You've never laid a finger on me in years." The Starlet's eyes immediately widen as if to say, 'that explains everything,' and their friends clear their throats and try not to pay any attention at all. "That is absolutely not true," he hisses, turning puce with rage. "Well, then, if it isn't," his wife seethes through a dangerously locked jaw; "I must have blinked and missed it," she concludes, before collapsing into sobs.

"About Worthington?" continues a know-it-all, who prides herself on a level head and a lack of emotion. "Cook in the back of the house saw everything. How could he afford to pay her? Serena, she used to sub him," The Know-It-All replies perfunctorily. "Anyway, she hears Teddy say 'Gentleman,' she hadn't even heard the door go, which was unusual, she told me, as she has excellent hearing. Anyhoo, next she hears him say, 'May I stand by the window?' Say what you like about Teddy, but he was a true gentleman. Impeccable manners…. Well, this prompts Mrs. Carter, the cook, to come out from the back kitchen and there he is, old Teddy, arms clasped behind his back, watching out of that Palladian window. She doesn't think anything of it for a second. Apparently he liked to stand there, bit of a habit," The Know-It-All shrugs. "Whenever she might ask what he was up to, because," she chuckles, realizing that she had liked him far more than she had thought, "you never had to stand on ceremony with him, he'd always reply with something witty to put you at your ease. Had a friend called Peter – ha, ha! – Used to have me in hysterics…

"But then," she continues, holding up forestalling hands, and adopting a graver tone, "the gunshot, straight through the back of the head. Gangsters. Owed them a fortune. They didn't see Mrs. Carter, thank God. But still she hasn't made any sense since Friday. She keeps on repeating, 'They closed the gate behind them,' and it's broken her heart. Seemingly, the only thing Teddy ever insisted upon was that the gate stay ajar. 'I'm waiting for the snow,' he'd say. 'But Mr. Worthington, it's July,' she'd protest. 'Yes, but miracles do happen. You never know, the snow might come…. I'm a philo-sophical optimist at heart.' And then he'd give her the Teddy smile; that hapless, boyish 'I've just broken the heirloom china with my tennis ball, but you love me really, don't you,' and it didn't matter he hadn't paid her in months, she'd only tut and walk back to the kitchen and hope Mrs. Lyons would visit that day. Sometimes she thought that Teddy did little else than stand watching that gate for her. She used to say that he could make it from the window to the door to greet Serena in less time than it took him to fritter away the family fortune…

"The real tragedy of it is that he could have saved himself," she says, suddenly overwhelmed by the sadness of his loss, despite how often she has repeated the story in the days since Teddy had died. "Apparently the only thing he owned of any value was a pair of diamond hair combs. But he refused to sell them, even when Mrs. Carter begged him to when times were so hard for him. And all he would ever say about it was, 'They don't belong to me. I'm only looking after them for someone else…'"

"So who was she, this Serena Lyons? 'Course, I've heard of her, of 'Little Newport' as we call it, but we've summered forever in the real Newport, and before that Saratoga, so this is the first gathering we've ever attended." Somebody superior comments to nobody in particular. "I'm so sorry, who?" replies The Nobody.

And at an upstairs door, The Host emerges, closing it behind him…And The Little Maid walks despondently down the staircase, stopping midway as if there is no real point in carrying on…And Anthony Duverglas arrives within inches of the great love of his life, Venetia Dryden…And Annabelle Adams brims with excitement at all of her tomorrows…And May Cook feels only relief that hers are behind her…And Rupert-Turner Hume looks up to find a girl, the living image of his dead wife, and thinks of first kisses and last kisses and all of those in-between…And the rest of the guests talk on, arranging and making plans and thinking of what they will do tomorrow and the next day and the day after – And now arrives the last and uninvited guest.

MAY COOK

"I am The Eavesdropper," announces May Cook to the crowd, well aware that not a soul is listening to her. "But, ssshh, don't tell anyone just yet," she smiles impishly, as the guests continue to pay her no mind. "It would spoil all the fun...

"I believe – and I say this with some authority and no small amount of pride—that, of all of us, I am the very oldest guest in attendance," she continues brightly, wrapping her hands around her cane. "But don't let that trouble you unduly. I consider it a virtue, because I remember everything. I have seen it all from my habitual chair, here in the corner of the ballroom, where I sit now, with all of you, as we wait for the party to end.

"Did any of you guess?" she asks, raising her eyebrows quizzically to the room. "Or were you fooled by the fact that I sometimes include myself in my columns? I suppose that many of you might judge me very harshly, especially considering what I've written about you... But I had to have something to do when I returned from Antibes all those years ago. I rationalized at the time that anything had to be better than dressing up as an Indian from the Shinnecock Reserve on Lake Agawam, to raise money for charity with the dire Dreadnaughts. Besides," she continues joyously, "hasn't it been such wonderful fun, these *Tales of The Summer Visitors at The Westhampton Leisure Hour and Supper Club?'* All of the gossip and scandal about you beautiful creatures that I have observed, here from my perch in the corner of the room, that with the help of my friend, the Editor in Chief of The Southampton Press, to whom I dictate my column, I have brought to you each Saturday morning of summer. Perhaps you might consider yourselves honored," she says, turning to a group of guests at her side, studiously looking anywhere but at this little old lady talking to herself in a corner, "he is the only one who is aware of my true identity. And now you," she beams to the scene before her. "Yet, I thought it so very important that we meet each other, at last: I did so want to say goodnight before I go.

"Do you know that I can hear practically everything that goes in this marble hallway?" she asks. "Something to do with an echo, or so I realized when, crippled with the vile arthritis that has so undone me, I was deposited here, next to the window, by my husband, on the evening of Serena's debut: It's one of those tidy and safe places, sufficiently out of the way, where the view is pleasant enough, but which does not invite others to tarry long. I'm sure you've come across ladies like me at functions before," she says, knowingly. "Perhaps you've even offered a sympathetic word or two in passing, before joining those more intriguing types, invariably in a gayer portion of the room, where the real fun is to be had. Those places where ladies like me once held court ourselves, but where we can no longer follow. Death begins here in these corners," she sighs heavily. "You find that your life swiftly starts to recede before you as a consequence of those failed romances, or disappointments, or illnesses, that first placed you in them and, by and large, the process of oversight begins. Soon, you cease to exist."

This is what happened to May after the tragedy, when she was wheeled off the ocean liner and confronted New York once more. "I was right back in the throes of it, as if I'd never been away; the smothering customs of The Social Guard still rigidly in place; the arranged marriages; the carping inane snobbery; the mistreatment of staff under the auspices of heritage; The Dreadnaughts bullying everyone into submission. The heartbreaking reality that never again would I see the sun glint off the Mediterranean Sea, or walk the steep steps to our house in Antibes to hear the sound of gypsy laughter emanating from a ballroom in the late afternoon; that I would never again, in my life, dance on the sands of the Camargue where the white horses run free. Have you ever danced a flamenco on the sands of the Camargue to the sound of a gypsy guitar?" she asks, lost in the memory all over again. "I have.... I cast off my shoes one evening in 1891 and danced in a way society would never have approved of...

"I used to dance with Patrick," she says, fondly. "Oh, that son of mine could dance, the grace of a swan, but not to frenetic songs like they have nowadays. No, we waltzed, he and I: I helped to teach him myself, in our ballroom in Cap D'Antibes, when he was a child. The usual tricks for dancing with children; he stood on my feet. We had a gifted instructor we would always hire for the summer, Arnaud. He was a gypsy from the Camargue region, devastatingly handsome in that French fashion: black hair, bluest eyes, the accent, of course, which rarely hinders. And he would come every afternoon, the sun washing through that gilded room at a low angle, the Mediterranean beyond, the olive trees, the breeze... We used to blow kisses to him off the balcony, after our lessons, Patrick and I. Heaven! How I adored those summers, but I think it may have been because I was in my prime; happy as a clam, so in love..." she says, noting with sadness how old her hands seem to her now, when contrasted with the recollection of holding those of her son's, when they had danced in Cap d'Antibes.

"I used to tease Helen Fitzgerald about it, whenever she'd try to one-up some poor soul by proclaiming, 'Summers on Gin Lane. Can there be anything more divine?' 'Yes, Helen,' I'd interrupt, 'Summers in Cap d'Antibes with a Frenchman called, Arnaud.' Ha! Her face! Priceless. So very strait-laced, Helen, but a firm friend to Serena – In the end," she adds shrewdly, but her mind remains fixed on Antibes... "They have a saying, the gypsies there, that you shouldn't stay in one place for too long. They say, 'One should always leave with some regret in one's heart.' Well, *I* did. I was inconsolable, but there was nothing to be done.... You see, my eldest daughter who was all of nineteen at the time, tumbled into folly-laced love with that impossibly good-looking Frenchman and he with her. I'd never seen him like that with anyone else. But I feared for her terribly; those gypsy hearts, they can be so very inconstant, you know.... He came to ask for my husband's permission. He had a boat; he wanted to sail it with her all through the Mediterranean. I remember when I heard that, I almost let her go; I thought of dancing on the sands, the freedom I felt, but it was out of the question: Better, we thought, to let her keep him only as a lovely memory. It was a mistake, of course; depriving the young of love always is. It ruined my daughter: She never forgave me. Instinct, you see," May clucks sadly, "and the first choice is always the best, to my mind; everything after smarts with disappointment. Why, just look at Kit and Serena....

SAMANTHA BRUCE-BENJAMIN

"I was only fifty though," she continues, regretfully. "Far too young for the corner to beckon, to be left here, an afterthought, unable to stand up by myself. To sit alone and remember how tall I had once been, tall like a light-house, he would say, because of my blond hair that went white in the sun, my searching eyes. No, that summer of my return, I vividly saw the future unfurl before me, understanding that the best of me was spent, and accepting that I simply could not survive the death of my heart. So."

May made up her mind to kill herself. At Serena's debut: arsenic, a tiny draft in her purse. She planned to drink it and fall asleep in the corner, where she sits tonight. She reasoned there would be so many people there that by the time anyone realized, it would be too late. She felt such relief as she settled in her chair that evening, *Soon*, she told herself, *it will be over*. The only small comfort May derived was knowing how happy Serena and Kit were going to be together; their courtship had been the only pleasurable aspect of her return: How heavenly it is to be them, she thought that evening, pulling out the vial, so much to look forward to....

But, it was then that Serena suddenly appeared, running down the staircase to Kit. Yes, this is how it should be, May thought, watching Serena, this type of passion, careless of constraint, unbound by decorum, a feast of emotion that defies all logic. May relished how scandalized everyone was, cheering Serena for her defiance. There it was in front of her, what May was about to leave: Life! The best of what it could be. She almost became Serena for a moment, living each second that elapsed with her, acutely aware of the privilege that awaited her beyond the door where Kit waited. But then the shadowy veil started to fall, obscuring brightness, reminding her of the shadows, of the betrayals, the damage she couldn't repair, the kind of love she would never know again. And then May couldn't bear to watch anymore: She fumbled the top off the vial with her stiffened fingers: *Not to see*, she prayed, raising it to her lips, *never to see again*.... But with the sound of the door slamming shut that reverberated like an alarm throughout the hallway, May dropped the vial in fright. And all that remained of her death was the vision of Serena sobbing on Teddy's arm, walking over the puddle of poison that had pooled at her feet. "No," May cried out in protest, but not for herself, for Serena: It was as if the veil had been lifted from her eyes. May saw everything to which she had been blind. And so she turned back from the precipice before she fell.

"Only to survive, my fellow guests," she reminisces, "only to survive: If I'd not written about Serena's parties, I don't like to think of how close I would have come to leaving my darling son alone for the five years that were left to him, before he died. Yet, after what I witnessed at Serena's debut, a new kind of heartbreak settled over me: Because of Kit, that beautiful creature, because of his smile. Do you see?" she inquires, scanning the faces of the guests. "Well, maybe you don't, not yet. The point is I had to stay then, if only for Serena. And so, the column was born. Of course, it was only later that it became what it is now, after the parties of 1917 when The Westhampton Leisure Hour and Supper Club was truly initiated. Before then, it was nothing more than amusing eavesdropping's from her parties, a mention here or there of Kit, the summer he had stayed with us. So that Serena might never forget. And, slowly and by degree, in helping her to live, I have arrived at the grand old age of eighty-one," she trills, proudly.

"Of course, some of you are quite young," she observes, directing her speech to the teenage girls and boys hip to hipping on the dance floor, "so you don't like to get too close, frightened it might rub off on you. But it will. You'll be old too, one day, I hope," she counsels, maternally. "I'd like for you to learn as much as I have, what I understand about life. It's like, I think, a carnival; all of us on the merry-go-round, perched on pretty, painted horses, waving and laughing; some of us crying because we are afraid, some of us praying, some of us, despite the fervent efforts of others, dead already; but what a wonderful journey, even if it only ever takes us in a circle, back to the very beginning; everything we see; the hearts to which we wave; up and down we go in gracious, leaping arcs, waving hello and goodbye simultaneously, turning for a last look at the faces behind us, sometimes not; a ride that goes on forever, new faces replacing the old, with different perspectives on the crowd, but, at its core, an endless cavalcade of promise. What a joy it has been to watch," she tells them, "despite how the spectacle sometimes disappoints, hurts, forces one to grieve, but what a gift to have been able to sit here for this long. I wish the same for all of you," she says, smiling over at them. "I hope that what you will witness in your lives exceeds your every dream.

"Naturally," she says, turning her penetrating gaze to the window beside her, where she can see the courtyard of La Doucette, "one begins to play back memories when people leave, especially central figures of any existence, around which we oscillate: Serena being the star, this evening. All of the recollections that pirouette through the mind when we remember her; Serena welcoming the President; Serena dancing with Teddy; Serena lost in thought at a window; Serena watching the children rush through the door; Serena gliding from guest to guest; Serena hearing the name, Kit, and coming alive again, if only for a second. Snapshots," she announces pointedly, glancing back at the party, "all we ever know of anyone; what they permit us to see. A picture can be formulated, but it is always unfinished: Serena's game of the Five Things, a perfect example. Do you have yours yet?" she asks a passing lady, who nods politely before hurrying away. "Perhaps not," she calls after her, "but sooner or later, you'll gather them and I will understand as little about you from them as you would if I were to tell you mine. There lies the answer. We none of us know anyone, even those we love the most.

"So we must say goodbye tonight," she concedes, sitting back in her chair. "But it's not so very sad, I assure you. It's like leaving a party; sometimes, you'll see the guests again, at others you will not. You younger ones might find this upsetting, the idea of losing promising faces in the tossing and turning crowd. But those of us who are older; we are resigned. For there is an awareness, as we age, as we learn, that there are other parties elsewhere that we will be invited to attend, and, perhaps, the last party, will prove to be the very best, for someone will arrive to lead us out. And it is that person's hand we will grasp, complete finally in ourselves, as we understand the why of everything that happened, when we are reunited, at long last.

"I have bid farewell to everyone I loved," she says, resignedly, "and those for whom I cared not a whit. I have woken on mornings, doubled up in agony for my son who died alone, whose courage, to run over the top of the trench, while the Teddy Worthington's of this world loitered behind, caused him to fall, face down onto an earth God gave him to bless; I have wept for the sorrow I caused others, for my husband for whom I felt nothing, despite how he adored me; for my daughter who loved a man she could never have, that one summer at her prettiest; for the love I left behind in Cap D'Antibes.... I have mourned the missed chances and opportunities that once were so readily available. But, do not pity me," she instructs the guests, rallying brightly. "I much prefer to watch now...And the things I have seen!

"I *loved* to watch Serena with those Chinese lanterns," she exclaims. "Kit at her side in Remsenburg Park. Yes, I did say Kit," she says, widening her eyes authoritatively to the crowd, "He was with her. He was always with her. I told Serena once; I think it helped. 'No, Mrs. Cook, surely you're referring to Teddy,' she said kindly – she was terribly kind, Serena; not a malicious bone in her body – 'No, I said Kit, Serena. Kit was with you. Kit is always with you.' Such a nerve I touched, her face visibly drained of color, but it's so important for people to learn of who waits at their side. Whether they believe it or not is entirely a different matter," she adds ruefully, shaking her head. "'But he's never come back for me,' Serena said. 'Hasn't he, Serena?' I asked. 'How can I explain this to you, my dear? It's like, I think, that entrancing clapperboard house you loved so much, that your father built over: the simple truth you always speak of that exists at the heart of La Doucette. Serena,' I said, 'there is a simple truth that exists at the heart, at the core, of all of us: It is called the soul. And if you remember only one thing of life, remember this: Always trust the soul, Serena: It knows. Instinct is its emissary. Who the soul loves first, loves last.' She continued to grasp my hand, a multitude of thoughts coursing through her mind, as she came to her own conclusions. Oh, what a perfect creature she was then," May says, remembering, "like a gazelle; To have ever been so pretty as Serena, what a lucky girl... To have been loved by Kit so deeply, even after he was gone.

"Of course," May admits, soberly, "we run a risk, us See-ers, when we confide what we see to others: premonitions of futures, of life and death, the ghosts who live amidst us. Perhaps Serena thought me mad, out of mind. Yet, if she did, she was far too gracious to let it show, because all she said was, 'Thank you.' Not dismissively, but contemplatively, as if there was an answer in what I had revealed that she had never considered.

"He used to chase her hats, you know...." she says. "She lost them on purpose, to see if he would," May chuckles. "And he did not fail her, as so many others did. He would have done anything for her, to guarantee her happiness. Well, he did, didn't he...?" she insists, sitting up taller. "I imagine that would be amusing to many of you, wouldn't it," she comments shrewdly. "It's too commonplace to speak of lost hats in the context of great romances, isn't it? Because all these years you've wanted a touch more than the story gave you. 'Tell me what he told her that Wednesday in June when he took her sailing at the end of Basket Neck Lane,' I've heard you beg. 'What did he whisper when he waltzed with her at Sara Wiborg's clambake?' Oh, such things, I can assure you. Not that you've ever asked me," she chastises them. "But sometimes, the instances that define great love, those to which we return forever on, *are* commonplace: derisory to some, those who like to sneer, and yet a perpetual comfort to those for whom it happened because, over time, they become something other, infinitely more precious. And there forever, when we look back, is encapsulated everything those who had the privilege to love completely ever sought from life and received for one brilliant moment. For Serena, it was the memory of a hat, lost, a boy chasing it. Enough? Well, yes. Because it was her hat, that boy, what it signified to her. For each of us, all great love is nothing more than a simple story that barely fills the pages of the history that constitutes our lives. Yet, it is enough.

"Of course, none of you have ever arrived at a satisfactory answer, have you, despite all your gossip?" May remonstrates, affectionately. "The perpetual question of the party: Why did she let the door close on him, why did he not follow her? What I witnessed, sitting in this very spot, having nothing to do with the circumstances involving Captain Lyons and Teddy....

"Well, I'll tell you now," she announces. "The night of her party, what they saw pass before them was their life together and its inevitable death. There emerged a truth that both suddenly understood; *There will come a day when I will have to live without this love and however will I survive then because nothing else will ever compare?* That notion proved so terrifying that both thought to turn away, to spare one another the agony; to flee from love, knowing they would be unable to survive its death. And, in this way, they told themselves, what they had owned together would prove eternal, for it would reside only in the memory where it could never die: It was an act of extraordinary courage and compassion, a recognition of their own frailties;

his smile, her outstretched arms offering welcome even as she permitted him to leave: acts of assurance and consolation they thought would never fail them, even in their darkest hours. But then...

"The story didn't end there, did it? Because the red front door was closing. Only then did it begin to dawn on them what they were truly giving up. Only then did something in Kit speak to him of his actual death, that I unexpectedly foresaw; an innate knowledge that told him he would die without her; the reason why he ran back to the door, after it closed, which I witnessed through the window, as he immediately thought better of the path he had chosen. And as Serena acknowledged the party within, life itself, she realized that she was about to lose the partner to her soul, with no guarantee that she might ever find him again. So she turned back. But it was too late, wasn't it? Their fates were sealed. The red front door had closed.

"So, do you understand now, why I had to write him down?" she asks again, sitting forward in her seat. "You see, The Westhampton Leisure Hour and Supper Club – *'The party, the party...,'* the column – is life," she reveals to the guests: "Life continuing even as it ends for others. Haven't you fathomed that yet?" she asks, as if it is the most obvious answer in the world. "Everyone shut out from the party, whether by choice, or the actions of others, or fate, died: Kit, Teddy, Serena, and all the other ghosts who are present tonight. So, this is why it was so very important that I continue on, to keep Kit alive; to make sure that Serena would never doubt the simple truth within her; that he was perfect host for her soul and herself, the perfect hostess for his. So that she would always wait at an open door, to admit him when he arrived again to take her home: Because there is never any surety in the path of the soul, especially when other people stand in the way, as they often do, intent on claiming such souls for themselves. And, sometimes, as heartbreaking as it is, those for whom we wait do not choose us in the end; they arrive for someone else instead..." she concludes, with a regretful smile.

"But then," May continues, reflecting proudly on her life's work, "on seeing the consolation Serena derived from his inclusion in the column. I thought to bring back into the party the many others who were left outside so early, so cruelly; to remember them as best I could as frequent characters in my column, so that they, too, might not be forgotten. Of course I changed the names – they became The Dancer, The Gilded Idol, The Dandy, The Last Resort; all dead and gone, but alive each week, so that they could live on in the hearts of those they were waiting to meet again, one day. And aren't you glad that I did?" she says, clapping her hands joyously. "Haven't we had such fun?

"And look," she exclaims, placing her hands on her heart as she looks to the window, "there he is now, that precious boy. Why, he's barely changed: Such a gentle soul, still the same radiant smile. And aren't we all rewarded," she says, turning her bright eyes to the room as if to search for a kindred spirit, "we who have faith in such things? All of us who pray that our one person will arrive at the door to lead us out at the end of the party? I don't know about you, but I take such solace in knowing that Kit left Serena the brightest star at the front door of this house, all those years ago, and now he has navigated back by that same star, albeit the one she has become in death: the one that has continued to burn so brightly, by honoring his memory, so that he might find her once more.

"Well," she exhales, contentedly, "How I would adore to watch this reunion, but I am terribly tired, you see. No," she nods affirmatively, "I stayed up long enough to see him get here, to prove myself right, but there's Patrick, now," she says, pointing to her son, walking toward her. "Did I mention him to you? I'm sure I must have. We have a long-standing date: He has arrived to ensure I get safely home. Can you see him," she inquires proudly of the group at her side, still resolutely ignoring her, "black hair, the bluest eyes; so very handsome, a touch of the French about him. Such things we will have to tell each other. It's been so long since we last met. I think I'll tell him about the villa at Cap d'Antibes.... I wonder if he remembers how I taught him to dance, his feet on mine, Arnaud, watching us on the other side of the room: Such a beautiful dancer, my son. He inherited that from his father.

"Well, hadn't you guessed...?" May confesses, tears glimmering in her eyes. "That's why I couldn't let my daughter have him. Those gypsy hearts can be so very inconstant, you know: I would have given anything to spare her what I suffered when he left me....But not to worry. I have it on good authority that he's waiting for her somewhere.... And so we waltz on," she says, wistfully, gazing one last time at the young people on the dance floor.

"Did I ever tell you that I once danced a gypsy flamenco on the sands and watched the white horses of the Camargue run wild...?" she asks, looking up at her son Patrick, standing over her. "I'm so old, you see, I'm sure I repeat myself..." she smiles, taking hold of his hand. "Well, then goodnight to you all," she says, waving goodbye. "Unfortunately, we won't see each other again now. But, as thanks for all you've given me, I blow you a kiss, you beautiful creatures. I blow you a kiss...." she says, as she gratefully embraces her son, and the last of the life ebbs from her soul in the chair that her dear friend, Serena Lyons, chose especially for her.

THE HOST

How many chimes has it been? he counts, looking to the clock on the wall, announcing the hour of seven, as he emerges from his wife's room to stand at the top of the staircase. He sees the men gathering at its foot, but Serena will not be brought down, as they had planned. For he knows that everyone in attendance this evening will be at the mercy of the waves, before the men ever reach the top. Yet, it would accomplish nothing to forewarn them, so he grants them the bliss of ignorance, just as he did with his wife.

He watches the clock, and thinks back to that afternoon in his study with Kit; the minute glass in his hand, explaining how it worked, marking life one minute at a time. What can you learn in a minute? he recalls. Everything, he considers. You can learn if there is hope or if there is not; if you are loved or if you are hated; if you will live or if you will die. It all comes down to seconds during which the answers to these fundamental questions are uttered, a simple yes or no deciding the direction we will travel. And who decides this for us? God, Fate, or our own Will? No, he concludes, knowingly, often the route we navigate in pursuit of fulfillment, is decided for us by others: by the secrets they impart of their immortal souls and those they choose to keep.

Incomplete: this is how it seems to him now, as he reflects again on Kit's Five Things; the contents of his soul that Captain Lyons insisted he confide that afternoon. A life yet to come, and how beautiful a testament because of that, in all Kit's youthful, questing spirit projected into a future that would never be. It is the same for Serena, too, he acknowledges, for her guests: These people who have congregated below me, who will be lost to the sea in seconds, and myself with them. Incomplete, he nods sadly, a ballroom full of unfinished lives.

How many conversations ended in mid-sentence, he wonders, or arms that failed to grasp those things for which they reached? What of the dances given up before they were mastered, or half-finished drinks left for others to carry away? And the empty tables, or tables for one, or tables too full; confidences murmured after one too many, the yearnings of hearts kept silent because it was not the hour to reveal them? And in this rolling tide of souls; an epic drift, back and forth; of desire and apathy, elegance and ugliness, pride and shame, luck and misfortunes, dreams and death.

Turn the page, find a name, he remembers: *William Paxton; Date of Birth; 10/10/1887; Place of Birth, Liverpool, England; Date of Death, 22/3/1907; Height: 5ft 10 inches; Color of Hair, Black; Eyes, Blue. Five Things: The sound of the sea after a storm; Saturday afternoons at the dog track; My son, George; My wife, Helen; That Sunday...* Turn the page, find the next name: *Simon Pearce; Date of Birth, 06/03/1875; Place of Birth, Lancaster, Pa; Date of Death, 05/28/1901; Height: 6ft 3 inches; Color of Hair, Gray; Eyes, Brown. Five Things; Baseball; Ma's cobbler; My dog Jack, The Pinnacle; When it snowed on my sixteenth birthday...* Turn the page, find the next name: *Christopher 'Kit' Peel; Date of Birth, 07/20/1886; Place of Birth, London, England; Date of....*

Turn the page. Life can be changed irrevocably.

It is with no bitterness that Captain Lyons has listened to the young bemoan their various disappointments. He has not sneered, as most would expect him to, at their woes or regrets. Instead, he has pitied them for what they will invariably learn, that what they consider to be a setback is merely a passing cloud in a well lit life that grows darker the older they get, the more they know. Disappointment should only happen to the old, he thinks. Men, like me, on the darker side of sixty; too young to die and yet too much time gone to expect anything more than the prized shards I have gathered from life's once glittering expectations. All that I remember of Serena and our years together, lined up like pieces of a jigsaw in my mind; a composite of rare instances of understanding, of nearly-missed joys.

He has not seen the good rewarded. He has not witnessed the triumph of the kind over the cruel. Time and again, he has observed those who deserve joy least receive it in abundance. Yet, when he was a younger man, Captain Lyons thought he could change these realities, by saving Serena from the truth, by allowing her to believe that the fact of her continuing with her life was her own choice, when, in fact, it was the destiny he had decided for her because of the secret he kept.

There was nothing Captain Lyons felt he could offer, save the party: The earth belongs to the living, after all, as he has upheld, and the party, in itself, provided reason enough for her to live. Yet, the occupation he sought for Serena was not of planning, entertainment, or distraction. It was the business of legacy: the lesson he learned from his first wife, Laura: "We are only as good as we are remembered." As Captain Lyons knows, there has never been another guest at this party but Kit. Each week his wife has anticipated his return, along with every other person who has ever passed through the door and heard the story of her debut. She has spoken of him, commemorated him in every possession, every detail. And so he has lived on, which is entirely as it should be, Captain Lyons believes: She belonged only to him. A fact he has honored, by denying himself the rights of a husband, despite how he failed himself in his treatment of her, as men so often do when they aspire to noble acts.

After Rupert's lie, he could have told Serena the truth, but he couldn't let her go, despite the nothing they shared. He has always considered it a strange thing to adore someone, to yearn for them, even in the face of their hatred, but she was everything he asked of his life and he was given her: Although, she has been mine, he recognizes now, only in my imagination. But then, with his promise to find her son, he orchestrated another bargain, one that would keep her near and safe a while longer. And in that fashion he succeeded in keeping her alive, nurturing his own vain desire that he might, at least, receive something from her, if only that she might see him for who he is and not who he allowed her to believe him to be. But she was lost to me after Teddy's letter, he accepts. The knowing did kill her in the end. I had cost my wife everything by trying to protect her: the secrets I kept, the memories I tried to kill. Just as I tried to kill the summer redbird when it flew overhead last Thursday, so that Serena might not be reminded of what could not be. But I could never have done such a thing.

Should he have told her that he died? That when he arrived in Nairobi, Kit's body had already been transported to England for burial? That the letter Serena found on his desk was the one Captain Lyons had written to her, after he found Kit in London; the letter he couldn't ever give to her because of what later happened with their baby son, his fear that she would kill herself. That if Serena had turned the page, she would have found not only Kit's Five Things, but also the lilac Captain Lyons has just placed in her coffin; the sprig Kit pressed between the pages of his favorite book of poems by Joyce that Captain Lyons found amongst his possessions, along with the letter Serena sent to Kit as a child. Serena would have seen the details; his name, date of birth, height and the date of Kit's death, but she would not have learned what Captain Lyons was told in Nairobi from that rude page; how Kit's face was turned to the window, how he believed she was with him when his heart finally gave out as a consequence of the Dengue Fever he had contracted: Serena, his incomparable wife, who died of a heart attack on the road outside this house last week, waiting for someone who could not come. And the reason that he never told her is because it would have robbed her of hope. And hope, he used to believe, is all that we live for.

Of course, he realizes, far too late, that he has been wrong about this. What we truly live for is certainty, he concedes, evidence of whether or not we have meant at least something, to the owners of the hearts we wish to command. And is there not a freedom inherent therein, to find another path before it is too late, as much as there is an incalculable reward if the answer is what we do so long to hear.

This past week, as he has questioned the correct course of action of whether the past should remain simply that: of whether he could bear to let her go, even now, Captain Lyons has come to understand that, for everyone, there is only ever one person, regardless of how hard you may try to distract any living person's heart from the star that guides them forward. For both Serena and Kit who died, with only her memory at his side, at the age of twenty-one in a filthy hospital in Africa, it was each other, despite how desperately Captain Lyons wished for her to change course and come to him. And so he has given Kit's Five Things to her now, to guide her safely on her way: It is, he tells himself for the last time, far too precious a thing to stay behind here with me.

Yet, it does not read the same as it once did: Kit hesitated over the fifth and last point of his soul; he did not tell Captain Lyons the whole truth. "Her hat," he said. Beautiful but incomplete, Captain Lyons acknowledges, smiling sadly. It is what remained written on the page until today, when he found cause to change the word to what it should be; to what he is convinced Kit intended to say. As he has so often said, "I have been a chronicler of those lives given to me to oversee, an unpaid editor of better men." He believes that he has done the right thing by so doing. In fact, it is the only decision Captain Lyons has ever made, of which he is certain:

I have done it for him, for her; for all that I stole from them both.

He waits now for the waves, to do with him, as they will.

THE UNINVITED GUEST

They pass through the screen door, the beautiful and the lovely, the golden and the young, an ebb and flow of grace. In and out, in and out, they come and go; a lilting rhythm that somehow constitutes the saddest melody man ever stills to hear, and yet what spiraling chords of awe formulate the sounds, so that all are rapt, struck dumb with love before its music.

He felt Anthony place a hand upon his shoulder, "You must come outside now," he said. And there he found him, that boy, amidst the cheering crowd. Kit followed, a spectator in his wake, as they carried the boy toward where Kit lived.

"Seventeen," someone said. "A sailor." He was not much younger than Kit had been. His name was Christopher.

He had Serena's hair, Kit's eyes; but he seemed more golden, somehow: a happy boy, so many friends. He is like her then, in that way, Kit thought, and he was glad that his son had not been alone, as he had been.

Kit touched him as he passed, when he tumbled from their shoulders and Kit caught him. "Forgive me," Kit said, through his tears. And their son replied, "There's nothing to forgive. It was an accident." "But you are so young," he mourned.

"There's nothing to forgive," he repeated, and Kit understood then that his son knew him. "I've always been loved."

He can still recall his son's warm and affectionate expression, the slight shrug of his shoulders, as if Kit was silly to worry. There is nothing to reproach yourself with, he seemed to say: My life has been happy enough. "But those were not our arms that held you," Kit said, "and they should have."

He turned and left and Kit watched him recede into that hinterland where the young go, when they can no longer live. Where they are cloistered and adored by those who arrived so much later, to remember what youth was, to honor its inconstancy. But Kit could not follow him back, not without Serena.

"I'll come now," he said to Anthony, at his side. "I'll come to the party." Anthony who, for years, had attended them, only so that he could be close to everyone again: "It consoles me," Anthony would say, whenever Kit asked how he could bear it, "being able to watch. I like to look at her. It is all I ask."

But fourteen years ago, when Kit first walked with him to this door, he could not cross over the threshold. He did not attend the first party, he will not attend this last, and that evening he was forced to wait outside, confined there by Captain Lyons, who chose to keep his soul locked away. So instead, Kit watched Serena through the windows of the dining room, lighting the candles on the table, as they had once imagined she would in their home. In the years, which, for them, never came.

We watch through the windows at those lives that continue on for others, Kit thinks, those we could not lead ourselves, and we ask only that they never forget. There is no shadow you can cast over those left behind that can ensnare them, to anchor them to one's side. It is the perpetual fear of those who leave, who, in parting, run the risk that those they cherished might forfeit the memories of that love, in the arms of another. There is nothing that can be done, except to wait, the prayer, with which we are born, when we encounter the person for whom there is no alternative, on our lips: *Remember me.* And that is what Kit said to her that evening, as he watched her light the candles in her life that carried on without him: "Remember me," he said. And although it was impossible that she could ever have seen him, Serena smiled at the spot where he stood and he knew that she did.

He is here now, at the red front door of La Doucette. Yet, despite the years, he is the same as he was then. He was only ever young. Not for him to age, to gather experiences and knowledge. All he has is what he took with him when he left, what impressed itself upon him for that brief while, those things in which he has believed. The summer is dying now, for everyone, and these are not last steps he walks, but first. He arrives here, not to say good-bye, but to hope for something more; to lead her away with him, toward the tomorrows he could not give her in life. He has waited for this one moment, before the end, when her soul might make its final choice, to be with him once more. And he says, as he promised he would;

"We will go then, you and I, in the night."

His arms fall open to welcome her in.

THE PARTY, THE PARTY!

The clock chimes for the fourth time.

"She must be coming. It's seven..." someone remarks. A forty-something year old from East Hampton, chin in hand, manipulating her shoe on and off her heel in utter boredom, turns her listless eyes to the French doors to see if The Starlet is still standing there, and is blandly heard to comment, "I don't have my glasses on, but is that a – "

"Vermilion!" decides a woman emphatically, who has recently moved to Remsenburg. "I'll paint the front door vermilion! It will look dinky next to the lattice windows, quite like an English –What on earth is that noise? Is it –"

It starts as an aside: "Is that a wave?" Then it builds to a chorus; "*Is* that a wave?" Some are silent, some are still...

The clock chimes for the fifth time.

The Summer Visitors will not see the dawn and devastation. They will never learn that they could have been saved if Charlie Reid, a young man in the weather bureau in Washington, who correctly mapped the path of this hurricane this morning, had not been dismissed for being too young and inexperienced to matter. They will never gasp again in horror at the inhumanity of men, who will pick over their dead bodies on the beach tomorrow, denuding them of their jewels that glisten so brilliantly around their necks. They will not shudder in fear at the nightmarish candlelight that will illuminate the dance floor of The Westhampton Country Club, where so many of them celebrated Labor Day two weeks ago, which will masquerade as a makeshift morgue for their lifeless bodies. All they will know is this final sight before their eyes: the wall of water they turn to confront, it's tendrils curls gleaming and crystalline against the night, seemingly so benevolent in its beauty, before it falls over them. And the sound of the hurricane's voice – this terrible fugue so distinct from the dulcet song of the birds that sang so sweetly for them at the start of this party: the deep bass of the sea, the high scream of the wind, the sustained organ-like groan that drowns out the sound of everything else.

It's. Just. Another. Step. Just. Another. Step, he thinks, a combination of unassailable yearning and need propelling him on: Anthony Duverglas, can no longer breathe, only reach. And he is reaching now, his arm feels as if it might be removed from its socket, his fingertips can almost touch her, but no one appears perturbed by his desperation. He calls her name, over and over, but none turn to hear it, and Venetia herself, does not acknowledge him. Instead, she listens graciously on to the Governor, descending into falsely modest bombast, – "I couldn't have reckoned on the ground-swell of support for my initiative, nor the praise for its originality. I can say, however…" – in an attempt to impress her with the ins and outs of city planning.

"A toast, I think, to Serena," announces her husband, arriving at her side. "Serena," she assents soberly, in dignified, if fatigued, acknowledgment of her husband's gesture; casting a glance up at him with practiced benevolence, timeworn from disappointment and resentment. A hollow, dull sensation pulls her mood down, as she confronts the emptiness of her days: How much more of this, she thinks dully. All it is, is this, standing next to him, being maligned by other women, and he only ever brags on, grandstands on, insists that I play along too. And I do. It's all I ever do. And yet, she sighs, It's so much easier this way. What other alternative is –

But it is now, on raising her glass to toast poor Serena, that she sees him: Anthony Duverglas, who she would have toasted with delight any day of the week, who she would have rushed to the gates to greet each evening, or up and down tenement steps should it have come to that. His eyes, she mourns, as they meet her own. Once they were the color of far-distant seas, what has happened here? And she accepts anew, what has happened to him and what will now happen to her.

In the seconds that follow, it begins. It is as if she is gliding back to the beginning, through the dark waters of a river, on either side of her the banks, light dappling through the willows over her head, violets, pansies, poppies, floating in the water, as she is pulled further and further back...And in her, a settling of the stirred up emotions and difficulties of years into something fundamental, elemental, as the cool water cleanses her of every care; drawing together the disparate facets of her personality – jostled, splintered and strewn here and there – into perfect alignment: a cohesion that enables her to breathe finally clear air, relief, as she casts her gaze skyward, leaving. *"There you are,"* she sings, his image in front of her, but it is a heart's hymn of departure: of grief and acceptance, of bittersweet acknowledgement that it is all so late, that she will be washed ashore momentarily; that she must reach for his hand and not let go. For Venetia Dryden understands that she is about to die.

And in the final minute of her life, Venetia confronts her soul mate, Anthony Duverglas, who once dressed impeccably and longed for her across rooms. Anthony Duverglas who killed himself on losing all of his money in the stock market, after trusting a deliberately bad tip by way of Douglas Dryden, through a friend, and with it any chance, he felt, of ever being good enough for her. She understands now that he has felt the same for her as she for him; that there is a new beginning that awaits them. Not what either of them would have chosen, but enough, perhaps, she thinks, enough...

Out stretches her arms, as if pulled from the water toward the skies, as if his hands could reach down and carry her up and out. And Anthony Duverglas lunges to make his final claim on her soul, the only woman he ever desired, the one moment for which he has waited, when an arm unexpectedly reaches around Venetia Dryden's waist and spins her away. That of her husband offering the security and devotion she has always craved, but which he has never once offered her. "No, no," she screams, "I don't want you. I want him," she pleads, her arms falling wide open as she tries to grab something of Anthony Duverglas, before she is turned away from him forever. But she cannot reach in time. And the last sight she ever sees is the broken heart of his ghost in front of her, as he falls at her husband's feet; his arms still outstretched toward her promise, her red hair, the Irish of her voice, her hand he had once had the privilege to clasp.

The Governor and Douglas Dryden contort in horror at the sight and sound of tragedy crashing through the rooms of La Doucette; arms spiking, pointing, twisting, entangling; legs kicking, bending, lunging, the scream that lasts for eternity, the collective intake of breath that expels to plead, *No*: The Host, at the top of the staircase, stands perfectly still, as if on the helm of a ship, in anticipation of the wave that will leap forward from behind him. Guests move to flee, others freeze in place, while still more turn in acceptance of what is to come.

The Little Maid, too young and innocent to understand the cacophony of noise emanating from the back of the house and what it signifies, watches from the stairs, forlorn yet enthralled by the young man she loved and a debutante, twirling on the dance floor, performing steps one only learns in private school. She stands thinking of trays of paste diamonds and silk shoes nestled in boxes that were never worn. Everything she will never own, because she is just a maid who will always be just a maid. But then, up the stairs he rushes, two steps at a time, a Yorkshire lad's foot on the Axminster carpet, imported from England – how far he has come from the working class street! "There's something I must tell her," Rupert Turner-Hume insists to The Little Maid, "Where is she? Please, let me pass through."

The Little Maid does not speak, in awe to the fact of him in front of her; that he should even remark her presence. "I lied," he protests, "I lied. I would never try to ruin love for someo–" But then, from behind her, he sees it. And the beauty of its undulating grace, its eternal command of the souls who charge it forward, like a chariot, impels him to remember why he has come; the reason why he has found himself at Mrs. Edward Lyon's last party. Not to atone for the lie he told Serena: the lie that broke what was left of her heart, as she was forced to accept that she had been forgotten by the only person she ever loved. No, he has come to turn The Little Maid away from the sight of Death.

And here, in her rosebud lips, those lips for which he has endlessly searched – cheap, thin, meager, to anyone else, but a perfect fit for his own – he finds his past, his present, and the future he will lead her toward. And in the one heroic act for which, had he lived, he would have been forever associated, he thinks not of first kisses and screen kisses and all those in-between, but last kisses, as he tips the young girl, so reminiscent of his first wife, over backward to ensure she will not see the wave, and so know no fear. And, in the last minute that is left to her, The Little Maid's breath mingles with the intoxicating ether of a makeshift God who finally makes her good enough: Rupert Turner-Hume who once talked to her at the first party she ever served at, before he was killed one week later in an aviation disaster, his golden head severed from his body.

"Who knew?" observes The Dandy, and there are tears in his eyes as he acknowledges The Little Maid's victory over the cruel: The Dandy who was killed in a head on-collision with The Last Resort in 1927. It was the evening The Last Resort had disappeared at a party with the boy she knew he secretly loved, out of spite for one of his jibes. What had led to The Dandy getting behind the wheel of a car, drunk on gin and malice and heart-break, and killing them both. The Dandy searches for the boy he loved in the crowd, but he has not been chosen to lead him out. And so when The Last Resort opens her tragic eyes, smeared with black Kohl, and whispers, "Don't leave me," he can't help but pity her, still unable to accept that she is no longer living. Here they are again, the last two guests without partners. "I won't leave you," he says. "But go back to sleep now. This is not for you to see." And The Last Resort, always so grateful to oblige, turns her face to the wall and tries to forget.

So, the wave, the last guest at the party – uninvited, unwelcome – makes its presence felt. It lunges through the walls; it caresses and admires the fine china porcelain arranged perfectly by Mrs. Lyons on marble and onyx mantles, before smashing it to shards, forgotten as it rampages toward more bewitching finery; it snaps into pieces the regency tables, shatters the glass lamps, maroons the Sevres rugs in a thousand stains from the bottom of the sea, that will never come out; lampoons the marble of the hall, catching strains of last words as it barrels its way through to the front door.

There, a man shelters in an alcove, clutching a woman in silver silk to him, the desire still a promise between them. His wife's blonde head rests against his neck, it is their first party as man and wife – oh the stories they have heard! How to say goodbye to her, he asks himself, because that is the only word left to them. What to say; something, anything – "It's like I told you once, if we never saw one another again…" "I know," she cries over the noise, understanding this, the last look, "It wouldn't make any diff—" And the sea takes the words, as it wrenches them apart.

So the sea takes the words, robs them from the lips of the parting, silencing the whisperings of souls beneath its surface. It takes the books, lining the shelves of the study of Captain Edward Lyons, dragging the souls of the men locked within them down to the seabed, instead of releasing them to the skies, where they belong. It snatches The Emperor from his captivity on the wall back to the world beyond it, where the families of deer who come to the steps of La Doucette to admire him will no longer wait. All gone now, killed by the ferocity of the storm.

Her life has only been lovely, so it is with eyes expectant and trusting that Annabelle Adams turns her youthful head to acknowledge the noise behind her. And it is now that she first glimpses the wall of water cascading toward her from the back of the mansion, the stories of which she has begged for and replayed over and over, longing for the day when she could see it for herself. The clock chimes again, for the sixth time, and she parts her lips that have never been kissed, to emit a murmur both innocent and agonizing. She accepts there will be no seventh chime before the clean rivulets of water, more crystalline than any she has ever before seen, will cover her. *Please not yet*, she begs, *I have not even lived. And no one is with me, to hold my lovely hand. It is all supposed to begin, with this party....*

Since she was a child, she has kindled a fantasy of attending one of Serena Lyon's parties and dancing with the handsomest man in the room: her silk scarf flying behind at her neck as he waltzes her around, as if she were her idol, Amelia Earhart, gliding through the air. But that will not happen now, she knows, the water flying toward her like shards of glass from a mirror that can only acknowledge her beauty. Yet, in these seconds before she is sucked under, it seems to her that the water holds her in loving arms, as if she is a baby being cradled with a lullaby, its touch like a warm embrace on her forehead bidding her to go to sleep. Annabelle almost feels as if she might sleep and that, when she wakes up, all will be well again. But now, with a sudden jolt, the water pulls her under, snaps her neck back and drops her to the bottom of the sea. And the gold daisies in her hair untangle themselves and rise above to the surface, a floral tribute, as if to say, "Do not trespass, This is where Youth sleeps." And as Annabelle falls deeper and deeper down, she remembers the boy who showed her the way to this place. And it is almost as if it is his lips that kiss her own; as she watches the reflection of the youth, float away above her to the surface; in commemoration of all she will remain, if anyone lives to remember her.

And Helen Fitzgerald, who has tried unsuccessfully to die for years, who stopped eating the day her daughter, Susannah, died, thinking of ice-cream and summers on Gin Lane, sits in a corner of an attic room, watching the children play, casting her protective shadow over them. But suddenly the door opens, and beyond beckons privets and the Halcyon Lodge she loved, tennis at The Meadow Club, and her darling child's hand in hers again. "My Susannah," she cries, as her baby girl comes rushing toward her, to pull her to the door. And the children all follow her as they run down the corridor, clambering up onto the roof, to avoid the rising water. Here they sit, huddled together, as the little boats they clutched – those that Serena Lyons had gifted to all of these children on their births – sail out toward a different horizon; all pinks and blues, both worn and unused, but every one special, from the vestiges of La Doucette.

So little will remain, for the waves have everything in their sights, and with each rampaging lunge, what exists, becomes what was; like images in picture books that speak nothing of the people who lived in these houses surrounding La Doucette; nothing of the people who bid the wealthy luck as they travelled to their summer swansong; nothing of the trinkets and the jewels and the china polished by the hands of people who worked here; nothing of the beaches and the games of polo that once crowned charming young boys champions; nothing of the parasols underneath which hid the lips of ladies that would be kissed, kindly and callously, gratefully and arrogantly; nothing of anything at all.

And the clock no longer chimes, for time is gone now.

The dead turn to their partners, those partners their souls have chosen to lead them out through the golden arch toward ended days, and hold out their hands to them. Hands that seem to the newly invited to be cast in marble: they are so fluid, elegant, and refined. And in their beauty they augur something of what it is like where The Summer Visitors are going now and so they grasp onto them with restored passion. Or is there simply false hope contained within the gleaming artifice of their elongated fingers, some suddenly fear? But still they hold fast, as their Hostess appears on the mezzanine above them, and all of the guests turn to welcome her.

Their golden feet, once clad in silk or kid-glove leather, are now bare. And in the cause and effect of their turning, their dresses swish with them, blurring their images, like snapshots fading to sepia, as they prepare to depart from this life. They pivot as elegantly, and with as much as innocence, as when they first opened their eyes, on the very day they first drew breath. And somewhere in them, something sounds, *The splendor*... as it appears before them once more.

Yet, whether they have abused it, forgotten it, overlooked it, or taken it for granted, it has not dulled; the luster is there still. It is etched in the marble floor beneath their feet, it is in the cool of their dresses; it is like gold smeared on the fingertips of a lover that suddenly reaches for a lucky girl's hand. It is in the memory of their good fortune; in summers on Gin Lane; in Vodka Gibson's at catered bars overlooking the Atlantic where only the privileged sip. It is in the pristine streets, well tended by others, over which they have driven. It is in the lattice windows of flawlessly emulated English country houses, into which they escaped, to play dressing up, for two months each summer. It is in the footfall on the platform of the financier returning for the weekend, sated by young lovers in the city, grateful to discreet wives in country houses in Georgica who knew how good they had it. It is in the old promise of a party on a Friday evening, held by a supreme hostess, who asked nothing of them, except their happiness; it is in the driveway lined by torches, the champagne spilling out of fountains, the drinks made especially for a guest's palate, remembered that way in a book Mrs. Lyons kept so that no-one was ever impelled to ask for anything twice. It is in the eyes of an Emperor that surveyed them, without judgment or anger, suspended there to be admired because Mrs. Edward Lyons felt it just. It is in the lilacs, the hydrangeas, the phlox, the lavender, the hollyhocks and the day lilies. It is in the sea that has claimed them.

It is all there, in everything they were fortunate to have been a part of; the knowledge of what it is to wake in a summer home of a morning, to feel the slight cool in the air before the heat of later day; the smell of sea spray misting around the edges of the flowers, somewhere at the end of the road, the colors of morning deepening from pale to bluer, but never too blue, a Hampton's blue; and the surging excitement of the thought that is always born, as if a favorite child: 'It begins! The day begins!'

"How lucky we have been," The Summer Visitors acknowledge, as they watch their Hostess descend the staircase, to lead them safely out from their last party. Arm in arm, they follow at her heels; departing in good favor from the lives they loved so well.

THE HOSTESS

All that we are, are the minutes: the time afforded to each of us that slips away so readily, sometimes before we are ready. There are only a handful of minutes in our lives that are of any importance; those ordinary moments around which choices are done and undone and paths changed. Yet, each one contains an event and a choice and, sometimes, a soul that determines our destinies.

Five minutes at the end of the day, Five Things: a recollection of time passing, this ritual I have shared with you tonight:

A lilac tree
A piece of lace tied to a key
Five things
A summer redbird
The road that leads to the sea.

I am leaving, but there is no time for regret. For all that is left is the love I remember, distilled into these minutes I have recounted; these minutes that benignly arrived, familiar yet unremarkable, but which came to contain the essence of whom I once was. There was the door closing forever, as my heart affirmed, *Yes, that is love*, on a boy for whom there would be no equal; the humble awe of my son opening his eyes to me, his mother, and the unnavigable tragedy of his loss; the searing beauty of a metaphor for life from the pen of an unpaid editor of better men; the bittersweet acknowledgment of the end of hope from the unwitting heart of my most beloved and yet inconstant friend; and then, the acceptance of letting go as I waited at the window of this, my last party. These are things that comprise me. They are who I understand myself to be. So, at the end, the lesson I have learned is that while knowing can kill you, sometimes it can set you free. It was the answer I came upon years ago, in my husband's study; the reward he finally placed in my hands this evening:

The dead are the stars by which we navigate.

Look, see how he waits for me.

I am walking to where Kit stands now, my last steps through the past I will leave behind. They do not come amongst us very often, these fair and delicate boys. Nor do we keep them very long when they do, for they are far too beautiful to stay. But they wait for us, they wait for us, their arms outstretched to lead us to the paradises where they dwell, with a question on their lips, to bring joy to all departing souls:

We will go then, you and I, in the night.

At the end, as at the beginning, there are those rescuing arms, the arms to which I cling as we fall deeper and deeper into our memories. As we relive the moments that have defined and brought us back to one another once more, we find the ultimate reward of these parties of our lives in this love that has never faltered. It is all there between us as the seconds slip by, everything we shared, everything we missed, as we walk out into a realm neither real nor false, but everlasting. Am I seventeen again? Is he twenty-one? Or is age, as time, irrelevant when all that matters is the soul. What the soul once promised, what it has reclaimed in the ebbing light of final moments: a light that is neither earthly nor celestial, but infinite in its benevolence.

And it seems just like those summer days we once loved so well. We see the light bouncing off the water over the edge of the lawn, there are so many things we will do...Yet, between us now are the stars, the points on our souls, that we cast in our wake as we leave. My Five Things joined with those of his; those my husband, that keeper of souls, kept safe for me:

When the shy star goes forth in heaven...

Shade of elms, her arm in mine...

Lilacs...

The summers I have lived with her; the summers I will live with her...

And this last, the eternal consolation I have sought and finally found. One single word: my name:

Serena.

Our arms linked once more, we walk on toward the destiny at which we all arrive. And it is now that it happens as he inclines his perfect face to mine: something again passes between us. It is a confirmation of all we were once promised, all we once searched for in bright upturned glances to the face of the other. We find the acknowledgment in our eyes of everything we will be, in the infinite space into which love projects its kindlings: the most exquisite promise any heart can make to another;

"Tomorrow," he says. "Tomorrow, we will...."

Yes, I smile.

Tomorrow, we will.

EPILOGUE

The girl in the Vionnet dress, curled up for safety on the floor of the ball-room, or what had once been the ground beneath her feet, opens her eyes, so innocent and trusting, and finds that she is still here. She is in the mansion where Mrs. Edward Lyons hosted her parties, every Friday evening of sum-mer. The house where the crowds of people had seemed to part in waves to welcome her – "Isn't she lovely," they had gasped, "Lovely!" – when she ar-rived on the arms of her parents, not moments ago. The house where she had taken her first sip of champagne, and accepted a cigarette from a charming man. Or so she supposes, because she realizes that the Florentine clock no longer ticks on overhead, nor has it chimed to mark the passing of another year: I must still be seventeen, she considers, looking around. Yet, it is not the sight of silk papered walls or fine boned Limoges china, or even of the sea, clearly visible through the wall that has collapsed at the back of Serena Lyon's enchanted house, that meets her eyes, but a complete vision of time past, playing out before her, as she sits here all alone.

It is as if she is five again, standing in the doorframe of her parent's summerhouse in Georgica, the black and white marble floor so cool beneath her bare feet, her hand held gently by her nanny. And before her, there is the brilliant white haze of an early summer evening, the pollen glowing in the light, the smell of the sea beyond the privets, a light breeze rustling in the leaves, her pink swing hanging from the apple tree. It is the hour before supper on a Friday, the hour each week when she watches her parents leave, to travel to one of Mrs. Edward Lyons' fabled parties at The Westhampton Leisure Hour and Supper Club.

There it is that treasured memory: of the tall, elegant figure of her mother as she places one of her glittering shoes artfully onto the white gravel driveway, the beads and chiffon and feathers of her dresses glinting winningly as she glides out into the summer evening to join her father, resplendent in black tie, leaning against the Packard. *"The party, the party!"* Annabelle thrills, looking up in excitement to her nanny, her red curls tumbling down her back. She revels in the romance of her father watching her mother walk toward him over their courtyard, his bashful acknowledgment of her beauty, the awe and graciousness of his expression, as if he is accepting the presence of a masterpiece beside him. Say something, Daddy; Tell her, Annabelle wishes, clinging more tightly to her nanny's hand, in anticipation. Always, she thinks he might; a flurry of loveliness and intoxicating sweet-nothings, such as she supposes husbands say to their wives... But instead, her father claps his hands, as if in applause, and announces, "I believe in you, Tinkerbell," as her mother, so blonde, so vivacious, affects a little curtsey before him; "Why, thank you ever so, Peter Pan," she demurs, as he opens the car door for her, with a ceremonial bow.

But now Annabelle's eyes sparkle again, because it is about to happen, her favorite part. As if thinking better of his actions, her father takes her mother's hand, kisses it, grips it tighter, and Annabelle's mother turns her long, white neck slightly to him, lowers her chin and casts her eyes up, in a lingering acknowledgment of his presence that ends always with a smile so special, her father never fails to place his hand over his heart. "Ah, that now that is love, young lady. When you grow up, you marry a man just like that," her nanny remarks, with an approving nod down to Annabelle. And Annabelle, so very young, nods knowingly too at that language without words that unites her parents in the love Annabelle will one day aspire to know herself.

They turn now, her mother and father, to wave goodbye, full of their weekly promises, which they always fulfill: the small piece of cake or a profiterole that she finds waiting on her breakfast plate on a Saturday morning, a gift from Mrs. Lyons, "who was enchanted by you when she met you that afternoon at Hildreth's, when we were buying linens. Do you remember? Mrs. Lyons was the lady who gave you the little boat...?" Yes, Annabelle always remembers Mrs. Lyons; so elegant and pretty, so terribly kind, smiling at Annabelle as she talked to her mother, whereas certain other ladies ignored her. And it was on an afternoon, when Annabelle was five, that Mrs. Lyons extended the invitation that would become her defining ambition: "Annabelle has a summer birthday? What a coincidence! It's the same as mine. Well then, Annabelle, you must celebrate your eighteenth birthday at my house: You have my word! Can you imagine, Rosemary, when everyone lays eyes on her? They will faint when they see how beautiful she is…"

So it had begun, the dream of the party ahead that Annabelle had been promised by Mrs. Edward Lyons. And, of course, before then there were the stories of the people, the dresses, the dancing, the gossip, for which she would beg her parents, every Saturday morning at breakfast. She came to know all of their friends and acquaintances intimately, like their best friend, Helen, who lived on Gin Lane; "a poor lady called Lucinda, who you must not laugh at, even if others do;" Teddy Worthington, "a decent chap," her father would nod kindly, "despite his problems;" the incomparable Venetia Dryden, "You know, Annabelle," and here her mother would smile conspiratorially, a little cheekily, and her father, knowing he would not win, would sigh and return to his newspaper, 'I always thought Anthony Duverglas was in love with her. The way he used to look at her! You would die to have a man look at you like that…"

And there they would arrive at her mother's favorite topic, Anthony Duverglas – "my second husband," her mother would wink at Annabelle, much to the affected distaste of her father. "Anthony Duverglas this, Anthony Duverglas that," she would sigh. His immaculate manners, the time she had sprained her ankle, dancing, and he had gone to the kitchen – himself! – for the ice… "Annabelle, I have never feared your mother running off with a sailor, but Anthony Duverglas, now I do worry about him…" her father would remark comically whenever his name was mentioned on a Saturday morning, lowering the newspaper and looking at her over the top with rueful eyes. And her mother would laugh, jump up from her seat, throw the paper out of the way, and sit down on his lap, her arms wrapped around his neck, "Annabelle, your father need not worry for a second, but Anthony Duverglas is, by far, the handsomest man I have ever seen," she would swoon, before kissing her husband square on the lips, and exclaiming, "except for you, Peter Pan!" And Annabelle, resting her lovely cheek on her lovely hand, – at six, at seven, at eight, at nine, at every age, of every summer, up until her eighteenth birthday – would laugh with them, and listen on in thrall to the glory of those summer parties, imagining what might happen the night she would be able to attend her first. If only she could dance, just once, at one of Mrs. Lyon's parties, in a gold dress, with gold slippers, with the handsomest man in the room, how sublime would that be! For that was how she imagined Serena Lyons had spent her eighteenth birthday, from everything she had heard from her mother. By all accounts, Mrs. Lyons had been so lucky; she had led such a lovely life.

But now it starts to fade before her eyes; that blessed memory of Annabelle's childhood: of Georgica and diamonds and profiteroles and heads of curls and rounds of applause for Tinkerbells. She can no longer see her mother and father in front of her, nor are they anywhere near, as she casts her eyes around the ruins of La Doucette. The party is over and it ended so terribly, she remembers. And all I was given was a minute of it.

Yet, as she starts to weep, she knows that she was somehow right to dream this dream: to be at the center of such a lovely world, with such lovely people. "But it's all gone," she says, "and I am all alone." And Annabelle Adams, dead at seventeen in the hurricane that claimed the life of every guest at Mrs. Edward Lyon's last party, save for six children who were found on a portion of roof that broke off and floated away to safety, buries her head in her hands and weeps.

But now, from above her, she hears someone call her name: "Annabelle," he says, "Annabelle..."

Annabelle Adams, still so lovely, for she will not grow old now, raises her trusting eyes, wet with despair, to find the impeccable figure of an extraordinarily handsome gentleman, standing over her. "You poor girl," he says kindly, in perfect comprehension of her sorrow. "Please don't cry. How is it that you were left by yourself?" he asks, crouching down in concern beside her on the floor. "I came by myself, except for my parents," Annabelle replies, tears spilling down her cheeks, "I thought I might meet somebod—" but she finds that she cannot finish what she wants to say; about the dreams she once cherished, that will not come true....

So beautiful, the man thinks, regarding her. He suddenly glimpses something from his youth, Annabelle's mother Rosemary jokingly flirting up a storm, her husband laughing at her side; all of them gathered around a marble cocktail table, champagne on ice, the jazz band, the silk dresses, the tuxedos, the dancing and the splendor of it all. "Well, as it happens, I don't have a partner either. So, it would be my pleasure to escort you, if that's what you would like," he says softly, "but, do forgive me. I appear to have forgotten my manners, I'm Anthony Duverglas," he introduces himself, holding out his hand to her. *The handsomest man in the room*, Annabelle remembers, her mother's bright voice sounding in her ears, as her hand, so young and tender, grasps onto his own.

"I am dead, aren't I?" Annabelle whispers, standing up to meet him. "Yes," he replies, sadly. "Are there other parties, where we are going?" she asks. "No," he shakes his head. "This is the last party." Annabelle nods in acceptance of his words and with a courage of which her parents would have been proud, acknowledges the devastation of La Doucette: the shattered porcelain, the broken clock, and the pink mist hovering over the sea as the light fades around them.

"I wish I could have danced, just once," she says, almost to herself. And it is now that Anthony Duverglas understands why he has been chosen to lead Annabelle Adams out, as his heart breaks for the years she will not live, and, too, at the memory she inspires; the hand he once crossed a room to hold in his own that he will never hold again. "You can, Annabelle," he says. "There is still time. Will you dance with me?" "But there isn't any music," Annabelle protests, terrified her dream might yet die. "There is," he assures her, recalling the Irish melody he has never forgotten, that reminded his beloved Venetia Dryden of home, "I know a song." And, somewhere in his heart, just for a moment, a field of meadow wildflowers blooms beneath his feet, as he gently draws the young girl, so reminiscent of his lost love, to him.

So Anthony Duverglas and Annabelle Adams dance together for the first and the last time: a hauntingly poignant waltz of regret and loss and longing.

Youth and Romance sway together, cheek to cheek, clinging to the vestiges of all their lives once promised, as the light suffuses their dying souls. The memories of everything they had once known resurge around them with the greater music that suddenly resonates throughout the ruins: a triumphant refrain spiraling up into the darkening sky, as the last of the light ebbs from the spot where they dance. It is a symphony comprised of the voices of the guests who once flocked to the parties of Mrs. Edward Lyons: the sound of their souls as they ascend toward heaven.

"The day I walked on my hands over the sands of Dune Road...The sea at twilight and Benjamin standing on the shore...Lucy, Lucy, Lucy...Just let me look at her...The crest of the hill on South Country Road...A meadow walk, a path of cherry blossoms...Morning...Margaritas at the Maidstone and Jemima in a blue dress...Summers on Gin Lane...Five things...Those were daisies, in her hair...The perfect air step...A summer storm in Amagansett...The time he held the cup up high...A villa in Cap d'Antibes...Gin...A blue beaded handbag... The Emperor...A boy, so fair and delicate, tumbling off his bike at my feet when I was twenty-one...Lilacs...The road that leads to the sea...Ta-ta, Love. Ta-ta... The party, the party...!"

They dance on, as the voices grow ever softer, so soft they can barely be heard, their music spinning out slower and slower toward the vista of sea beyond. Until silence falls over the shores of Long Island, beyond the echoes of time past resonating within its waves as they crash, timid now, onto the beaches. Nothing is left of all that once was: nothing of hostesses, or parties, or last guests, or kisses, or waltzes, or dreams.

All that is left are the stars.

Made in the USA
Lexington, KY
01 July 2015